SHADOWS CHANT

PAUL OUTRAM

WOHLER PUBLISHING

ISBN: 978-1-0684620-0-9

Disclaimer:

This story and its characters are entirely fictitious. Certain locations and establishments are used in the context of the characters' journey. Unless otherwise indicated, all names, characters, businesses, places, events, and incidents in this book are either the product of the author's imagination or used fictitiously. Any resemblance to actual persons, living or dead, or actual events is purely coincidental. The author strongly recommends consulting medical professionals for any injury, whether minor or severe. The events, actions, and dialogues within this book are intended for fictional purposes only.

All rights reserved.

Printed and bound in U.A.E
by Wohler Publishers

The paper and board used in this book are made from wood
from responsible sources

WOHLER PUBLISHING
www.shadowschant.com

FOREWORD

In this story, you will be taken on an emotional journey with a young girl named Aeona, who faces a number of traumatic events. Some things happen to her by accident, while others, due to her age she is too young to fully understand.

These moments are all part of growing up. We all make mistakes, no matter how old we are. Don't let anyone put you down, demoralize you, or discourage you from being who you truly are, flaws, quirks, habits, and all. Embrace yourself, as you are.

Aeona carries both physical and emotional scars, but she will overcome them, and so will you! Remember, no matter where you are, there is always someone on the other end of a phone who is there to listen, without judgment or blame.

For support, please visit:
Child Helplines – A Global List
https://home.crin.org/child-helplines-a-global-list
https://befrienders.org/find-support-now/saath/

ACKNOWLEDGMENTS

A special thanks to all the SAR teams, paramedics, doctors, and nurses worldwide for their dedication to helping others. Additional thanks to the Mountain Bothies Association for preserving the memory of John Gregory. May he rest in peace.

Thank you to my wife, Gilan
For helping me through the
dark days.

CHAPTER ONE 'LOSS'

It was a wonderful start to life for Aeona Squire and her twin brother, Christopher, growing up on the outskirts of a large town with the whole world ahead of them. Every morning, their loving father, Thomas, would kiss them goodbye, get into his car, and reverse out of the drive. He always made sure never to leave until they'd run to the living room and blown him kisses from the window.

It was a cold September morning, and the big day had arrived: the first day of a new school after the long summer break. The twins quickly ate their cereal and dropped the bowls in the sink. Their mother, Anwen, shouted, 'Last one up is a stinky duck!' then bolted out of the kitchen and bounded up the stairs three steps at a time before the two children could react. Christopher slammed into his sister to gain ground, causing her to ricochet off the kitchen cabinet.

"Cheater! Cheater!" she protested, trying to grab at his leg. "Not fair! Not fair!"

By the time she chased him to the bedroom, he was already rejoicing, jumping up and down on the bed with a pillow in hand, ready to defend himself from the loser.

"Stinky duck, Aeona! Stinky duck, Aeona!" he teased.

"Mum, he cheated… he pushed me! He pushed me! That's not fair! It doesn't count!" she scolded.

Their mother gently told him to apologise and give her a hug to say sorry. Anwen always tried to make them bond and wouldn't tolerate any bickering about silliness. Like all siblings, they had their disagreements, but it was clear that they loved each other very much. Aeona always stuck up for him and defended him in many ways.

"You two shouldn't fight; you need to look after one

another," Anwen said, giving Aeona a stern look. "What am I always telling you?"

"Sorry, Mum," she said, as Christopher jumped off the bed and into his sister's arms. "Not sorry, Aeona," he whispered, kissing her on the cheek.

Trying not to laugh, Anwen put her hands on her hips and forced a frown. "I asked…" she repeated, "What am I always telling you?"

The two stood to attention like little soldiers.

"You… always… say… Mummy and Daddy aren't going to be around forever," they chanted, "so you must take care of each other, no matter what!"

Their smiles were enough to make their mother's heart melt. "So nice," she beamed, wrapping her arms around them.

"You can let go now, Mummy," they giggled. "I'm sure we've got somewhere to go."

"Just a minute longer!" Anwen said, as a tear of happiness rolled down her cheek.

After a long sigh, she gave a slight cough, wiped her face on Aeona's pyjama sleeve and rhetorically asked, 'Why do you need to grow up so fast?' With a pause of composure, she asked the question again, "Okay… Now… who wants to go to school?" To Anwen, it felt more like eight short moments rather than eight years since she had been blessed with them.

The move to a new house over the summer had made everything quite new and exciting, especially as the family had moved to the other side of town for a better school. She had thought the twins would be nervous about going to a new one and that they would give her a hard time, but it was quite the opposite. She had explained to them that it was best for their future.

At the bottom of the bed were their neatly folded uniforms:

burgundy jumpers with green apple logos on the breast pocket, cream long-sleeved shirts and blouses, and two pairs of long grey trousers.

Aeona had wanted a skirt to make her feel more grown up, but her mother explained that the weather was far too cold for it at the moment.

"Come on, get your jammies off and let's do this!" she cheered.Five minutes later, Aeona and Christopher were laughing at the bottom of the stairs, putting their shoes on. They then sat patiently, bags in hand, waiting for their mother to come down.

"Mum," they called, "we're ready! Come on! We don't want to be late!"

It took her another five minutes to come down, as usual. She put on their coats, zipped them to their chins, and got ready to leave.

"Year Four, here we come!" Anwen smiled, pulling the door shut behind them as the children laughed and skipped ahead down the side of the road. The sky was a dull grey. Although the weather forecast said it wouldn't rain until late in the evening, Anwen took her umbrella with her just in case; the weather was always unpredictable, even for a short walk to the school at the end of the road.

As they walked hand in hand, the twins questioned their mother, trying to get as much information as possible. They wanted to be able to answer all the questions they guessed their new teacher would ask them.

"Mum," Christopher asked, pulling at his mother's arm. "How many days until our birthday?"

"I'm not sure," she answered. "February is only a few months away. Why do you ask?"

"Nothing really, just thinking about what I want," he smiled.

"We haven't got through Bonfire Night, Halloween or Christmas yet. Are you seriously thinking about your birthday?" she said.

The school, a charming building that had once been a nursing home, had been converted to accommodate the increasing number of children in the area. Its quaint rustic charm, with ivy climbing up the walls, gave a warm welcome as they drew nearer. When they arrived, they entered the gates and were greeted by the smiling teacher, Mrs Jenkins.

Without giving her a chance to welcome them, Aeona ran forward with her rehearsed greeting. "Good morning, my name's Aeona, and this is my brother, Christopher. We're twins, but I'm four minutes older," she grinned.

"Good morning, Aeona. Good morning, Christopher," the teacher laughed. "It looks like someone's excited to come today! In you go, my lovelies, in you go!"

The teacher smiled at their mother, who stood at the side of the gate, feeling somewhat left out by the scene. "They're in safe hands," the teacher beamed. "You'll have them back sooner than you think."

With a nod, Anwen turned from the gate, feeling a little dejected, but a second later a joyous cry behind her returned a smile to her face. "Bye, Mummy!" the twins called together, followed by, "Love you!" from Christopher.

Before Anwen knew it, it was three o'clock and time to collect the twins from school. They came out all smiles, and so it appeared to be a great start to the school year.

Early in the evening, Thomas arrived home after a long haul down to London to drop off pallets of cement, then across to Swindon for a pick-up before returning to his depot in Warrington. He was always exhausted from driving up and down the country and had been searching for another job for over a year, but nothing had come his way. On his homeward stretch, he looked forward to coming home to his wife and his beautiful twins, and he couldn't wait to hear about their first day of school.

As usual, as soon as they heard the key, they came running to meet him at the front door, screaming, "Dad's home! Dad's home!" Once he had thrown his bag in the corner and taken his jacket off, he fell onto the couch with a happy groan.

"Hey, my little knights, how was it? I bet it was awesome!" he smiled. "Come on, tell me all about it."

Once they'd started, there was no stopping them. The children went on and on, from new friends and tricky maths, to weird school dinners. Aeona missed her old school and friends, but she didn't want to say that out loud. Not when her brother was bouncing around excitedly like he'd just got off a ride at the funfair.

It was only when Anwen said, 'Come on, children, you've had a long day. Leave your dad to get changed. You have to wake up early again tomorrow,' that they paused.

Thomas didn't care; it was the only real time he could play with the twins, especially now that school had begun. His job had him travelling up and down the country, so if he ran into roadworks or an accident, they would be asleep by the time he got home and he would only see them at the weekend.

He grabbed hold of Christopher and buried him under a pile of cushions. 'Come on Aeo, I'm the dragon, are you just going to let me kill your brother?" he growled. "Girl, draw your sword and get ready to battle the beast!'

Aeona jumped into action, pretending to wield a sword. "I'm coming Chris… hold on!" she screamed, ready to run at her father to save him.

'Come on Chris, quickly get out. Let's kill it!' she shouted, laughing as she picked up a cushion and pretended it was her shield, swinging her imaginary sword.

"Tom," Anwen called in a stern voice, "not before bed, you're supposed to be winding them down, not up!"

"They'll be fine. Won't you guys?" he laughed, falling off the couch and pulling them with him. "No, get them off me, Mum! Grrrrrrrr!" he roared, tickling them until they were in stitches.

"Thomas! My dear!"

"Oh-oh! She used my full name," he joked. "You know your mum's right," he beamed. "Come on, me twinnies, up we go!" He threw his little girl over his shoulder, cupped Christopher under his arm, and marched up the stairs with the two still in fits of laughter.

"One, two, three, four," they all chanted, counting the stairs with Anwen behind them.

"Now, in we go my superheroes!" Thomas screamed, lifting them high in the air as he ran down the squeaky landing to their room. "You guys are getting a bit too heavy for this!"

Anwen always scolded him for the way he put them to bed, but he didn't care or listen. He loved them dearly and never wasted a second showing it.

He swung Christopher over his head like a wrestler and slammed him flat on his back on top of the duvet. Then, spinning Aeona around several times, he did the same. However, he handled her more gently, but deep down, he knew his beautiful princess was as tough as her brother.

"Mayday! Mayday! We've been hit. We've been hit, CRASH! Aeo down, Aeo down!" She landed on her back with a flop.

"Have you finished?" Anwen growled, standing at the door.

He gave them one last tickle as they lifted their legs to slide under the duvet. "I think so, Mummy. All ready for you, captain!" he saluted with a wink.

As was routine, Thomas always tucked his daughter in, while Anwen did the same with Christopher. After kissing them goodnight, they stood silently at the door, arms wrapped around each other, savouring the moment.

"We'll leave the landing light on and the door ajar for now, okay!" smiled their father.

"Goodnight. Sleep tight, don't let the bedbugs bite!" both called.

"You too, Mummy, Daddy. Love you," the children whispered back from the dimly lit room.

***

Around two in the morning, Aeona woke restlessly, a feeling of dread settling over her as her bladder cried out for relief. Eyes wide, she realised she wouldn't be able to hold it in and slid out of bed as quietly as she could. The urgency made her scramble for the door. As she yanked at the handle, the door protested on its creaking hinges and the landing light sliced into the dark room. Christopher whimpered, rubbing his tired eyes, stirred from his sleep. "Where are you going?" he asked.

"Shhh! You'll wake Mum and Dad," Aeona whispered. "I need to go pee!"

Annoyed by the disturbance, he groaned, closed his eyes, flopped back onto his pillow, pulled the covers over his head, and went back to sleep.

Aeona listened for a second before tiptoeing past her parents' room to the toilet at the end of the landing. She made sure to hop over the loose floorboard by the spare room. Then, slowly opening the door to the toilet, she sneaked in and quietly lowered herself onto the cold seat.

The night was deathly silent; even the sound of the disturbed water echoed off the tiles like a thunderous waterfall.

When she had finished, she sat listening for her parents for a minute or so, but luckily the coast was clear. She thought it was best not to tempt fate by flushing the toilet or washing her hands, as she knew her light-sleeping mother would be woken. Her father could generally sleep through anything.

She looked down the landing as if it were an assault course. The mammoth task of getting back to bed seemed all the more daunting now her bladder was empty. She held her breath and edged gingerly towards her room. Halfway there, she looked down to where the dreaded loose floorboard was. The light above cast a line of shadow across where the carpet was pushed up like a little ridge. She couldn't understand why her father never got around to fixing it.

Then, curiosity about the spare room took hold of her. Her mother had told her that when she was nine, she would be able to have her own room, but at the moment, Christopher was too attached to his sister to sleep by himself. Hopefully, by her next birthday, she could persuade him to let her go. The thought of having her own room, with new wallpaper, bed covers, and shelves for all her dolls and teddies. It would be the best birthday ever.

She stopped at the top of the stairs and smacked her lips lightly, trying to decide if she could chance going to the kitchen for a glass of water. "It'll be alright," she whispered under her breath. Her hand was already on the bannister rail, pulling her towards mischief. She edged down as best she could, putting all of her weight on the banister when she got to the creaky fifth step. The landing light aided her secret descent. From the hall, it was an easy tiptoe through the living room, past the utility room, and into the kitchen. And the further she went, the dimmer it became, the landing light fading with every step.

In the dark kitchen, the appliances stared back at her with their glowing red eyes, humming and groaning as if disturbed. The refrigerator's clock cast a distorted light across the cupboards, creating foreboding shadows, shapes and silhouettes like ominous creatures lurking in the dark. She stood hesitant for a moment, shook off the imaginary demons, then crept towards the sink to get a glass. But as she did, she stepped onto the leg of her sleeping cat, Jinx, who let out a loud squeal of pain and bolted under the dining room table in alarm. Aeona fell backwards with fright, twisting her ankle, which gave way beneath her. Losing balance, she fell against the knobs of the cooker and lay sprawled on the kitchen floor, clutching her ankle with one hand and her shoulder with the other.

"Stupid cat!" she cursed.

Through the torn sleeve of her pyjamas, blood seeped through her fingers; the strange warmth comforted the pain, but brought focus to her ankle. She tried to move, but excruciating agony shot up her leg. She sat up sobbing quietly, thinking about what her mother would do if she found out she was downstairs, but the damage had already been done. Aeona couldn't move and whimpered on the floor, watching the clock on the refrigerator. The 02:20 bled into the night… five… ten… fifteen minutes flickered ominously forward.

A strange smell hung in the air.

Her loving father wouldn't have punished her, but in her mind, the thought of losing the promise of the spare room was more than enough to make her push through the pain. She wanted to be brave, but the tears began to stream down her cheeks. She knew she would get into trouble if she called out, but what else could she do? She thought she could say Christopher had wanted some water and that she'd fallen over one of her toys. Then half of the blame would be on her brother and the other on the toy instead of her.

"Come on, Aeo. You can do it," she coughed through gritted teeth, dragging herself across the kitchen tiles towards the dining table. The strange hissing smell grew heavier, clouding and confusing her mind. She swung her elbow onto a dining chair for leverage to get up, but the heat rising in her swollen ankle was nearly unbearable.

The red lights of the screaming clock… 02:45… distorted the swimming pain. Her mind grew foggy to the point of calling for her father. Then the pain shifted from her ankle to a dagger stabbing at her temple. She couldn't take it any longer. She breathed listlessly, coughed, and forced herself to stand.

"Where… cough… am… cough… I?" The disorientated question hung in the room. Why is the air so thick? "Da…" she coughed. "D… ad." She gasped. The gas hugged her tighter and tighter, enveloping her with its lethargic comfort, hissing ominously. The red eyes around the room watched her every move, smiled at her, warmed her… spoke to her. 'Sleep Aeona. Sleep Aeona. Sleep Aeona!' they murmured, but she shook her head in disagreement and shunned them.

"Dad, hel…" she cried. Tears poured down her cheeks from pain, from fear, from helplessness. She couldn't take the darkness anymore. The light switch was not far away. She hopped as best she could, trying to support herself on the edge of the table. She pushed the curtain aside, reached for the light switch, and pressed.

The poor girl didn't have time to react as a spark erupted into a piercing light. The blast punched her through the kitchen window into the garden. The pane shattered as her skull hit the double glazing, her body blasting through the second sheet, taking fiery debris with her. She hit the grass with such force that she rolled and slid like a fallen meteor, leaving a trough in her wake. Her motionless, burnt body lay buried in the remnants of the room she had just been in.

The shockwave engulfed everything in a fireball. The kitchen instantly burst into flames, vaporising the curtains and everything it touched.

Upstairs, Thomas and Anwen were thrown from their beds as the floor buckled and shattered like a derailed train. The fire alarm screamed from the landing. They scrambled to their feet as flames licked around the landing. Thomas ripped open the door only to be knocked back into the bedroom by the sheer blast of heat that hit him full on.

"Christopher! Aeona! Christopher!" they screamed.

It was no use: there was no escape. Thomas ran and threw the window open as far as it would go. He leaned out and peered to the right, trying to see if he could spot the children at their window, but it remained shut.

"No!" he screamed, his eyes wide with terror. "ANWEN, JUMP!" he begged.

"WHAT ABOUT MY BABIES? WHAT ABOUT MY BABIES?" she cried, trying to push him out of the way in an attempt to get to them.

Inside, Christopher was cocooned under his duvet and didn't react to the alarm nor to his parents' screaming. The cover offered little protection from the creeping death that approached from above; his breath was slowly being stripped from his lungs by the smoke that seeped through the fabric. His coughing disturbed him in his sleep, but by the time his body reacted in self-preservation, it was already too late for the poor boy. Half-dream, half-nightmare, he became aware of beings surrounding him, calling, 'Come to us! Come to us!' In fear, he shunned them and clawed at the covers in an attempt to escape to the outside world, only to be met by the blackness that swam around him. In his final moments, he gasped at the acrid smoke once… then twice… and then, the lack of oxygen sent him into a lucid dream, which faded into death.

At the bedroom window, Thomas snatched Anwen's shoulders and gave her a rough shake, trying to break her blind panic. Smoke now billowed through the gaps around the door.

"I WILL GET THEM, NOW JUMP!" he ordered. "Go… Please, Anwen, you have to go!" he said tenderly, as he forcefully edged her out onto the window sill. Shock had taken hold of her senses, and there was nothing else Thomas could do but push. In a gasp of confusion, she fell onto the car roof in the drive with a screeching clank, slipped, and bounced off the windscreen to the asphalt with a jarring thud.

He jumped back, picked up the stool next to the dressing table, and quickly climbed out, edging his way along the gutter to the children's room. He stopped just short of the twins' window and swung the stool as hard as he could against the pane, searing a crack up the glass. It needed another blow before it gave. Shards of glass exploded with the heat and impact, falling inwards into the void. Black, ominous smoke welcomed the release.

"No!" he cried, letting the stool drop.

It smashed just next to his sobbing wife and the car's headlight in the drive. "CHRIS! AEO! GET OUT! GET OUT!" she wailed.

He looked down to see Anwen screaming, pleading, praying, helpless tears streaming down her face. He grabbed at the jagged teeth of glass, blood pouring from his hands in unfeeling pain. Fighting through the seething smoke, he climbed in.

The sorrowful look in his eyes as he entered would haunt her for the rest of her life as he disappeared into the inferno. That was the last time poor Anwen saw her husband, and the memory of her beautiful children's last words, 'You too, Mummy, Daddy, love you,' hung in the burnt air.

The whole street rushed out of their homes when they heard the blast rip through the house. There was nothing anyone could do but watch in horror. People stared in disbelief over their garden fences as Thomas scrambled towards the bedroom window. There was no time to shout, except his name.

"THOMAS!"

With outstretched arms and gasps of, "No!" They watched him disappear through the broken window. They waited, breathlessly, for him to emerge with the twins in his arms.

But he never came out.

They clung to the fragile hope that he had found another exit. Yet deep down, they knew.

The dancing flames within extinguished all hope.

The Wilsons at number four, next door, were lucky to get their family out through their front door. Now, they stood on the opposite side of the road, dumbfounded, watching as their house disintegrated before their eyes. The father had tried to rescue his car, but burning debris had already fallen onto the convertible's roof. Pieces of molten plastic dripped like fiery raindrops onto the driver's seat, preventing any chance of saving his beloved car.

It took more than ten minutes for the fire engines to arrive, racing as fast as they could through the winding country lanes. They sprang into action, ushering people to safety and dragging the heartbroken mother to the other side of the road, into the arms of other residents. But Anwen was incoherent and too distraught to comprehend anything further through the night. The hoses attacked number five with as much water as they could throw at it, in a desperate bid to halt the flames from spreading down the cul-de-sac. It was too late for number three; everything Anwen had ever loved was lost forever in its ashes.

A team of firefighters broke through the side fence to reach the back of the house, where the kitchen had once stood. What greeted them was pure carnage. The house, and the poor souls who perished within, were lost. At this point the firemen didn't know if any occupants were inside, but the fire had a firm hold and the hope of anyone escaping diminished by the second. Hoses battled the inferno, while other firemen attempted to move anything flammable as far from the house as possible, throwing broken chairs, window frames, and plaster to the far corner or over the back fence. Neighbours tried to help but were told to stay back.

They lifted a window frame and, to their shock, they discovered a burnt body lying beneath, covered in broken glass and smouldering debris.

"We've got a kid!" shouted one of the firemen, ripping off his gloves to check for any vital signs. "I've got a pulse!" he yelled with urgency, as the fire intensified, hissing in fury at the water. White steam erupted into the air. In one fluid movement, he crouched, scooped her up, and ran to the far end of the garden, away from the intense heat, and out to the road. Once clear, he thrust the charred girl into the arms of a waiting paramedic, who froze in shock. She grimaced at the young child. The unexpected horror only lasted a second, but the image would stay with the woman for all of her life. It was difficult to shake off, but she spun around and sprinted towards the ambulance.

The ambulance crew, Jo and Geoff, had worked as paramedics for a number of years and had attended multiple car crashes and other medical emergencies, but the sight of the young girl, of maybe six or seven, burnt to a crisp, was the toughest yet. They had to work fast if the child had any chance of survival: her blood pressure and heart rate were low, and her oxygen levels were extremely poor. Jo pulled at the radio to call for air support. The response came fast; ETA fifteen to twenty minutes came the answer.

"I was hoping for ten," she barked back, looking to her partner, ripping the first aid bag open.

Across the road was a farmer's field where the helicopter could land. The police, who had arrived just after the fire brigade, cleared the field of spectators and had marked the side of the road with cones. The incoming chopper prompted the ambulance crew to prepare the patient for transfer as it approached.

"You ready, Jo?" the paramedic called to his partner.

"Hang on, let me just lift the O2," she said, sliding the tank next to the girl's leg. "Okay, ready!"

"One, two, three… up she goes," they grunted together, lifting the stretcher, then making their way towards the field. But along the edge of the farmer's field was a line of broken hedges and a wide ditch blocking their path.

"Shit!" Jo spat as she looked up and down the road for a way across. There was none. The thicket of brambles ran the entire length of the road. "There's no way around…" she cursed, "Hey, you!" she screamed to a couple of police officers. "You're going to have to help us get across."

They looked down at the ditch, about three metres wide, with freezing, shallow water running through the sludge and overgrown weeds.

"Erm… Right, how are we going to do this again?" one officer asked at a loss.

The paramedic wondered the same. "I… I… I don't know, but we're doing it,"

The two officers looked at one another, shrugging their

shoulders. "Well, don't just stand there!" she shouted.

To her surprise, one of the officers jumped into the water, up to his knees, and shivered. "They don't pay me enough for this! Come on, if I can do it, so can you!" he scolded his colleague.

"No! Wait. I'll need to pass it across to you," she instructed, holding her arms high in the air to reach for the stretcher. Slowly, he edged it down. When she had a firm grip, he let go and jumped into the ditch, splashing ice-cold water over the officer and the underside of the stretcher.

"Right, now let's feed it across… easy… easy… easy…" she guided. "Geoff, get down here while I climb the other side."

In no time, they had traversed the stretcher over the ditch and were carrying it quickly through the ploughed field to the waiting air ambulance. Now, it was up to the crew to take the child to the nearest specialised burns unit in Manchester. Jo quickly briefed the critical-care paramedics while they secured the girl for the flight. "You better step on it, Mike. Get on the blower to Manchester Royal, tell them we're on our way with a burn victim!" Within ten minutes, it had covered the twelve miles and approached the pad. All through the flight, the paramedics battled to stabilise her, but the outlook wasn't good. Only time would tell, and the sooner they had her down the better.

"Royal, this is G-PICU, inbound with a paediatric burn patient," radioed the pilot.

Emergency care responded seconds later, "G-PICU, Royal, copy. What's the patient's age and condition? Over."

"Approximately six to seven, female, approximately fifty per cent third-degree burns to arms, chest, and face. She is unresponsive, but we've got her breathing stabilised at present. IV fluids administered, oxygen on board. ETA five minutes, over."

When the copter landed, the resus team immediately transferred the girl to the waiting stretcher, rushing her into the emergency resuscitation bay, where the best went to work on her.

Back at the house, it took the firefighters over an hour to subdue the blaze. Only then did they discover the charred remains of Thomas, with little Christopher in his arms, lying on the living room floor after falling through the ceiling. It was then that the police turned their attention to the distraught mother, standing in the arms of a neighbour on the other side of the road, silent, eyes wide, frozen in disbelief. She was quietly led to the ambulance, covered in a silver emergency blanket, which shimmered in the flashing red and blue lights, its brightness standing in stark contrast to the chaos and outpouring of grief around her. Heads bowed, hands over mouths, silent gasps and whispers conveyed unheard sentiment for Anwen, but she was mentally in another world. The ambulance took her to Warrington Hospital for a broken collarbone, a few cuts and bruising. The doctors thought it best to keep her in for observation, due to the shock. Anwen couldn't remember much; she had shut down, her memory of the event blocked out the terror.

A couple of hours later, her sister, Melanie, arrived in utter disbelief of what had happened. But Anwen was too distraught to respond, only repeating the echoing words, "You too, Mummy, Daddy. You too, Mummy, Daddy. You too, Mummy, Daddy!" and the image of her husband fading into the swirling flames. She didn't know that her daughter had survived, nor did her sister, until the police came the following morning. When the doctor released Anwen, wearing a sling and a small bandage for her lacerated arm, Melanie drove them straight to Manchester to see the poor girl. The sight of Aeona through the ICU window compounded the sheer horror. Her baby was wrapped in bandages, tangled in wires, surrounded by beeping machines, the heart rate monitor spitting out erratic spikes, with the specialised staff rushing around the room, each action a reminder of the desperate situation they faced. With the severity of her head injury and the flash burns from the initial explosion, her condition kept everyone on edge. Her broken body sometimes gave in, but each time the call rang out, "CODE BLUE! ICU! CODE BLUE!" echoing through the hospital, every hand was on the poor girl, helping her fight for life.

She spent the next five days on the ventilator, and then, suddenly, her eyes flickered open to the desperate screams of "DAD… DAD…" But then she was gone… Seconds later… "CHRIS!" she whispered, fading back into the beeping monitors. Over the next twelve hours, the doctors weaned her off the ventilator until she was able to hold her own. Now, it was up to her to fight her way out of her stupor. When she finally managed to open her eyes and keep them open, she lay silent. Then, her mother's face came into focus.

"Mu… mmy," she whimpered, her throat sore from the ventilator. "Whe…re am I?" she asked, slowly taking in the surrounding murals of giraffes, elephants, and other brightly coloured animals that blurred into the machines. The vibrant walls drew her gaze away from the monitors and wires around her.

"Shhh… It's okay, baby, Mummy's here, lie still!" Anwen comforted softly as her daughter faded back to sleep.

∗∗∗

Aeona was in ICU for another two weeks, constantly

monitored and CT scanned on numerous occasions, with Anwen never leaving her side. The girl couldn't remember anything of what had happened, but she knew it must've been something terrible. She looked at her wrapped hands and bandages, then at her mother in a sling, bandaged and bruised on her cheek. She looked around for her father and brother, but the doctors had advised Anwen not to tell her the truth about what had happened… for the moment. Focusing on her healing was the most important thing, and being faced with the mental trauma of losing her father and twin brother would exacerbate her recovery. Luckily, the doctor explained, Aeona had been somewhat protected by the curtains in the initial blast, but the scarring to her face would need skin grafts that would take a great deal of time to heal, both mentally and physically.

Aeona had just finished another round in the CT scanner to check her skull fracture when they rolled her back into the unit. A sudden pain stabbed at her temple, causing her to wince.

"Sorry, we'll have you settled in a minute," a nurse said. They slid her into bed and began to plug her back into the main monitors when the next sharp pain thrust her into reality. Her pupils dilated, and blood drained from her face. The memory of the explosion hit her: vivid images… toilet, spare room, stairs, Jinx, pain, hissing, smell, FLASH!

"NO!" she screamed.

She couldn't grasp the chronology, but the shocking fact she couldn't deny was that it had happened. There was no doubt about that, and the purity of her heart came flooding out.

"No! I'm…" she sobbed, burying her head in her hands. "I'm sorry, Mum. I'm sorry, I'm sorry, Mum."

Anwen quickly rushed to her side. "It's okay. It's okay… I'm here Aeo… I'm here! There's nothing to be sorry for! I'm here!" her mother comforted, unsure of where to touch or pat for all the bandages. She softly wrapped her arms around the distraught girl. "It wasn't your fault. Sometimes, things happen, and we can't stop them. You can't blame yourself."

"But it was my fault!" she wailed, beating the bedsheet and pounding her knees. "Why did I? Why did I?" She struck her legs harder, her voice growing louder with each cry. "Why?" she begged, her voice breaking. The nurses tried to intervene and prevent the girl from ripping at the wires.

"Shh, my love, it's okay," Anwen whispered to her inconsolable daughter, trying to put more pressure into her hug while conscious of the bandages. "Shh… Shh… Shh," she continued, rocking back and forth. "It's okay! It's Okay!" Anwen couldn't hold back her tears any longer and let them flood down onto Aeona. It had felt so long since she had held her daughter. The sound of 'Shhh!' drowned out the machines.

Then, Aeona pushed back with a look of earnestness and asked bluntly, "Where are Christopher and Daddy?"

"I… I…" stammered Anwen, "I… don't know what to say, Aeona," she cried. "But… but… they're gone, my love."

She knew there was no way her father or her brother would have left her in the hospital all this time without rushing to her side. "Gone?" she asked, wanting to hear the words. "Gone?" she repeated.

Anwen swallowed, lowering the hands that shielded her face. The slow intake of air failed to calm her constricted chest. The words screamed in her mind; the pain of saying the reality reverberated in her throat. "They're gone… Daddy, Chris, the house… everything, Aeona. Gone!"

Aeona screwed up her face in confusion. "Gone? Gone where?"

Anwen didn't want to break it to her like this, but there was no other way. "The house went on fire; that's why you're wrapped in bandages. Don't you remember?" she sobbed. "They…. they… d… didn't make it out!"

She stared at her feet jutting from beneath the blanket as if they belonged to someone else. Her lips parted, but no sound came. A thin thread of unnoticed saliva trembled at her chin. The world pressed in, shrinking to the roar in her ears. Her heart battered at her ribs, a scream she couldn't quiet. "But… who will feed Jinx?" she stuttered.

The machines beeped on.

The question threw her mother off guard. "Oh, I'm so sorry, Aeo," wept her mother. "But, Jinx… I'm sorry, he's gone too." She mumbled, placing a hand on the girl's foot. "It's going to be okay. It's going to be okay." That's all Anwen could add.

"It's not okay! Christopher and Daddy would be here if I…" she paused, "If I… never went downstairs," she cursed, pulling her foot sharply away from her mother's hand. She then looked directly into Anwen's eyes. "I… I…" she said, hating every word. "I stood… on Jinx… and made the cooker go on."

"Jinx? What? I don't understand, Aeo," her mother asked in confusion. "What has Jinx got to do with the cooker? What do you mean, cooker?" She sat up, trying to see the connection, remembering that the fire inspectors had said it was a gas explosion, a leak or something, most likely from the cooker. "Sorry, did you say… cooker?"

The anger returned to the little girl. Her hands half over her face, she sobbed deeply. Raw emotion turned physical in self-hatred, her fists slamming the mattress in blame, but this time, her mother didn't stop her. She sat and watched in disbelief. The nurses ran over as fast as they could upon seeing the commotion.

Anwen quickly stood up, facing the child. "Do you even understand what you've done?" she questioned, forgetting she was just a mere child… her daughter! "Your dad, Christopher! They… they're gone, Aeona, GONE because of you! How could you?"

The girl shrieked uncontrollably. "Mummy, please… I didn't mean to… They can't be gone?"

Anwen lowered her gaze, lost in the moment. "Sorry, doesn't fix this! It doesn't bring them back! If you'd just stayed out of the kitchen…"

"Gone… Gone… Gone… Gone… Gone…"
Aeona screamed over and over again, lost in the flash of the fireball and desolation.

The image of her daughter, lying broken in the hospital bed, was a reminder of her failure. Her hands trembled, not just from grief, but from the unbearable truth screaming in her mind that her daughter had caused this. A nurse at the side of the room spotted what was happening and called to a doctor, who quickly ran over to the screaming mother and the hysterical girl pounding at the sheets. "Mrs Squire, Mrs Squire, I need you to leave now. You're making things worse for her. You need to calm down."

Anwen turned her fury on the nurse. "Worse? Making things worse? She's the reason they're dead! Why should I leave? She deserves to hear this!" She wasn't listening to anyone anymore.

"Mrs Squire, I understand your grief, but Aeona's in a fragile state. This is dangerous for her. I've got to insist you leave."

Anwen threw her hands up, palms raised to the heavens. "I ca… I can't believe this. My whole world's gone… because of you!" she spat at the terrified girl.

Behind her, a number of doctors and a security guard rushed in. The nurse already had a firm grip on her shoulder, her other hand on the door. "A little help," she begged, as they were quickly surrounded by the others.

One of the male doctors stepped forward, demanding, "Let's step outside, Mrs Squire. This isn't the place."

She tried to get past him to pound on the door. "She shouldn't be here. She shouldn't even be alive…" Her venomous curses ricocheted off the cold walls of the corridor until she was pulled away to the exit, but the damage inside the ICU was yet to unfold.

The young girl, hyperventilating in panic, rambled to herself. "I'm sorry! I'm sorry! It's all my fault! Dad… Chris… I'm so-so-so-so-so-so-so-ssssoo-sosos so sorry!" she wailed. She slipped from the world around her into a dark realm of demons, screaming and thrashing. "No! I didn't mean to! Water! I didn't mean to! Cat! I'm sorry! I'm sorry!" The monitor rang out its alarm as her heart rate spiked; she was breathing, panting, gasping as she deteriorated rapidly. The doctor skidded around the bed with a syringe in his hand and administered it into the IV. It took only a couple of seconds, but it felt like a frozen horror for the girl until her body and mind went limp, as she fell back onto the pillow.

"There we go, Aeona," said the heart-torn nurse, brushing back the girl's hair. "Rest now, little one."

"You okay?" the doctor asked solemnly, patting the nurse on her shoulder. "Let's monitor her closely and make sure Mrs. Squire doesn't come back in until we're sure she's calm."

Aeona was discharged from the ICU ten days later and moved to a ward with other children. She still had a little way to go before they let her out, and they said there was a light at the end of the tunnel. They never told her how long the tunnel was, but she could guess it would be longer than she liked. After all, her bandages needed to be changed painfully every day, and although she was moving her fingers again, the pain was still there. A bonus was that her head was all mended, and her face was largely unscathed. "Still a beautiful, lucky angel," the nurses told her.

She had only seen her mother about four times since the outburst of blame, not up close, as you might think, but through the window at the far end of the ICU. She never entered; she just watched without emotion, staring at her in the bed. All the other children got visitors who brought them toys, some sweets, and… attention. All she got was the love of the nurses.

In the end, Anwen stopped appearing at the window, fading into depression and solitude. Whether it was from losing Thomas and her beautiful little boy, anger for not having done more, or blame, it was difficult for anyone to speak to her or get anything coherent from her anymore.

Aeona was left in recovery with only a doll she had been given so long ago. She had no recollection of how long she had been in the hospital; she had lost count of the number of nights she'd spent looking at the ceiling, longing to see her brother and father. Their absence was a constant ache in her heart.

She blamed herself every now and then, especially when she woke screaming from the nightmare of the explosion: her finger on the switch, the spark in slow motion, and then the white light. Other times, it was when she would hear the laughter and voices of children playing in the distance. Her self-blame was a heavy burden she carried, a constant reminder of her role in the tragedy.

Finally, the day arrived when they said, "No more bandages or medicine," and the joyous words of the doctor doing his rounds, "You can go home tomorrow." However, there was no home to go to… not a conventional one anyway. The following morning, she woke to two ladies smiling at her from the bottom of her bed, holding a brown file with her name.

"So, little…" one lady began, looking at the top of the file, "…Ae-ee…on…a. Sorry dear, how do you pronounce your name?" she queried. "I've not seen it before."

Aeona expected to see her mother and glanced at the door. She sat up, confused and forlorn. "What?" she asked. "It's Ae-own-er," she answered, pronouncing her name slowly. "Why?" But she knew the answer; it was etched into her burnt hands and face. Nothing could take away that fact. The compliment from the nurses hung in her mind.

"Such a beautiful name, it sounds quite lovely," the woman smiled. "Do you know what it means?"

The young girl didn't answer. She stared into the void, blinked a few times, and slowly brought herself out of the darkness, making eye contact with the woman, then at the file in her hand. The younger woman sat at the end of the bed and said nothing.

The room was alive with children, but Aeona heard nothing. Silence surrounded her. Some children to her left were sitting in their beds hooked up to various monitors, whilst a couple of the older children were over at a table in the centre of the ward, playing with what looked like a board game.

"Umm?" Aeona murmured.

The woman asked again, "Sorry, I asked, do you know what

it means, my dear?"

Aeona gave a pause. "What does what mean?"

The woman repeated, a little confused, tapping her finger on the label of the file. "I asked, do you know what your name means?"

The girl paused again, turning her head towards the door, "My mu…" she started, squinting at the window, "…I was told by… it means 'long beauty', but I don't… remember who told me," she added expressionlessly.

"Nice, let me see if I can say it right, A-yown-na," she grinned, trying to make some connection with the child. "Was that better?" she questioned but again got no response. "It says in my little folder here that your family name is Squire. I bet I'm saying that wrong, too," she chuckled, with the other woman joining her in laughter. Aeona remained solemn, observing the two ladies.

"Now I know your name, would you like to know mine?" she asked, waiting for a response that never came. She paused. "My name is Samira, and this is my friend Naomi. We're here to talk with you for a little bit. May I ask, how are you feeling today?"

Aeona thought for a minute, but this time she never turned back to the door. She gave a long sigh. "Nobody likes me."

She knew exactly what was happening. Abandoned by her mother when she needed her most to help her through the pain, burnt, head broken, no father, and no twin brother. No one could even begin to understand the pain of losing a twin unless you're a twin yourself. It felt like she had lost herself; a part of her… was just… gone. She couldn't explain how it felt. It was just unexplainable… an unquestionable emptiness within where there used to be something… a beating heart… love. But there was nothing.

Samira softened her tone, placed the file on the cabinet beside the bed, and sat beside her colleague. "Aeona, Naomi and I work with people who help children like you. We know you're a fearless girl, and we're here to make sure you're safe and ta-?"

"Like me?" Aeona coldly interrupted.

"Sorry, dear, I mean children who… need a little help…" She hesitated. "We understand that things have been a little tough for you lately. You've been through a lot. Our job is to ensure you have a place where you feel comfortable and cared for."

The girl shuffled in the bed, her whole mannerisms changing as the tension increased. "What do you mean? Where am I going? So, my mum isn't coming, is she?" she asked coldly.

"Sorry dear, but I'm afraid she isn't. But we're working on it… she's getting a new home and making it ready for you. We're going to take you to a place where there are nice peo…"

"What?"

"…ple who can look after you. It's called a home, and other children will be there, too. It's just until we figure out the best place for you to be."

"Why can't I stay here? I want to stay here," she said sternly, banging her fists on the bed.

"I know it's hard to leave places, we really understand, but this is a hospital for sick children, and you're all better now, sweetie. Would it help if you brought some of your things with you? What's your favourite toy or book? You can pack a bag, and we'll make sure it comes with you."

Aeona slowly looked around. She was still dressed in hospital pyjamas, and everything she had was destroyed in the fire.

"I burnt everythin…"

The sentence was lost in sorrow as she buried her head in the sheet and cried into her knees. "Chris…" she wailed.

A nurse who waited at the side gently sat and held her shaking body until the wailing became sobs, the soft sobbing became weeping, and then, finally, it subsided to an exhausted, spent cry. Then, when the time came, the nurses who had cared for her for so long whispered their loving goodbyes, saying they would miss her terribly, while the two social workers made their way to the doctor to discuss discharging the little girl into their charge.

Nurse Gina dressed the girl and led her by the hand to the door, kissed her warmly on the cheek, and placed the doll her mother had brought in under her arm. "Be brave, little one. It's going to get better," she said, trying not to shed a tear.

The social worker carried a bag containing a few things the nurses had bought from a collection they'd had; enough money to buy her a few clothes, a teddy, and a couple of books she liked. At the door, Aeona stood still for a second. Then, with a gentle pull on her hand, the two ladies led her down the corridor and out of the hospital.

This is where she left the last remnants of her mother, as the automatic door bumped open… tried to close. Bumped open… and tried to close. Bumped open… unable to close as the doll lay on the threshold, blocking its way.

The only thing Aeona could see from the back seat as they bounced along the country road were the tree-tops whizzing by towards the unknown. The car smelled of overuse, a musty odour that emanated from sweet wrappers and lingered with the stains of crushed juice cartons littering the floor. To add to her discomfort, the seatbelt choked her, and for survival she held it away from her chest in order to breathe. She wanted to just get out before she caught some nasty thing.

The sound of the tyres grated on the gravel as the car ground to a halt, causing Aeona's head to loll forward and the seatbelt to slice into her throat. An unexpected gag shook her out of her dream-like state. She didn't have any expectations of where they'd stopped; she just wanted out. With curiosity, the girl unbuckled the belt, slid over beside the door, and peered outside.

The house, if it could even be called that, stood in the middle of a long terrace. The row must've been nice in its day, but now, the boarded-up windows and graffiti painted a picture of despair and hopelessness.

Samira, in the passenger seat, looked down the forlorn street and grimaced. "Are you sure this is the address?" she asked.

Naomi reached down and switched off the engine, before pulling out a file from beside her seat and resting it on the steering wheel. "Yep, it's what it says in here… right address," she answered, leaning the page towards her for clarification.

The depressing house mirrored the dull sky above. Black clouds swam amongst the grey, and thunder grumbled in the distance. Running across the front yard, vertical daggers of the broken fence stabbed outwards at various angles. A fitting welcome for the monstrosity before them, with its end posts barely able to hold the gate on its hinges as it swung in the gale.

"How the hel..." she gasped, stopping short. "...Oh! Sorry," she apologised, upon remembering the girl was sitting in the back, her head visible in the rear-view mirror. Samira leaned slightly towards her colleague, lowering her voice to a whisper. "How the heck are we going to drop her off in that?"

"I can hear you... I'm not two, you know," Aeona scowled from the back. Her eyes pierced into Naomi's as she glanced in the mirror, who didn't bother to lower her voice. She had a little more respect for Aeona's intelligence than the other. "I called the council, and they said they tried. This is the only place available for a child of her age, at the moment."

The air thickened with silence. Everyone stared at the house.

It was Samira who got out first and walked to the back of the car to open the boot. Naomi gave a hard sigh. "Sorry, Aeo, but this looks like it for now. I'm sure it's much better on the inside."

"It's not Aeo… it's Aeona! Only my dad calls me Aeo," she scolded, pulling at the handle, her defiance shining through.

The wind outside was relentless; great gusts welcomed her to the street. She had to hold her cardigan closed with both hands, its buttons pulled to breaking point, as the cold bit at her through her thin top. It couldn't get any worse for the little girl, standing in front of a house she was being forced to enter. That was until blots of rain began to spatter on the pavement around her. Then it fell like a cruel addition to her misery, making her feel even more vulnerable and alone than she already was.

Naomi was the first to run from the downpour, leaving Samira standing at the side of the road, holding the small bag of Aeona's possessions. She ran up the path to the front door, seeking cover beneath the porch. Her colleague's groans were carried away with the wind in disgust.

As it poured, Aeona felt the weight of her brother and father's absence. They had left her, abandoned her to this unknown place. How was a young girl supposed to cope with this? She was too young to understand the situation fully, but she knew one thing for sure. She had no family or home to speak of, just the unwelcoming sight before her.

A rough-looking woman in her mid-forties opened the door, her unkempt hair highlighted and bleached long ago. White roots contrasted with the faded auburn. She kindly made eye contact with the women before focusing on Aeona.

"Come, come, come, little one," she pressed, beckoning her to enter. "It's pouring down, oh my gosh, you'll catch your death!" Aeona stepped gingerly in and lowered her head.

"This won't do," the woman said sternly to the two social workers. "You should be ashamed of yourselves. All wrapped up in coats, and this young girl... What's your name, my lovely?" she asked, holding out a hand to greet the girl.

"A-Yown-Na!" she answered, somewhat shocked at the anger aimed at her chaperones.

"Aeona… just wearing a thin cardigan and no coat," she slyly winked at Samira. "Not good, not good at all." She shook the girl's hand and led her down a hallway to a dining room at the end.

"Come sit, let's dry you off," she said warmly, and in one fell swoop, she bent down, picked her up, and sat her on the dining table. Then, she got a towel from the laundry and threw it over the girl's head, rubbing it around to dry her hair. When she had finished, she threw it on the floor near the washing machine. A slight smile appeared on Aeona's face. "Oh, now that's better; that's the girl I want to see." She smiled back. "Now, my name's Mary, but you can call me 'Mar', 'Ma', or just 'M', whatever you're happy with," she chuckled. "I know I seem a bit rough around the edges, but I'm on your side, and woe betide anyone who crosses us!" She added, lifting her from the table. "You wait here, sweetie. Let me go and give those two a piece of my mind!" And off she stormed, back down the hall to the front door, shouting. "Now, this is unacceptable"

Aeona looked around the dining room. There were many pictures of children on the walls, possibly other unfortunate kids that had had to stay here. The look of the place, she couldn't think of why anyone would want to stay here unless they were forced to. Along one wall stood an old wooden cabinet with glass doors, its shelves cluttered with ornaments: a delicate lady in a flowing purple gown, captured mid-dance, her porcelain feet barely touching the ground, her arms stretched upward, frozen in graceful movement as though caught in the swirl of music. Beside it, a knitted doll with uneven stitches sat propped up against the back, its button eyes a little too large for its face, its hair a messy tangle of yarn like it had been attacked by a dog, its small arms outstretched as if offering anyone who could possibly show it any attention.

"Why would she keep a creepy doll?" she pondered, as she heard the front door closing. She turned her attention to the hall and waited. A second later, Mary appeared, with a frown. "I gave those two my two pennies' worth, so welcome to my home."

It was a line Mary had delivered countless times to Samira and Naomi. It was all just a show, a carefully scripted act she had perfected over the years of caring for troubled children. The façade generally worked, a little moment of light in an otherwise grey world of the children who came through her door: a little hope, a little love, just enough to make them feel like someone was on their side, even if it was for only a moment. Each child had left their mark on her, some more permanent than others. And with each new tear and sorrow, she had grown accustomed to the perfect charade, masking the exhaustion and the quiet heartbreak that came with caring. Despite the emotional turmoil, she enjoyed her job and wouldn't change it for the world.

Aeona looked up at her, then back at the knitted doll. Mary noticed the glance, "She hasn't got a name, you know. I've always just called her Dolly."

Aeona didn't quite believe her. It seemed too old not to have a name. "I did think of naming her Ronald, though," the woman added with a wink. "After my husband, before he ran off with…" She chuckled heartily. "I'm pulling your leg. Go on, my girl, make fun of me all you want. Yes, I know it doesn't look like a Ronald." Her laughter echoed warmly in the quiet house. She stepped closer to the cabinet and tapped her finger on the glass. "Oh, and that little lady dancing? That's one of my favourites. But my favourite, favourite is that one there. That's George and the dragon. See the way he's fighting it. That's been in the house for as long as I can remember…"

Mary paused, hoping Aeona might take the bait and add to the conversation, but she just stood quietly, staring at the ornament. A knight astride a rearing white horse, his spear striking home as the dragon flared its wings, jaws wide in the fight with its tail coiled ready to strike. The cliché of knights and dragons didn't entertain the girl enough to warrant a comment.

Mary broke the silence with a grin. "Okay! Maybe we can talk about them later. Now, who's hungry? I know I could do with a cheese sandwich or something. Come on, let's see what we've got in the fridge." She gently reached out, offering her hand.

Aeona hesitated for a moment, then slowly took Mary's hand with a quiet sigh.

The woman glanced down with a smile and opened the door to the kitchen. Suddenly, Aeona froze, fear washed over her, her eyes widening, her breath caught in her throat, sealing her lungs. This was the first time she had stepped foot into a kitchen since the accident. The horror of the explosion in pinpoint detail seared through her mind.

The painful squeal of Jinx as he ran under the table. The sting of her shoulder as she fell onto the cooker. Hissing - smell - FLASH! "No!" she choked. Unable to move at the doorway, her hand fell limply out of the woman's hand as a warmth seeped down her legs to the carpet. She gasped in short, panicked bursts, constricting her chest.

Mary panicked herself; this wasn't something she'd read about in the girl's file: Nothing medical… no epilepsy or anything else. In desperation, Mary gently placed a hand on the girl's shoulder, but the moment she touched her, the child recoiled violently, cracked her head against the door frame, and with a sharp cry, she spun, fell to the floor and scrambled back into the dining room to curl into a ball beneath the table.

Mary, in shock, stood motionless at the doorway. She quickly looked around to see if there was any danger that she was unaware of, but finding nothing, slowly lowered herself to the carpet, using the table leg to stabilise her aging knees. Aeona lay sobbing in bursts of convulsions and screams of remorse.

"Shh… shh… It's okay," Mary soothed, sitting a metre or so away from the poor girl, her voice barely above a whisper.

The prone girl cried her little heart out so much it brought tears to Mary's eyes. When it looked like it wasn't going to subside, the heartbroken woman edged slowly forward and gingerly placed a hand on Aeona's foot. She threw her leg back, uncoiled like an exploding jack-in-the-box, and looked around in confusion. Then, Mary came into focus.

"Shh… shh…" Mary hushed with palms open. "It's okay. Nothing's here to hurt you." Through glazed eyes of sadness, it took a minute for Aeona to register. It was then that the silent tears began to stream and fall hopelessly onto her lap. Mary said nothing; the act didn't warrant it, but her beckoning hand gently coaxed the girl from under the table onto the carpet. With her head bowed, Aeona slid out with fragile-embarrassment. Mary softly deflected the event, "Shall we go and get you cleaned up?"

Aeona gently nodded, reluctant to look the woman in the eye. Mary wrapped an arm around the girl's shoulder for comfort, and as she did, her hand felt the dampness. Confused as to whether it was sweat or not, she slowly looked down at her bloodied-hand, wet from the gash at the back of the girl's head. She reached across the floor and picked up the towel she had used earlier to dry the girl's hair, and gently placed it over where she suspected the cut was.

"May I pick you up and put you on the chair?" she asked. A second affirmative nod came from the shaking child. Mary couldn't at the moment understand what had triggered the episode, but whatever it was, it had something to do with the kitchen.

"I think the best place to start…" Mary comforted, "…is to sort out the little cut you have on the back of your head." Which, upon close inspection, thankfully was only a break to the skin. After the bleeding had stopped, Mary gently cleaned it and dripped a couple of drops of iodine on it for good measure. "Right, now we've got that sorted. What do you say we go upstairs for a change of clothes, hey?" she asked calmly. She was about to say something else when the dining room door swung open.

The motionless frame of an older girl stood in the doorway. Her form seemed to engulf the space around her. Long black hair hung straight like a curtain, obscuring her sharp cheekbones, which stretched and pushed at the skin that covered them. Her eyes, dark and unblinking, scanned the room with an eerie stillness, as if she were seeing things others couldn't. Her clothes reflected her inner darkness; worn, black lace sleeves peeked out from a tattered leather jacket, ripped tights, and boots that thudded softly with each step. A silver pendant hung from her neck, nearly hidden beneath the layers of her dull, dark clothes. It was as if she didn't belong in the light, and she didn't care. Whether in the corners or the dark, she was at home.

Surprised to see her emerge from her bedroom of shadows, Mary welcomed the distraction. "Hi Nyxa, happy to see you. We've got a new visitor. Why don't you say hello? This is Aeona."

The girl gave a single nod, barely a movement at all, with an almost inaudible, "m…" given in recognition to the child on the chair. Mary avoided Nyxa's gaze, not out of fear, but because there was something about her that felt like a riddle that was better left unsolved. Mary had tried to connect with her on numerous occasions, but the teen seemed to linger as if the light itself was reluctant to touch her. Most of the time, Nyxa wouldn't respond to any small-talk and had an uncanny ability to blend silently into the shadows whenever the woman tried to have a conversation.

Mary knew some of the story behind how she'd come to stay in the Home, from her file. It read differently from Aeona's in many respects, but it was no less heart-breaking. The heavy hand of her father on her mother and her older sister, and then eventually on her. The memory of her father's fists still haunted her, even though he was long gone. It was in the way she flinched when someone raised their voice or the way she closed off when Mary asked questions.

Nyxa's restlessness, the need to escape a past that still haunted her. The first time she ran away, Mary was at her wit's end and called the police. They spent a great deal of time searching and questioning all of her known contacts to no avail. Only for her to turn up a few days later without any explanation of where she'd been. By the fifth time she'd run away, the police brushed off frail leads and said, "let us know if she doesn't come back in a few days." Mary knew she was a good girl and wouldn't do anything the other feral children did like drugs and other worse things. In the end, Nyxa wasn't much different from Aeona in that they both had nobody to look after them.

Mary could see the reflection of herself in the two girls and understood far too well what it was like. She too was from a broken home, a tragic echo of the countless other children she'd taken in. She couldn't understand why some parents put their own children through so much hell. All she had was love for the poor orphans. She was no saint by any means, but had never raised a hand in anger in her life.

The stillness of the encounter hung silently in the air until Mary broke it and bent down to pick up the bloody towel from the floor. Nyxa saw the chance and without a word, walked into the kitchen to retrieve something from the refrigerator. Mary turned quickly to block the view of the kitchen as Nyxa disappeared through the door. Then she took hold of Aeona's hand and led her upstairs to her room. It didn't take long to have Aeona cleaned and changed and resting on her bed, drained by the whole experience.

"You rest here for a little while I go and make you something to eat. I'm sure you must be hungry," Mary stated. Aeona, still feeling somewhat embarrassed, gave a murmuring nod.

"Good, I shan't be long," the woman smiled and headed downstairs, leaving the girl to take in her new room.

When she was halfway down, Nyxa rounded the corner to stop on the first step. Mary glanced over her shoulder before whispering. "Nyxa, please."

The teenager looked at the bottle in her hand and the packet of biscuits in the other, then back at Mary, "I'm sorry," is all she could muster.

"You've been here long enough. You know the drill. I don't need to say," Mary said softly.

"Yes, I understand. I'll make it up to her tomorrow." Nyxa answered apologetically.

"Please. You know how it is when a new kid arrives," Mary explained, before shifting focus, not wanting to over-do the issue with her. "I'm making dinner, please save the biscuits till later, okay."

"I'll try," Nyxa smirked, skirting passed her on the way up.

At the top, she glanced to the end of the landing where the new girl's room was. Nyxa couldn't hear the usual crying all new kids tended to do, and didn't want to push her luck. "Tomorrow," she whispered to herself, retreated to her own room, and closed the door behind her. She leaned backwards onto the pile of clothes that hung on the door and waited for her eyes to become accustomed to her dimly lit room. The window failed to exist; the curtains remained forever closed. Gradually, the furniture presented themselves to her from the darkness. The bed, black like the curtains, with its grey sheet pulled from its mattress. The creases ran like black veins showing that it had not been made for quite a while. Plastered on every wall, posters depicting creatures and mythical beings, with piercing eyes that seemed to follow the timid around the room. No one else dared enter, except Mary on the odd occasion, to pick clothes from the floor and remove plates of half eaten food.

Her desk sat near her chest of drawers nestled in the corner with numerous shelves scattered around for her books and paraphernalia she liked to collect. Overcrowded spines of dark literature, all perfectly organised by size or colour, snaked around the room. To Nyxa, they were more than just stories; she loved everything about them. Through each page, she could push away her own demons and chaos, if only for a little while. She didn't have to fight for survival in those worlds. There she could wrap herself in the safety of the pages and the solace of her dark thoughts. It helped her to drown out the yelling and screaming of her father, her mother's cries at the brunt end of his fists in another unwinnable argument, her sister's tears from being caught in the crossfire. Nyxa was too small to intervene; a split-lip and a scar on her eyebrow had taught her that.

She settled on her bed and had munched her way through most of the biscuits when Mary knocked on the door to bring her a plate of food. She then disappeared to take the same to Aeona on a tray. That was the last she saw or heard of her for the rest of the night. Nyxa didn't like wasting time on her phone like most teenagers; she only used it primarily for telling the time or using it for night-reading. Indelibly burnt into her mind was that the room-light would give her away. Another thing she had learnt as a young girl; cruelty taught her to stay out of the way. With the plate slid onto her dresser, she pulled out a random book from above her bed. In the evenings, it didn't matter which book it was; she had in fact read them all. None could be considered to be night-time reading. Tonight's would be 'The Banshee', the harbinger of doom in Irish Mythology, supposed to foretell the impending death of anyone unfortunate enough to hear their sorrowful cries, or so it said in the preface. She didn't believe in the stories she read, not in their entirety, but the thrill of gothic-horror intrigued her.

She flicked over the first few pages until she came to chapter one: 'Omen of Impending Death.'

The word reverberated over and over, "impending death, impending death, impending death, impending death, impending death," which grew louder and louder until it screamed at her. She clasped her hands over her ears in an attempt to drown it out. The book slipped off her knees and fell to the floor. Then, the screaming abruptly stopped.

She waited, not daring to lower her hands, until the words slowly faded into the void. Cautiously, she opened her fingers as if daring herself to listen again. "I must be getting sick or something," she said, raising her palm to her forehead to check if she was hot.

Then, a low rumble, almost words but indiscernible, ever so quietly at first, difficult to place. She readied herself to quickly block her ears for the next onslaught. But this time she didn't hear its warning; she felt it thumping from somewhere under the bed. It was unmistakable.

'thud, thud, thud.'

She scanned the room for an answer. When none came, she pulled at her duvet, flipped onto her stomach and edged over the side of her bed to peer into the darkness.

There it was again; she was sure it came from her dresser.

A bead of sweat slowly ran down her forehead to the tip of her nose.

"Come on, Nyx… What the hell are you doing?" she scoffed at herself, trying to shake off the uncomfortable feeling of dread. What else was she to think, 'impending death' thundering in her ears and now the 'thud, thud, thud' from her dresser?

She had read enough to know when the jump-scares were coming, but this was something else! This was not on screen, not in the text; this was real.

'It's definitely in the room,' she thought to herself, cocking her head to one side in an attempt to lock onto something.

Then, a single 'thud' was all she needed.

"There… got you!"

She crept out of bed and knelt on the floor in front of the dressing table as if urged to do so. She pulled the bottom drawer from its runners and placed it beside her. In the space, hidden from prying eyes, was her box in which she hid all of her special things: a few photographs, some horror magazines she thought Mary wouldn't approve of, and a book.

Silence.

"Come on, what do you want?" she questioned, waiting for the sound.

'Thud'

Nyxa jumped backwards in surprise as the book seemed to slam itself against the side of the box by some unseen force. When she had composed herself, she gingerly reached into the box, hand shaking, and picked it up. It had never done anything like this before. But, then again, she had never brought herself to read it either.

She had bought it online from a place lost from memory. She had tried to search for the website again, but no matter how hard she tried, it always drew a blank. No reference to its title; 'Shadows Chant' nor any of the chapters.

It was the cover that enticed her: old and tattered, with its title snaking across the bottom. The picture depicted the back of a child looking toward some old ruins in the distance. It was difficult to discern whether it was a boy or a girl, but with the shoulder length hair Nyxa surmised it to be a girl. Red stained-ivy entangled her feet, as if pulling her through an archway to the unknown, with claw-like fingers taunted from above.

In truth, Nyxa had ordered on a whim, not thinking it would

actually arrive. But for only the price of a burger, she thought it was worth the risk. To her surprise, about a month passed and the bell rang, but by the time she got downstairs, the person had left, and on the step, there it was. Excitedly, with it tucked under her arm, she ran upstairs two-steps at a time, jumped onto her bed and opened the package.

When she finally managed to open the heavily taped box, it was clear it was a book, but it was covered in brown-sacking and tied firmly with thick-string and a big knot. She couldn't think why, but it added to the mystery of the contents.

She thought it was a new book on the website, but looking at the actual thing in her hands it was all battered with bent corners. She turned it over to see if it had a blurb. On the rough back was a simple quote: 'Dark stories, evoking suspense and mystery of the disappearing ones.'

Nyxa didn't know what to think, except to flip it back over and begin.

The contents page was also a strange read: some spells, creatures, summoning, and a couple with quirky titles that didn't stir any emotions, scary or otherwise. "Okay, so, Chapter one, Candle burnt." she read.

To the side of the title was a small etching of a black candle with someone's fingers holding a match, drawn irregularly to illustrate a shaking hand, and under it was a short blurb to interest the reader.

'Fire is fire, melting wax and time. Extinguished souls of those who seek the past.'

"Pretty cliché," she thought to herself, defusing the tension it was supposed to create.

As she turned the page, her heart missed a beat, and her mouth fell open with a sharp gasp.

There, right on the page was a face… her face, Nyxa's face stared back at her. Her piercing eyes, filled with terror, tears streaming as if pleading for help as if she was looking straight into a mirror. It was unmistakable. On the page was a girl holding a blood-soaked knife, her hand slick with blood. Mouth wide open mid-scream, "No!" seemed to reverberate from the page.

Panic surged through her, causing her to slam it closed and throw it across the room. She sat motionless, her hands shaking, eyes wide, questioning what she had just seen.

"What the fuck…" she whispered, her voice tight with disbelief. "How? How's it even possible?" Her mind spiralled, struggling to make sense of it. But looking at it was like staring into her own soul: the same nose, jawline, hair and those eyes! "It couldn't be a… a coincidence?" she questioned, "What about the kni…?" The trigger fired into hatred, a memory she couldn't push away. She threw herself backwards onto the pillow, nearly cracking her head onto the headboard.

She was twelve again, standing in the kitchen, her hands wrapped around a knife as she washed the dishes. Her mother hunched over at the counter, shielding herself from her father's cruel words. The ghost like sound of slaps, the dull thuds of fists. Nyxa had grown numb to it over the years. Her sister had left her to the violent wolf. The memory of her retaliation came flooding back.

Her mother collapsed to the floor, her nose broken, dripping in transfixed slow-motion. Its drip-drip-drip exploding in her ears. The terror in her mother's eyes ripped into Nyxa's chest. 'I can't let him do this anymore.' A fierce, uncontrollable surge of anger rose within her. She watched herself, like an out of body experience, reliving every second.

The knife in her hand, slick with soap, but in that moment,

everything was about to change. She lunged at the monster without thinking. He stumbled back, clutching his stomach, gasping at the unexpected ferocity. It wasn't deep enough to kill him, but as she withdrew the knife, its blood-soaked blade dripped onto the tiled floor.

He thrust his hand onto the slice that quickly turned red, screaming, "I'm going to kill you!"

Nyxa didn't flinch or move. She bared her teeth and hissed at him with seething fury.

"Get out, you bitch! Get out!" he screamed.

She grabbed her mother's limp form, lifted her off the floor, and dragged her toward the door, without breaking eye contact, waving the knife at him. Her hands shook, but this wasn't the time for hesitation or backing down. This was survival.

With a frantic burst of energy, struggling to hold onto her mother and the knife at the same time, she put the knife in her left hand, grabbed the car keys from the table and carried the floundering woman outside. She bundled her into the passenger seat and slammed the door. He was already at the front door behind them.

She turned and squared up to him, ready for his advance down the path. But he didn't dare; Nyxa wasn't like her mum or sister, he knew that. She stood firm for a second and then when he turned his attention back to his blood-filled hand, she saw the chance and ran around to the other side to jump into the driver's seat.

She didn't know how to drive, but had observed the monster on many occasions. The adrenaline surged through her in a wild, reckless need to escape. Her father had got his second wind. He ran to the car and dove onto the bonnet, pounding and screaming vile curses at her. His voice barely audible over her pounding heart in her ears.

With a turn of the key the engine fired up. Nyxa yanked the gear stick to R and slammed her foot on the pedal. No mirrors or look back. With a screech of tyres, her world changed forever.

Nyxa didn't notice the oncoming lights of the HGV bearing down on their driveway as she lurched into the street. The truck driver didn't even have time to react, hitting the side of the car with such terrifying force. The deafening impact of twisted metal sliced through the saloon like a butter-knife. The crumbled mass was punched twenty metres down the street where it barrel-rolled into the ditch with the mangled occupants still inside.

When she eventually opened her eyes, Nyxa was in the hospital, alone. Her mother paralyzed from the neck down, spine shattered, unable to move, and… unable to care for her. Ashley nowhere to be seen, left Nyxa with nothing but the wreckage of her past, broken and lost, just like the twisted car.

The sickening memory left as fast as it came. It left her propped on her pillow with sweat streaming from her brow. She'd not thought about the event in a long time, but seeing that picture must've triggered the suppressed memory out of the dark. It took a few minutes for her to compose and meditate herself away from the crash. She couldn't think about it anymore; she shook herself and buried it back down to where she'd hidden it.

"What the hell is wrong with me? It's just a stupid coincidence." She forced, focusing on the book again. It called to her, had a picture of her, and made noises, but she would rather face it than her dark memories of her father and what she had done to her mother.

With a deep sigh, she climbed out of bed and picked the book up. "Stupid thing," she muttered, nervously put it back in its brown-sacking and wrapped the string around it as many times as she could. She placed it back in the box and slid the drawer back into place. That night, sleep came in fits and starts, haunted by her ghosts unwilling to let her find peace.

Early the next morning, at the other end of the landing, Aeona woke early and sat in her bed listening to the birds outside her window. She didn't want to go wandering around in a strange house and so waited for the woman or the strange girl to make some noise to indicate that they were awake.

It didn't take long for her to hear approaching footsteps and then came a knock on the door, which slowly opened followed by the head of the woman.

"Oh, you're awake," she smiled, noticing Aeona sitting up in bed. "Good morning, did you manage to sleep well?"

Aeona returned, "Yes, thank you," with a faint smile.

Without a fuss, the woman walked in, opened the curtain and unlatched the window to let some fresh air in. She then pottered around the room pretending to straighten things up. It had been a long time since Aeona had been in a house and didn't know what to do except sit watching.

The woman felt she had lingered enough to make her presence settle on the girl before breaking the awkward silence. "So, what about breakfast?" and not waiting for a response followed it with a loose order, "by the time you've been to the bathroom, I'll have it on the table, come on, out you get." She then promptly walked out of the room, leaving the door open. Aeona was left in her own thoughts as Mary disappeared downstairs, and a minute later, she was followed by the other girl from the other end of the landing.

There was no point waiting for the woman to come back upstairs to see where she was, so it was better to just follow along until she could find her place in the Home. After the toilet, with no toothbrush to call her own, she headed down to start the day. At the bottom of the stairs, she was met with four closed doors and not knowing which to enter, she stood listening. A radio played in one, but it was difficult to discern which. It was on the third attempt she found the dining room and walked in to find the woman sitting at the table alone. In the middle was a plate of hard-boiled eggs and next to it, some already made toast and a plastic tub of margarine. Mary met her with a warm smile, picked up the knife and proceeded to eat her breakfast. "Come along my dear, before it gets cold. Have a seat."

The woman carried the conversation by herself with the occasional nod from the girl until they had finished and Aeona drank the last of her milk.

"Thank you for eating with me," she gestured to the girl, and then nodded her head to the vacant chair pushed back away from the table. "Nyxa usually doesn't like my small talk, but it's okay. Each to their own. Now why don't you have a wander around and get familiar with the place, while I go and clean up in there. That's the kitchen," she pointed, "just so you're sure?" She remained seated, putting the empty plates and knife on top of one another, waiting for Aeona to make her leave. Mary didn't want to open the kitchen door until she was sure Aeona had left. She thought it better to be safe than sorry until she could figure out what the trigger was to last night's episode.

"Thank you," Aeona said, pushing her chair in and walking back out into the hall.

The door to her right was a downstairs toilet and the one to the left was a small cloakroom full of old musty coats and umbrellas. That only left the one at the end to explore, which she could only guess to be the living room. She turned the protesting knob and entered.

The room had the usual couch, fireplace and coffee table but it was difficult to see anything clearly due to the curtains still being closed. Aeona walked to open them and bring some clarity to the dimly lit room, and was about to pull them aside when she was stopped by a voice. "Leave 'em," it resounded.

Startled, she spun around to see the dark form of the other girl sitting in an armchair nestled in the corner of the room.

Aeona stood still for a moment before sitting herself on the couch on the opposite side to observe the teenager. She peered silently, trying to figure her out.

Nyxa sensed her staring and subtly glanced up from her book, then lowered her eyes again.

"I like you," she whispered.

Aeona eased her frown, unsure of what she had just heard. Nyxa glanced again to see if the girl was still glaring at her. Thick liner framed her foreboding eyes, which rapidly shot across the page as she read. And every so often, a long spider-like nail, painted in the same jet-black shade as her lips, would slowly turn the page. The truth was that Aeona had never seen a girl like her before.

Nyxa's words drifted in a ghost-like breath and snaked their way across the room to her, "You read?"

Aeona pursed her lips. She liked them and imagined whether she would look as intimidating as her. Then she plucked up the courage, trying to imitate the girl's mysterious tone. "I can read..." she growled, shyly adding, "a little." It was clear that they were both testing each other, wanting to trust but neither wanting to let their guard down.

"You like playing with fire too?" Nyxa tested.

Aeona tried to hold herself, "Don't," she spat.

"Don't what?" she asked, not raising her eyes from her book.

"Just don't!" This time, Aeona forced the words through her

piercing eyes.

The older girl continued reading, showing no interest in the disdain thrown at her from across the room. Then she said something that threw Aeona off guard.

"It looks good on you."

Aeona couldn't think of anything to say, not knowing how to take the comment, and sat quietly.

Nyxa had seen numerous children come through the Home. She had herself tried foster parents, but it never worked out. The whole happy family charade always felt fake. She couldn't help but feel sorry for the people who took her in, only for her to put them through hell until they eventually asked the social workers to take her back. And so, as Mary often said, she was "part of the furniture." She liked being in this run-down house. Mary seemed to understand her painful history and left her to her own devices, always providing just enough care, just enough love, and just enough distance to make her feel comfortable. A kind of loving rope which kept her close without smothering her. Now came a new stray who felt different from the others. Aeona came off as tough, battle-hardened. Whether it was the scars or her mimicry was yet to unfold.

The two girls sat silently. Aeona's eyes never left Nyxa as she studied her closely, noting how her fringe fell over her eyes like dark shadows framing her moonlit skin. Whenever Nyxa glanced her way, a flash of pure whiteness lit the room like a lightning bolt, beautiful and blinding. Eventually, Nyxa glanced at the girl and held the stare, both locked in competition to see who would blink first. The teenager had never lost to anyone, but it looked like she had finally met her match.

"Come, read," Nyxa ordered, patting the arm of the chair and coaxing the girl into the dark.

Aeona shook her head gently, wary of the strange girl.

"Come… but I might bite…" she teased, her fingers tapping the arm again. "I dare you."

Aeona couldn't back down now and slowly slipped off the end of the couch, taking the invitation. She carefully edged forward towards the tapping finger as if it were an X on a map. "Jump up, I bet you can't," the older girl grinned, her dark character on full display.

Nyxa twisted the book so the girl could see the page. Aeona was hit with a grotesque image of a woman in a long black dress, blood flowing down from a cut in her neck, which caused her to flinch backwards in horror. "Not funny!" she said sternly.

Nyxa gave a little smile, "Read!" she demanded.

The second time seeing the picture, Aeona forced herself to be firm and not give the other girl the satisfaction.

She began to read to herself, but halfway through the first sentence, Nyxa stopped her.

"I can't hear you. Read it aloud," she ordered.

"Okay… so…" Aeona hesitated. "The vampire moved closer to the crying girl, cornering her against the wardrobe, unable to move." Aeona thought that was enough for now.

"Carry on," Nyxa pressed, her dark eyes bore into Aeona, "continue."

Aeona read on, her voice faltering as she did. "The vampire pressed a finger to the girl's lips, silencing her. 'Shh…' she hissed, slowly turning her prey's head to one side before sinking her fangs in… Urgh!" She finished, repelled by the text. "What's this?" she asked, her face twisted in disgust, while Nyxa let out a quiet snigger.

"You don't you know what a vampire is?" she asked, her tone teasing.

Aeona shrugged. "Of course, I know."

Nyxa flipped to the front of the book and ran her finger down the contents list. "Stop me when you've heard of any of these: Annabel… Catherine? Claudia? Dracula?"

"Stop," Aeona interrupted. "I know that one. We used to watch cartoons with that guy. The man with sharp teeth, I remember."

"Nice…" Nyxa smiled, her eyes glinting with mischief. "What do you mean, 'we'?"

"I mean… my dad and… and… my brother," she paused, the words caught in her throat.

"Okay, nice," Nyxa acknowledged, but she didn't press the subject. "Next… you read," she continued.

"Okay, so… that's… Edith, Emily, Eu… la… lie, Eulalie… is that how you say it?" Aeona asked.

Nyxa's nodded in agreement.

"Frankenstein… I know that one too, Madeline, Mina & Lucy, Morella, Rebecca, Sophie… and the last one, Vampiress."

This was how Nyxa introduced Aeona to her gothic world. Over the next few days, the two girls sat in the living room, quietly reading. With each dark tale, a new mystery unfolded, pulling Aeona deep into a realm of Nyxa's books. Aeona found herself captivated, drawn further into a world of shadows and secrets.

CHAPTER SIX 'AEO'

The social workers, Samira and Naomi, popped in every now and then, always smiling and sitting with Mary in the kitchen. Aeona never cared to guess whether they sat there because they knew she wouldn't venture in or because they just enjoyed the place for tea and conversation. Regardless of the reason for their visits, Aeona found profound comfort in Nyxa. They never broached the subject of their losses; their bond formed over time and became unbreakable. They both understood the subtleties of their relationship: they had endured hardships better left alone. Their journey from solitude to finding solace in each other's company was a testament to their emotional resilience.

One evening, the two girls were in Aeona's bedroom, looking through some of the things Nyxa had amassed from her online orders. There were classic novels like Frankenstein, Jekyll and Hyde, and Stoker's Dracula, to name but a few. Others were magazines depicting 1900s serial killers: Jack the Ripper, Burke and Hare, Margaret Waters-Williams. The one she loved the most was Sweeney Todd, the Demon Barber, but she knew he was just a fictional character.

At around nine-thirty, Mary called them down for supper. The usual toast was on the table waiting for them. When they had got through the first piece and were about to start their second, Mary got up, went into the kitchen, and called Nyxa to give her a hand getting something from the top cupboard. Once in the kitchen, Mary pulled her aside. "Please don't be upset," she whispered, "but could you calm it down with all the horror? I don't like what you're letting Aeona read."

"It's okay, I'm keeping that stuff away from her," she said reassuringly. "We're only reading scary stories. No blood."

"Please keep it that way, okay," Mary ended, giving her a concerned nod, and then waved her off to return to the dining room, calling 'thanks' after her to make the premise a little more believable.

Once the two girls had finished, they ran upstairs to flick through some more magazines before bed. Frankenstein was the focal point of their night's discussion. Laughter filled the room about the pictures of the Monster strapped to the table in the laboratory in a tangle of electric cables. Aeona knew nothing about it, except what she had seen in cartoons on television. This prompted her friend to paraphrase the whole story, but in fact, Nyxa had never got around to finishing it.

"I know, it's stupid, but it is, what it is," she said, turning the pages. "Anyway, Frankenstein sews all these parts together, then zaps it to life with electricity. The Monster ran around killing people, and then I got bored. I never finished it," she chuckled. "So, I don't know what happens in the end. I can only guess the people kill it." The cliché had the two of them erupting into laughter, which was brought to an abrupt halt by Mary shouting from the bottom of the stairs.

"Come on, you two, it's getting late. ten minutes to get to the bathroom and into bed, okay?" Mary called.
"Shhh, we still have lots of time. She'll forget about us once she puts the TV on," Nyxa whispered mischievously, before continuing, "So, this one here is a little different." She reached across the rug and pulled a fairy tale from the bottom of the pile, a story about dragons. "I like some of these stories," she said softly.

After all, she'd promised Mary she had it under control. 'Calm down the gore and superstition right before bed,' Mary had scolded her, or something along those lines. Nyxa's outward appearance didn't reflect the torn teenager beneath; she was just a normal girl who had been dragged through the dirt. "Ok, this one's about a dragon," she said, showing Aeona the front cover.

"Dragons? Dragons aren't real," the young girl stated.

"What makes you think that?" Nyxa asked, going through the book.

Aeona reached across and stopped at one of the pages. Her finger fell onto an image of an 'Assipattle'. "Now look at it," she laughed. "Come on, look at it. Does that look like a real creature to you?"

With a grin, Nyxa couldn't help but agree: "Yes, I know, but they didn't have cameras then, did they, and I suppose… they couldn't draw either," she laughed.

"And," added Aeona between fits of laughter, "What are you going to call it, an Ass-dragon?"

The two were now practically rolling on the floor, clutching their sides as they desperately tried to stay quiet.

"We're so dead if Mary hears us!" Nyxa shushed.
Aeona's eyes widened in jest. "Listen, footsteps!"

With a sharp gasp, Nyxa's breath was stolen from her lungs. Her face drained of colour, and her whole body tensed as she seized Aeona's arm. Her pupils widened as if frozen in a memory. She wasn't with Aeona anymore; she was hiding under her bed, listening for her father's footsteps.

"Nyxa… let go… you're hurting me!" Aeona yelped. But Nyxa wasn't there. She was lost in her own body. Tears streamed down her face. Her nails dug deeper and deeper into the younger girl. Nyxa trembled violently, and Aeona shook with her in a helpless, brutal rhythm she couldn't break free from. She tried to pull away, but the force of Nyxa's grip tore into her, sending jolts of pain deep into her arm.

"Nyxa! I said you're hurting me, let go! Let go!" Aeona cried, the desperation in her voice.

But Nyxa wasn't listening; she had to be quiet, he was coming.

Her older sister echoed in her mind. "Hide, Nyxa, hide."

The phantom of Ashley pushed her under the bed, and then came the sound. The stamping of her father's fury just outside the door, cracking his belt on the banister. She knew he was going to find her.

Aeona's sharp cry cut through Nyxa's haze, piercing the wall of memory that surrounded her. It struck her like a thunderclap, jolting her back into the present.

"Nyxa!" Aeona shouted in desperation, trying to shake herself out of the vice-like grip.

Suddenly, Ashley's cries faded into Aeona's tears…
"Please, let go."

It took a moment for Nyxa to loosen her grip, and then, when the terror subsided, she stared at Aeona, half in disbelief, half in embarrassment.

"Aeona…" her voice cracked, thick with raw emotion. She looked down at her hand grasped around the girl's arm and quickly let go when she realised what she had done. But the damage had already been done. The evidence, on the verge of drawing blood, stood like claw marks on the child's skin.

"Please… Aeo… I'm sorry," the distraught girl wept. Her hands shook as she pulled Aeona into a hug. "I'm sorry… I won't let him hurt you. I won't." In truth, she was still locked between the two worlds, conscious of the now, but the past was trying to pull her back.

The pent-up emotion flooded over Aeona's shoulder as Nyxa released everything. The pain, the suffering, the blame. The two girls sobbed in each other's arms, locked in a mutual search for comfort.

How long they remained like this wasn't important. Physical

exhaustion made them fall away from each other. Nyxa exhaled, slowly, her breath easy now.

"Aeo…" Nyxa whispered, taking the girl's hand gently.

"Thank you," Aeona whispered back. Nothing needed to be explained. She jumped forward and threw her arms around the older girl in a tight hug. "I'm happy I found you.

As Nyxa held Aeona close, a quiet realization settled in her heart: she was no longer alone. The weight of her past, the ghosts that had haunted her for so long, no longer had the same grip on her. In Aeona, Nyxa found not only a companion but a source of strength. For the first time, she understood that she didn't have to carry her burdens in isolation. This shift, this understanding, was a quiet but profound moment of growth for both of them. Nyxa wasn't just the protector; in essence, they were protecting each other, a bond forged in shared pain and mutual resilience. In that moment, she knew she could face whatever came next, because they were no longer two broken souls, but two halves of a whole.

February arrived, bringing a gale that howled through the trees and rattled the windows like restless spirits. The heavy clouds that followed brought with them a blanket of white.

For the girls, the thought of venturing out never crossed their minds. They heard the distant laughter of children playing in the street and pulled back the curtains to watch them throw snowballs, but they couldn't quite understand the appeal. They preferred to stay indoors, curled up in their rooms playing or reading, with the occasional break to the living room to watch television. Mary liked these moments when the two girls came to join her. It felt like she had a family again.

Her children had long left the nest, finished university, and travelled to warmer climes to begin their lives. They visited once or twice a year depending on work schedules and the cost of flights. She wanted the best for them, but the winters felt colder since her husband passed away a few years ago. Even with radiators on full and the presence of the girls, there were nights when the house felt unbearable, and loneliness buried her deeper than any snowfall outside.

In the evening, the girls sat in Nyxa's room reading through some new magazines when Mary entered to collect their plates from supper. "Come on, ladies, it's nearly ten," she said. "Who's first to the bathroom?" Not waiting for a reply, "Rock-paper-scissors if you're going to argue about it," she added, giving Nyxa a smile as she looked down at the magazines spread across the rug.

"You first, Aeo. Let me tidy these up," Nyxa said, shuffling the magazines into a pile. Mary couldn't help but raise her eyebrows at how softly Nyxa spoke to the young girl and was even more surprised by the shortening of her name. It warmed her heart. Nyxa had been with her for a few years now and had expressed no feelings toward any other children who had come through the door.

Mary held the door open with one hand and a tray in the other. Aeona got up, ducked under her arm, and headed to the bathroom. Mary sighed warmly at Nyxa.

"What?" she asked, questioning the look. "What did I do?"

"Nothing, sweetheart… nothing at all," Mary replied, turning to take the tray down to the kitchen.

Nyxa knew what she meant by the words, but they felt like a soft blade. Her father used to say those words to mask his manipulation. He'd say 'sweetheart' before his demeanour would shift and turn sharp. She clenched her jaw, refusing to let the thought settle. It wasn't easy to untangle the damage his words had left behind. Shrugging it off, she placed the magazines onto the shelf and climbed into bed. She picked up a book from her bedside table: The Banshee.

Opening it, she ran her finger down the contents, trying to find something she hadn't read. "So, okay, page 27 looks like you're it," she said, turning the pages.

"The Washer at the Ford," she read, yawning. "A Banshee is sometimes seen washing blood-stained warriors' clothes just before they're about to die in ba…" she stopped as the door creaked open.

"Nyx… Nyx… are you still awake?" whispered a voice. A small hand reached around the door, followed by Aeona's head.

"Hey Aeo, yeah, come in. What's wrong?" she coaxed.

Aeona gave a coy smile. "I can't sleep. Can I come in for a bit?"

Nyxa patted the bed and swung her blanket to one side. "Sure, quick, get in, it's cold."

"What are you reading?" the young girl asked.

"I'm not sure you should see this one. It might keep you up all night," Nyxa warned, thinking about what Mary had said.

"I will just lie here, and you read it aloud," Aeona explained. "I'm sure I'll be fine. I know it's just a story."

"I'm not sure, but okay," she whispered. "You go to sleep, and I will read." She covered her with the blanket, pulling it to her shoulder.

"Chapter 4 - The Washer at the Ford," She read.

'The lake glittered beneath the moonlight, its surface broken only by the slow, rhythmic movement of the cold hands of the ghost-like apparition. The sound of a dress slapping against stone echoed through the night, wet and deliberate.

Donnacha O'Rourke was returning home late from a village gath...'

'Thud!' Nyxa fell silent. 'Thud, Thud...' followed by indiscernible whispering.

Aeona sat bolt upright. "Did you hear that?"

"Hear wha.." Nyxa froze, looking at the dressing table as it started again.

'Thud, Thud!'

"That?" Aeona questioned, her eyes wide in alarm. "You're messing with me, aren't you?"

"Yes," she rasped, hoping it would stop. "I'm just playing with yo..."

"Stop lying..."

'Thud!' Aeona jumped and withdrew her feet from the edge of the bed. "...it's coming from over there,"

'Thud.'

"Stop!" Nyxa cursed, slipping out of the bed and kneeling in front of the dressing table. "What do you want?" she spat.

"Who are you talking to?" asked Aeona.

Nyxa inhaled sharply, not answering.

'Thud!'

Nyxa slowly opened the drawer to nothing but a pile of underwear and socks. Aeona shrugged her shoulders and peered closer, expecting a faulty toy or something, anything that would make a noise. It was then that Nyxa slid the drawer all the way out and placed it on the floor beside her. She then nervously reached in, picking up the bundle of wrapped parchment, and as she did, it fell silent.

Aeona frowned at the object. "What's that?" she asked inquisitively.

Nyxa glanced over her shoulder, reluctant to speak. "I don't really know what it is. I've only ever opened it once, and I can tell you, out of all the books I've read, I don't like this one!"

"Is that why it's tied up?" the younger girl asked. "Come on," she whispered. "Let's read it. I'm not sleepy anymore," she pressed.

"I don't know, Aeo," she paused. "I…" The thought of seeing the page again came flooding back to her. "I think it's better if we don't, and I promised Mary I wouldn't read this stuff to you before bed," she said, glancing at the door.

"It's okay. I got your back, Nyx," Aeona encouraged, taking the parcel from her to sit on the rug in the middle of the room. Nyxa stayed where she was, not willing to move just yet. She mulled over the idea of snatching it from Aeona and throwing it out of the window.

"You said it's just a book. It can't hurt you!" she smiled, pulling at the string.

"Aeo, I," she stopped, "I think we should just throw it out or something," Nyxa hesitated at the thought of the face that looked back at her. She knew she had brushed it off as a coincidence and tried to push it to the back of her mind. But something gnawed at her insides.

Aeona unfurled the parchment to reveal the cover. "It's very dirty and looks kind of old," she described, "and, it's got a picture of the..."

Nyxa interrupted, "...back of a girl looking toward some old ruins in the distance. Red stained-ivy around her feet as if pulling her through an archway to the unknown. There are also claw-like fingers taunting the girl from above."

"Oh," Aeona paused, taken aback, not knowing how to take having the words stolen from her mouth. "Yep, you're right. So, you've read it?"

"I've seen chapter one!" she exclaimed.

"Okay, so let's start at number two then?" Aeona said, pointing at the open contents page.

Chapter One: Candle Burnt.

Chapter Two: Gone in One.

Chapter Three: Chant Become.

Chapter Four: Dead Up Now.

Chapter Five: Life Spirit. She stopped reading any further and looked at Nyxa, who was sitting quietly, lost in thought.

"Which one?" she asked. "You choose."

Nyxa didn't respond at first and then glanced back at her. "Not Candle Burnt, okay," she said with a shake in her tone.

Aeona put the book in her lap and turned to the beginning of Chapter Two: Gone in One. On the page was an illustration of a crow's foot and a dark shadow of a creature coiled around a cauldron. On the opposite side was the text. It was in a Helvetica font, meant to warn, not scare, but its crisp letters on the tea-stain--ed page didn't soften its warning.

"This looks like a dark story," Aeona grinned at Nyxa, but she wasn't her usual self for some reason. "What's wrong?" Aeona asked softly. "Should I not read it?"

Nyxa looked deeply into her eyes, searching for a reason not to, but the pureness of the little girl comforted her and calmed her soul. "No, I'm sure it's going to be fine. Go ahead, read on," she said, forcing a smile.

"Chapter Two: Gone in One… A WARNING," Aeona cooed. "Great start; I think we should stop!" she giggled, placing a hand over her mouth to quiet herself.

"So," she continued, *"A WARNING: To those who read Gone in One, you must never read it ALONE! ALWAYS with someone who's got your BACK. Never FALTER, Never STOP, Be mindful CHANT BECOME leads to ONE.'*

They both shuffled nervously and looked at each other.

"Do you understand anything?" quizzed Aeona.

"Well, it is a strange beginning, I'll give it that," Nyxa prodded. "Carry on," she added curiously.

'Seraphim had been told love was forbidden. Not by law, not by her father's hand, not even by the guards who shadowed her steps. It was something older, something carved into her blood before she was even born. Her family carried crowns heavy through history, yet none of them were carried through love. The kings and queens ruled. They endured. They grew old and bitter. But for her, she felt that she would always be alone and for Seraphim it was truly an unforgiving thought. She wasn't like them. She didn't want to be them.

Curses cannot be broken. She had heard about all the warnings since she was a little girl. The old maids repeating the same tales over and over again. No love beyond the blood. It will not last. It cannot last. You are royal blood. They said it so many times it stung at her ears. The curse devours all who try to subdue it. And she believed them for a time. She believed them until the day she saw him in the garden.

He was dirty, with sweat along his brow, bent to the soil working the land, instead of being at her station. He noticed she smiled at him from afar, as if she were not a princess, as if she were simply a woman. And for the first time, Seraphim felt something her family's halls had never given her.'

Nyxa placed a hand on Aeona's knee; something in her gut wanted her to stop, but nothing sinister was in the tale. Aeona looked puzzled at her friend. "It's pretty cliché and not a great beginning. Can't we just jump to the next chapter?" she asked. "I'm sure it'll be better than this."

"No, we're good, for now," Nyxa answered in a monosyllabic tone, raising her eyebrows. Aeona gave a nod and continued.

'Love. A small word. A dangerous one.

They tried to keep it hidden. Behind silks, behind secrets, behind the mask she wore in the court. Love isn't meant to be hidden. Their love pressed on the verge of breaking through. Forfeit of their lives was a fair price in her mind. He warned her no, but high people, high places control order. His love was true, he knew his welcome. But, she didn't know its folly. The thought of losing him, of letting the curse swallow him whole, became something she could not endure. She would not sit a throne with an empty heart. She would not let her name be added to the list of queens who ruled without ever being touched by love. Him she wanted, and without, the throne was not a reward.

She began to quietly search. Whispering voices from her attendants would be loyal in her quest. Not knowing some things should not be touched.'

Nyxa sat up at the sentence. It was subtle, but there was a shift in the tone. Something just didn't sit right with it. She leaned forward and read the line to herself. Aeona had already moved on.

'... dutiful daughter, the smiling heir, the jewel on display. But when the sun cowered from the land, she quietly stole her way to the undercrofts. A candle in her delicate hand, to read through scraps of parchment that had been locked away.

Their words remained, some faded, all forbidden. She whispered chants that cracked her lips and soured her tongue. She cut her palms and fed her *prayers with her coin. But nothing rang true for her searching heart. Further chests revealed stories of sisters, who were not made of flesh but of something worse than shadow. To be found where the last breath of sun gave way to night high on the heath. Many sought them, but they did not give freely, and when they did, their price was cruel.*

But Seraphim no longer feared cruelty.'

Nyxa had heard enough. "Okay Aeo. I think we need to stop before it gets going," she said, trying not to put a shake in her tone.

Aeona gave a nod and a look that begged for just a little bit more, and continued.

'The land out of her world was unknown, but her concierge searched true, until one night she slipped barefoot from the palace. No guards, no handmaidens, no light but the moon. The gnarled oaks and brambles whispered their warnings as she pressed on. Her gown shredded and heavy with mud. Forward she kept. Step after step, until the air itself hung strange, until silence pressed so deep into her ears it felt like the world closed in around her.

That was where she found them.

The shadows narrowed and twisted their form, waiting, watching. Seraphim's knees sank in the mud and she whispered the only prayer she had left.

"We know what you seek, but…" they counselled, "…your childish heart fools you."

"I… I… give you all," Seraphim unfaltered by their unheard direction. "I am tired of it all, please."

The violent storm howled through the trees as if it welcomed the words.'

"Aeona, please stop," Nyxa pleaded, unable to move, frozen on the carpet, unable to intervene. But she spoke to the emptiness. Aeona wasn't in the bedroom; she was upon the heath, bound by the lines on the page. She read on.

'The ghostly whispering of the chant. It shan't be spoken, but beg she

did. The essence was in silent gasps of exhaled damnation congealed in the stagnant shroud of air.

The weird sisters, they called them, up on the ruins, but Nay, ONE was the doer. Green mist swirled in the cauldron as demons writhed and clawed their twisted limbs in the frothing spew.'

An unnatural darkness enveloped the bedroom.

'Seraphim knelt, hands clasped tightly before them, supplicant to the dreadful apparitions for the chant, "Please, I give you everything," she wept.

Once… twice… thrice… the dark sister turned away, chances of repentance she gave. The purest evil within cared for those who begged. Three times it declined, but upon the fourth, it gave that which should not be given.'

'Three say you, one shall give, GONE in THREE,' the vile woman croaked. 'Say you not?' it questioned, shaking its head.

Seraphim repeated, sobbed she did, 'GONE in THREE.'

'Two say you, one shall give, GONE in TWO,' it croaked again. 'Say you not?' it pled.

Seraphim looked up from her tears. 'GONE in TWO,' she repeated in acceptance.

The shadow stretched forward its skeletal hand, palm to Seraphim… WARNING, before the third she gave. 'ONE say you, one SHALL GIVE,' it croaked, with a pitying glimpse in sorrowful eyes. 'Say you not?' it said with elation.

Seraphim looked into its piercing eyes, uttering what should not be said. 'GONE in ONE!'

Into the dark, oblivion went she.

Nyxa leant forward and took the book from Aeona to look through the pages. "Is that it?" she asked, flicking to the next page and back again. "It looks like it," she said. "So, Seraphim falls in love with this guy and is angry the king and queen won't let her marry him because of some curse or something. She hates the world. She goes to the witches and says, Gone in Three… Gone in Two," she paused, scanning the page for the next line, running her finger down the page. "Ah… 'One say you, one shall give,' but then this woman says, Gone in One!"

The book shook violently, causing Nyxa to jolt backwards and shove it onto the carpet.

The two girls looked at each other and then at the open pages. "Well… we've had a long night. Let's just put it away," yawned the older girl, opening her mouth in a pretend yawn.

Aeona didn't pick up on the cue. "No, no, no. Wait… let me just finish. We still have the poem."

"You want to carry on reading? What's wrong with you?" Nyxa said nervously. "Mary says… Oh, Nyxa, be careful what you read to Aeona before bed, don't do this, don't do that… She's vulnerable, she says. Like shit, you are!" Nyxa reached forward to get the book from the carpet, but she was too slow for the younger girl, who had already set her sights on it. Aeona dove forward, snatching it, then hugged it tightly.

"Look Aeo, I'm telling you, we need to stop!" Nyxa said sternly, not caring if Mary heard or not. "Let's call it a night!"

"Okay, I'm sorry, but let me just read the poem?" she asked. "I promise."

The older girl looked into her manipulative, doleful eyes and then at the book. "Okay, and not another word. Promise?"

"Promise!" Aeona beamed, content that she got her own way. And slowly opened to the page, giving a little cough. "Really quickly."

'Silent step, shadow's kiss, Gone in Three, don't read me.' Aeona couldn't help but whisper in rhythmic rasps. Nyxa felt a light stab at her temple, wanting to scream, DON'T.

'*Slip away to the void's abyss, Gone in Two, don't read me!*' A tear rolled down Aeona's cheek. Nyxa sat wide-eyed, frozen, screaming, DON'T!

'*Whispers call, unseen be, Gone in One, trapped you'll be. DON'T READ ME!*'

Instantaneously, the girls were blown backwards from the blast. Nyxa, with no time to register pain, exploded against the wall with such ferocity that her body disintegrated, leaving an imprint in the plaster. Aeona smashed into the wardrobe, its mirror slashing her body with a million shards as she landed in a pile of blood-spattered wood and broken hangers.

Mary heard the loud bang and ran upstairs as fast as she could, throwing open the door and shouting, "What the hell happened?" Looking for an excuse or apology, none came.

She was stopped dead in her tracks by the silence of the empty room.

The wardrobe leaned against the wall, split down the middle with one of its doors hanging off by a thread of metal. Strips of its splintered remains were scattered around the room, with clothes strewn in a mass in front of the broken shell. The shattered mirror covered the carpet, the bed, and the chair with specks of blood like loose confetti.

It was then that she looked down and saw a delicate foot sticking out from the bloodied clothes and hangers. "Nyxa!" she cried, yanking at the girl to pull her out of the entanglement. When she saw it was not her, but Aeona, she screamed and dropped the foot in alarm. Hand clasped to her mouth in horror, frozen for a second, she shook herself out of panic, swiftly turning to the bed and swiping at the debris. As she knelt to lift the girl, shards of glass stabbed at her knees, causing her to wince in pain. The dead weight of the girl was too much for her. "Nyxa!" she called, "Nyxa… where are you?" she shouted, hoping she would come running from the toilet or somewhere. With all her might she tried to bundle the girl onto the side of the bed, but it was impossible.

A movement of the curtain caught her eye. "Nyxa!"
Getting back to her feet, she ran across the minefield of glass to the window and tore at the curtains, only to find the window closed. Nothing stirred in the street; there were no cars, no people, just dark and silence. "Where could she have gone?" she worried, quickly going back to check on the unconscious

girl. Aeona was unresponsive, breathing in slow, shallow pulses. "Wake up… wake up!" she screamed, and as blind panic began to set in, she gave the girl a sharp slap, but she didn't stir.

At the end of her wits, she grabbed her phone and stabbed at the screen. "Come on, Nyxa. Pick up!" The phone at her ear gave no reward. Her heart stopped as the melody came from somewhere inside the room. Lowering the device, she honed in on the sound to find it under a book lying on the floor under a shattered drawer.

"What the shit… NYXA!" she shrieked, hitting the screen again.

"Hello, 999, what's your emergency?"

"AMBULANCE… AMBULANCE… Quickly!" she shouted.

Instantly she was put through, and within a minute, they had all the information they needed. "Please stay on the…" Mary didn't wait for what she had to say.

"NYXA! Quickly, Aeona's hurt!" she called to no one listening. Except, near silence enveloped the house.

The indentations on the wall between the posters remained unnoticed. The halo of red in the plaster across the room and the two smaller indents to the sides. Nyxa's elbows, thrust outwards as the back of her head slammed into the softness of the cold wall, were all that remained. The dimly lit room kept them hidden, preferring to throw shadows at the carnage scattered around the room instead.

The distant siren brought some comfort to Mary, and soon after, the vehicle's lights cast themselves onto the bedroom ceiling in a kaleidoscope of blue and red. A second later, voices called from the front door. "Hello! Paramedics, may we come in?" they shouted rhetorically.

"Up here," the distressed woman called down, "In the

bedroom!”

A rapid succession of feet ascended the stairs. “Here,” she indicated again, “at the end!”

“Hi, I’m Paramedic Liam, and this here’s Amy. Let’s take it from here; could you step away, please?” he requested, kicking the drawer across the room.

Mary sat on Nyxa’s upturned bedside table and began to pick at the glass stuck in her blood-soaked knee, while the paramedics went to work. “What’s her name and how long has she been like this?”

“Aeona… her name is Aeona,” Mary winced, “erm… maybe fifteen minutes, I guess.”

He began rubbing her breastbone firmly and shaking her shoulder. “Aeona, princess, I’m an ambulance man. Can you hear me? Come on, wakey-wakey!” He lifted her right eyelid to check dilation and was about to do the left when she moaned and pushed away his hand. This was all he needed to give his colleague the cue to unfold the carry-chair, and within no time, they had Aeona in the back of the ambulance.

Mary followed and stood watching from the back of the vehicle, shivering against the cold wind. She was torn between the young girl on the stretcher and Nyxa, who had just… disappeared. Yes, she was a loner, an introvert who usually avoided others, but this made no sense. She never usually went out without telling her, especially not in the middle of the night. Mary looked up and down the road, trying to understand, but there was no movement. Only the flickering triangles of light from curious neighbours watching from their bedroom windows, their faces eerily flashing in the glow of the emergency vehicle.

She didn’t know how long the paramedics would take to make a move, but she hoped there would be enough time for her to run back into the house to get her coat and phone. Quickly, she ran to the dining room. On top of the cabinet were some sticky notes and a used coffee jar full of pens. She quickly wrote a note and stuck it to the fridge door.

From the kitchen, she ran upstairs, threw the robe she was wearing on the floor, grabbed a pair of jeans, and pulled a jumper over her head. Coat on and keys in hand, she slammed the front door behind her, just in time to catch the paramedics. "Are you coming with us or in your car?"

She didn't blink at the offer and climbed in.

Upstairs, hidden behind the curtains, a small, seething creature listened to the sounds of the strange world it had entered. It sat in the dark, growling quietly, waiting.

The ambulance pulled into Accident and Emergency with its sirens off. Aeona, now conscious, lay tight-lipped, looking at her guardian. Unable to say anything, she was at a loss, thinking about her friend.

When the ambulance had ground to a halt, the paramedics gently unbuckled her and took her into Resus to leave her in the capable hands of the nurses. In the cubicle, Aeona buried her head into the fold of her elbow, shielding herself from the stinging brightness of the overhead lights. While the nurses were checking the girl's vital statistics, a doctor appeared from around the curtain and began poking and prodding her. He gently took hold of her elbow in an attempt to look into the girl's eyes, but Aeona fought him off. When he had finished he turned to Mary and informed her that the war-torn girl was otherwise in one piece, and that the cuts were superficial and nothing a couple of butterfly-stitches and a bandage couldn't fix. However, he would place her under observation for a few hours or possibly overnight to be sure.

Mary looked at Aeona and nodded to the doctor as he left.

"Close your eyes and get some rest. It's going to be alright," she said through a soft smile and then turned her attention back to her phone, whispering, "She must've seen the note by now?" and quietly dialled the landline again.

Mary didn't know what had happened. She would never understand what happened in the bedroom or the kitchen. Aeona's file didn't have any other history, except to say there was a house fire. The conversation Aeona had with her mother in the ICU didn't happen; who was to tell? The nurses? It was the only thing that indicated why her mother had abandoned her in the hospital, but it wasn't documented anywhere.

Aeona watched Mary tapping at her phone, raising it every now and then to her ear, listening to the unanswered melody. Then, the girl couldn't hold it in any longer. "Where's Nyxa?" she asked coldly.

Mary raised her eyes and looked at the bandaged girl. "I don't know. I really don't know," she answered with a puzzled look on her face. "You two were reading last night, weren't you?" It was more like a statement of fact than a question. After all, it was all the girls did, night after night. Aeona stammered, rechecking the event in her mind. She was just about to say something when the prying question came to an abrupt halt, as one of the nurses shuffled through the curtain pushing a wheelchair.

"The doctor has written for her to go for a CT scan just to check on her head. Better to be safe than sorry," she smiled, pulling the blanket away from Aeona's legs to take her to the radiology department.

As she lay on the cold plate, she was slid into the machine while the strange whirring sound began. It grew louder and louder until it screamed in her ears. She tried to let her mind wander to shun off the claustrophobic feeling of being trapped inside the cylinder. "There must be something, literally anything I can remember," she scolded herself, but nothing came to mind except that she was reading with Nyxa in her room. The machine paused, then whirred again, but the sound missed a beat: thud, thud, whistle, thud. At first, she thought it was the scanner; however, the sound shifted focus: clank, thud, thud, thud, thud.

The chronology hit with foreboding clarity. "The drawer!" she jolted, banging her head on the top of the cocoon she was in.

"Keep still please, we're almost done!" blurted the nurse's voice on the speaker.

"But how?" Aeona thought, trying to remain motionless. "She was right in front of me. If I was in the bedroom, where did she go?"

The machine stopped and moments later a faint voice from somewhere in the room spoke to her as the flat-bed slowly slid out from the tube.

The hours waiting in the cubicle passed slowly with the lingering pain thumping in the back of her head. Slowly she began to piece the events together: from the noise in the drawer, to the old parchment wrapped around the book. It took her a while to remember some of the chapter, but when it came, it flooded over her and the haunting words hit her hard.

The hours hung in the sterile air with the nurses checking in on her every now and then, but generally she sat alone waiting to leave. Mary, tired of pacing up and down in the confined space, disappeared for some time and then returned to sit on the bed again. But with nothing but a dead phone in her hand, all she could do was stare at the grey wall and count the tiles on the ceiling.

Aeona, bored and groggy from the pain, faded into a restless dream that snuck up on her from the back of her mind. It was about to devour her with its demons when she woke with a start. A nurse placed an oxygen monitor on her finger. But still lost in its darkness, Aeona began to ramble in a cacophony of delirium, reasoning and consequences. "Nyxa told me to stop. Why didn't I listen? I had to push, DIDN'T I!" she cursed herself with loss. "I killed my father… I killed my brother… and now I killed Nyxa." The thought ripped at her heart.

The woman stood sharply, cold at what she was hearing. The nurse, mouth wide, lost mid-breath, left her side and ran out of the cubicle.

Aeona didn't stop! "How can I tell her? How would I start? How would she believe me anyway? She'd brush it off as complete nonsense and tell the doctors I was insane. They'd probably lock me up in a crazy hospital, too." Rivulets ran down her face, dampening her gown.

Mary rushed over to her side, "Shhh… Shhh… Aeona… Shhh," she calmed.

"The last time I told the truth, I was abandoned. I was thrown out like a stray. What if she knew about the cooker?"

Silent tears streamed out of the girl, soaking the pillow as she threw herself backwards. No wiping would ever stop them. No tissue would bring her family or her friend back. To add further to her suffering, she remembered Jinx… The thought of the cat didn't add to the sorrow; it fuelled her anger and dark thoughts. THE CAT! "What if that… stupid cat wasn't on the rug?"

It started as a whisper that grew and grew. "The stupid cat – the stupid cat!" rang in the darkness. 'Stupid cat – stupid cat! Stupidcat-Stupidcat!-Stupidcat-Stupidcat!Stupidcat-stupidcat-stupidcat-stupidcat-stupid-stupidcat-stupid-stupidcat!' She started panting sharply and shuddering with rage.

"Aeona, shh…shh… what cat?" Mary questioned. "What are you talking about? You're going to be fine… The doctors said you're going to be fine." But Mary saw the shift. It was like what she had observed at the house: the kitchen. "Shhh!" she continued, "Everything's going to be alright…. NURSE!" she shouted. "… breath, Aeona… NURSE!" she shouted again.

Aeona saw it all in her mind: Every fine detail; spark; death!

A nurse came running through the curtains, followed by another, and another. "Shh… It's okay, it'll pass. Shh…" a nurse tried to soothe her while the other poured some water onto a tissue and quickly put it on the back of the girl's neck.

"THE B….!" The sensation of the cold-shock did its job and jolted the girl back to the room. She let out a sharp yelp and threw her arms out in alarm. Her eyes darted around until they fell on Mary.

"I'm sorry… I'm so, so sorry!" she cried, throwing her head into her hands.

In the early hours, a doctor came to her bed. "You're a very lucky girl. The ambulance men said you fell through the door of a wardrobe. Did you slip, or were you sleepwalking?" he smiled.

He got no response from the girl; she just stared blankly at him. "Is she okay to go home, doctor?" Mary asked from the side of the bed.

"Sure, she's good to go. The CT is clear. In a couple of days, you can remove the bandage. I'm sure the minor cut to her scalp will be fine," he reassured her, then turned to Aeona again. "Lucky young lady, you gave your mum a bit of a fright!" he said, wrinkling his nose.

The look on her face changed in a flash. "She's not my mum… I haven't got a mum!"

The junior doctor jumped at the ferocity of her return. "Sorry, dear, I thought." He said, turning his attention back to Mary. "Erm… I'll fill in the discharge note; you can collect it from reception. I'll also give you some painkillers and a little bottle of iodine if you don't have any at home."

When he had left, Mary slowly pulled back the blanket and lifted Aeona's legs out of the bed. "That was quite rude, Aeona. There was no need for that,"
she gently scolded. "Come on, let's get out of here."

They waited a little over fifteen minutes in the reception for the taxi to arrive. Mary hung her coat over Aeona's shoulders to keep her warm and slid off her slippers for her to wear. It was seven in the morning by the time they got home. Mary helped Aeona upstairs and into her bedroom. She glanced down the hall to Nyxa's room, expecting to see her, but the curtains were as she'd left them. Tucking Aeona into bed, she yawned, "You got a nasty bump on your head, and we've both had a long night. Let's get some rest for a few hours." She then asked, "Do you want anything, a drink of water or something?"

"No, thank you," the girl said, shaking her head.

Mary closed the door behind her and, instead of going to her room, she turned and quietly stopped at the door of Nyxa's room. With the curtains closed, it was difficult to see the extent of the destruction. The light switch brought no joy to the room; the stem of the shattered bulb hanging from the wire in the ceiling looked dangerous.

Skirting the wall in an attempt to step over some of the

broken mirror, she edged to the window and opened the curtains. In the daylight, the devastation unfolded before her. Many questions left unanswered swam around her head, but what she couldn't understand was the phone. 'There were no scuff marks or footprints on the windowsill, but why would she climb out of the window?' she queried.

She pulled her phone out of her back pocket and scrolled through her contacts until she found Linda, another carer who didn't live too far away. Mary had taken Nyxa around to her house on a number of occasions, and she had become friendly with a couple of the girls who lived there. Possibly Nyxa went to her house to see one of them.

"Hello?" came a voice.

"Hi Linda, I'm so sorry to call so early. It's Mary."

"Good morning, Mary. No need to apologise; I'm just about to get the kids out of bed for school. What can I do for you?" she asked.

"Has, by any chance, Nyxa stayed over at yours last night? She left, and I don't know where she is."

"Sorry, Mary," Linda apologised. "The last time I saw her was a few weeks ago… Hang on a sec…" The line went quiet for a minute, but Mary could clearly hear the screams from the bottom of the stairs.

"Ava… Maisie … get out of bed and get down here, I need you pronto… Sorry, Mary, give me a second," she apologised again. "Morning, you two. When was the last time you saw Nyxa? Come on, out with it, Mary's waiting," she questioned the bleary-eyed teenagers.

Maisie rubbed her eyes and yawned. "I dunno… Maybe the last time she was around here. You saw her… Can we go back to bed now?" she faded.

"What about you, Ava? Has she messaged or anything?"

Linda continued.

Ava just glanced at Maisie and shrugged her shoulders.

"Sorry, Mary. Maisie hasn't seen her either…" she then had to turn back to the girls who never listened to anything she said. "No, bathroom and get ready for school," she scolded the two girls.

"Thanks, Linda," Mary ended. "Maybe she's gone to another friend. Thanks again." She hung up. Mary could barely keep her eyes open any longer and made her way out of the room and down across the landing. Unknown to her, a creature watched from under the bed as she left.

CHAPTER NINE 'MEMORY'

After the long night at the hospital, Aeona and Mary slept through the day. The sun came and went unnoticed, and the evening drew in. Aeona slowly opened her eyes and sat up in the dull light. The coldness of the empty space where Nyxa used to sit on the carpet stared back at her. She curled her knees up and hugged them to her chest, trying to comfort herself. She had sent her away. A whirlpool of unanswered questions ran through her head.

Reading the book had been a terrible mistake. She hadn't meant for it to happen. She never wanted to hurt anyone, least of all Nyxa. Yet, deep down, she couldn't escape the feeling that she had killed her. 'It was me. I made it happen.' Every time she closed her eyes, the whispering gnawed at her, reminding her that she was to blame. It was as if she knew what was going to happen? Nyxa had told her that she didn't want to read chapter one, so it was obvious that she had read the book before, but she never told Aeona why.

With guilt and confusion buried under layers of regret, she just wanted to scream and make it all stop. But every time she tried to block it out, the horrible burden seemed to crack open again, leaving a hole of sorrow and blame. No one understood, no one cared. Everyone saw her burnt face with pity, but to her, it was the mark of blame. On her face and her hands. The scars were there, but that was nothing compared to the scar on Aeona's heart.

The weight kept her from sleeping, from eating, from feeling like she was anything but the girl who had made awful mistakes. It didn't matter that no one had seen Nyxa's departure, that no one knew about the chant, or the strange evil that hung over her like a curse. No one would believe her anyway.

That was the problem. If she told, they would only think she was crazy, all over again, like at the Unit. She had done something terrible. And no matter how much she cried, no matter how much she begged, she couldn't take it back. In slow, rhythmic movements, her mind took over and she began rocking, lost in the nightmare.

Late in the evening, Mary gave a little knock and backed into the room, carrying a tray of food. "Good evening, Aeona," she said quietly, flicking the light on and setting the tray on the bedside table. It was then that she noticed the girl sitting locked in a frozen stare.

"Aeona," Mary said softly, "Aeona… dear…" She sat on the end of the bed, not daring to approach until she was able to gain her attention. She had learnt that from the incident under the dining table. Mary tapped gently on the footboard with her fingernails, whispering, "Hey, Aeona!"

She didn't respond; she just rocked gently back and forth until the tapping got louder and louder in her ears. Until she begged it to stop, throwing her hands over her ears. "STOP!" she screamed.

Abruptly, it did. "Aeona, it's Mary," came a voice, a soft murmur that she'd heard before, but it felt distant, as if it were coming from afar.

"Aeona," it called again from the light. "It's Mary, Aeona… come on, dear, push out of it."

Something in the air shifted, a sharp snap, like the world suddenly coming back into focus. Aeona's eyes locked on Mary, but the connection didn't register at first; everything around her felt like it was happening through a fog, muffled and slow.

The woman's presence slowly began to break through Aeona's daze. The thick veil of her internal world began to part, inch by inch, as reality slowly bled through. For a moment,

Aeona blinked, unsure if she was dreaming or waking from a nightmare. One blink, then another; the cloud slowly lifted from the girl's eyes as she brought the present into focus.

Mary gave a gentle smile. "I thought you must be hungry. I've made you some sausage and eggs," she gestured to the tray.

Aeona, still in a state of confusion, seemed to have retreated back into the sad little girl she had been when she first arrived. She gave a little nod and looked at the plate.

Mary slowly got up and made her way out to the landing.

She thought it best to leave Aeona to soothe herself back to her surroundings, rather than encroach on the space she needed. Mary had been looking after children for far too long not to see the signs of when a child needed space to become aware of themselves after an episode.

Mary made her way to Nyxa's room to see the extent of the damage. She had tried to clean it earlier, but worried the noise might have woken Aeona, she decided it could wait. She stood at the door, looking at the mess, trying to picture what had happened.

"Did Aeona trip or fall? Did she step on something? Or were they playing and… No… Is that it…" she paused. "Nyxa… what did you do? Were you fighting, and you pushed her? But… I didn't hear any arguing, though… That must be it," she speculated. She had quickly turned from being the carer to judge and executioner in a matter of seconds. "Oh, Nyxa, what have you done?" she said, shaking her head. Then she headed downstairs to get the hoover and some bin bags.

Aeona finished a sausage but couldn't eat any more; her mind was on other things. She placed the tray back on the table and sat running through the sequence of events again.

"So, I went into her room… that I know! And we were in bed, reading, when…" She sighed heavily in frustration. The memory hovered just out of reach. "When… when… come on, remember!" Nothing. A blank. She couldn't understand it. "Why?" she murmured to herself.

The when-why-what-which-how, all swam around her mind in utter confusion, so she thought it better to get her notebook from her bedside and begin writing things down.

On the stairs, Mary struggled to carry the vacuum cleaner, banging it against the wall with every step, and once at the top, the squeak of wheels echoed as she pulled it along to Nyxa's room.

It took a long time for Mary to get most things straight, shaking the clothes free from the broken glass of the mirror and removing the doors from the destroyed wardrobe. The only thing left was to vacuum the whole place.

As she stepped on the button, the vacuum came to life. Mary didn't notice the terrified creature as it ran as fast as it could to get away. It slammed into the bedside cabinet and bolted out the door, desperate to escape the bellowing monster. Seeing an opening, it shot down the landing and darted into Aeona's room.

Aeona caught a glimpse of something black streak out of the corner of her eye. At first, she thought it was her mind playing tricks, but she knew it was real when it smashed into the side of her bed.

"A rat? But we don't have any rats?" she questioned.

Placing the notebook beside herself, she spun around and lay on her stomach. Half terrified, half curious, she edged precariously off the side of the bed. Gripping the sheet with one hand, she slowly pulled the duvet up. It was hard to make anything out in the dim light, but as she peered upside down, she made out something sitting motionless at the far end, shimmering in the dark.

She shifted her hand to get a better grip on the bed when, suddenly, the thing growled and snarled, backing away to hide in the shadows. She fought not to fall off the bed, but in shock, there was no stopping her. With a thump, she landed headfirst on the floor. The vacuum still roaring in the distance. It was too big for a cockroach or a spider, and never in her life had she heard either of them growl. She knelt, willing herself to lift the duvet to get another look, but the creature saw an exit and ran to the opposite corner of the bed. The scuttling sound sent Aeona skidding backwards into her dressing table.

The drone of the vacuum faded and went quiet; moments later, Mary's footsteps approached. Aeona quickly picked herself up and jumped back into bed, pulling the covers over her legs.

"How's it going in there?" Mary asked, entering and looking at the tray of uneaten food. "Why?" she quizzed, "Not hungry? How are you feeling now?"

"I… think I'm okay," she responded, rubbing her head, deflecting. "Has Nyxa come back yet?"

"No, I really haven't a clue where she has gone," she replied, her voice tinged with concern. "I don't know, but I'm sure she'll be back soon, though. She's never gone off and not come back."

"I hope so," Aeona said, her voice trembling on the edge of tears, but the thing under the bed was on her mind.

"Aeona, I know you two have become very close lately, so… please tell me, do you know where she's gone?"

The word 'Gone' hung heavy in the question, and then she couldn't hold back the guilt. "I.. I.. I don't know," she cried, starting to tear up.

Mary sat beside her, seeing if she could place an arm around her for comfort. Aeona didn't react or flinch, so she moved closer to calm her down. When the tears had stopped, Mary lifted the child's chin. "It's going to be alright; everything is, you'll see." Forgetting to take the tray, Mary turned to the door. "I've got to pop out to the shop to get some things. Would you like anything while I'm there?"

Aeona shook her head, slumped back onto her pillow, and said nothing.

Mary went downstairs to get ready to go out. It was true that she needed to get some things from the shop, but she also needed to check on a few things for herself. She needed to go to the other carer's house to see if Nyxa was there.

She had dealt with Linda on a few occasions and knew how she worked. Sometimes, a stray girl or boy would weave their magic and manipulate a carer into giving them a safe haven when, in reality, they were the ones who should be looking after the child's best interests. Children, at times, can be very crafty and play one off against another to get their own way. Mary had been a carer for far too long, and there was no pulling the wool over her eyes.

In the bedroom, Aeona waited until she heard Mary pull out of the drive and the sound of the car fade into the distance. She then lifted her knees to her chest, slid out of the duvet, and crawled as quietly as she could to the end of the bed. She was too frightened to get out on the left or right, as she didn't quite know where the thing was.

She guessed it was just by her headboard, but didn't want to chance it nipping at her ankles. Once at the bottom of the bed, she gingerly slipped off and tiptoed to close the door. The hesitation of closing the door and the thought of it climbing onto her face while she was asleep sent shivers down her spine, but at the moment, she thought it was better to confine it to her room rather than have it running around the house.

"Now what?" she asked herself.

She couldn't hear anything: no pitter-patter, no snarling, nor growling.

She wasn't scared of insects; her father had taken her to the woods behind their house on many occasions, where they'd played with all sorts of creatures, from slugs to butterflies. But this thing, whatever it was, made her feel different… connected… in a way she couldn't fathom.

In order to try and get a better idea of where it was, she picked up the tray, placed it on the floor, and slowly lifted the bedside table out of the way. Hopefully, she thought, it would stay where it was if she did it nice and easy. She was about to let go when she picked up on a sound, a very low movement of feet that scraped at the carpet to her right. Not daring to move, she froze.

Out of the corner of her eye she could see the black, insect-like thing watching her with curiosity, cocking its head from side to side.

The element of surprise was lost under the weight of the bedside table as the unbearably heavy load made her calves scream for mercy. She swung it to one side and dropped it with a thud. It was either jump back onto the bed or hide. Neither would have been a solution, so she slowly knelt on the carpet. The thing remained where it was, watching every move. Glancing at the plate, Aeona very slowly reached across and ripped at one of the eggs until a piece broke off, and in a smooth, deliberate motion placed it on the carpet in front of the thing.

It didn't move.

Aeona reached again, and slowly tore off a small piece of sausage, tossing it toward the thing. The creature flinched as the food bounced on the carpet towards it. Inquisitively, it smelt the air. And with one eye on the girl and one on the food, it edged forward until it came out into the open.

Aeona could make out that it was about the same size as her phone, pure black, and glistened like glass. It had a bulbous head and a zip-like line cut along its front; she could only guess were teeth. It edged nearer. 'Don't bite, don't bite, don't bite' raced through her pounding heart. It opened its mouth in a yawn-like movement before flicking out its purple-black tongue from between its serrated needles and eating the sausage. It then stretched forward its elongated neck towards Aeona's hand, as though it was capturing the scent of the terrified girl. It was difficult to see if it had a nose; whatever it was didn't appear to have any nostrils. Horn-like pieces of black scales blinked rapidly, jutting out from the sides of its head.

Aeona couldn't stop herself from questioning, "Nyxa, is that you?" She never consciously thought of it, never intended to say it; the words just came out of her mouth, an utterance under her breath.

It took a little over twenty minutes for Mary to drive across town to Linda's house. She parked in the street and saw the woman's car in the driveway. Then she sat watching the windows to see if she could spot any sign of Nyxa, whether walking in the living room or up in one of the other girls' windows. After a few minutes of nothing, she turned off the engine, walked to the front porch, and rang the bell.

Linda's cheerful face appeared through the window, and she answered with a smile. "Nice to see you, Mary. Come in, come in, come in," she beckoned, shaking her head as the brisk February wind forced its way into her home. "It's too cold to be out in this weather. What are you doing here? You should have called."

She stretched out an arm and swung the door closed behind her visitor. Mary took off her coat and handed it to her.

"Any sign of your girl yet?" Linda asked.

"Nyxa, you mean? No sign of her, and I'm worried. Do you think the girls are covering for her or something?" she quizzed, looking around the living room for her coat or bag, the mystery of Nyxa's disappearance hanging in the air.

"Mary, you know me, come on. Don't play that game. If she were here, you'd be the first to know!" she defended. "What happened? Have you spoken to the social workers about it? Possibly, she's gone to them, you know, wanting to move to another foster home or something." She fished for any possible answers to the girl's disappearance herself.

"I don't know, Linda. Are the girls home from school yet? Maybe they know something… anything. Have they given hints or possibly mentioned other friends in their circle, about Nyxa's whereabouts?"

"They're not due home for another hour or so," she said, glancing at the clock on top of the fireplace. "Have a seat. Do you want a cup of tea or coffee?" she asked.

Mary wasn't focusing on Linda's words as she opened her bag to retrieve her phone to call the social workers: Naomi or Samira.

"Coffee it is, then!" Linda said, as she turned and went into the kitchen.

Back at the house, Aeona was still locked between moving and running. She'd never seen anything like the creature before. It defied logic. This thing was millimetres away from her right hand. She could almost feel its warm breath. She knew what was going to happen. She anticipated it, but to her horror, it was worse than she had ever expected. Its tongue sprang out of its mouth and stuck to the ridge of her hand as if she were an enormous fly. She couldn't help but spring backwards with a scream and pull her hand away, but as she did the creature came with her. Frantically, she ran around, waving her hand in the air, trying to get it off. The creature swung around as Aeona screamed. With a high-pitched squeak, the creature's tongue let go, sending it ricocheting off the top of the bed. Its scaly black body writhed as it tried to regain its footing.

Aeona jumped backwards and slipped on the tray, sending the plate in one direction and the food in another. The girl landed on the arm of the computer chair, which spun around on its casters. The creature desperately ran up and down the bed, too small to jump off.

Aeona, in panic, reached down, picked up the egg, and hurled it at the snarling and snapping creature. The egg landed squarely on its face, causing it to screech in fright and bolt headfirst into the headboard before it tumbled off the bed and landed with a crunch into the rubbish bin. Aeona gasped with a hand over her mouth in alarm. In any other circumstance, it would have been comical if it was a kitten or a puppy, but this was far from it. A mixture of crinkling, rustling, and smacking lips came from the bin as the creature tried to remove the egg from its face. Aeona, half hanging on the chair, listened as it tried to claw its way up the smooth metal sides of the bin. Aeona let out a sigh of relief when she realised that it was trapped.

She stood up and peered into the bin at the creature that squealed for help. Aeona, feeling more confident, kicked the bin to see how it would react. It went silent, frightened by the girl who towered above it. Once she was sure it couldn't escape, she crouched slowly and knelt to get a better look. Using a couple of pens like chopsticks, she began pulling out as many things as she could: paper and discarded sweet wrappers. Every now and then, the creature would jump, snapping at her fingers, but she managed to stay out of reach.

It tried as best it could, running desperately in circles, jumping up the side in a feeble attempt to escape, but it was too small to escape its prison. Not believing what she was actually saying, "Nyxa… is that you?" she whispered. The creature paused, stopped running around, and listened to the large thing that spoke to it.

Aeona couldn't believe what she was seeing. Every time she said Nyxa's name, the thing would stop, take an interest and cock its head from side to side.

She crawled to the other side of the room, picked up the last of the remaining sausage, and shuffled back. "Let's see what you are," she asked inquisitively, pinching off a little corner of the food and dropping it into the bin. The creature slowly went over, sniffed, then flicked its tongue out and sucked it in with a sharp gulp. The girl let out a joyous yelp. When she was down to her last piece, it sat in the middle and looked up at her. It closed its mouth, and with its teeth hidden from view, it looked like a small black frog, albeit a little deformed. No bigger than a runt kitten, scales ran all over its gleaming black body, with frills that ran down its spine.

The black slit for a mouth cut right across its pointed head, held by a crest that ran around the back of its head. To the girl, it was like a frog-crocodile with short, stout legs that didn't look strong enough to hold its body weight. Its hands and fingers, if they could be called that, had blunt nails at the end of its long fingers. Two large hunches stuck out on its shoulders and pushed at its taut skin.

"What am I going to do with you?" Aeona asked with a curious grin.

Mary and Linda sat in the living room waiting, and it wasn't until late afternoon that Linda's foster children came home. The front door opened with a commotion about who was going into the toilet first, followed by a mad scrabble of throwing coats and bags, a fight and scuffle of pushing each other, and the stamping of feet as they both raced up the stairs.

Linda shook her head and turned to Mary, "Do you see what I've got to deal with?" she smiled. "It's nice to see them getting along."

As with most children who came into the Home, these girls were no different from the rest. Their files were no bedtime reading, filled with emotional stories of broken homes and hardships no child should have to go through.

Mary rose and moved towards the door, but her friend stopped her. "Leave them alone for a second; give them a chance to get home. Then we can call them down to see."

It didn't take long for Ava and Maisie to come running down the stairs to see what was for dinner. "I won!" Maisie screamed as she threw open the door and stopped dead in her tracks.

"Oh, sorry," she apologised and composed herself on seeing Mary. "Oh... erm, Hi Miss," she smiled before being hit sharply in the back by Ava, who thundered after her. "Stop," Maisie scolded, "Miss Mary's here!"

"Oh, Hi, Mary," Ava waved, skidding to a halt.

"How was your day at school, girls? I hope there was no trouble today?" Linda asked, rolling her eyes.

"Nope, we were good today... except Ava swore at Miss Wilkins in history," Maisie laughed, pointing at her.

Linda could only shake her head, glancing at her phone. "That's not going to ring later on, is it?" she frowned. "Anyway, it's good to see you two smiling. Erm, Mary has a couple of questions. Come on, sit down for a sec, and then I can get the dinner on."

Mary asked them the 'what, where, when, why, who, which, how,' but every answer drew a blank. The girls were sincere in their answers, and it was clear to both women that they seemed to be telling the truth. Nyxa had last contacted them two weeks ago, but that was to wish Ava a happy birthday.

Mary thanked the girls for their help and got up to leave.

"Thanks a lot for the coffee, Linda. If you hear anything, please let me know." In the hall, Linda handed her the coat, thanked her for the visit, and closed the door behind her.

Mary sat for a minute in her car thinking about what the girls had said and had to believe them, as their tone and the responses didn't seem to be rehearsed in any way. No body language or facial expressions gave them away. They were telling the truth, so what now, she thought. She called Nyxa's social workers and they said the same. They had been through the running away scenarios and said precisely the same as the police always did, "Call us in a few days if she doesn't turn up."

Mary started the engine and headed back home, but before

she did, she would need to stop at the shops for some things.

Aeona and the creature sat staring at each other for over an hour, each trying to make sense of the other. The girl had never seen anything like it, and the creature, in turn, had never encountered a human, well not up close before. They were locked in a Mexican stand-off.

"I'm not going to hurt you," she said softly with increasing courage. "What harm can you do… you little froggy-lizard thing?" Slowly she edged her hand onto the side of the bin and slowly tilted it to one side. "Please don't bite, please don't bite, please don't bite," she whispered repeatedly.

The creature slid to the bottom of the bin and glanced at the edge as if ready to make flight.

"No, no, no, no, no… don't run… it's okay, it's okay, it's okay!" Aeona cooed, fighting the urge to flip the bin over and trap it beneath, but, 'what good would that do? It would only terrify the creature and undo the fragile bond they had built over the last hour,' she thought. Edging the bin further and further, Aeona tilted it until the thing slid out and clumsily rolled onto the carpet. It sat up quickly and curled its black tail around itself like a puppy, waiting for instructions. Aeona couldn't help but smile. The creature mirrored her, revealing its tiny, needle-like teeth, causing Aeona's smile to falter with nervousness. The thing sensed the change and closed its mouth in response.

She slowly got to her knees and crawled to the other side of the bed, the creature following close behind. She then slid the plate towards it, hoping it would be interested in the last remaining scraps of food or if it wanted to lick the plate clean. To her delight, it did the latter, darting its tongue out in rapid succession all over the plate.

"So…" she spoke tentatively to the creature, "I think you can understand me, and… I don't know but... please tell me… you're Nyxa, aren't you?" she asked, more to herself than to the black thing. Whenever she said, "Nyxa," the creature stopped and looked at her.

"But how?" The memory of yesterday still eluded her.

Just then, a noise from downstairs alerted her; Mary was back. Aeona panicked, waving wide-eyed at the creature. "Quickly, hide!"

The creature saw something was wrong with the girl and, not knowing what it was, bolted back under the bed and hid.

Aeona jumped into bed and threw the duvet over herself when the door creaked open to the song of…

"Happy Birthday to You, Happy Birthday to You
Happy Birthday, Dear Aeona, Happy Birthday to You…."

Mary held a small birthday cake with a lit candle in one hand and a small box covered in wrapping paper in the other. "Happy birthday, Aeona. Did you forget?" she smiled. Aeona hadn't realised it was. Mary let her smile dip, "Hey, sweetheart, it's okay. Nothing major... forget about yesterday. Don't worry about anything," she comforted her gently. "A nasty bump on your head, but the doctors said you'll be fine in a day or two. No more of that sad face... it's your birthday. Come on, open your gift. I hope you like it."

Aeona already had a special gift, and unbeknownst to Mary, it was hiding right under her.

Mary spent most of the evening wondering where Nyxa had gone, but by midnight, there was still no sign of her. She tried calling Linda again but couldn't get an answer, and she presumed her friend would have been asleep anyway. She left the light on in the living room and the backdoor unlocked. If anything, the girl would try the front door and then, with a great deal of common sense, come in through the back.

It was a pretty safe neighbourhood, rough around the edges, but Hollins Lane was on the rural side of the town and considered a little up-market for the area. That's why, to her surprise, none of the neighbours spotted her walking down the lane: after all, it wasn't that late in the evening when she left.

Mary also couldn't understand that Mrs Tomlinson, who lived a few doors down and was always at her window, didn't spot her leaving. She was better than having a neighbourhood watch. Anything amiss, the ninety-eight-year-old would be the first one on the phone to call her or the police. Mary had been on the wrong end of the phone with her a couple of times; as soon as any of the children she was looking after did anything untoward, like climbing a tree or speaking too loudly, the phone would ring.

Aeona sat quietly in her bed, listening for the creature, who remained under the bed, unwilling to leave the dark. There was nothing but silence all around. An occasional car drove past, but there were no footsteps. She knew Mary had left her bedroom door ajar in the hope of hearing Nyxa come home. She didn't want to chance having her walk in if she was talking to the thing under her bed. So, she just lay there trying to remember what had happened with Nyxa between the nods of approaching sleep. She already knew they were reading and had guessed it had something to do with the book. She remembered a blinding light and an incredible punch, then nothing. But she couldn't separate the memory of the gas explosion from the incident with Nyxa's disappearance. Mary had told her she must've been sleepwalking and accidentally fell into Nyxa's wardrobe in the dark. It was how she was found, buried underneath the clothes and broken carcass of wood. She couldn't put any other explanation to it or speculate on anything else.

The following day, just as the sun brought its early light above the curtain pole, Aeona, still in a dream-like state, felt something push on her chest. It wasn't to the extent of affecting her breathing, but she felt the weight all the same. She let out a restricted grumble of not wanting to be woken, but forced herself to open her eyes slowly. Through her squinting sleep, she could make out something dark moving through her flickering eyelashes. Whatever it was, the dark silhouette was very close to her face. Its breath seemed to suck at hers. She tried to force herself away from it, but could only push her head further back into her pillow. She blinked her sticky eyes a few times and waited for her bedroom to come into focus.

It was the black creature that stood nose to nose with the girl on her chest. In panic, the girl threw her hands at the thing, knocking it to the floor with a squeal, making the thing scurry under the bed in fright.

Aeona quickly came to her senses and realised what the dark thing was. "Sorry… sorry… sorry…" she repeated softly, jumping out of bed and crouching on the floor apologetically.

Over the next few days, she tried to build its trust in any way she could. The only thing it seemed to respond to was when she threw little pieces of food. It seemed to like them, and over time, the creature took the offering quicker each time.

Eventually, the creature would come out and sit curiously at the edge of the bedside table. One day, Aeona was sitting on the carpet, drawing a picture of it, when out of the corner of her eye, she saw it edging its way closer and closer to her hand. She placed the pencil beside her foot and stretched out a finger to gently touch its front paw. It didn't flinch or back away.

"Nyxa, I'm glad you came," she whispered. "We're going to figure this out, okay!"

And that was the start of a new beginning for them both.

Time brought them closer together. Finally, some normality contrasted with the pain of guilt, neglect and blame the young girl carried. Now Aeona had a friend to call her own.

The next few months, they grew close. Mary never suspected a thing, or so Aeona thought. When Mary went out, they would play in the garden and once risked venturing into the woods behind their house. No one ever went in the woods, or not that Aeona could see from the back-bedroom window. A narrow stream ran through the centre. Aeona made mud pies and dammed the stream with sticks and clods of soil. It made her forget about her past. A place where she could be free of her troubles and just play with her new friend.

It was in the bedroom where they bonded the most. Aeona tried teaching it to read, but it was no use. The creature could only, if any, remember some of the letters of the alphabet. Aeona couldn't understand it; Nyxa could read, so why was it so difficult? She guessed it was because she had changed from a human to a creature. "It might be how brains work. Animals are somehow different from humans," she would tell it. One day, Aeona got the shock of her life when it repeated what she said, "This is your book, Nyxa. You remember… book?" Not expecting any response, it barked, "Bok. Bok." The scream of laughter from the girl nearly had Mary running up the stairs.

The first tears of joy the girl had felt in so long. The feeling overwhelmed her.

There were no pictures of it on the internet and she could only presume it was some sort of black lizard with stumps on its back.

Mary let her borrow some books from Nyxa's room until she returned, going through them to make sure they were appropriate for her. Aeona finished them soon enough with the creature as motivation. She didn't step foot inside Nyxa's room since her disappearance. It just didn't feel right, even though she was with her in a different form.

For Mary, the days went to weeks, and the weeks went to months. The police just said they had not heard anything, and they had added Nyxa to the list of ever-increasing missing teenage girls in the United Kingdom. So many young children just vanished into thin air, and they said they had no resources to search for them all.

Months into their friendship, Aeona and the creature were playing hide-and-seek in the garden. It had learnt how to camouflage itself in the shadows of the flower bed, making it almost impossible to find.

"Nyxa, you're too good at this," she called. "I can't find you anywhere. Come on… let's play inside. It looks like it is going to rain."

"Boo!" The creature jumped out from behind the rockery, sending Aeona reeling back onto the lawn in fright. "Me good… yes!" it beamed, "Yes… Yes!" it hopped around her in a circle, laughing at its new-found skill.

"Come on, let's go to my room," the young girl said to her friend. She didn't want to lose track of time and knew Mary could come back from wherever she went any minute, so it was safer for the pair to retire to the bedroom, just in case. The girl made a good call. Just as the growing thing bounded up the stairs, Aeona heard the car pull into the driveway. The creature knew the drill and skulked behind the wardrobe and under the bottom panel to wait quietly, listening for the girl's voice to announce it was all clear.

The door opened with Aeona sitting on the bottom step waiting. "Hey, little lady. How has your day been?" Mary asked, holding a bunch of flowers. "Could you give me a hand bringing the shopping in from the car?"

"Sure," the girl responded coyly, listening for any noise from upstairs, following her out.

Mary opened the car door, and on the back seat were several things for her to carry: a large bundle of toilet rolls, boxes of tissues, and a little bag that was just as light as the other two. "That bag is for you," she smiled. "I thought you might like them."

The girl tried to look into the bag but was stopped short by the smiling woman, "Not until you've finished taking everything in."

She quickly ran in with the things and returned for the little bag. Mary kicked the car door closed behind her and thanked her for her help. "Now, while I'm making dinner, you toddle off, and I will call you when it's ready. Okay? Oh…" she remembered, "Please do not eat anything in the bag until after dinner. I'm making your favourite, some fish and chips! It won't be long."

"Thank you, Mary," she smiled and then ran up the stairs to her room and tipped the bag upside down on her bed. Out fell some sweets, a small packet of biscuits, some bubbles and a bar of chocolate. She listened for a second to see if Mary was coming upstairs, but when everything was quiet, she called her friend to come out to see what she'd brought. Not being ungrateful, but she couldn't help tell the creature, "How old does she think I am, five?"

The creature jumped on top of the bed and smelt the packets.

It took an interest in the biscuit, so Aeona couldn't help but rip it open so it could have one. "You can't have any of the chocolate, remember. It's bad for cats and dogs. So, you, being an animal, more for me," she explained. The girl broke small bits off the biscuit and put them onto the carpet. The pointy teeth still scared her a little, even though she knew the creature would never bite her. However, all the same, she liked to keep her fingers as they were.

After about fifteen minutes, she heard her name being called from the bottom of the stairs and got ready to venture down for dinner.

"You stay here and leave the biscuits alone," the girl smiled. "I won't be too long. Then we can teach you some more letters. Please be quiet; don't knock anything over. Okay! I got to go," she waved, closing the door behind her.

At the bottom step, she stopped, took a breath, and ran her fingers through her hair with both hands to straighten herself up. At the dining table, Mary waited for her to come down, and greeted her with a smile. "Come-come. Let's get started before it gets cold," she said, nodding to the plates of steaming fish and chips.

They sat quietly eating, with Mary asking her a round of questions, nothing in particular, about how the girl was and whether she liked what was in the bag. Aeona finished, placed her knife and fork on the side of her plate, and was just about to slide her chair back from the table when Mary stopped her.

"How's the reading?" she asked, "You must be ploughing through everything; you spend so much time in your room."

"I'm getting better," the young girl said shyly, "Some of Ny… it's… books…" she stammered, and quickly lowered her gaze. She didn't know why she changed what she said to 'it' and hoped the woman didn't pick up on it. She quickly added to the distraction, "Some are very thick. I'm managing and using my phone to help me with the difficult ones. The stories are excellent, though," she rambled on and on. "I like the new ones better; they're quite scary. The old ones like Frankenstein, Dracula, Jekyll and Hyde, Wuthering Heights, Dorian Gray…" Mary had to jump in.

"Nice… My gosh! You've got through so many," she interrupted, changing her tone to a softer one, and forced the question, "I know we've not discussed it before but… erm, so… how are you feeling about Nyxa leaving?" she asked hesitantly. "It's okay to talk about it. I'm sorry, but I'm still in a state of shock, myself." She said, bowing, waiting to see the girl's reaction.

Taken aback, Aeona was lost for words and didn't know what to say. She'd thought she'd heard her playing with the creature upstairs. The girl didn't know how to play it, to be distraught, sad, or carefree. She unconsciously glanced at the ceiling, realising the obviousness of the action, then looked back at her empty plate. She nervously picked up her fork and started to draw in the ketchup with one of the prongs. Mary reached over gently and placed a hand on top of the girl's. "It's okay to be upset, you know."

The truth was she missed Girl-Nyxa so much and didn't know the how or the why of it, but she knew her friend was still here, yes… in a different form, but all the same, she was upstairs waiting for her. She thought carefully about what to say. It needed to be middle of the road, not too sad, not too happy.

Mary waited patiently for her to speak. She expected sadness or loneliness and knew they had become quite attached over their short time together. Then the young girl responded, taking Mary completely off guard.

"I know she is going to be fine, so don't worry about her," Aeona mumbled.

The woman's mouth slowly dropped open, lost mid-breath, lost in thought. "I… I… … I hope so. I hope you're rig…"

"Can I," Aeona said, sliding her chair back from the table, "… go now."

"Oh… I suppose… erm… yes, fine… good, you're fine. Okay!" the dumbfounded woman stuttered, as the back of the girl's head left, closing the door behind her.

Mary was left, lost in her thoughts at the dining table alone, tapping her fingers on the side of her plate. "Well, that went… unexpected, I do say." She pushed her chair with the back of her legs and stood to clear the plates and take them to the kitchen. She picked up Aeona's plate, and as she did, the knife and fork slid onto the table, splattering ketchup on the tablecloth. She put the plate down to pick up the stray utensils when she noticed the picture of what looked like a lizard or a crocodile the girl had doodled on the plate. "Seems like she's alright. Good talk, I suppose," she smiled uncomfortably.

Aeona stood motionless at the bottom of the stairs again, thinking about what had just happened. She looked back at the door, trying to imagine what Mary was feeling, and then looked up the stairs thinking about the creature. She crept back upstairs as quietly as she could, making sure to jump over the fifth step. She tried to sneak up on it, but it was nowhere to be seen. "Good girl, I was just testing you!" she smiled.

The biscuits, the bubbles and the sweets remained where she had left them, albeit minus a couple of biscuits.

"It's okay. The coast is clear; you can come out!"

The creature's rounded snout appeared from the corner of the wardrobe. "I did good?" it smiled.

"You did, girl," Aeona praised, picking up the bubbles and running the small tube through her fingers. "I don't think Mary knows how old I am. I haven't played with these…. since," she stopped.

"Since what?" the creature asked, cocking its head to her.

"Since… Chris. We used to play in the garden together before…" she stopped.

"Who is this Chris person?" The curious animal pried.

A tear escaped and rolled down her cheek. "He used to be my brother. We played together all the time," she answered, trying to suppress her emotions.

The creature sensed the intensity of the girl's feelings and couldn't help but care. "Why you cry?" it asked sincerely.

"Oh… it's nothing… anyway, let's play. You're going to love these!" she shook a smile back onto her face.

She sat on the carpet in front of her friend and twisted the top of the bubbles. Then, twisted some more… "What the heck? It's stuck solid," she grunted. "How's a kid supposed to open this?" She raised the bottle and held the top in her teeth.

She bit and twisted it for all she was worth until her jaw hurt. "Don't look at me. You try?" Aeona scoffed in defeat, handing the bottle to it.

It took it in its claws and ripped at the plastic top, which split down the edge. "Here you go, muscles!" it laughed.

"Now, how am I supposed to close it again, genius?" Aeona frowned, taking it back off the creature. "Right, are you ready for some magic?"

Aeona placed the lid on the floor and pulled at the silver cover to reveal the soapy contents.

"Hey, are you ready?" she laughed. She put in the wand, stirred it, raised it to her pursed lips, and blew gently.

The soapy film pushed forward and began to form. It grew until it formed and floated gracefully into the air.

Suddenly, at the sight of the sphere the creature froze in terror. The fully formed bubble hovered above its head. Eyes wide, with a sharp gasp, unable to exhale, it remained motionless until the bubble lost momentum and slowly drew nearer to it. It let out an almighty shriek, screamed in panic, and slammed headfirst into the side of the dressing table, trying to escape. It ricocheted off the wall and dove behind the wardrobe.

"Bad-bad, very bad!" it kept repeating, shaking in fear.

"It's Okay," she comforted, "You have seen these before."

"Yes, I was!" It growled and spat, "Evil things!"

Aeona wanted to smile but looked more confused, lying on the floor, trying to speak through the small gap at the bottom. "What do you mean… I was? Please come out! I'm sorry. It was just a bubble!" The young girl couldn't understand.

It didn't matter what she said; the creature refused to leave the safety of the wardrobe, even when she tried to entice it with biscuits. She pushed little broken pieces under the wardrobe with a pencil, but a second or two later, they would be pushed back out again.

In the end, the girl thought it best to leave it to calm down. She was sure it would come out eventually. Maybe it has a phobia of bubbles or soap, she thought.

It wasn't the best way to end the day, with the bubbles disturbing the creature to the extent that it remained under the wardrobe and wouldn't come out. After Aeona had been down for her supper, she came back to her room to sleep.

"Good night," Aeona whispered, tapping the side of the

wardrobe.

It skulked onto its cushion and wrapped itself up, quietly whispering back, "You too, my girl, you too."

Aeona settled on her pillow, pulled the duvet over herself, and closed her eyes. A minute later, she felt something push at the side of the bed, and without bothering to move, she slowly rolled over and opened her eyes.

The creature stood on its hind legs and looked at her over the side of the bed. "Aeona," it whispered.

"I'm sorry. Please forgive me!" she returned gently. "What's wrong?" she asked.

"Can I ask you a question?" it paused.

"Sure. Of course, you can," she waited.

"You call me this… Nyxa… name?" it asked softly. "Do you want to name me?" it sincerely asked. "I like it. It fits well wit…"

"Sorry… what did you say?" Aeona sat up questioning.

"I don't have a name!" it responded, "or at least I don't think so… I didn't want to stop you because it seemed like you… liked calling me it. I will be Nyxa from now on," it smiled.

The girl jumped out of bed with a bolt. "What are you saying?"

The creature quickly retreated to its cushion.

Aeona slid onto her knees, nearly catching herself on the corner of the cupboard. "Did you say you AREN'T Nyxa?"

"Well… yes… I don't know who that is?"

"Then who? What happened? What? No wait. You're not Nyxa?" Aeona couldn't believe what she was hearing. "So, what happened to her and where? Oh!" She stopped herself. "Where did you come from?" She had so many questions.

The creature sat up on its cushion, looking up at her. "I don't... have any answers," it said, puzzled.

Aeona knelt for a minute without saying a word, trying to get to the bottom of her memories. Something had to make sense! "What… no why was… I'm in… Nyxa's room, and how come Mary… said she found me… …in the wardrobe?"

The creature, unable to understand half of what she was rambling on about, just looked up at the confused child, waiting for the girl to tell it or find the answers to her questions, herself.

"Sorry, I can't help!" was all it could say.

The creature grew quickly over the next few months and was only just able to sleep on the cushion, out of view, near the back of the wardrobe. For now, it was still okay if Mary happened to check on her in the middle of the night while she was sleeping, but for how long, Aeona thought.

It was a hot night and the sweat soaked Aeona's pillow as she slept. The duvet was pulled high to her chin. Her dreams swayed to the rhythm of her breath. Her steady chest rose and fell in the controlled calmness of the night, only to suddenly become a panting fury as she was dragged into the pits of pain and suffering of her past. "No!" she gasped, waking with a start, disturbing the creature from behind the wardrobe. It bolted out to her and stood guard by the door as if ready to fight.

The sodden bed felt like ice as her wet pyjamas clung to her skin. She kicked the duvet off as well as the nightmare, which tried to keep its hold. She reached to her stomach and pulled her wet shirt away from her body, and realising the discomfort, she got out of bed. The bedside light exposed the contrast between the dry sheet and the dark patch that framed her body on the mattress. "Urgh," she sighed and opened her wardrobe to get a change of clothes. She threw her wet underwear and pyjamas on the floor and looked at her bed in disgust.

She looked around for any possibility for her to sleep on the carpet but even the duvet was damp. She looked down at her friend and then at the door. The landing light spilled into the room and it was then that the only solution came to her: Nyxa's room.

"Shhh, come on," she whispered to the creature, "I'll have to sleep in the other room. Be quiet!"

The landing didn't have any loose floorboards so it was an

easy jaunt to the other girl's room. It felt very strange entering Nyxa's room, especially after so long. She pulled back the blanket, slipped into the cold, dry bed and closed her eyes to go to sleep. The creature scampered behind her and jumped on after her. Aeona felt the weight of it near her feet and gave it a gentle nudge. "You can't sleep there, can you?" she yawned, "Go and find somewhere to hide."

The creature, a little put out, jumped off the end of the bed and found a discarded cushion beside Nyxa's chair. Its open zip was too enticing for it not to slip in and snuggle into a ball and settle to sleep.

The world was silent, except for the distant sounds of nocturnal animals tearing at discarded bin bags, rummaging for food, or the flit of a bat as it hunted moths on the wing. Suddenly, there was a soft, dry rustle that stirred somewhere in the bedroom. The creature sensed it, gave a growl and pricked up its ears. Even the animals outside froze in alarm. The rustling of paper was followed by a dull Thud which made the creature stand and flick out its tongue to smell the air for the cause.

Then the silence was broken when something fell off the shelf and made a loud triple-thud as it bounced on the carpet. Instantly the creature was on it, shaking its head side to side, ripping at the thing.

Aeona groaned and sat up in the commotion, leaned across and turned on the bedside light. The creature was next to the bed worrying something in its mouth as it growled and clawed at the object. The girl blinked a few times before she caught a glimpse of what it was. "What are you doing?" she mumbled with tiredness, getting out of bed and reaching down to pull the object out of the creature's mouth.

Aeona looked at the string and torn wrapping around the

book in her hand and didn't care to question how it had fallen off the shelf. "It's a book!" she groaned to the snarling creature. She never heard the rustling or sound prior to being woken up by it and was too tired to put two and two together.

"Come on, please go to sleep," she begged, putting the tattered parcel on her bedside table and climbed back in to sleep.

A moment later, the book slid to the edge of the bedside table. It wasn't much of a disturbance but it was enough to make Aeona roll over to tell the creature to go back to sleep. As she did, its pages rustled in the still air. The creature didn't want to be scolded again and buried itself further into the warm stuffing of the cushion and closed its eyes.

The book gently fluttered again.

Aeona refused to entertain it and pulled the covers over her head to drown out the disturbance. In response, the book flapped violently, causing it to fall to the floor with a sharp thud.

"Will you go to sleep!" she snapped, understanding that if she didn't give it a stern look, within a minute, it would be playing again.

She reached over and flicked the light on. Nothing moved; she sat listening, unable to understand what had disturbed her. When she couldn't see or hear anything, she brushed it off as her mind playing silly games, and reached back to turn off the light. With a sigh, she lay quietly for a minute and then slowly closed her eyes, but as she did, she let out a gasp. The realisation of the empty bedside table hit her. With sleep stolen from her, she jumped up and dove across the bed to the light again.

She was right, the book wasn't where she'd put it! She looked around; she could've sworn she'd put it on the cabinet. Looking over the side of the bed, to her alarm, there it was on the floor staring back at her. She hesitated at first, questioning the notion of whether she had knocked it off by accident when she reached for the light the first time. Without getting off the bed, she stretched as far as she could and managed to wrap the tips of her fingers around the corner of the cover and pulled it up. As she flipped herself the right way up, she leant back onto her pillow, and as she did the book fell open on her lap. The pages fluttered, drawing her to read.

On the first line it read: *The grandmother asked the prince, 'Are you sure you want to marry this maiden?'* which was all it needed to bait the girl into its pages. She reached behind and lifted the pillow to get comfy. Then propping the book on her knees, she felt for the corner with her index finger and she slowly turned to the beginning of the chapter.

'Chapter 4: Yfel two... Three'

'Once upon a time, a young maiden named Evelyn lived in a village far away in the mountains with her father. She would help him tend to the sheep day and night, dreaming of knights in shining armour, who would come and rescue the maiden and take them to live in a beautiful white castle and become queen of the land. Like many before her, she was no different in wishing it were so.'

Aeona paused and gave a little tired smile. This story was different; it was calming and settled her mind with peaceful thoughts. She gave a warm sigh and continued.

'On a beautiful spring morning, the prince was riding through the mountains and came across their little cottage. The father, Henry, welcomed his highness and his entourage and introduced his daughter Evelyn. He had never seen such a fair maiden in all the land and took it upon himself to ask for her hand. However, when word travelled to the castle, the queen would not hear of such nonsense in her son marrying a peasant girl who

tended filthy creatures.

She sent an envoy for the prince to return to the castle at once for counsel.'

Every time Aeona's head faded forward as if she was being pulled to sleep, the book jumped, causing her to open her eyes in shock, not realising it was the book that was forcing her to read against her own will.

Softly it teased. *The prince knew his mother's mind and thus, before he would be drawn into the confrontation of royal blood, he ordered his servants to take him to the coastal fortress of his grandmother's abode. She had taught him the ways of princedom and he was forever grateful of her care. So, it was only right that he would seek her opinion on the proposal to marry the young commoner. The old woman would know how to work her magic on his mother, so they devised a plan to bring the two heart-bound children together.'*

Aeona struggled to stay awake again, as her chin lolled onto her chest with a grunt. The book refused to let her go and closed sharply, snapping her thumbs together within the cover, making her cry out in alarm. Each time, she would take a deep suck of air and continue. Part of her screamed stop, but it was impossible to put it down.

"Bring Evelyn to the castle just before sunset," his grandmother ordered.

As the last remnants of the night were pushed away, he told his soldiers to bring the young maiden to the castle side-wall. In she snuck through the dark tunnels to be met by the waiting candle of Grandmother. "Come, sweet Evelyn," the grandmother said, "Much I know of your longing."

Aeona gave a heavy sigh, distracted by the sound of a passing car and its dancing lights as it cut across the ceiling. The page fluttered, annoyed at her distraction. 'Read,' it whispered. Aeona obeyed and turned the page.

The Grandmother asked the prince, "Are you sure she is your maiden of choosing?"

"Of course, grandmother. I will do anything," he bargained.

The woman lowered her gaze. "Your mother will follow," she warned.

He knew she would, but by then it would be too late, they would be wed.

Little did the prince know, her guise hid her true form. Grandmother she called herself but Yfel she was.

She raised her hand beckoning him closer.

"One time you beg, Yfel will give," she warned.

"Please, grandmother, she will listen to you. Will Yfel give?"

The hag turned her back, "Two times you beg. You say, Yfel will give."

"But grandmother, I love her. I beg you, please, Yfel will give!" The prince fell to his knees, hands clasped together, pleading.

The hag stretched out her skeletal hand, palm drawn. Payment she sought for the false warning she gave. Suppliant to his wish, before the third she gave. With fallacious-pity in her eyes, she croaked, 'What say you? Yfel will give.'

She paused in quiet elation, 'Say it boy… Yfel WILL GIVE!'

The prince caught the subtle disdain, rose and turned to Evelyn. Her joyous eyes met his. Boundaries broken by Love. "Thank you," she mouthed. They would finally, be together.

The vile hag repeated the curse, sensing their desperation. "Say you, Yfel will give!"

He looked deeply into Evelyn's eyes, took her by the hand and turned back to the witch, and repeated, "Yfel will give."

Into the dark oblivion they went.

Before Aeona had time to sense what was happening, an explosion punched her in the chest, blowing her backwards into the headboard with such force it snapped in half. The bulb imploded from the pressure and the blast-scorched duvet blew off her legs, taking the bedside table with it. The cushion in which the creature slept violently smashed into the wall and spewed its crimson stuffing over the carpet.

Semi-conscious, she rolled herself out of the clinging mass of wood and padding, groaning from whiplash. She twisted and fell off the mattress with a bang, slicing her knee on the carcass of her lamp, and scrambled as best she could towards the blood-soaked cushion. To her relief its stained fabric ruffled and a head slowly emerged from the torn opening. "Are you alri-" she stopped.

Out of the rip emerged a form so vile Aeona gasped in horror. The abomination heard her breath, jerked its head loose and scanned the silent room for its prey. Instantly, it locked eyes on the girl and went for her throat. With nothing more than her smouldering duvet for protection, she snatched it and threw it at the demon, catching it mid-flight. The mass landed on top of her, furiously slashing and tearing at the material with its talons. Aeona quickly scuttled backwards, kicking and screaming as she tried to put some distance between her and the buried monster. In blind panic, she turned and bolted for the door on her hands and knees, unfeeling to the glass in her palms. She wasn't quick enough; as her hand went to yank at the handle, she was hit squarely in the back and was slammed face first into the frame. As she ricocheted off the wood, the demon caught the rebound. It bounced off and fell to the floor, which gave just enough time for her to pull open the door and dart down the landing.

"Mary!" she screamed. "M..." she stopped.

She knew she was dead when she heard the hell-born shriek behind her.

She thought it would be on her in an instant, but it didn't. It knew it had won. It lowered itself into a crouch like a cat about to pounce, waiting for her to attempt a feeble escape. It let out a low, glutinous rumble, goading her to run, but she couldn't. Where could she run? Nyxa's room was farther down the landing, with Mary's opposite: she could make neither. The stairs? She had already passed them; to attempt she'd have to turn and face the demon. Possibly she would make it three, maybe two steps before it would be over the bannister and at her throat. The only place left was the bathroom to her right.

Her legs shook violently in terror at the thought of not knowing when it would attack. She closed her eyes and imagined its breath inches from her nape, and then without control, a warmth trickled to the floor, audible above her shallow panting. Her mind faltered in acceptance of death, but conatus whispered through her body, and her arm lifted, trembling as it reached for the handle. The first creak snapped like a starting gun as the worn mechanism twisted in agony.

It remained crouched at her bedroom door, rocking its body in a deliberate rhythm, waiting for Aeona to make her move.

Her self-preservation started like the effortless shunt of a steam engine, as she drew in the cold air through her nostrils. She exhaled and repeated, willing her failing body to move. 'Time, time, time, time!' she silently screamed; she couldn't hold it in any longer. The demon unsheathed its claws into the carpet and gave a victorious grin, unmasking its serrated teeth. She felt the door give with a click, as the catch released its hold. The monster had stalked its prey enough. It shifted its weight and coiled into its hind legs, ready for the kill. Suddenly, the girl burst forward, slamming her shoulder into the door. She tore her hand from the handle, nearly wrenching her wrist, spun, and caught the door on the rebound before slamming it shut just as the black abomination struck. The frame shuddered under the impact; a shriek of rage split the air as claws ripped deep into the wood.

Aeona hurled herself against the door, bracing her weight as she rammed her foot against the bottom to hold it shut. The flimsy door trembled under the fangs and claws outside. It was only a matter of time before the flimsy barrier gave way. Her eyes snapped to the handle as it jerked downward, the demon wrenching at it from the other side. "No!" she screamed, "Mary!"

Mary shifted uneasily in her bed, brushing aside the dull thuds and muffled cries behind her earbuds and mask. The night wrapped her in a false silence, and shielded her from the impending death on the landing.

Abruptly, the demon stopped, stood on its hind legs and looked up and down the landing. Then to the bottom of the door where Aeona's foot was locked in desperation. With a snarl, it drove its claws into the soft plaster of the wall and began to climb to the ceiling. Over the thunder of Aeona's pounding chest and gasps of panic, she heard the unnerving claws creeping higher, closer. Then came the muffled crack as its fist punched through the ceiling, showering white grit to the floor, leaving only the thin wooden laths between it and the girl.

Aeona quickly looked up to where the scraping was coming from and then over her shoulder to the small slat window. She would have to climb into the bath, open the window and drop to the garden some four metres to escape. The monster was at the top of the wall near the ceiling, slashing at the wood. It was only a matter of time before it would enter. Trying to move as fast as she could, reluctantly she released her hands from the only thing protecting her and nervously edged to the bath. She lifted her leg over the side and was about to step in with the other when the lath splintered in her ears, followed by an ear-piercing shriek of triumph from the malignant hell spawn.

In a heart-stopping scream, Aeona emptied her lungs, "HELP!"

The pitch of the cry tore through Mary's earbuds. She sat bolt upright, pulled at her mask, and ripped out one of the plugs in her ear. The dull room was silent. Then she heard it again.

"MARY!"

The woman fell out of bed, ran for the door and bolted out into the landing. "AEONA!" she shouted, stopping dead in her tracks at the sight of the dust and debris scattered on the carpet before her. "MARY!" came the scream again.

The slashing claws at the ceiling stopped. It dug in its talons to prevent itself from falling and slowly edged its body back out of the hole to see where the other cry came from.

Mary looked up at the movement and froze. Horror seized her as she stumbled backwards into the wall; a blood-curdling scream tore from her throat as the monster flew at her in an instant. The ferocity of the blow slammed her into the door frame of Nyxa's room. She fell in disbelief before she had a second onslaught of the demon's fangs. Aeona didn't know where it came from, but the sound of Mary's fight on the landing lit a spark in her. Her eyes shot around the room for something to defend herself with. She pulled her leg out of the bath, wrapped a towel around her arm and grabbed the toilet brush. She took a sharp, deep breath then ran out into the landing with a battle cry. Mary was on her back, thrashing her legs out at the demon, trying to kick it off. The demon turned in confusion and locked eyes on the girl, who realised her mistake.

It recoiled its hind legs and launched itself into the air. Aeona instinctively threw out her arms in defence. Luckily, she struck home and sent it hurtling into the opposite wall. She fell back into the bathroom and jumped into the bath, reaching for the window. The latch refused to budge. "Come on," she screamed, turning to climb back out of the tub. But it was too late; the demon was already in the room.

There was no escaping it. The brutal impact sent them flying into the bath, pulling the dolphin-print shower curtain and pole with them. The beast, cocooned in a frenzy of girl and plastic, bit at the dolphin. It let out a scream of frustration and ripped at the curtain for release. Its claws found an opening and it pushed its way out to search for its target. Aeona froze. It stood on the side of the bath, confused at where she'd disappeared to.

Just then, Mary stumbled into the bathroom, only to be knocked backwards into the toilet by the demon. Her legs buckled under the impact and down she went, with teeth clamped into her shin, tearing flesh to the bone. She kicked in terror and shuffled out into the landing towards the stairs, but it continued its attack. Left and right, it jumped away from each kick. It saw its chance and clamped its fangs into her foot. Eyes wide in excruciating pain, Mary flung her leg into the air in an attempt to shake it off. Suddenly, something had to give; the agonising sound as the back of her foot tore off in an eruption of red and disappeared down the cavernous throat of the abomination.

Aeona, now free, stood at the door of the bathroom, pointing the broken pole at the demon. It turned its focus away from the screaming woman and fixated on the girl, with blood and tissue dripping from its gaping mouth. Aeona shook violently, glancing left and right, but now there was no retreat, nowhere to run. She slowly retreated to the end of the landing and stood waiting for the Yfel to end her life. It growled and snarled in its blood-lust victory, its teeth gloating at the prize before it.

The girl's chest heaved and struggled in the thick air.
She was ready for her demise. She didn't care anymore. She aimed the broken pole at the abomination and closed her eyes.

In one powerful leap, it lunged for her throat.

As it hit, the momentum sliced the end of the rod through her bloodied hands and jammed it into the wall behind her. The pole stabbed through the demon's chest, causing it to shriek in shock. It fell to the girl's feet, squirming and writhing in agony. In a gasp that questioned her fate, she looked down in total disbelief at the green pus streaming around the embedded pole. Quickly, she leapt over it and ran along the landing to Mary, who was pale and lying motionless. Aeona retched at the flesh that hung from the woman's foot and the sodden-red carpet that surrounded it. Then she bolted to her room to get something to stop the bleeding. But the shift in focus was short lived, as the demon wasn't finished yet. It struggled to its feet with the pole still protruding from its chest. Now, the unforgiving spawn was bent on one thing only. Disinterested in the woman's squirming body, the demon saw Aeona's legs disappear around the corner of her door and crawled in pursuit.

Inside, Aeona couldn't find any towels to use as bandages and so bundled under her arms as many clothes as she could get from her wardrobe. Then shouted for her friend, "Creature!" she cried, "I need your help! Quickly!" But it didn't emerge from under the bed. "Where are you?" she asked, before running back to help the woman.

She was too late. The demon was standing next to her unconscious body, growling. Aeona stopped in her tracks and let the clothes fall from her arms. Without thinking, she spun around and ran for her window.

She yanked it open; the night air swept in with its cold welcome. Tears streamed down her cheeks; "Why won't you die?" she screamed at it.

There was nothing in her room to defend herself with. She had to jump! Quickly, she looked out at the precarious drop to the front garden. Then jumped to lift herself onto the sill, just as the demon went for her. Her foot slipped under her wet socks, and she fell backwards. The demon missed, catching her pyjamas with its talons, before it fell through the window and landed in the front garden with a loud scream as the shower pole jarred further into its grotesque body. She quickly clawed herself up to see it crawl out from under the bushes and snarl its rebuke, before it ran out to cross the road.

She watched as the headlights of an approaching car bore down on it. The demon froze like a rabbit as the car slammed on its brakes. It was a swift reckoning. The hell spawn's skull shattered the bumper before it fell under the front wheels. The travelling tyres dragged it under the skidding wheels, leaving a trail of black and pus. The tyres couldn't hold onto the filth, lost grip, and threw the broken mass to the rear wheels, which ripped at its limbs. The vehicle behind couldn't stop in time and ploughed into the back, causing more damage to the already dead creature, its torn body squashed between the bumper and chassis.

The drivers got out to evaluate the damage and argue about who was at fault, when they heard a frightening scream erupt from the house opposite the accident. The drivers instantly looked at the girl in the window and back at each other, then ran towards the house. Aeona ran to the landing as fast as she could.

Mary was conscious, yanking at her sleeve to use as a tourniquet in desperation as her life slipped away.

'Thud! Thud! Thud,' slammed a fist on the front door.

The woman's screams rang out again, sharper than the first, as she wrapped the make-shift bandage around her foot. Her shins streamed with bursts of blood.

'Thud! Thud! Thud,' "Open up! Open up!" shouted the men outside. 'THUD! THUD!' they banged. One quickly backed to the middle of the lawn, cupping his hands and shouted to the window. "Open the door! Open the door!"

"Towe….. l" cried the woman, a hand grasping in the air towards the bathroom.

The terrified girl bolted into the carnage of the destroyed bathroom and seized a towel from its hanger. Mary, unable to see through the tears of pain, lay on the carpet, slipping in and out of consciousness. The towel was no use in stopping the blood spewing from the woman. The girl pressed as hard as she could, but the towel dripped remorselessly, sodden with dark liquid. Her hands flowed red as the woman's life streamed over her fingers. The banging and shouts from downstairs came into focus.

She got up and sprinted down the stairs, crying, "Help!"

The men stepped back in shock upon seeing the poor girl covered in blood. "Come quickly," she shouted, leaving the door and running back upstairs. Stopping half-way, she quickly glanced over her shoulder to check they were following. "Here, here!" she pointed and ran into Mary's room to get the phone.

One of the men dropped to his knees beside the failing woman and pulled her hands away to see the damage. He instantly regretted it. Flesh hung ragged from her shins and calves, and blood surged in rhythmic jets, each pulse spraying her life across the floor. The man looked around in shock. "What the fuck… did this?" he choked, on the verge of vomiting. He had never seen so much blood in his life.

The panic in Aeona's eyes, the whiteness exploded from her sockets. "It wasn't me… It wasn't me… it wasn't me!" is all she could scream.

The other man had already called the emergency services, cupping his hand over the phone to inform the other man, "Ambulance on its way! Should be here soon…" he grimaced, looking down on the poor woman.

"Large cat-thing…" Mary panted, in excruciating pain. "it… was… a…"

"Is that what that thing was?" asked the man, "rest assured, it is well and truly dead. I just ran over it."

"Was… a… was… a…" Mary's head began to fall backwards as the loss of blood started to take its toll.

"Come on lady…. Stay with us… Stay with us!" the man kept saying, patting her hand frantically. "Where the hell are they? If they don…." He trailed off as the sound of the siren echoed in the distance.

"Hello… Hello…" called a paramedic from the bottom of the stairs.

"Up here!" the driver yelled, "Hurry!"

Heavy thuds followed and then stopped abruptly as the paramedic stood in shock at the amount of blood on the floor. "What on earth?" she gasped. "Just how? CLAIRE, get up here… NOW." she shouted. "You!" she ordered the man. "Get me towels… anything… CLAIRE!" She screamed, searched for a pulse, "Where are you? where are you? There… shit…come on Claire," she cursed as she came bounding up. "I got below 40 bpm; we got to work fast. She's lost that much; it looks like she's in hypovolemic shock. We've got to stabilise her here!" she looked at her partner with a stare that said: this isn't a great start to their shift. "Get everything on her! Where are the damn towels?" she screamed. He was trying to find out where they were kept in the strange house.

The paramedics worked as fast as they could to hook her up to the monitor and search for a vein for the IV. Mary was slipping fast at this point. They tried to stop the blood loss with QuikClot and tourniquets but it didn't look like she would make it.

In the bedroom, Aeona pressed herself against the wall, as far from the blood as she could get. But it was no use. It clung to her, smeared across her pyjamas from head to foot. She looked down at her hands. In slow, deliberate strokes, she wiped them on her breast, once, twice, each movement more frantic than the last. Too much red. Too much everywhere. She couldn't get away from it. The more she wiped, the more it spread. Her chest rose and fell in ragged bursts, quick and shallow, the metallic tang of iron heavy in her nose. Then the room tilted; the paramedics' voices grew faint, slipping farther away.

'Run, run, run, run, run,' screamed in her mind.

Beyond her world, the paramedics rushed to prepare the woman for the ambulance. "Get the stair-chair, this can't wait… we can't stabilise her here."

Moments later, a police car pulled up, siren wailing. The paramedics barely glanced up, too busy with their work, and simply pointed toward the two men standing in the doorway. They hadn't moved. Their eyes were wide, their faces blank, as if the scene was still replaying behind them: crash, scream, blood. The wrecked cars mattered less than the wreck inside their minds.

The officer got out and walked slowly to a small gathering of neighbours and the two men. For a moment, no one spoke. The blood on their clothes and stone expressions required silence.

The night sky still held its summer hues, but the calm was torn apart by the strobe of emergency lights. The ambulance wailed into the distance, its fading glow painting the houses in passing flashes. The police car sat in front of the wreckage, blocking the road, its blue lights washing across walls and windows.

"So… where should I start?" the officer asked at last.

The two men exchanged glances, then looked at their cars, and at their blood-soaked hands.

Officer Knowles slowly reached into his breast pocket for his notebook, ready to jot down the details of the accident and the reason for the ambulance.

The driver of the first car didn't feel the need to defend himself, as they both knew the one who had rear-ended the other was usually at fault. Besides, the other man was drenched in blood and too shocked to speak.

"That rabid cat there… or what's left of it," the driver pointed, "…came out of nowhere. I didn't have time to stop. I hit it, then he hit me. We both got out and heard screams from that house." He gestured towards the door. "We ran inside and found the woman. The ambulance just took her. She was on the landing, covered in blood, a lot of it. I…"

"Sorry to stop you, sir. What's your name?" Officer Knowles asked.

"Karl. Karl Cronson."

"Would you mind spelling that for me?"

Karl swallowed hard, then stammered, "Oh, there was a girl at the window." He turned to the other man. "There was a girl, was there not?"

"I don't… yeah, I think so," the man muttered.

The police officer glanced into the hallway, but there was no sign of any girl at the door, and then he continued with his notes.

"Okay, so cat, rear-ended, you two have insurance? Sorry, I'm just writing all this down. So, did any of you manage to call the AA or anyone to get these cars towed?"

The neighbours didn't have anything to add apart from stating that they had heard an almighty scream, which was ultimately the reason the police were called. Once the ambulance had left and there was only the police officer and the incident of a dead cat, they returned to the quiet of their houses, leaving the three men in an uneasy silence until the recovery vehicles arrived. After exchanging information, the shaken drivers went on their way.

Knowles stood alone on the quiet street, staring at the mix of skid marks and the mangled cat. To him, it was nothing of importance. A cat was a cat. The carcass was little more than scraps of fur and flesh ground into the tarmac, unrecognisable. In his eyes, it was just an unfortunate animal, and the drivers were the unlucky victims of its stupidity.

He turned his attention to the house.

The open front door cast its light onto the path, which led the officer towards the scene that now demanded his attention.

"Hello, is anyone home? Police," Knowles called, pausing for an answer that never came. "Police, I'm coming in," he added as he stepped into the hall.

Silence. Too much silence. No footsteps, no voices, only an oppressive stillness pressing in on the walls. "Is anyone home?" he called again, his voice less steady now, as he crept down the hall towards the kitchen to find no one. He skirted through the living room and then headed to the stairs.

"Hello! It's the police. I'm coming up. Is anyone home?"

Still nothing.

On the landing, the sight struck him like a wave.

Blood.

Everywhere he looked. It pooled on the carpet, smeared across the walls in jagged streaks. Thick drops glistened as they slid down a torn plastic shower curtain which lay crumpled near the bathroom doorway. The stench of death filled the air, clinging to his throat, making him gag. "How the hell did this happen?" His stomach lurched. "Hello," he managed, choking on the metallic scent that seemed to cover his whole being.

Nothing. Then a faint whimper reached him from one of the bedrooms. "Is anybody there?" he asked.

He had never experienced a sight like this before. He had heard from other officers that the city had crime, but in all his years on the force, nothing had prepared him for this.

The silence amplified the grotesque vision on the landing, and the unknown location of the sound unnerved him.

He edged closer to the bathroom, trying not to step in the pools that blocked his way. Small bloody handprints and footprints tracked across the tiles. Half of the shower rail lay snapped by the toilet, streaks smeared where the curtain had been dragged across the floor. A few tiles on the wall were shattered, and he guessed the broken pieces had ended up in the bath.

Along the landing was another bedroom with nothing untoward inside. The bed was unmade, and the duvet had been thrown back as if someone had been sleeping in it. One slipper was near the door, and another, shredded, was by the wall on the opposite side of the landing.

"How many times am I going to write 'blood' in this report?" he stammered to himself. There it was again: a whimper with a faint creak of furniture, but it was not in the room he was in. He leaned out into the landing, listening, holding himself still.

Aeona had retreated to the safe haven of the wardrobe, rocking herself back and forth, wrapped in the safety of her own grasp, whimpering softly to herself.

Knowles heard the creak again and gingerly made his way towards the only room he had not entered. The unreal, intermittent sound came from within. The officer consciously held his breath, trying to use all of his senses to pinpoint where the noise was coming from.

The child's rocking made the wardrobe door move in and out as if the whole thing was sighing in distress. He approached, not sure what to expect. He coaxed himself to reach forward, and with the tips of his fingers, he cautiously edged the door open a few centimetres, ready to slam it shut if anything should fly out at him. To his relief, there was only darkness. He breathed deeply. "Nothing more, nothing. Wait," he gasped as his eyes quickly adjusted to the dim light.

At the back was the young girl sitting amongst bloodied clothes. The officer reached into his pocket, took out his phone, and tapped the torch on. The shock of seeing the child's stone-white face made him jump backwards and throw the door closed.

Her animalistic pupils, black and wide, stared vacantly into nothingness. She panted in sharp, shallow breaths; her teeth contrasted with her purple-blue lips that cut across the terrified girl's expressionless face. The ferocity in her eyes was amplified by the blood and sweat that streamed into her matted hair. He froze, sitting on the carpet. He wanted to back away, go downstairs and wait for more officers to arrive, thinking it was above his pay grade, but he told himself deep down that it was a child, just a frightened child. He didn't like how it was playing out: the silence, the blood, the creaking, panting, staring. A typical horror film scenario; he knew the outcome, and it was not going to be good… for him.

"Come on, pull yourself together, John," he scolded himself, biting the inside of his cheek.

Slowly he plucked up the courage and reached for the wardrobe door again. "Hey, it's okay, I'm a policeman," he whispered.

The girl didn't react.

Knowles gently waved his hand in front of her eyes to see if she would focus.

She didn't do anything.

"It's okay, I'm a policeman," he whispered again. "Let me get you out of here," he said softly, reaching towards the girl and placing a hand on her knee to see if he could wrap his fingers around the back of her legs to try to slide her out.

In an instant, the girl exploded and leapt at the man, her teeth clamping onto his hand, snarling and ripping at his face with her nails. Knowles keeled backwards onto the carpet with the girl on top of him, tearing and slashing at his eyes. Instinctively, he punched with both hands, hitting her square in the chest, sending her back into the wardrobe with a terrifying scream as she dragged the door closed behind her.

"What the fuck!" he yelled, throwing himself backwards onto the dressing table, the metal handles stabbing into his back.

Aeona, disorientated and confused, pushed herself into the dark corner. The fight-or-flight response sent her deeper and deeper into the emptiness of her mind. She was broken, and a pat on the knee was all the trigger she had needed to fight. The poor girl pulled and tugged at her hair, and clumps of congealed hair lay on her knees, detached from reality.

Knowles sat for a minute, catching his breath, pulling a tissue from his pocket to place over the bite on his hand. It was not too bad, but it was deep enough to draw blood. Luckily, he had managed to keep her hands just out of reach of his eyes. She had caught him on his cheeks several times, but they were only scratches and would heal in time, unlike the broken child who whimpered and shook in the wardrobe before him. It would take much more time to pull Aeona out of her mind.

He reached for the radio. He didn't know why he hadn't called it in earlier, but it had just been a simple car accident; he hadn't been expecting a bloodbath and a physical assault.

Within twenty minutes, several other vehicles and an ambulance arrived with no sirens, but a stream of blue and red. The neighbours couldn't understand why they were being disturbed for a second time in the night and stood at their doors or leaned out of windows with interest.

The emergency services couldn't believe what they saw upon entering. The police dealt with the landing, the bathroom, and clearing the lane of the debris from the cars on the road.

It was the paramedics who sat in front of the wardrobe door, quietly trying to coax the frightened girl out. Aeona was unresponsive to anything they said. She never removed her hands from her face, but whenever a woman moved forward, the girl reacted venomously, spitting and clawing in all directions.

Slowly, opening her medical bag, Jackie retrieved a thermometer and stethoscope to see if she could distract the girl with them.

"Is the poor girl here all alone?" she asked Knowles, who was sitting to one side, already wary of the feral child.

"Yeah. The two men in the car accident said that the ambulance rushed a woman to the hospital moments before I arrived," he answered.

"Is that whose blood is on the landing?"

"I presume so. Let me go and find out who she is," he said, getting to his feet, nervously glancing at the girl and then walking out to greet the blood again.

The paramedic played with the stethoscope, thumbing it through her fingers, but Aeona was lost in her own world. "Would you like to have a play?" she asked, placing them onto her own chest. "Here," she said, slowly placing them at the foot of the wardrobe.

The girl hissed.

"Could someone try to contact her mother?" the paramedic whispered to her colleague.

As soon as the woman uttered the word, Aeona launched herself out of the wardrobe. Jackie, like Knowles, didn't have time to react. The girl lashed out, hitting her full-force, screaming and ripping at her face and hair. Jackie was knocked flat onto her back. The other paramedic rushed at her and grabbed hold of the back of her T-shirt, trying to yank her off the cowering woman. As the girl turned to attack the man, Jackie, swiftly seeing the opportunity, wrapped her arms around the girl and held her tightly.

"Shh... shh... shh..." she cooed. "Shhh, you are safe. Shhh…

no one is going to hurt you." She lowered her voice to a gasping whisper, repeating over and over again, "No one is going to hurt you."

The girl fought for all she was worth, but Jackie had three girls of her own and knew she was not going to let this chance go to waste.

"Let us breathe together... Shh... shh one, shh... shh two, shh... shh three, shh... shh four. That's it, my girl... shh... shh five, shh... shh six."

They stayed in this position for more than ten minutes while the girl struggled and kicked at her. "Shh... shh one, shh... shh two..." She didn't care how long it took; Jackie felt the girl's pain, her fear, and her struggles.

Aeona couldn't break free and stared blankly into nothingness, breathing rapidly and trembling in the woman's arms. She was unable to hear the outside world and had shut down. She could only sense the intense whistling and her own thumping blood that tore through her veins. It was her own doing, to throw herself into the darkness and claim it as her home. No one would hurt her there, nor would she allow anyone to bring her into the light. The downward spiral into the darkness after the fire had been left unchecked by those who should have seen the signs and put something into place to help the young girl, but everyone had failed her. She took the blame and told the one person who should have understood it was an accident, but that person never comforted her, never took the guilt away from her. That person cast her into the pit of despair without a second thought. That person was now dead to her. She refused to call her name; refused to acknowledge that she even existed. Without giving her the dignity to even be called by her name, Anwen or mother, she didn't deserve either. If she saw that person haunt her dreams, it would become a nightmare. She would force herself to wake and tear herself from its clutches until the vile thing that called herself 'mother' was nothing but darkness itself.

Nyxa was no different. She drew her in, then spat her out. Aeona had slowly become attached to her, liked her, loved her, and needed her. But then she left her all alone, with nothing but the dark literature, evil demons, and the pitch that she was fed. It was her plan all along, to throw her to the black wolves so she could be eaten from the inside.

She didn't need to anticipate Mary's words; she already knew. The events stabbed at her soul and raged through her young mind. This was no different than going downstairs for the glass of water that killed those she loved.

She was the cause of it all.

The bathroom was like the cooker, ready to release its destructive anger. The demon was like her cat, Jinx, and the switch was like the ripping fangs that tore at life itself.

Blood and death, death and blood, laughing at her, goading her, punishing her.

Everything was too much for the girl, and without any control or mental capacity, she fell lethargically into a nightmarish sleep in the paramedic's arms.

Jackie felt the release and gently rolled onto her side, laying the girl on the carpet and placing the poor child in the recovery position, while Ryan quietly slipped the elastic of the oxygen mask over her head. Jackie knelt beside her to check her observations and gently stroked her forehead, questioning how and what had led to such a sorry sight.

If only she knew. But, for a mother of three beautiful girls, already tucked in bed at home, it was better she didn't. Dealing with horrific car crashes and other emergencies was nothing compared to the young life of the one that lay before her.

It was not long before the girl was in an A&E cubicle, being cared for by kind hands.

She woke feeling confused and disorientated, hooked up to beeping machines, the hiss of oxygen, and the intravenous drip in her arm. She glanced around for a minute and then faded back into the unknown.

She was stable, to say the least.

Samira, the social worker, was informed by the police that a young girl had been rushed to the hospital in a traumatic state. There was no adult at home, nor could anyone be contacted. The person looking after her had also been rushed to the hospital with some unknown injury.

As soon as they told her the address, Samira couldn't believe it and asked the officer to confirm. She called her colleague, Naomi, straight away. They both jumped into their cars and raced to the hospital to see what had happened, calling Mary's friend, Linda, on the way.

The three arrived at the hospital at the same time. Linda's car screeched to a halt in the car park. She jumped out and ran to the others, calling, "What the hell happened?"

"We haven't got a clue. The police called Samira, and she picked me up on the way," Naomi reported. "They said Mary has been rushed to theatre, something about her foot and blood. That's all they said."

Linda was visibly shaken. She had known Mary for over fifteen years, and she was always a stickler for being careful, so she couldn't for the life of her guess what had happened. Fallen down the stairs or something silly, like cutting herself with a kitchen knife, but why would that need an ambulance? she asked herself.

In the theatre, the surgeons had Mary on the table, the room filled with the best staff they had. "Whatever animal did this was unclean," said the lead surgeon, trying to think of all the possible scenarios. The foot was already turning a green and sickly colour before his eyes. The Doppler couldn't find anything. All arteries were negative, the calcaneus destroyed. There was no viable tissue left to reconstruct. The damage was too extensive. The foot was beyond saving. Silence stretched between them. "Best chance is a below-knee amputation," the surgeon said with finality. "Plus, that shin does not look good either. By the way, that colour is shifting; I think we'd better act now, or there isn't going to be a life to save."

When Aeona arrived at the hospital in the ambulance, she was stabilised in Accident and Emergency. Although her cuts and scratches were superficial, the doctors and the assessment team decided that she might become more aggressive and possibly self-harm, based on the report from Officer Knowles and the paramedics who brought her in. The doctors felt it best to keep her under observation and sedate her for her own safety. And so, the Paediatric Intensive Care Unit (PICU) offered the safest environment, with continuous observations, access to specialist paediatric care, and the ability to intervene rapidly if her condition deteriorated.

In a room by herself, on the other side of the hospital, Aeona slowly opened her eyes. The overwhelming smell of antiseptic, the bright lights, and the soft hum of the oxygen mask seemed to suffocate her. She didn't know what was happening nor how she had come to be there, but she had done her fair stint in a hospital to understand where she was. She reached up and pulled the mask from her face to breathe. The nurse, her back turned, heard the noise and quickly swivelled around to find the girl with her hand on the side rail, leaning to climb out. The nurse quickly pressed the call button and gently held a hand on the girl's shoulder to keep her in position. Moments later, other nurses entered, one of them holding a soft restraint behind her back. The senior nurse crouched beside the bed, her two hands on the top rail. "Hi there, sweetheart," she said. Her dark blue uniform contrasted with the others. "We know you are frightened, but we need to make sure you are safe. You are in a special unit where we can help you feel better and relax," she smiled.

Aeona didn't know why, but the overwhelming feeling that she was not in a 'normal' hospital led her to look for an escape. The blinds were half closed. The light softened as treetops peered over the window sill. The door, blocked by a doctor and another nurse, led to a corridor of gleaming white that hurt her eyes as she looked out at the long rows of doors.

The Head Nurse spoke calmly again. She could see that Aeona was becoming increasingly agitated as the seconds passed. "We're going to help you calm down." She glanced at the two nurses to act. One reached forward to shake the girl's hand, and when Aeona instinctively opened her palm, the nurse quickly slipped a padded restraint around her wrist, whilst the other did the same for her left in the distraction. Now, there was nothing she could do; she was well and truly tied to the bed.

"Do not worry, we'll stay right here with you, Aeo…"

The girl erupted in pure rage, arched her back screaming, fighting to get her hands loose, to rip, bite and gouge. The woman jolted backwards in alarm, her unbalanced crouching position unable to save her. Like a rabid animal, Aeona pulled and ripped at the side rails.

"Shh… it is only temporary… it is only temporary, Aeo."

Instantly, the girl exploded again, "DO NOT CALL ME THAT!" she spat.

The doctor quickly moved forward, swiftly removing the syringe from his pocket, whilst one of the nurses reached forward to push her onto the mattress.

"She is going back into shock!" one of them shouted.

"No choice. Forget the sleeve," Dr Lanston didn't hesitate. He uncapped the needle and jabbed the Olanzapine straight into her upper arm.

The girl let out a scream, fighting like a demon, bucked once, then twice; then her body fell victim to the drug. The tension began to ebb, and a ripple of calm waved over her. Her chest relaxed, her fists unclenched, and her face went peaceful, almost too peaceful.

Lanston took a heavy sigh and patted the child on her shoulder. "I'm sorry, little one. I'm so sorry."

Aeona awoke from the sedation, free from the restraints in the quiet room. She squinted her eyes and looked around. It was strange, unlike the hospital rooms she had been in before. The soft yellow walls calmed the atmosphere, and low music played in the distance. A soft chair was pushed up against a small table in the middle of her room. It also had its own en suite to one side, next to a narrow, frosted-reinforced glass window that brought in diffused light from the outside world.

She sat up slowly, feeling a little groggy, rubbing her sore wrists. The room was unthreatening, but a clean isolation hung in the air. Seeing freedom, she quietly got out of bed, uneasy on her feet at first. She held the side for support and when steady she tottered to the door, but the handle wouldn't give. It was locked from the outside and had no latch to grasp from the inside. The camera in the corner of the ceiling winked its little red light at her from above. She couldn't see out of the plate glass window in the door, and cupping her hands over her eyes didn't change the fact. She turned with a sigh and returned to the bed. She was just about to climb in when there was a knock at the door.

A woman dressed in a green PICU polo shirt poked her head around the corner with a smile. "Good morning, dear. I see you are up. You look much better today. How are you?" she asked softly, slowly stepping into the room.

Aeona looked her up and down. "I'm okay… I suppose."

The nurse walked to the centre of the room and pushed the chair to the table before going to the window without a fuss.

"So, you have been here a while, and I think it is time I gave you a tour. Are you up for it?" the woman asked.

"A while?" thought Aeona, then directed at the nurse, "What do you mean, a while?"

The woman deflected without answering, "My name is Lucy.

If you need anything or feel upset or worried, you can always talk to me," she paused.

The girl had no recollection of time. In truth, she had been in the unit for just over three days, severely stressed and most of the time under sedation for her own good.

"Come on then, out you pop," the woman ordered, holding the door open. "I think you might like it out there rather than in here."

Aeona was unsure at first, but the room was empty, with only the bed and a small table and chair; that was it. She looked past the nurse into the other room and then at her own bare feet.

"Cold, is it not?" smiled the nurse. "You had better slip those on." She pointed to a pair of white Velcro trainers tucked just under the side of the bed. "Let me first show you to the bathroom to freshen up, and then we can get dressed."

The girl was set into a routine that ran like clockwork: wake, wash, breakfast, followed by therapy sessions with the doctors, psychologist, therapist, or nurse-led discussions. There was never time for herself; she was always made to do something. The doctors said she needed to be occupied and engaged until bedtime. By the second week, she was introduced to lessons in the unit, mainly art and colouring, which she began to enjoy. It was a time when she could lose herself being creative, but there were moments when the horrors would manifest in her mind and spill out through the crayons. Ghosts from books and events screamed to get out. On a number of occasions, she had to be restrained and sedated. But as the weeks passed, the episodes reduced and lorazepam was reserved as a last resort. The nights were terrible for the girl. At times, they were wrought with dark creatures and nightmares, amplified by the screams of the other children in the unit.

It took over six months before Aeona was able to bury her anger. She no longer stared at the ceiling, and the thoughts of darkness dwindled, pushed deep, deep down, covered under the sediment of time, routine and therapy sessions.

Now, it had come to the time when she wanted out. "The nurses say I'm better now, so when can I go out?" she asked the doctors in her session.

"I can see you are much better," smiled the doctor. "So, let me see what I can do, okay?"

Another month blurred into the next, and the girl lost all track of time. Awake at 7 am, routine, bed at 9 pm, and repeat. There were many meetings with the social workers, Child Services and the discharge planning team. Mary couldn't look after children anymore; the demon had stolen that away from her through injury and trauma. She tried to convince herself it was a rabid cat, but she knew what she saw. The remains were shredded beyond recognition, under the wheels and washed away with the rain. What was left were vile pickings for nocturnal animals to eat; their hunger was short-lived, and they didn't survive the night.

The social workers searched for a foster home for Aeona up and down the country, but the only ones who had a bed were in questionable areas or places Naomi and Samira didn't feel were fit enough to take anyone in her condition. The two social workers sought the help of Aeona's aunt, Melanie, explaining that there was nowhere for the young girl to go. It was under emotional blackmail that she finally gave in. Images of unfit foster homes and hostels did the trick. Melanie had two children of her own, but they had left for university. So, in truth, she had a place for Aeona, but how it would play out with her sister was going to be a difficult juggling act. Melanie had been through the thick of it, from the house fire to the struggle with Anwen. But, she knew she was partly to blame for Aeona's grief. She never sought a balance between her sister and her niece, and the young girl was thrown to the side lines. Melanie had tried to talk sense into Anwen many times, but it seemed she couldn't cope. But now, more than a year after the accident, Melanie couldn't leave her niece to a life of never-changing foster homes when she had a place for her. She didn't know whether to tell her sister or not, but she decided on the latter for now. She crossed her fingers and hoped it wouldn't backfire on her. Now it was only a matter of time, paperwork and procedures to make it happen.

Christmas came and went. The nurses tried their best to bring some happiness, but it was devoid of any real cheer. New Year was just another day of routine and therapy. But, around one in the afternoon, Aeona was sitting in her room with nurse Lucy in quiet time, talking about the nurse's favourite book, when there was a quiet knock at the door. The doctor entered, gave a wink to the nurse and addressed the girl. "Come on, Aeona, do you not think you have been here long enough?" he said, with a smile. "I might have a surprise for you. I hope you'll like it."

The nurse stood, stretched out her hand, "Come on, let us see what he has got," she said.

They followed him along the corridor to the office at the end. Aeona gently squeezed the nurse's hand in apprehension as he opened the door. Inside sat two nurses and a person she had not expected to see: her aunt, Melanie. The girl rocked forward on her toes, wanting to run and throw her arms around her, but the other half of her hesitated to react, whether through fear or anger.

"Hi, Aeona," her aunt said softly, waving coyly. "I've been told some good things about you and… I hope… you know why I'm here."

The girl didn't know what to think. She didn't say anything at first but glanced at Naomi and Samira with questioning eyes.

"They say if you want to, that is, you can come and stay with me," she said with a nervous smile, not knowing what to expect after all this time, but deep down, she knew she had betrayed the young girl.

The social workers smiled and raised their eyebrows in silent approval. There were no other favourable options. It was either this or move Aeona to the south of England, far away from everything and everyone she had come to know.

She remained silent.

Melanie didn't want to begin with apologising and what-ifs because she thought it would cause Aeona to go into defence mode, and she knew it would bring out all the resentment and hatred she had for her mother and possibly herself.

Naomi broke the silence, "Come on, Aeona. Let us go and pack your things, and we can go with you to your new place. It would be nice for you to show us around your new bedroom. What do you think?" she coaxed, standing and moving to the door, giving the nurse a pat on her shoulder.

"That sounds lovely," the nurse added. "Do you mind if I come too?" she asked, to which Aeona reacted with delight.

Nurse Lucy took her back to her room to pack and say goodbye to some of the other children. It was not generally allowed for a nurse to accompany a child to their new home, but due to the girl's attachment to her over the last year, the doctor thought that by letting the nurse go, he would make things easier for the girl. She had been in the hospital for so long that she had forgotten what it was like to be in the outside world.

It took just over an hour to drive from the hospital to Melanie's house. Aeona was quiet most of the way, occasionally whispering to the nurse a few things about whether she was going to leave her or not. The nurse said she could stay for a little while but would come back in a day or so to check on her.

Melanie had emptied the room of her daughter's things, put them in the garage, and redecorated it, ready for Aeona to move in. Naomi and Samira had packed all Aeona's personal belongings from Mary's house and placed them in a small cardboard box.

"This is a new beginning, little one," said Melanie, sitting on the end of the bed, watching Aeona look around her new room.

Melanie was thoroughly briefed by the social workers and doctors at the unit. She tried her best to keep to the routine, but she had to admit it was tough going. Her children had grown up, and having another child in the house took it out of her. The social workers had said it was imperative, at least for the time being, to stick to the routine until the young girl was brought out of herself. Melanie had to complete a journal on a daily basis to keep notes of any mood swings or anything that triggered an outburst. Melanie felt it was a little too much.

Waking up at seven o'clock in the morning every day was impossible. On weekends, she threw the routine to the wind, refusing to wake up early, especially on Sundays. It was also challenging for her to manage lunch and dinner: her home was not big enough to have a dining table. She usually ate sitting on a stool at the breakfast bar, but was told to keep the girl out of the kitchen. She made a point of buying trays so they could eat in the living room in front of the television. Supervised free time was next on the agenda. She couldn't understand what on earth it was supposed to be. Did they have to be in the same room? Twice a week, a nurse would check on the girl. Melanie suspected it was to check on her, so she would run around the house, frantically cleaning to make sure everything was just right. There were set times for everything, including medication Aeona had to take three times a day.

The more time they spent together, the more Melanie grew tired of all the rules. She took it upon herself to decide that her niece didn't need most of what the social workers were forcing her to do. Without their knowledge, she slowly stopped the tablets altogether and abandoned the strict schedule. She saw Aeona flourish as time passed, and she had to admit that she enjoyed having the little girl around. She was settling in well, and so Melanie decided to give the girl some freedom from the strict regime. Summer slipped away, and the new school year loomed.

The social workers suggested to Melanie that Aeona could start by spending one or two days a week at school. It would do her some good to finally mix with children her own age. Aeona was reluctant at first, but once dressed in her little skirt and matching burgundy polo shirt and jumper, she thought she looked grown up.

On the first day, Melanie took her to the reception to introduce her to her class teacher, while Naomi went to see the principal. She had already spoken to him on a number of occasions about Aeona's tormented past. From the outset, it didn't go well. The school did everything they could to welcome her into class. However, to Melanie's surprise, Naomi brought her home at lunch time.

When Melanie opened the door, Aeona bolted in and ran up to her room, leaving her aunt speechless, looking at Naomi for answers.

"So, what happened?" Melanie asked.

"A long story," she explained. "The teacher said they were doing art, and a boy next to her was drawing monsters or something, and then she just picked up her chair and started smashing it on his table. Unfortunately, she hit him in the process. She then ran to the corner of the class, hid in the cupboard, and wouldn't come out. It took them about thirty minutes to get her out, and then the deputy head said Aeona became extremely violent. So, they physically carried her to the nurse and called me. So… yeah. We'll have the nurses check in on her… I will give them a call."

At dinner, Melanie didn't mention the incident, thinking it

was best left alone and that Aeona would tell her what happened in her own time. Later in the evening, the nurse from the hospital came and had a little chat with Melanie, saying she should keep her off for a day or two. Aeona refused to go on Wednesday, Thursday, and Friday, and by the end of September, she wouldn't go at all. Sometimes, she would get dressed in her uniform and stand at the front door, but then she would turn around and return to her bedroom. Ultimately, Melanie decided to home-school her for the time being. Melanie arranged for tutors to come to the house, but Aeona said she didn't like them. In the end, Melanie gave up trying, leaving Aeona to fall into her books.

A few days later, Melanie came home with a hamster for Aeona to look after. She thought it would bring some comfort, and that by asking her to clean, feed, and care for it, she would be giving her niece a little responsibility. Small, but it was something.

She grew very attached to it. When she was not reading, she would play with it on her bed or make mazes for it to navigate through. Melanie sometimes sat with her on the carpet when they were having dinner. The little creature would be trying to climb over the sides of their trays; Aeona would giggle and laugh, gently pushing it away with her finger. Melanie made her daily entries in the journal about a positive change in the child. The routine was really working, and Aeona was making a lot of progress. Hopefully, she would have another try at going to school in the new year.

Autumn passed, and winter blew in with Christmas approaching. The radiators kept the cold at bay, but the frost and snow made them battle in vain. Melanie couldn't afford the rising bills, so they confined themselves to the living room or bedrooms. All other rooms were closed, with towels at the bottom of the doors to keep the draught from invading.

Melanie was putting some clean clothes into Aeona's wardrobe when the doorbell rang. "Aeona love, could you get that?" she called.

The girl was playing with her hamster and watching television in the living room. "Okay!" she shouted up the stairs, getting up and placing Fluff in his cage. She made her way through the hall to the front door.

At the frosted window, she could make out the top of a green woolly hat with a multi-coloured bobble, the face blurred by the glass. Aeona guessed it was the nurse and groaned inwardly, hesitating to open the door. She went to the bottom of the stairs, calling up to her aunt.

"It's only the nurse again. Should I let her in?" she shouted.

In the bathroom, Melanie was emptying the bin and changing the toilet roll with the door closed. She didn't hear her call from the stairs.

Aeona listened for a response, but when the bell rang again, she turned the latch and opened the door.

At first, the person was difficult to recognise, their face hidden by a thick scarf against the harsh wind and drizzle. The girl had barely opened the door a crack when the woman shouted joyfully, "Happy Chr…"

The two locked eyes, and the air ripped from their lungs in a simultaneous gasp.

Anwen. Aeona. Mother.

Her body stiffened, and a sharp, cold wave of disgust, anger, and panic flooded her. All she could do was turn and vomit. Clumps of half-digested food, streaked with blood, splattered onto the bottom step. Melanie froze at the top of the stairs, wide-eyed in horror. Her nails dug deep into the bannister. Then she ran as fast as she could to the child.

Aeona's stress response kicked in with an almighty jolt of adrenaline. The surge of emotions and sheer shock overrode her body's control. She didn't register the feeling of warmth running down her legs. Humiliation turned to burning hatred. Aeona fell to her knees, slipping on the river of vomit on the step, spitting acrid bile onto her aunt's bare feet.

Melanie stared in disbelief at her sister, not knowing what to say. Anger welled in her. She leapt over the heaving child and slammed the door in the woman's face. She then turned quickly to the girl, patting her back. The girl threw back an arm in revolt, hitting the woman in the ribs with her elbow. Melanie grimaced in shock, seeing the girl sitting in her own vomit. She ran down the hall to get some tissue and a glass of water from the kitchen. Melanie ran back to find Aeona shaking uncontrollably. "It is okay… It's okay," she shrieked, but the girl didn't understand where she was.

Anwen was standing in her own torment, frozen in horror, on the doorstep with the cries of her husband and Christopher ringing in her ears. Melanie was to blame for this, having kept it hidden from them both. Confused about how or when to say it, she had looked after her niece. Anwen had never visited her before, so why now? The question ran through her mind over and over again. She had hoped to bring the mother and daughter back together slowly. That was why she agreed to take in the girl from the unit. It was her intention, but now it had exploded in her face. She had no idea this was how it would play out.

Aeona refused to acknowledge it; her mother's presence was already too much, and she felt small and powerless again. Then something in her ignited; the hatred burnt brighter than her shame. She refused to let tears run down her cheeks, refused to give her the satisfaction of a reaction. Her mother was a vile thing she rejected, like the pungent mixture she sat in.

Over and over, Anwen slammed her fists on the door. "How could you?" she raged, rattling it on its hinges. "I had to bury my son and husband because of you!" she thundered. She didn't care that they were the girl's father or twin brother.

Out of all people, Anwen had seen it with her own eyes. Once, Christopher went to school while Aeona lay sick in bed. Just after lunch, Aeona started to cry. He had fallen over and hurt himself. The mother had brushed it off, but five minutes later, the telephone rang.

The dentist, the hot water, the bicycle; they had been connected repeatedly. No scientific proof could explain it, but it was there.

And, on the day of the fire, it was there. Whether by fate or cruel luck, the child, burnt and broken, was unconscious beneath the rubble in the garden. She was spared from the agony and suffering that would have torn through her tiny body. She never heard his screams. She never felt his pain. She never said goodbye, as the bedroom they had shared was engulfed, taking half of her soul with it.

Melanie began to wipe the drips of spit from the girl's chin and then raised the glass of water to her lips. As soon as it touched her, Aeona flew into a rage, snatched it from her, and threw it at the door. The glass hit the door, shattering over the carpet.

"You should have died, not them!" Aeona cursed.

In a panicked frenzy, Melanie yanked Aeona up by her arms, hoisted her over her shoulder, and sprinted up the stairs. The girl fought like she was possessed, but the woman clung on. It took all of her strength to carry her into the bathroom and drop her into the bath. She twisted the tap with shaking hands, switching it to the shower.

A blast of ice-cold water struck Aeona's skin. She gasped, her body jolting, a silent scream wrenching from her throat. Water streamed down her face as she struggled for breath. Then, a sharp crack. The sharp echo of a slap ricocheted off the tiled walls. Melanie's open palm left a stinging imprint on Aeona's cheek, snapping her head to the side.

Aeona froze. For a heartbeat, she was suspended in the moment, her pinprick pupils locking onto her aunt's. A flicker of recognition surfaced. Her breath came in shallow bursts as she whipped her head around, confusion clouding her face as if the spell had been broken.

Then, to Melanie's utter shock, Aeona lunged forward, flinging her arms around her. The force sent them both tumbling backwards onto the cold, wet floor. Aeona clung to her, trembling violently, her tiny body wracked with sobs.

Melanie wrapped her arms around the child, holding her tight. For a long time, they stayed like that, two souls caught in the wreckage, lost in the moment. The pounding at the door faded. Her sister was gone. Whether in anger, shame, or indifference, Melanie didn't care. Aeona had been through enough. She wouldn't let her suffer at her mother's hands any longer.

As Aeona's sobs softened into quiet sniffles, Melanie gently lifted her chin. Their eyes met. "I'm here for you," she whispered.

"Whatever happened downstairs… I'm so sorry. I didn't know she…" her voice broke. "I'm sorry."

Tears streamed from Melanie as guilt tangled in her chest. She had dragged the girl back into darkness, but she swore she wouldn't let her slip away again.

"Come," she said at last, brushing damp strands of hair from Aeona's face. "Let us get cleaned up… and then we can play with Fluff."

Later that afternoon, Melanie sat on the edge of the bed, phone in hand, debating whether to call Lucy, the nurse. But fear gnawed at her. What if they took Aeona away? What if they decided she was not fit to care for her? She couldn't risk it.

She never saw her sister again. Over time, she heard whispers that the woman had sunk into her own world, drowning in medication and despair. Perhaps, at last, she understood the torment she had inflicted on her daughter. But Melanie doubted it. Eventually, Melanie and Aeona made amends, and the visits from the nurse were reduced.

Melanie's daughters, Olivia and Cassidy, came and went during university breaks, but were warned by their mother to be careful about what they said in front of the girl. Melanie had told them specifically not to mention that they were twins. Cassidy was to say that she was two years older than her sister. Being typical siblings, they argued about who looked older, but settled it in the end. They stayed for a few days, playing with Aeona and Fluff in the bedroom, and also managed to coax her into going with them to the mall. To Melanie's delight, they all went to the cinema to watch an animated film. Then, after a couple of weeks, they had to go back to university, leaving their mother and Aeona to settle back into their daily routine.

Two birthdays came and went for Aeona, with Olivia and Cassidy taking the time to come down from Scotland with presents, books, and a few things for her hamster.

Aeona tried to break out of her solitude, but it became unbearable. Everything seemed to hurt, no matter what she did.

She refused to go to school; she couldn't explain the underlying reason to Melanie, but she just couldn't. She wrapped herself in her books, burying herself in the dark stories she read.

Olivia and Cassidy, Melanie's daughters, helped in some ways. They told their mother that it was a part of healing, so Aeona's room was brought to life by the themes and characters in her books. The supernatural was plastered everywhere, from floor to ceiling. Her shelves overflowed with well-thumbed books about things a girl her age shouldn't be reading.

At times she would stand at the window, fists clenched. "I just want to run away!" she growled under her breath. She didn't care if anyone heard. She felt invisible and helpless, an object to be moved around, with no control over her own life. She didn't want to deal with the looks of pity, the unspoken words, or the overwhelming guilt that was eating her alive. The world outside seemed like a distant place, one where she could escape and finally breathe, away from all the pain and the loneliness. She fought the overwhelming urge to climb out of the window when Fluff, behind her, knocked over his water bottle, spilling water across the desk and sending it into the toy box beside her bed. The dull sound of glugging water made her groan inwardly. "Oh, come on, Fluff! What are you doing?" she said, picking him up and putting him into his cage.

She pulled at the bottom of the bottle, but by then, all the water had emptied itself into the toy box. She couldn't just leave it. Then, a call came from the bottom of the stairs.

"Aeona love, are you nearly ready for bed?" Melanie called.

She reached in, feeling the dampness of the soft toys, and then the hardness of a corner of a cardboard box. Her heart skipped a beat. "No!" she exclaimed, urgently pulling at the things within reach to get to the books at the bottom, her curiosity piqued.

She peered in, and at the bottom was a large cardboard box. She couldn't remember putting it there; it was probably her aunt, she thought. Lifting it out, luckily, only the right side of the box was wet.

Just then, Melanie popped her head around the corner of the door, "Hey, it is past nine." She stopped herself when she saw all the things over the floor. "Oh my!" she smiled. "You have been busy. What happened?"

"Stupid Fluff knocked the water bottle over," she said, flashing a smile back. "It is ok. I will clean it up and then go to bed."

"You need any help?"

"Nope, I've got it," Aeona replied, placing the box on the carpet.

"Oh, I remember that," she said in surprise. "You never got around to unpacking it. The social workers brought some of your things over from the other house...." she stopped.

Not picking up on what Melanie said, she thanked her and lifted off the lid to check the contents. "I'll just make sure everything isn't wet, and I will look at it tomorrow."

Placing the lid beside herself, she gasped with joy. There must've been over fifteen books, with mesmerising titles running down their illustrated spines. Melanie saw the gleam in the girl's eye from the door and smiled, "Good night, Aeona. Sleep tight!" She then closed the door and went to bed herself.

Aeona carefully lifted the books, checking each one for dampness and placing them in a pile on the desk next to Fluff's cage. As she read the titles, her eyes kept glancing at the posters on her walls. They were all classic novels, nothing unexpected, until one book stood out. The name on the spine was familiar, but she couldn't place where she had seen it before: 'Shadows Chant' meant something to her. The name called out to her, and she felt a mix of dread and curiosity. It was extremely dirty, creased, and had folded corners. It was different from the others, with a piece of string wrapped tightly around it, holding it shut.

The back of what looked like a young girl or boy was on the cover, about her build, looking through an arch. In the distance, an old castle or building appeared, distorted by fog, possibly with ramparts. Around the bottom, red plants snaked around the figure's legs and branches with clawed fingers reached out to grab the child.

She was curious about the contents, but a yawn told her it could wait. The remaining three were 'Encyclopaedia of Myths and Legends,' 'Loch Ness,' and 'The Banshee.' All of these were dry, so she placed them on top of the rest.

Aeona threw the wet box beside her bin. After making sure her hamster was asleep, she climbed into bed, reached over, and flicked off the light. "Good night, Fluff," she said with a yawn, and closed her eyes.

The wind whispered through the empty lane. The night was still, save for the quiet rustling of nocturnal creatures scavenging for food. Above, bats screeched in amusement as a fox leapt, trying to catch them in vain. High on the wall, a black cat sat perched, its glowing eyes tracking the fox's every move, and inside, Aeona slept soundly.

An hour or so later, Fluff crawled out of his straw bed, had a little food to eat, and jumped into running on his wheel. The clanging of his claws on the metal grid and the squeak of the bearings troubled Aeona in her sleep. She didn't need to open her eyes; she knew exactly what it was. Usually, she unscrewed it from the side and let it lie on the cage floor until morning but had been too distracted by the wet box to remember.

Rolling over, she groaned, "Fluff, please stop." But the damage had already been done; she was awake.

Not bothering to put the light on, she waited for her eyes to adjust to the faint darkness. Then she slid out of bed, slowly made her way to the cage, and unscrewed the wheel, letting it fall inwards on the sawdust. Fluff sat looking at her in disgust.

"Just go to sleep," Aeona returned with a scowl, returning to bed.

She lay on her back, staring into nothingness. The drone of an approaching car sliced its headlights across the walls in an arc as it sped past. Listening to it disappear, she rolled onto her side and slowly began to drift back into her dreams when there was a thud behind her.

"Oh, come on, Fluff, please go to sleep."

Usually, he was quiet, barely a presence in the dark. But sometimes, he became restless, scratching, gnawing, rattling the bars just enough to needle into her thoughts. The only way to silence him was to drape a t-shirt or an old blanket over his cage. Darkness subdued him; he would stop playing, stop eating, stop drinking. Instead, he would burrow deep beneath his straw house, vanishing into stillness until morning.

Aeona exhaled sharply, frustration prickling at the edges of her exhaustion. Then, a noise echoed in the room just as she was about to fade off again. She clenched her jaw and pulled the duvet higher, willing the night to be quiet, but there was nothing for it; she had to get out of bed. She quietly opened her wardrobe and grabbed the first thing her hands could find. Her toe struck something unexpected as she gingerly made her way toward the cage. It was not hard enough to hurt, but the sudden jolt caught her off guard.

She attempted to throw her pyjama top at the cage but missed entirely. Then, with a groan, she got up to turn on the light. The pile of books she had placed on the dressing table earlier had toppled over, and in the middle of the room was the culprit she had stubbed her toe on.

Fluff was standing on his hind legs, looking at her through the bars. The ironic thought of whether he was questioning why he had been disturbed from his sleep went through her mind. She straightened the pile of books on the dressing table and bent to pick up the book that lay open on the carpet, with its brown ruffled pages curled over at the ends, beckoning to be read.

Turning it over, she remembered looking at its cover earlier, 'Shadows Chant.' Still having her finger in the middle, she flicked her thumb to the open page out of curiosity.

Darkness Dawn,' she read with a soft sigh.

Fluff gave a little squeak, yearning for attention. Aeona took the bait, poked her finger through the bars, and gently rubbed his head. "You silly thing," she smiled, "now go to sleep… naughty." He dropped onto all fours, gave a little blink, and scurried across the sawdust to bed.

Aeona climbed into bed, propped herself up on her pillow, and pulled the duvet over her legs. She sat enthralled by the cover for a minute, trying to remember where she had seen it before. She had no recollection of the sort except when she first retrieved it from the box. Her thumb was still on the page, and she flipped it open.

"Okay, so let us see if this can put me to sleep," she said.

CHAPTER FOUR: DARKNESS DAWN

From the earliest days of their infancy, Antoinette and Cylis had found solace in the woods, a realm unfettered by duty and decorum. Now, at eleven years of age, they knew its every winding path and whispering bough as intimately as the lines upon their own hands. Here, amid the tangled embrace of nature, they might shed the burdens of their station and be. The palace, grand though it was, had ever been a gilded prison, endlessly attended and enclosed within an unyielding lattice of watchful eyes and ever-present servitude. The stark contrast between the two environments was a testament to the relief they found in the woods, a breath of fresh air in the suffocating confines of their palace life.

They contrived to slip away upon a morning of singular beauty when spring's gentle breath stirred through the awakening earth. With a modest parcel of bread and cheese, they stole through the palace grounds and ventured southward, following the river that fled, as though in rebellion, from the towering stone walls of their ancestral home.

As they ventured deeper, the world around them transformed. The dense canopy above, in its noble defiance, shunned the sun's golden touch, leaving a chill that clung to the air like a ghostly whisper. The ground was thick with the detritus of nature's decay, leaves sodden with age, twisted roots and crumbling bark, and among them, mushrooms of an unnatural sheen, their smooth, poison-laden caps standing in silent warning. No creature of fur or feather dared disturb them, yet children, innocent and fearless, are creatures apart from the wisdom of the wild, their innocence a beacon in the shadowed woods.

At length, they reached the river's edge, where the gentle current murmured its eternal refrain. Antoinette knelt, her small hands unfolding the cloth that held their humble fare, spreading it carefully upon the soft earth. Cylis, grinning, reached into the folds of his coat and withdrew a handful of bluebells, their delicate petals trembling in the breeze. The beauty of the bluebells filled the air with a sense of wonder and appreciation for nature's gifts, their vibrant hue a testament to the artistry of the natural world.

"These are for you, Antoinette," he said, pressing them into his sister's palm.
"They are lovely," she murmured, smiling as she smoothed the fragile blossoms. "Come, let us eat. I am quite famished."

Aeona paused, absently scratching her cheek as she pondered the text's peculiar style. There was something unsettling about it, something that stirred at the edges, but still, she read on.

Outside, the wind rose, a restless force that seemed to have a life of its own, rattling against the world. It was a cold wind, biting and relentless, that made the leaves shiver upon their uneasy branches. A rubbish bin knocked over in the distance, startling the leaves even more. She exhaled softly, a quiet sigh in the hush of the room.

'Cylis regarded his sister, then cast a thoughtful glance toward their simple repast.
His eyes brightened with sudden mischief. "I have a notion," he declared, and without another word, darted toward the clearing's edge.

Above them, upon a withered, contorted bough, something watched.'

Aeona thought the story would put her to sleep, but it did quite the opposite. She sat forward as if she was being drawn into the tea-stained pages. She knew something foreboding was coming. It read like a Victorian novella, dark, mysterious, and sinister. Her eyes flitted left to right and then shot to the other side, the pace pushing her on.

'Cylis returned, a golden mushroom in hand, the beauty of the umbrella mottled with crests of white.

He thrust them toward the excited smile of his maiden, who shrieked in glee. He ran his tongue over his lips, the ghost of an acrid bitterness lingering upon them. The mushroom had borne a fragrance most deceiving, a rich, almost nut-like warmth; its cap a smooth and beguiling brown, marred only by pale, wart-like blemishes. Somewhere, in the recesses of his mind, he recalled an idle whisper of knowledge, that some fungi, when prepared with due care, might be rendered harmless. Some, it was said, could be endured with practice, a tolerance if one were bold enough to cultivate it.

But in truth, it had been a gamble. Eat, he did!'

Aeona gasped with Cylis, unsure, only to have the answer thrust at her from the page.

'Within mere minutes, an unholy fire ignited within his gut, searing its way through his innards with cruel deliberation. A sudden, violent nausea seized him, and he barely had time to stagger forward before he was bent double, his body betraying him in a fit of wretched retching. A viscous spatter of bile and the half-dissolved flesh of the fungus befouled the forest floor, steaming in the cool air. Antoinette was beside him, her hand on his back. "No jest!" she begged.

He gazed wide-eyed, questioning, into hers. His limbs trembled beneath him, his joints moving not as his own but like a puppet whose strings were pulled by some unseen, malevolent hand.
Then came the visions.

The trees swayed, not with the wind but with a terrible, animate hunger. Their gnarled bark twisted into tormented faces, and their roots stretched like fingers, eager to grasp, consume, and claim. His breath faltered, the act of drawing air becoming a struggle against some unseen, merciless force. His heart, once steady in its ceaseless toil, now faltered, skipped, then thundered in frantic bursts, a desperate instrument played by a mad conductor.

A piercing whine arose within his skull, swelling until it became an unbearable shriek, as though some unseen force sought to split his mind asunder. A fevered itching crept over his flesh, a dreadful sensation like something wriggling, burrowing, multiplying beneath his very skin. His nails raked at his arms, yet no relief could be found, only raw, burning agony.

A seizure ripped through him. His spine arched violently, his limbs flailing in gruesome contortions, his body now nought but a vessel for chaos. The force of his convulsions dashed his head against the cruel earth, yet even this pain was swallowed in the tide of suffering that raged within him.

His vision fractured. The sky above him flickered, now brilliant daylight, now an abyssal void. His limbs no longer obeyed him, instead twisting and jerking in grotesque spasms. His muscles fought against themselves, his frame bent and wrenched by misfired impulses, a marionette caught in the grasp of a careless, unholy hand. Foam frothed at his lips, and his teeth clenched so tightly that they threatened to splinter.

And then, silence.'

"No!" Aeona begged. It was as if she was standing beside them. Hands outstretched, but unable to help. "Cylis!" she gasped.

'He collapsed. His body, still trembling in weak aftershocks, lay discarded upon the loamy ground. His breath came in a final, pitiful rattle, barely more than a whisper of life. His heart, once a ceaseless, faithful servant, now hesitated, forgot its rhythm, stuttered, ceased.

His unfocused and empty gaze found the sky, or was it merely the darkened confines of his mind folding inward upon itself?

And then, at last, nothing.'

Aeona sat up in alarm as 'Antoinette bent over her lifeless twin…'

"No… no… no…" Aeona sobbed uncontrollably, "Why Cylis?" she choked through tears. The word 'twin' cut deep.

'The shadow stirred in the trees; down it came on all fours, claws gripping the bark.

"A shame," it croaked, startling the wailing girl. "Sadness, I see." The dark figure raised itself onto its hind legs and straightened.

She pulled at her brother's hand, dragging him towards her. "You shan't take him!" she screamed. "He is mine!"

"That is not yours to say; I come with my task, you go with yours," it growled.

"Never," the two girls screamed, turning the page as fast as they could to see what the demon demanded. Antoinette and Aeona in a desperate battle for the soul of Cylis.

"There may be a way of atonement," it whispered, interrupted by the girls. "I may be able to h…"

"We will take it!" they spat at the vile creature that bargained before them.

"You say not, I warn you thrice: Whisper of Shadow, Darkness and Fly,"

Antoinette remained silent, but the reader spoke. "Whisper of Shadow, Darkness and Fly,"

"You say not, I warn you twice, Through the cracks where the whispers lie."

Antoinette remained silent, but Aeona said. *"Through the cracks where the whispers lie."*

"I warn you now, do not say I want him; you need him. It is a dire price you pay, I warn you last – but you want to say, "By the dawn, By the dusk, By the fading light. One must go, and one must stay."

Aeona whispered the breathless words. *"By the dawn, By the dusk, By the fading light. One must go, and one must stay."*

Instantly, Fluff exploded through the cage's metal bars, spraying fur, sawdust and entrails across the wall. Shredded organs cascaded down to the skirting board. All that remained was a crimson flower, a grotesque remnant of the girl's beloved pet.

Aeona was thrown backwards in the blinding flash, her wide eyes covered in innards and freckles of blood, sprayed across her face. She stared, cowering; the vile book lay on the floor, gloating in pleasure. A deathly silence hung in the air, except for something crouched in the corner, watching, waiting for the moment to pounce.

When the girl slowly came to her senses. Her eyes prowled blindly. The flash had stolen her sight. A foreboding darkness enveloped the room, and then a shuffle echoed, but from where? She sat bolt upright, her eyes searching. She knew something lurked somewhere, but this time, she had nothing to defend herself with. The memory of Mary overwhelmed her, and panic-stricken, she accepted the outcome.

In the corner of the room, a creature slowly shifted its paw as if it were ready for the kill.

Fight or flight tore at her insides. Heart racing, her hand trembled uncontrollably in hesitation, reaching to tap the screen of her phone. Half of her didn't want to see. The other half wanted to look death in the eyes. She couldn't take it any longer; the fear was too much. She fell to the floor, waiting for her throat to be ripped out. She hoped it would be quick, not giving it the satisfaction of seeing her face.

The creature rose from the dark corner, claws scraping at the carpet as it approached. Teeth gleamed in the dull light, and then a low growl emanated from it, "Remember me?" it questioned softly.

"How could I forget?" whimpered the child. "But you died? The cars?" she questioned. She had heard the crash; she had watched from the window… "How? I saw you die!" she spat on the verge of her last breath.

"Aeona, what are you talking about?" it said. "Come on, up you get." The creature spoke softly to the girl, unsure of her reaction.

The coldness contrasted with her boiling blood. Flashes of broken memories and sadness flooded over her. "I know you," she cried as the realisation swept over her. "Why did you come back?" she spat. "You broke me," she sobbed. "I sent you away."

The monster edged forward, pity in its movement. Its body shivered and pulsated. "You sent me away," it said, changing its tone. It softened, almost unbefitting the beast that loomed above the crying child.

Her face streamed with blood and tears; streaks distorted her features. She looked at the stains of drying blood on her pyjamas and ran her fingers through her hair. Clods of flesh and fur and wood rained down onto the carpet, causing her to retch in disgust. The creature watched her with patience. There was no malice in its stance, no predatory hunger lurking in the curve of its wicked grin. Instead, there was something softer, something ancient and knowing.

Its half-folded wings shifted slightly, sending a ripple through the air that carried the scent of soaked earth and something else, something indescribable, like the crisp air before a storm or the hush of a forest at twilight. It was a scent of familiarity.

Aeona hesitated, but the creature didn't move. It simply waited as though understanding her uncertainty, as though it had all the time in the world for her to decide.

Up close, different than before, its skin was not just dark but layered, textured like smooth stone with the sun's warmth. The pulsing glow along its spine flickered in a slow, steady rhythm as if matching her own heartbeat. The tendrils of energy that curled from its crown flickered like candlelight, responding to the invisible pull between them.

She reached out carefully. The moment her fingers brushed against its skin, a hum of energy resonated through its frills that ran down its back. A warmth spread through her fingertips, travelling up her arm and chest, settling into something she had not even realised was empty.

It had been waiting for her, locked away in the void. It didn't know where. Its mind was hazy and confused. The weight of that understanding settled over Aeona like a protective cloak. The loss seemed distant now, unimportant. The darkness pressing in from all sides was no longer an enemy to be feared but a quiet companion held at bay by the creature's presence.

She exhaled a breath she had not realised she was holding. She glanced back at the book. "It forced me." she gasped, "It tricked me… us," the reason dawning on her. "The damn incantations," she swore.

"I think that's how you must've come back," she said.

It looked at the book, still on the floor. "So, if I came out, did anything go in?" it asked.

"Do you think I always paint my face in blood?" she said, shaking her head and pointing to the cage's bent bars and Fluff's splattered remains across the wall.

"How can I forgive you? No one understood; the doctors, the psychiatrists, the medicine, they thought I was crazy," she explained. "How could you?" She slammed her fists in anger, pounding on the creature's chest, her anger turning to love. "I've been trying to forget about you,"

"But I never forgot about you," it consoled, and with a sincere smile, it changed the subject, "You've grown, my girl."

"When did you grow wings?" she asked, staring at the wreckage, surprised her aunt had not come running.

"What are you then? A dragon?"

The creature glanced at its wings, tilting them left and right. "I don't know the name you would give me. I guess so."

"It doesn't matter," she said softly. "The thing before you was evil. I'm just glad you're back." Her voice cracked. "I don't want to stay here anymore. I'm just so, so tired of everything." Tears brimmed, spilling as her shoulders trembled.

"It's dark outside," the creature whispered, its heavy steps padding toward the window.

Aeona sniffed, fighting to steady herself. "It's dark inside."

"Climb on," the creature said. "I need your help."

Her gaze lingered on the cage and the broken body of her hamster. A weary sigh escaped her lips. She stood frozen for a heartbeat, then pulled herself onto its back.

The creature lowered itself, wings unfurling with a leathery snap that filled the room. The crest along its neck rose, shielding her like a living shield. Muscles bunched beneath its skin as it shifted its weight.

Then, with a violent thrust, the wings struck backward. Wind howled through the shattered room, scattering papers and snapping curtains against the air. Wood splintered, stone cracked, and the window frame gave way in an explosion of dust and debris.

The creature surged into the night sky, carrying half the wall with it, Aeona clinging tight as the world below fell away in a storm of rubble.

Aeona clung tightly to the crest on the back of the creature's neck as they took to the brisk autumn night.

"This is amazing!" she screamed as wisps of thin clouds rushed past them, creating vortices that danced and swirled in eddies behind them. Beautiful hooks and strands of horsetails stretched across the sky, painted in the soft hues of morning cirrus. The blue-purple of the pre-dawn sky was a welcome cloak to hide them. They remained hidden for the time being, but that would soon change when the first rays would make them stand out in the emptiness and silence of the sky. Aeona felt calm in the freedom of the sky: no hurt, no pain of the world below.

"How about north?" asked the creature. "Shall we go north, my girl?" Its wings reflected no light and contrasted against the changing hues of purple and navy. Onwards they flew. The towns and villages of the English countryside glittered below, where the pinpricks of street lights and cars were the only signs of how high they had risen. It turned its head to glance at the girl and said, "I've got somewhere." Then, it raised its dorsal crest which slowly wrapped around the girl's back to form an arch-like seat. The caudal tail thickened and stretched like a knife edge, while the wings formed a ridged black blade. "Faster than lightni…" The swiftness of the shockwave that exploded from the thrust caught the girl off guard. Firmly held in place by the dorsal seat, she fought to reach forward, arms flailing as she tried to regain her grip. With her eyes shut tight, she groped blindly for anything to hold on to. Finally, she managed to place a hand on the frill and gripped it with all her might. Fear began to take hold. She grimaced, her skin taut and her teeth clenched, then tried to speak. "Drer… gun… slerw doon!"

Her words came out forced, like a novice ventriloquist who could barely open her mouth. She tried again. "Slerwww dooooooon!"

The dragon sensed her struggle. It eased off, released the tension in its tail and broadened its wings to steady her. Just behind its ears, a flight panel opened. When fully extended, it deflected the rushing wind away from the girl. She gave an exasperated thumbs-up and forced a smile as she tried to make her mouth obey. "Do we really need to fly so fast?" she asked.

The dragon's tone turned sarcastic. "Shall I carry on?" it asked. Its hearty laugh echoed through the vast blue sky as it rocked left to right. The girl swayed in rhythm to the dragon's silent song. "My girl. I can't believe you are back." The girl felt its heart, the words resonating from deep within its chest.

The girl stroked the dragon's neck, feeling its warmth beneath her hand. "I searched for you too, but I locked myself away and refused to come out." She wiped her nose with the sleeve of her pyjamas as a tear rolled down her cheek. She shook her head, forcing herself out of the dark thoughts. "But we found each other now..."

Nothing else was spoken for an eternity. Nothing needed to be; the silence that followed carried everything.

The world below was a painted picture of rolling fields, a patchwork blanket of green, yellow, and gold. The autumn harvest was ready for reaping, and it seemed to look up at them. A river snaked its way below, its pale gold surface contrasting with the sharp lines of the land on either side. Clusters of clouds, some dark and others pure white, drifted at the whim of the wind, deciding which farms below would be blessed with rain as they made their way north. Their shadows glided across the land and, every now and then, gave it the mottled skin of a boa, bringing the river to life. Aeona and the dragon sailed through the calm air.

The river led them to the horizon into the unknown, or so the girl thought. The dragon knew where it was heading. It gave a slight cough to clear its throat. "Let us get going, shall we?" It waited for the girl to answer, but she sat deep in thought, looking down at the world below.

When no response came, the dragon continued, "Let us fly!"

The girl patted its back. "Where are we going?" she asked.

"It is a bit too early to say, and I need your help. But first, let us put some distance between us and the destruction we left behind," it explained.

They journeyed onward into the dawn, the dragon pulled by a sense of purpose toward an unknown destination. The girl was oblivious to how she could help, especially since she didn't even know what it was. Caught in the moment of escape, they fell silent, needing no words, just flying as one. The dragon, so accustomed to his own needs and instincts, had never truly considered what a human might require. It had only ever thought of flight, of the landscape, of the horizon ahead. But now, with the girl voicing her hunger, he was forced to think beyond himself. Aeona decided to break the silence, "I'm hungry," she mumbled.

The dragon cocked his head to one side, taken aback. It couldn't, for the life of it, think of what humans eat. Dragons eat practically anything, but was that the case for a human? "Hmm, never thought of that," it said aloud.

"Never thought of what?" asked the girl.

"What do you eat?" it asked, with all sincerity.

"I never thought about it before," she said, and they both laughed. "They had me so drugged up, I do not remember what they fed me." She tried to remember, scratched her head, and thought a little more. "Nope, got nothing, dragon," she went on. "I recall toast with crisps, but nothing else. What do you suggest?"

"I'm a dragon," it said. "I can rustle up a cow or sheep if you like, there are quite a few in the fields." Peering below, it spotted a small village a few miles to the north. "There is a place not far from here; let us head down there." It pulled its wings back, slowed, and descended toward a bend in the river. When they were about two hundred metres from the ground, the dragon made a sweeping movement toward a forest just outside the village. It carefully surveyed the surrounding area to ensure an inconspicuous landing. A clearing at the forest's heart offered the perfect place to land. Stretching its rear legs toward the ground, it arched its wings, and with a plume of dead leaves and earth, they came to a halt. It gave one more look around and listened for anything that might give them away. Once it was sure their landing was secure, it said, "Come on, my girl, let us get you some food."

The clearing was a small copse in the middle of towering oaks, a good place to stay hidden for now. They made their way to the edge of the clearing and entered the trees. Birds fell silent at the intruders. The faint rumble of a tractor in the distance told them they were not entirely alone. It was difficult for the dragon to move through the forest without the eruption of snapping twigs and branches underfoot. The girl turned to it, with palms outstretched, with a look of seriousness. The dragon could only shrug its shoulders. "What can I do? Look at me, stupid branches," it said, giving pitiful eyes. It looked at the mass of broken twigs littering the forest duff. To avoid the minefield, it searched for small clearings free of branches and bounded from one to the next. At the outer rings of trees, the two of them stood motionless.

The village was about a hundred metres ahead and was an

easy jaunt if they followed the thicket hedge to the right. It seemed unnervingly quiet, almost abandoned, but a couple of vehicles gave it away. Old stone houses lined the entryway. The black and white of the Tudor cottages stood out on the left, juxtaposed with the autumn peach dahlias, violet asters, and multi-coloured hanging baskets, breaking the mood. Water trickled along the stream that ran under a mill. The waterwheel, once a symbol of past industry and craftsmanship, now stood still, the stream too weak to set it in motion.

The girl led the way, beckoning. "Come on, dragon, follow me." They stayed as close to the hedge as they could, scurrying on without hindrance. When they had made a good fifty metres, a cast-iron telephone box, gleaming red with its eighteen small windows, stood as a proud relic of the 1940s. Beside it, an odd-looking post box, matched in style, marked that they were close. Just beyond stood the shop, post office, and police station, all housed within one convenient cottage. The girl crouched under a dogwood hedge, its red berries giving her some cover. It was only then that she looked down at her pyjamas. "Dragon," she whispered.

"Not now, my girl. Let us listen."

"Dragon," repeated the girl.

A little agitated, "Shhh!" came the response.

"It can't wait. Please listen." Her voice was more audible than before. "What is it? Can you not see, we're undercover?"

"I know, but have you not noticed I'm wearing pyjamas," she explained. "So?" it quizzed.

"Pyjamas are for sleeping; they don't have any pockets."

Even more confused, now it was the dragon's turn to shrug its shoulders and turn its paws to the heavens, "So?"

"I don't have any money," she explained. "How am I supposed to walk in there and buy some food?"

Putting its paws over its eyes and snout, "Seriously, now you tell me!"

In normal circumstances, if they'd not been under the hedge, trying not to blow their cover, they would've been rolling on the ground in tears of laughter. But now wasn't the time.

"Umm!"

"Umm…" That was all the girl could think.

They sat for a minute, collecting their thoughts. Someone must be looking for them by now. Parents and, most likely, the police. After all, a girl had gone missing, an enormous hole was ripped through the side of a house, and cars and debris lay damaged everywhere. They were sure of it.

A robin flitted into the hedge, puffed out its red breast at the thoughtful pair, and was gone again before they could take in its plumage.

"Are you still hungry?" the dragon asked, hoping the girl was not.

Aeona's stomach rumbled its answer. She patted the dragon's paw. "I'm fine, dragon, no need."

"Well, you need food, so you're going to be my angel on the run," it said, studying the girl closely.

"On the run?" she asked.

"We're going to break into that shop and get you some food," it went on, "no ifs or buts; everyone is searching for you, so let us give them a reason."

The girl got to her feet, not thinking about blowing their cover to anyone nearby. "I thought you were a good dragon," she said.

"I am… I was. But after what they did to you… us," it fumed. Now, it was the dragon's turn to get to its feet. The street was deathly quiet. Nothing stirred, nothing moved.

"Come on," urged the dragon as it made off at a fast pace

towards the village.

They stood at the corner of the first house, taking in the aroma of the flowers in the hanging baskets at every house in the now-empty street. The colours of cyclamen and pansies were even more vivid nearby, surrounded by carex of yellow-bronze and blue-grey, with ivy cascading toward the ground. But this didn't calm the dragon; in its mind, it had one goal now: to get food for his girl. Only five metres away lay all the food they could ever hope to carry.

"An easy in and out, break window, climb in, grab food and off we pop," it told the girl. "As simple as that."

The dragon was cut short when the door swung open, striking the bell at the top of the door as a person backed their way out of the shop. In sheer panic, the dragon bolted for the telephone box and struggled to hide inside. It pulled the door as best it could behind it. The darkened windows made the red glow even more striking. The girl didn't have time to react. With nowhere to run, she froze in front of the shop, her pyjamas making her look entirely out of place. The old lady called in a rough, squeaky voice, "Why, thank you so much. Geoffrey, give my love to dear little Helen for me, such a sweetheart." She turned, almost bumping into the girl, who stood motionless in front of the shop. "Oh! Sorry," she stammered, nearly dropping the bag containing her eggs and milk.

"You're going to catch your death, lass," she continued. The woman couldn't help but wince at the sight of the side of the girl's face.

"Sorry, I… was not looking where I was going," she said.

"No worries, my dear. Please put a coat on or something. How have you come into the street dressed in your pyjamas?" She smiled and shook her head. "It's getting cold; winter is coming… Oh! I haven't seen you before. Are you Janice and

Frank's daughter, from number 28?" the elderly lady asked. It was obvious she wasn't, since the woman knew nearly everyone in the village. "No, sorry, but I… seem to have forgotten my… money. I had better go home and put that coat on as you suggest," she stammered, glancing around for a place to run.

"No need, my love. Here, take this." The old woman reached into her purse, produced a pound coin, and swiftly pushed it into Aeona's hand. "Nip into the shop and get what you want quickly. Run home, my love." She winked, waved her walking stick and walked off. The telephone box door edged open to reveal the dragon, firmly stuck inside. "How long must I wait? All the feeling in my tail is gone," it groaned, toppling out onto the street with a thud. The woman was spared the sight of the creature's graceless exit.

"It is a stroke of luck that she gave you some money, my girl.

Now go and buy something to eat, and let us go," it said with a smile, giving her a gentle push towards the door. Aeona followed the momentum and pulled the door open to enter the shop.

It was like stepping back in time. Floor-to-ceiling shelves lined the shop, a wheeled ladder running along the top rail. Near the top of the ladder sat an elderly gentleman; he glanced over his shoulder as the bell chimed to mark her arrival. "Good morning, my dear lass," he called, climbing down from his perch to serve the girl. "Dearie me, dearie me. You'll catch your death. This will not do at all. How? Just how? I should give your parents a piece of my mind for sending you out shopping in your pyjamas." He looked the girl up and down, shaking his head in dismay. "No coat, no coat, come in, come in. How may I help you?" The girl approached the counter and searched for anything a whole pound could buy. Hopefully it would keep her going until the dragon planned another ill-fated smash-and-grab. She picked up a packet of biscuits and a chocolate bar, placing them on the counter. "Just these, please," the girl said.

"That'll be one pound twenty-five, thank you."

"Oh, sorry. I only have a pound. I'll just take the biscuits," she said, putting the bar back where she had taken it from. It is better than stealing, she thought to herself, glancing over her shoulder to see if the dragon was peering in. Through the window, she could see the blackness of the shadow hidden at the end of the hedge.

"You know what? Take the chocolate as well. You look like you've had a bad morning," the shopkeeper said with a smile. "Go on before I change my mind. Now, run home before the weather turns."

She smiled at the man, gingerly picked up the chocolate bar, said thank you, and then turned to leave.

Only when she stepped outside did she think of going back to throw it at his face. That was what she had become: every glance, every comment from others felt like too much to bear. But in light of her situation, even though she wanted to say something to him about not wanting or needing his pity, she had to go with it and try to calm down.

The chill hit hard after the brief warmth of the shop, the sudden shift cutting through her thin pyjamas. She was used to the English weather, but when she realised, thanks to the concern of the elderly man and woman, that she was outside in only her pyjamas in autumn, she suddenly felt the chill of the misty morning hills. She looked down at her red and green slippers, "Umm…great!" She smiled to herself. Her eyes lingered there for a moment before she slowly looked around, half-expecting someone to mock her for walking the street in pyjamas and slippers.

Not walking directly towards the dragon, the girl crossed the lane and followed the pavement toward the forest, in case anyone might glance from their window and take an interest in the stranger. When the dragon realized this, it skirted the hedge a few metres behind, trying to stay in the shadows of the scarlet berries abundant on the skimmia bushes.

The lane, a patchwork of cobblestones and asphalt, blended the new with the old in the picturesque village somewhere in the north of England. The girl didn't know where she was, but it felt different from the city she had lived in, or used to call home. When she reached the end of the hedge, not far from the village's edge, the dragon appeared, covered in crimson berries, juice running down its body. It smiled at the girl, lowered itself as if crouching on its front legs, then, starting at its head, shook with a ripple running down to its tail. The girl jumped back with a start. "Nooooo! Get away!" she squealed, waving her biscuits and chocolate bar to fend it off. Once it had finished, the dragon then sat back on its haunches, tail wagging with puppy-like enthusiasm. "We did good, did we not?" it beamed.

"Come on, let us get out of here." The girl smiled back.

Back in the village, the two elderly people went about their day. One went home, and the other continued to go through his daily takings, getting ready to close his shop for the day. The old woman took her coat off, walked to the kitchen with her eggs and milk, and put them in the refrigerator before she put the kettle on. Then she sat at her small dining table and looked around the room. Photographs of her late husband, Ronald, with her sons and grandchildren filled the walls, capturing family moments from holidays, birthdays, and ordinary days alike. "October is nearly through, Ron, anniversary next week; what have you got me this year?" She smiled. "I hope our sons pass by and pay us a visit with the little 'uns. That will be nice, will it not? Anyroad, I'm sure they're busy pottering around with summut or other." Not expecting an answer, she reached across the table, next to the vase and ornaments, where the remote control lay on a doily she had crocheted. With a press of a button, the television flickered to life, and channel one, by default, blared out of the speaker. The usual volume for an elderly lady, not entirely deaf but hard of hearing, was the term generally used. She took no notice of what was on, she stood up and attended to the kettle.

Geoffrey, the old man, finished counting and cashed off for the day in the shop. He gingerly tottered to the door, flipped over the sign and turned the numerous locks to secure the door for the night. No crime had happened in the village for as long as he could remember, but old people did their due diligence for peace of mind. The good old days had long passed when he could leave his door open day and night without a care in the world. He went to the back of the shop and slowly climbed the stairs to his little bedsit above the shop. He knew the stairs like the back of his hand: number four was the creaky board, and number five was the loose carpet he always promised himself he would nail back down one day. He flicked on the light, sank into his old leather recliner and reached across the table to where the remote control lay on top of a doily his late wife had crocheted.

The television had been in his possession for over thirty years and was as good as new; he kept telling himself there was no need to buy a new one. It took a minute or two for the enormous television to flicker to life and another minute for the screen to warm up. While he waited, he glanced around the room: dusty picture frames lined the walls, along with a wooden fork and spoon. Faded wallpaper, mottled green and brown, ripped at the edges, dated to the war era and reminiscent of the railway children of old. Within the frames, his daughters, who had long left to begin their own lives, married with children, married with children. He didn't see much of them anymore, once or twice a year, if lucky. Eventually, the image on the screen faded into view.

Channel One, by default, played a film or program that entertained the old man for a while.

"Rowwwwww! Rowwwwww! Rowwwwww!" bellowed the Viking. "Come on, men! Rán does not want you this day!" The screen depicted a crew, soaked to the skin, heaving with all their might. Oars dug deep, then pulled in unison, powering their ship forward. The men on either side, enormous and grunting, strained against the fury of the storm. The Viking ship struggled to keep its course. The captain looked to the port, then to the starboard, to see only blackness, broken by the raging waves, as if furious black horses stamped and waited for their chance to drag the vessel under. The man on the rudder fought to keep them straight. He stood fast, heels locked into the bulkhead, the steer board firm in his grip. "Vidar, there is only one thing I can d…"

"Enough of that," the old man said to himself and pressed the button.

Channel Two: lions, giraffes, elephants. CLICK.

Channel Three: science. CLICK.

Channel Four: music. CLICK.

Channel Five: "Oh, I remember this," said the old man as a black-and-white movie lit up the room. CLICK.

Channel Six: the news. "Here we are," he murmured, "let us see what's happening in the world."

On the screen sat a presenter behind a desk, surrounded by images of wars, floods, fires, and every other disaster the world had to offer. He read out the headlines while shuffling through papers. "Hurricane Elisie is heading across the Atlantic and is expected to hit landfall in Cornwall and the south-west tonight. The police and emergency services stress staying indoors unless it is vital to go outside.

"I live in the Lake District. How is this relevant to me?" Geoffrey muttered at the screen.

"Other news from further north," continued the presenter, "a ten-year-old girl has gone missing, and police are asking for anyone with information to call the hotline on the screen. The girl is approximately 137 centimetres tall, has short brown hair, and has distinctive burn-scarring on the right side of her face and neck. She was last seen wearing a pair of red and blue pyjamas. Her disappearance happened around 4 am this morning, and we can go directly to our reporter who is at the scene in Winwick, Warrington."

"Good evening. We're going live to Peter at the scene. Peter, what can you tell us?"

A short delay occurred in the feed, then: "Yes, Sebastian, thank you. I'm standing here in Winwick, Hollins lane, where the disappearance happened around four this morning. The police still have the area cornered off. Debris still litters the area. They're not allowing us to get any closer until they have conducted their full investigation. Still, they have said a gaping hole had been torn out of the upper floor, which they suggest may have been caused by a small gas explosion, though this is unconfirmed." he continued. "I managed to speak to some residents who stated that they were woken in the early hours by a large crash, which set off several car alarms in the area. Those living next to the property have been asked to stay with family or friends until further notice."

Back in the newsroom, the presenter interrupted, "Sorry to cut your report short, Peter, but we've just had an update on the event. The police have just released an image of the young girl they're searching for, and they want the public to be on the lookout for anything suspicious or of her whereabouts. Please call your local police or the hotline on the screen," he alerted.

A photograph of the hotline number below appeared on the screen. The photo looked more like a mugshot than an appeal for a missing child, cold and clinical beneath the hotline number.

"Now, over to Alec, for the weath"… CLICK.

"All doom and gloom," Geoffrey yawned and looked at the clock. "Seven o'clock already!"

Channel Seven: Dad's Army.

"Here we go," he smiled, settling back in his chair, singing along to the theme.

If you think we are on the run,
We are the boys who will stop your little game.
We are the boys who will make you think again.
Cause who do you think you are, kid…'

The old man stopped abruptly. "Kid… Kid… THE KID?"

He quickly picked up the remote control and pressed the channel button many times in panic. "Damn! Channel Two! Back to the news. Work, you bloody thing!" he spat, jabbing the remote.

In quick succession, he scanned through the channels.

Channel Two: Crocodiles… CLICK.

Channel Three: Space… CLICK.

Channel Four: Scooby-Doo… CLICK.

Channel Five: Black and white film…CLICK.

"Come on, you stupid thing," he cursed. CLICK. CLICK.

Channel Seven: Tom and Jerry.

"Tom and Jerry," he paused, "What happened to the news?" he puzzled.

It took a second for it to dawn on him: "Six! Six! Six! You fool!" He clicked back in a frenzy.

The final moments of the football results were being read out on the screen. "Liverpool four, Aston Villa three. That's the end of the sport. Back to the headlines."

With that, the photo of the girl appeared on the screen again. His heart thudded against his chest. There was no mistaking it: the girl from the shop. "That's you, my girl. Hope you enjoyed my chocolate… lass!"

He got up as quickly as he could and shuffled over the chest of drawers near the door. He reached for a piece of paper and pencil, knocking them all over the floor. "Bugger it!" he said, cursing under his breath.

He then turned quickly and wrote down the hotline number from the bottom of the screen just before it vanished. "I hope you are safe, my girl," he said, lifting the receiver.

At the same time, the old lady on the other side of the village was dialling the last two digits of the hotline number. Her telephone rattled back and then returned to the start position. Placing her finger in the hole of number nine, she rotated it to the metal bar and let go. Clack, clack, clack, it went, then hit home. Holding the receiver firmly to her ear, she waited.

"Hello, emergency hotline. How may I help you?" the police officer said.

"Good evening, my dear. I hope I'm not bothering you," the old lady said. "But I've just seen the young girl on the news, and I think I saw her today."

"Many thanks for calling in," the operator replied. "Every call is important. I will pass you on to my superintendent. Please stay on the line."

The walk back to the forest was a joyful one. At the end of the lane, they made a beeline towards the copse of trees, thirty metres to the north. The thought of being caught slipped their minds for a while. The grass and heather were easy enough to walk through, and a mixture of deep green foliage and mauve and orange flowers coloured the way. To the right, a couple of hares stood watching, ready to take flight if the need arose. They rose up on their rear legs, ears bolt upright, listening to the pair's low chatter.

"Well, that went better than expected, dragon," the girl reported as she attempted to open the end of the packet of biscuits. After several pulls, she decided to use her teeth and ripped the end off, losing one biscuit in the process. She caught the next between her teeth and pulled it into her mouth. The taste of sweetness exploded with saliva. She chewed it into a mass, swallowed, and took another. "I don't suppose dragons eat biscuits, do they?" she questioned.

"I've never had the pleasure, my girl. I don't think I have," it smiled as it glanced over at the packet in the girl's hand. "They don't look very tasty, though." It lowered its bottom lip and made a little grimace, indicating its thoughts of dislike.

"Why don't you try?" the girl said, holding out her hand, a biscuit pinched between her thumb and forefinger. "Here."

The dragon hesitantly opened its mouth and stretched out its long purple tongue, where she placed the biscuit. The dragon withdrew it and waited a second before reluctantly closing its mouth. It didn't take long for it to melt in its mouth, and in an instant, the dragon was coughing and spitting the contents all over the grass. "What on earth!" it spluttered. "How can that be any good for you?" It looked at the girl in confusion. "Out of everything in the shop, that's what you chose to come out with? What's wrong with you?" It curled its lips in disgust and scurried away to the left, leaving the girl slightly amused at the dragon's reaction.

"More for me then," she called after it, then raised her hand to eat another.

A minute later, the dragon returned with a hare in its mouth, ears lolling in the air. "Would you like to try one of these?" it grinned.

"What's wrong with you?" she returned. Now it was her turn to curl her lips in disgust. "The poor thing!"

With a quick jerk of its neck, the dragon tossed the animal into the air, and in one swift gulp, the hare was gone. "That's what I'm talking about," it retorted. "That's what I'm talking about, my girl."

When they entered the forest, they made their way to the far end, as far from the village as possible. By this time, it was already dark. The nocturnal animals had started to make their way to hunt for prey. Tiny Pipistrelle bats darted around, picking off small moths and insects. They weaved to avoid the larger Daubentons and Noctules swooping above. The dragon watched intently at the flurry of wings beneath the tree canopy. The forest was a symphony of life, with other creatures of the night around them going through their nocturnal motions, unhindered by their visitors, as long as they sat quietly.

Male Tawny owls occasionally called to mark their territory with a 'toowit,' followed by the sharp 'ke-wick' of a female in response. Rodents scurried into cover, grateful for the warning the owls had unwittingly given. A foraging badger clambered out of its sett onto a fallen log, pausing to eye the dragon with uncertain curiosity. The black shape didn't alarm it. After a curious glance, it padded along the log, snuffling for grubs and beetles, perhaps even raiding a squirrel's stash of hazelnuts.

Above them, a mass of stars glittered in the moonless sky, while a glowing wave slashed across the heavens. Millions upon millions of pinpricks of light brought peace to them. They sat silently in awe, not wanting to steal the moment from each other. The stillness was broken only by a beam of light from a passing aeroplane, its path angled toward the silhouetted mountains in the distance.

The hare had whetted the dragon's appetite, and with so many creatures stirring in the forest, it was a wonder it didn't hunt for more. Meanwhile, the girl's sugar rush was fading, and a small pang of hunger crept in. Beside her lay the unopened bar of chocolate that she was saving, but the temptation was getting the better of her.

"Dragon, I don't suppose you're allergic to chocolate, are you?" she asked with a hint of concern.

Still gazing at the stars, it answered simply, "I don't know. Should I be?"

"I was told that dogs can't have chocolate," she recalled, "but you're not a dog, are you?"

"It is good of you to notice, my dear girl," it laughed, "very astute."

"I think it's best if we don't take any chances, though," she said, raising her intonation. "What do you think?"

"You may be right. I think the excitement of nearly being stuck in a telephone box took its toll. Besides, I did have a hare, so I'm good for now. You go ahead and tuck in." The dragon returned its gaze to the heavens.

Aeona became lost in thought as she ate. The food in front of her was barely touched, her thoughts drifting elsewhere, far away from the forest clearing and the mundane task of eating. In the back of her mind, she knew that someone must be looking for her, the police, her aunt. But the thought was fleeting, like a shadow, quickly slipping away. No one would find her here, would they? No one would come to take her back.

"Hey, dragon, remember the fun we used to have? I was thinking about how we played in the woods behind my house, just the two of us. I'd like it to be like before… you know. Anyway, we need to decide what we're going to do. But not now. I think we should get some sleep, and tomorrow we can make a plan."

Dragon seemed to be away in its thoughts.

A hedgehog made its way under a pile of leaves nearby, causing them both to look in its direction. "What are you doing out so late?" Aeona asked. "Are you not supposed to be hibernating by now?" It stopped, looked at her in annoyance, and scurried away.

Aeona let out a yawn, wiping away a tear. "Come on, dragon, are you not tired?" she asked.

"Not really. You sleep. I will rest when I know it is safe," it said softly. "I'm sorry we left in such a hurry; you do not have anything besides what you are wearing. Forgive me, my girl." It then wrapped its body around the girl, curling its tail to make a soft pillow. "I hope this keeps you warm?"

"I'm sure it will, my friend," she smiled. "Thank you for coming back." She stroked the dragon, yawned again, and closed her eyes.

In the village, there was a firm rap and then a ring of the bell at number 36. It took a short while for the old woman to reach the door. "Who is it?" she called. "It is very late."

The man in the police uniform raised his voice to make himself audible to the old lady through the door. "Good evening, Phillis, it is Constable Williams. You rang about the missing girl.”

“Oh, yes, yes,” she answered. “Just a moment, just a moment, my dear.”

The sound of the chain sliding into place and then the lock clicking. Gingerly, the old woman opened the door ajar, with the chain pulled tight. She peered through the narrow gap, one cautious eye glinting in the porch light.

“Constable Williams… I know it is late, but this is urgent.”

“Good evening, Gary, do not ‘Constable Williams’ me. It has been so long; do not worry about the time. How are you and Emma?” She swiftly unhooked the chain and pulled the door open. “Come in, come in, do not forget to wipe your feet.”

“Would you like a cup of tea? The kettle has just boiled.” she asked.

The constable chuckled to himself. “Sure, Phillis. I would say no, but I know you would thrust one on me anyway.”

Shuffling her way to the kitchen with the man in tow, she went straight to the cooker and turned the knob to light the flame before making sure the whistle was in place. “Now, Gary, what can I do for you?”

“Well, Phillis, you called about the young girl. You told the lady on the phone that you saw a girl matching the description on the telly,” he explained. “And I’ve come to ask you some questions, just to see if it really is the girl we’re looking for.” When he finished, he took a picture from his breast pocket and slid it across the dining table towards her.

The woman reached across to collect the photograph and raised it to her face. “It is hard to say, Gary, but... Oh, let me get my glasses.”

The constable let out a sigh. “It is important, Phillis. We had another call from Geoffrey, from the shop, saying the same thing, so, it can’t be a coincidence that two people in the same village report the same sighting."

Phillis was not taking the slightest notice; she was too busy hunting for her glasses. She moved things around the coffee table in the living room, then the sideboard, then the ottoman. "No, no, where on earth have they popped?" she muttered. "I was wearing them watching the telly just before you arrived." She paused to think. "Ah… the hat-stand beside the front door." She turned and headed to the hall. "That's where I put them." She chuckled.

"Phillis," groaned the constable. "They're on your head, you daft old bat," he said with a smile.

With confusion in her eyes, she reached and had a feel around her hair. "So, they are, Gary, so they are," bringing them to rest on her nose. "Now, where is that picture you want me to look at?" Placing it in her hand this time, Constable Williams began again, "Is that the girl, Phillis? You know, the one you called about."

After a few seconds, she looked concerned. "I'm afraid it is. That's the little one I bumped into outside the shop. Dressed in her pyjamas, I thought it was strange, in her pyjamas, and not forgetting the terrible scars. They made me wince a little, so without a doubt, it was the poor lass," she replied, shaking her head. "I knew something was up."

"Do not worry about the tea, Phillis; I will have to pop up to see Geoffrey and see what he has to say on the matter," he apologised. "I'll tell Emma you sent her your love. Thanks a lot for the call."

Phillis couldn't help but ask, "The lass's parents must be worried sick, but how on earth did she get so far from home in her pyjamas?"

"I've no idea, Phillis. We're looking into it. Thanks again."

He let himself out and called back to her, "Phillis, come and lock the door, love. Good night."

Not far along the lane and a left turn was the shop. Constable Williams had lived and worked as a police officer for over twenty years and knew everyone in the village. He went to school with Phillis and Geoffrey, and he should have retired a long time ago, but the constabulary kept asking him to stay on. After all, nothing ever happened in the village. At most, a letter would go astray, and old people, being old people, needed to find the culprit. This was the most exciting thing that had ever come Gary's way, in the form of actual police work, so a sense of urgency hung over him.

The constable knocked on the door and called up to the window, 'Geoffrey! Geoffrey! Get down here and open the door, Gary here!'

The curtain fluttered, letting through a slice of light, and the old man peeked out. The curtain drew open, and the window swung out.

"What do you want, you old sod?" he shouted down. "Have you any idea what time it is? Give me a second; this better be good. I will be down as fast as I can."

"Should I come back tomorrow? It'll take you that long," he called back as the window closed.

After what seemed like a lifetime of standing in the empty lane, the old man finally appeared at the door.

"A long time, no-see. How are you, Gary? I hope all is good!"

"Sorry to bother you this late, Geoff," he apologised, "but I got a call from the city saying you had seen the girl that went missing. You know, the one from the telly," he said, handing him the photo of the girl.

"Let me see," he said, pulling his spectacles from the pocket of his robe and looked carefully at the picture. After a minute, he glanced back at the constable and nodded. "I have to say it was her, Gary, sure of it. She looked a little more windswept, with her hair all over the place, but I'm certain it was her." he nodded again. "How can anyone forget her? The poor lass, you know her face and neck. Nearly broke my heart. Such a beautiful young girl and then… shame, poor shame."

"I do not doubt what you are saying, Geoffrey, but I do not suppose, by any chance, those cameras of yours are working?" he asked, glancing up at the corner of the ceiling.

"I think so. I've not checked them in a long time, Gary," he responded. "I think they record over themselves every week or so."

"You do not mind if we take a look, do you?"

"It is well past my bedtime, but this is exciting stuff." He grinned. "Like the old days, Gary, like the old days."

"Nothing like the old days, you crazy bat," he laughed. "Where is that video recorder?"

The pair of sleuths made their way to the back of the shop.

"Now, do you remember how this thing works?"

"Not really, but how hard can it be?" Geoffrey replied, picking up the dusty manual that had not been moved in years. He sucked in a breath, coughed, then blew sharply, sending dust everywhere. The dust flew all over the place, causing them both to cough.

The constable gave him a dirty look, snatched it off him and flicked to the contents page. "Here we go… page five, how to replay. Okay, so I think I should go to recording seven, it says here. I'm presuming that means seven o'clock."

Geoffrey followed his instructions, first pressing the stop button and then rewinding. The machine screeched loudly as it rewound the tape. The two men bent forward and stared at the counter, spinning around, waiting for the right time to press the button.

8:00

7:55

7:50 and so on…

7:10

7:05

7:00… By the time Geoffrey pressed the button, the machine wound to a halt at 6:55.

Pressing play, the video appeared on the small television in the corner. It was black and white but served its purpose. On the screen, Geoffrey was sitting at the counter doing the crossword in the paper. The men watched as Geoffrey, in the recording, chewed the end of his pen for a minute, deep in thought. The two men glanced at each other, and Gary held the forward button, not wanting to endure the tedious wait any longer. Although still visual, the screen sped up with flashes of distortion across the top and bottom.

One customer came in and went, whom the shop owner quickly identified as Florence from number 75, purchasing sugar. Then, about twenty counts further on, Phillis appeared, buying her eggs and milk in fast forward. The old lady moved gracefully around, picking up the items she needed, paid, and edged toward the door.

"Let go! Let go!' Gary shouted, in a panic.

The video recorder groaned to normal speed, but for the old men, time seemed to stand still.

On the screen, they could see movement outside the shop just before Phillis made her exit. They could make out a black form to the left that seemed to be moving toward the shop before quickly disappearing when Phillis made her exit. Although the window advertisements obscured the view outside, Phillis was clearly talking to someone.

"'Wait, wait, wait…,' called Geoffrey. "She is going to come in now."

Sure enough, a girl entered and stood transfixed by the counter. The video quality was blurry, but they could make out that it was the girl in the photo.

"I told you it was the girl, that's why I called." He jumped with joy. "Now, what's our plan?"

Gary's solemn face didn't share the joy of his friend. "This isn't good, Geoffrey… not good at all. This means I've a lost girl in my village. I've got to call this in. Where's your phone?"

It took the dragon a while to shake off the thoughts swimming around its head before its eyelids grew heavy and it drifted off to sleep. The background noise of the creatures and insects sang through the night, and the gentle rocking of the dragon helped the girl feel safe from harm.

The nocturnal world went on around them, as it always had.

A few hours later, the dragon awoke to find the girl curled in its tail, enveloped like a blanket.

Slowly, it raised its head to look around. When they had settled for the night, it was too dark to fully understand where they were, but now the dawn had arrived. The navy and deep orange-red glowed behind the silhouetted horizon of rolling hills and treetops. Morning dew glistened like diamonds on the ground. Mist hung in the stillness, waiting for the sun to hide it for another day.

The dragon slipped gently free from around the girl and made its way out of the forest. The morning brought with it the woodland birds and the drone of distant cars, a low, never-ending hum in the otherwise tranquil place. Aeona stirred out of her sleep and, with a shiver, squinted and sat up with a groan. Moving her tongue around, she clicked, trying to moisten her dry mouth. Then, she arched her back, the cracks in her spine echoing in her ears.

She got to her feet and looked around to get her bearings. A squirrel barked its annoyance from above, then darted from branch to branch into its nest as a twig snapped from the approaching dragon, which had a bundle of something in its mouth.

"Where have you been? Catching hares for breakfast, no doubt."

"Not quite my girl, not quite," it said, laying the pile of what appeared to be laundry at her feet.

With a look of confusion, the shivering girl probed, "What's this?" bending down to investigate. On the ground lay a pile of clothes: a jumper and a pair of jeans wrapped up in a scarf and woolly hat. "Where did you get these from?"

The dragon bowed its head, looking a little coy. "Well, when I was jammed in the red box, I heard the old woman say that she thought you lived at number 28 and something about Frank and Janice having a girl. So… I… just thought I would go and have a little look," it said bashfully.

The girl stood holding the pair of jeans up to see if they were her size. "A little big, but they will do, dragon," she said, "so, we went from not breaking into a shop, to stealing clothes.

Great job!"

The dragon interrupted, "Where we're going, you had better put them over your pyjamas, my girl. It is going to get a little colder than this."

"Thank you," she said, quickly pulling them on. "How do I look?' she asked, giving a little pirouette.

The air was broken by the cries of birds taking flight and the frantic scurry of a hare bolting for cover. She looked over to see what had startled them.

She froze, then quickly ducked for cover.

"Dragon! Look!" she croaked, pointing.

Police officers and several people, most carrying hiking poles, spread out across the field. Some, with dogs, were on the verge of entering the forest. When folks in the surrounding area had heard that the girl had been sighted in the village, they came out in force.

The dragon swiftly looked left and right for an exit. "Quickly, get on," it demanded, crouching low on its stomach. The girl, staying as low as she could, crawled on its back. The dragon then skirted for cover and crawled behind the fallen log and under the curtain of ivy just in time. Scanning the forest, it spotted a stream that ran through the dense undergrowth. Quickly, the dragon snaked its way to the bank and slid into the water, lifting the girl high to keep her dry. Then it followed the gully upstream away from the search party.

"AEONA!" With dogs running here and there underfoot, the searchers shouted, "AEONA!"

The dragon ran along the side of the stream, making light work of the brambles and nettles that tried to hinder its way. Although the girl was now wearing pyjamas and jeans, her slippers didn't provide much protection from the stings and tearing thorns of the bushes.

The dragon continued to push through, and every now and then, they came to a clearing, dashing ten or twenty metres before being stopped by another tangle of brambles or a fallen tree.

"HERE, HERE, WE FOUND SOMETHING!" several people called. "A biscuit wrapper, looks new! OFFICER… OFFICER… OVER HERE!" One of the men from the village beckoned.

The police officer made his way to where the items had been found, reached to his chest radio and pulled it towards his chin. "Officer Collins to station, Officer Collins to station. Come in."

A second of silence went by before the speaker responded, "Officer Collins, go ahead."

"We've found the biscuit and chocolate wrappers the girl bought from Mr. Butler's shop last night."

"Good work, Collins. I'll notify HQ straight away," a woman responded, "Bristow has dispatched a Search and Rescue helicopter from Kirkbride; it'll arrive shortly."

The AW189 aircraft, with its distinct HM Coastguard red and white banding, had taken off a little over thirty minutes ago to complete the one hundred-nautical-mile flight to the search site. The call sign, SAR-912, was painted under the cockpit windows on either side in bold capitals, which contrasted with the red of the fuselage. Captain Thomson, seated on the right, piloted the craft, while Winchman Hackley occupied the left seat. Their bright orange flight suits and yellow helmets were visible through the cockpit windows as they headed towards the Lake District at speed. For over ten years, working side by side on countless missions, and this call was no different from the others, they knew minutes mattered.

Just outside the forest, Constable Williams arrived from the village to join in the search and parked along the dirt track. He had lived in the area for as long as he could remember and knew the ground like the back of his hand. He always had his Wellington boots in the back of the police car. Getting out, he popped open the boot, slipped off his shoes and sat on the boot sill to pull them on, tucking his trousers into the tops. "Right, let's see what Collins is doing." He stamped his feet to settle them in place. Williams had heard most of what was happening through the car radio but missed the conversation about the helicopter heading their way.

Williams ambled over to where the officer was standing near a few fallen logs at the edge of the forest. "Good morning, Collins. Found anything else other than the wrappers? Any tracks?"

Officer Collins was on the radio with HQ to respond. "Will do, sir!" he answered. Then, turning back: "Good morning, Constable. Glad you could join us." He then turned to the group of people standing around. "Well done, everyone. Hopefully we'll find her soon, and that she is all right. Keep searching, maybe she isn't far."

The radio call gave the dragon and the girl a head start, letting them slip farther from the searchers. They quietly reached the clearing of the forest to the north. "That was close," the relieved girl said. "Earlier, you said you needed my help. What exactly did you mean?"

"We're not clear yet," replied the dragon.

"Please tell me that was not supposed to be a joke. Do not, just do not," whispered the girl. "You said we're going somewhere colder. Is that why you got the clothes for me? That means you have a plan, does it not?" She paused and waited for the dragon to respond, but an answer didn't come.

"Wait, my girl, do you hear that?"

Aeona sat silently, cocked her head from side to side and looked around, but she couldn't hear anything except the pounding in her chest. The people had stopped calling, and the dogs were quiet.

The dragon froze on the spot. 'Not good, my girl! Not good at all!" The girl continued to listen, but still, there was just the sound of the occasional bird and the trickling stream behind them. Something troubling disturbed the creature. It must be something the dragon sensed, the girl thought. "We'd better get out of here!" it warned.

Then, a faint hum caught the girl's ear far in the distance. "I hear something, dragon, but I think it is from the cars over there."

At first, she couldn't place what it was, but as it got closer, the distinct …tocca-tocca-tocca, tocca-tocca-tocca… as the blades slapped the air. It dawned on her why the dragon was concerned.

"We'd better get out of here!" she shouted, her worry too great to keep her voice low.

The helicopter's rotor blades beat the air in heavy rhythm, its turboshaft engines roaring above the trees. Potta-potta, potta-potta, potta-potta, potta-potta. It circled the area once, then steadied itself, hovering directly above the police.

"Go! Go! Go!" Aeona pleaded.

Almost on cue, the helicopter swept outwards in a wide circle around the forest's edge, hovering motionless at intervals as it searched.

"SAR-912 above, please identify your party's position so we can eliminate your signal from our instruments," the pilot requested over the radio to Officer Collins below.

"Officer Collins-356, we're all on the west side of the forest and in the adjoining field."

"Got it, thanks, coming around." Captain Thomson flew over to where they were and gently swung inward toward the forest's centre, sweeping left and right.

The dragon ran further north for a group of trees as fast as it could.

"Not good, not good, not good," it muttered, then came to another halt.

The helicopter came around again with its thermal camera on. Each time the pilot released the microphone, the radio gave a double beep.

"I'm not picking up anything at the moment. Take it right," Winchman Hackley requested.

"Nothing for it, my girl. We've got to go up!" it panted. "You'd better hold on tight." The dragon waited until the helicopter's tail rotor pointed towards them, and then it launched itself into the air. It spotted a small cluster of stratus clouds, featureless grey and white, not far above them. The cloud offered some protection, but it would fail them if the wind shifted or rain began to fall. "Okay, that was easier than I thought," it shuddered, trying to hover in the thin vapour clinging in the drizzle, beating its wings carefully to avoid scattering the cloud. The dragon made its way gently to the outer edge, doing its best to remain within the cloud's cover.

In the field, a couple of teenagers from the search party took more of an interest in the police helicopter than in helping to look for the missing person. As a matter of consistency, Stephen, from number 28, the one the dragon had stolen clothes from, noticed it first. "Hey, do you see that?" he motioned to his friend, pointing towards the helicopter.

"You mean the helicopter?" she asked. "Awesome. I'd love to be a helicopter pilot."

The boy pointed, shaking his hand vigorously from side to side. "No… I mean behind the helicopter," the boy pressed. "Look past it, at the cloud, just to the left. Is it a plane or something?"

The girl squinted and put her right hand above her eyes to protect them from the distorting light. "Oh yeah, I see what you're looking at," she said, joining him in pointing. Interest spread through the crowd, and soon others were peering into the sky. The dragon was getting ready for another jump to the next cloud, unbeknown that the crowd below was taking an interest in them.

"Three, two, one!" it counted, then with a sharp beat of its wings, it tore through the air, once more to be hidden again in a veil of grey, or so they thought.

Stephen jumped with excitement, next to the girl. "Did you see that? Did you see it?" he cried. "It jumped to the other cloud!"

Everyone stared and pointed into the sky. Officer Collins, busy searching for tracks, emerged from the forest to find everyone peering into the sky. "What are you all looking at?

We've got a job to do; we're not birdwatching!" he complained, turning to see what the distraction was. The teenagers had now changed the focus from the ground to the air.

"Collins-356 to SAR-912 come in."

"SAR-912 to 356, found anything?" crackled the pilot, circling above.

"Not really, but everyone down here is taking an interest in something in the clouds to your right? You see anything?"

With a gentle touch to the cyclic stick and a press of the left pedal, it swung around in the direction the people below were now pointing. At first, the pilot didn't notice anything untoward. Then he noticed a small black object appear. "A few birds maybe, not enough for a murmuration," he muttered to himself, staring.

Looking down at the crowd and back again, the pilot crackled over the radio, "It is probably a few large birds, but I can't be sure from here," he reported, "Let us get back to looking for t…" He stopped abruptly as the solid object lurched out of the cloud and burst into another, some distance ahead. "What the…" he cut himself short, "SAR to Collins. Di… di… did you see that?" Without waiting for confirmation, the pilot pitched the rotor blades forward, and the helicopter increased its attack angle. "I'm going to check it out," called the pilot.

The dragon slowed its wings in another attempt at keeping the stratus together and edged forward to get a better look at their next move, but the noise of the helicopter was gradually getting louder. "We've got to move," Aeona pleaded, almost to tears, "now dragon, we're running out of cloud. Go!"

"No, wait, I've got something."

"We've not got time, we've got to move NOW!" she pleaded.

"Quickly, lie down on my back and face forward." The dragon ordered.

"WHAT! Are you serious?"

"Do it... hurry!" it begged. "Quick!" The urgency in its voice deepened her dread of what was about to happen. She twisted precariously, throwing her legs backward over the dragon, scrabbling to clutch at anything. "I've got nothing to hold on to!" she squealed. Though the thousand-foot drop lay hidden by the cloud, she knew it was there. Her chest tightened as panic surged, breaths coming in sharp, ragged bursts. No matter how she tried, it was impossible not to imagine the emptiness below, an unforgiving plunge into certain death. "What should I do now?"

she cried, her voice trembling.

The dragon's response came swiftly. At once, its spines shifted, rippling in a wave along its back. They curled around her body, down her legs, and finally clasped her ankles, holding her firm. She was locked tight against its back, unable to move.

"Is this to help you fly faster?"

"No," it snapped, "dragons are myth and legend, but who said anything about a flying girl?"

"How on earth are you going to pull this off?" she asked. "After they get over the shock of seeing a dragon, they will see a girl lying on your back, tied up as if you were carrying me off to be eaten. Is that your plan?"

What happened next took her by surprise: a kaleidoscope of colour rippled and then pulsated through the dragon's body. The quiver of light began at its snout and flowed to the tip of its tail. The once-black mass flashed grey at first with a symmetrical pattern that mirrored itself and blended with the cloud. The scales throbbed grey to blue, then back to black and began to intermingle with an effect of the surrounding air, within the wisps of stratus, where they had taken refuge. Then, all of a sudden, the dragon was gone.

"You see?" it whispered.

Terror ripped through the girl as the cloud thinned beneath them, and the dragon vanished. The sight of the ground far below hit her like never before. She could feel the dragon's back under her, but her eyes confused her sense of reality. Her lungs pumped rapidly, chest heaving with ragged gasps, as panic seized her. Triggered by the severe panic attack, she began to hyperventilate. Her panting quickened until dizziness made her head swim, and tingling numbness spread through her hands and feet. The dragon felt the shift as the girl struggled on its back. "Aeona, what's wrong?" it questioned.

It was no good; she was not listening.

It changed its tone as it tried to reassure the worsening girl.

"Girl," it said softly, trying not to panic. "Listen to my voice. Count with me. One… two… deep breaths. Three… four… that's it, breathe." The dragon's back pulsed in rhythm to its counting, one… two… three… wanting the girl to mimic its movements.

It was no good; she was not listening, the pain in her chest was too much. The breathless body of the girl became unconscious, limp and motionless, lying face down on its back.

It was the dragon's turn to panic. Spinning in the air, beating its wings violently, it bellowed, "What do I do? What do I do?" The only thought in its mind was to get down as fast as possible.

The cloud erupted in all directions, scattering into the air. Instantly, the scales pulsated again to mimic the hazy sky around them. Then the dragon plummeted headfirst with the ferocity of a peregrine falcon, wings tucked tight, legs pulled close.

The helicopter, sixty metres away and closing fast, saw it

clearly: a girl tumbling from the cloud, head and arms lolling like a rag doll. Thomson yanked the cyclic, flaring the craft violently in alarm. It took him a moment to stabilize the craft, and then he quickly looked across to his co-pilot. "What the fuck?" he shouted through the mic. "Please tell me that isn't a kid?" There was nothing they could do to prevent the inevitable. In their eyes, the girl was dead for sure. Travelling at over two hundred miles per hour, in free fall, without a parachute, there was nothing on earth that could save her.

"Three-five-six, come in. Collins, do you copy?"

"Collins here."

"Are you seeing this?" the pilot stammered.

"Negative, not from here. What have you got?"

"You'll not believe this, but from what I can make out, it is a kid. I repeat, a falling kid!" he gasped, trying to think whether eyes were playing tricks on him.

"What do you mean a kid?" the police officer scoffed, "Did you say kid?" With this, Collins cupped his hands over his eyes as if to make a pair of makeshift binoculars to block out the surrounding light. "It is just a black dot to me," he muttered to himself, "what does he mean a kid?"

The girl plummeted toward what looked like certain death. Or so they thought.

Almost vertical, the dragon dive-bombed, hurtling toward terminal velocity as fast as it could.

From a thousand metres down to five hundred, it screamed through the air. The unconscious girl's mouth opened, and her tongue whipped helplessly in the wind's force as the dragon sliced through the air.

Down it went… Four hundred… It had raced to save Aeona.

It was at this point, unbeknown to the worried creature, the dive forced blood back into her brain from her extremities. She slowly became aware of the loud, unbearable sound of the tornado around her. She screwed up her eyes tightly and pulled her mouth closed, still disorientated and confused. The sight of the farmer's field hurtling toward her at breakneck speed only worsened her panic. She cried through her gritted teeth, "Wha… is… happenin…?" The articulation broken by the accelerating headwind.

Three-hundred…

"You're awake!" the relieved dragon shouted. Instantly, it arched its back and threw out its wings to pull itself out of the dive, decelerating rapidly. The teardrop shape unfurled as it extended its wings. "Do not worry, my girl, I got you! I got you!" The ground rushed towards them, "Up, up, up," the dragon continued to arch.

Two-hundred…

"We're doin' it, we're doin' it."

The sheer force of the pull-out sent the girl back to unconsciousness as she was pushed against the dragon's back.

One-hundred…

"I may have misjudged this, my girl," it yelled, "all under control. I got this, I got this," it tried to reassure itself.

It had never done anything like this before. Taking off and landing came easy, but it had never had to evade a predator or face an emergency landing until now. "Come on, Come on…" Using all of its strength, it pulled up; its outstretched wings caught the air as its feet skimmed the surface of the water. The shock wave of its low entry carved a sharp, straight wake across the dark water. Thankfully, the dragon misjudged its intended landing spot; if it had not, it would have smashed into the tree canopy of a forest just to the left. "Told you I could do it, my girl." It exhaled, following the shoreline, looking for a secluded stop to land.

"Aeona, you still with me?" the dragon asked, its body still streaking like black lightning.

She never answered.

"Aeona!" it said again, but this time it rocked side to side, trying to rouse her. "Aeona... please, can you hear me?"

It had not realized until now that the girl lay motionless, unconscious on its back. With a violent roll, it swung its tail and darted toward the bank of Malham Tarn. Legs outstretched, it crashed into the water with an enormous splash, rocks and mud exploding in every direction. Unfurling its frills and lowering its hind legs, the girl slipped from its back and dropped beside an exposed tree root. "Aeona, wake up, Aeona." The dragon's voice cracked with panic. "GIRL! What do I do? What do I do?" it repeated in fright, using its snout to nudge her cheek. It checked for breath, then watched her chest rise and fall in gentle rhythm. "Good, so now what?" it said to itself, looking around.

Being a dragon, the only thing it could think to do was roar straight into the girl's face. The blast rippled her cheeks with its rushing breath. The crows cawed harshly in fright and took to the air in all directions; other woodland animals cowered and took cover where they could. At last, a flicker of movement. Aeona rolled weakly onto her side and groaned, screwing up her eyes, "What are you screaming for?" she croaked, "Quiet down... my head hurts."

A flood of emotion ran through the dragon as it danced in a circle. "Sorry, my girl. You had me worried for a minute. Rest now... rest."

CHAPTER TWENTY 'PROTECT'

From the cockpit of the SAR helicopter, Captain Thomson and Hackley watched in disbelief as the girl fell to certain death. Five hundred… four hundred… three hundred… But they knew something unnatural was happening when she flared out of the dive. From two hundred metres, they were able to follow it down, losing sight of it at around forty metres. They guessed its impact trajectory as it disappeared behind a clump of trees on the north-west shore. The pair glanced at each other and back at the water, utterly confused.

In their minds, they argued silently over whether they had seen a girl or something else entirely. No girl could have done what they had just observed, but it was what it was; they couldn't explain it. Either way, they were inbound and needed to investigate or at least recover the body. From the east, they followed the shore and hovered over a jagged outcrop that jutted into the water, with the 18th-century Malham Tarn House to the north and continued slowly west.

Dragon froze when it heard the rotor blades whirring as the chopper approached over the trees, not too far away, scanning the shoreline for any sign of the remains. The creature didn't know whether to run, stay or hide.

It thought about scooping the girl up again and flying, but they would surely be seen. "Damn it, why did I not move sooner?"

it cursed. The noise got louder and louder; it was so close that it was visible through the thin canopy of sparsely covered branches. With no time to spare, the dragon dove into the undergrowth of nettles and wet leaves that littered the forest floor. It held its breath, fearing the helicopter's searchers might hear it, even over the roar of the rotors overhead. Then, the helicopter swung out over the mountain lake looking for the girl.

It was the winchman who spotted the girl first. "There she is," he called, pointing to the tree line. "There Thomson, two o'clock!" Sure enough, the girl lay motionless on her side, one slipper lying a short distance from her limp body beside the fallen tree.

The captain nudged on the stick and pressed the right pedal, rotating the nose in the direction Hackley had gestured to get a better visual. "Looks in one piece, at least." Thomson sounded through the headset, "No point, winching down; let us set it down in that clearing to the left." The captain turned and manoeuvred into place, bringing the bird to the ground. Hackley exited his seat, slid the door open and jumped out.

"I will radio in when I get there," he called back to his partner.

Although it looked close from the air, it took him more than five minutes to reach the woods and another five to locate the girl. Hackley didn't know what to expect; a fall from a thousand or one hundred metres was all the same; it was not going to be a pretty sight. He had responded to many vehicle accidents and mountain falls in his career, but it never got any easier, especially when children were involved. He never had any children of his own, but it always hit harder than if adults were involved. When he could see the girl about ten metres ahead, he paused, took a deep breath, and then made his way towards the body. He knew this was not going to be a case of life and death, but a recovery.

He reflected for a moment on how fragile life was. You were here, and then you were not. It had become meaningful to him in the last few years, not because of the job, but because retirement loomed closer with each passing day. He was six months from hanging up his flight suit, then another year in the control room before full retirement. Shaking the thought out of his mind, he raised his eyes to the heavens, then proceeded forward, following the lapping waves to the girl.

It was standard procedure to make mental notes for his report later on. The child was lying on her right, clothed in a brown jumper and jeans, one foot bare, the other half-slipped into a muddy blue slipper, its pair lying on the pebbles to her left.

Hackley looked around but couldn't see any scuffs on the ground where the girl had bounced or slid upon impact. There were other tracks and imprints on the sodden shore, but these were not related to the girl. The child looked like she was sleeping against the log, fitting for the beautiful scenery. He caught himself thinking, bitterly, that it was a beautiful place to die.

At first, he took his time surveying the area, not wanting to disturb the girl but faced the inevitable and made his way over to the lifeless form. He gently reached down placing a hand on her shoulder, almost afraid to confirm what he already believed.

Aeona groaned at the touch.

"What the hell!" Hackley yelped, stumbling back on the wet ground. Regaining his footing, he gasped, "You are alive... You are alive? How?!" He stood shocked for a second.

Heart pounding, he flipped into response mode. Muscle memory came with the job. He quickly regained his composure, jumped forward and checked the child's vitals. Fingers on carotid... count... one, two, three... "Pulse good: seventy-five. Hands and feet a little cold, but colour okay." He then reached for the girl's face; her cheeks were a little pale. Making sure not to move her, he lifted one of her eyelids... her pupils reacted to the morning light quickly enough.

"There is no way Thomson is going to believe this," he muttered before pressing the button on the radio. "Thomson, come in. Over!"

There was a short delay, then… "Hackley, come in. Did you find the body?"

"Yes, Thomson, I found her, but you are not going to believe this. It's not a body."

"What do you mean, yes, BUT it isn't a body?" quizzed the confused pilot.

"She is alive! I repeat, she is alive!" he said, aghast. "Her breathing and vitals appear to be stable. Come back."

Thomson went quiet, "What… How? Hackley wouldn't joke about anything like this. Sure, he has got a crazy sense of humour, but this…" he said to himself. "No… Would he?" pausing again… "Hackley, repeat… did you say…alive?"

"Yes, alive," he continued, "but unresponsive. We'll have to stretcher her out," he advised further. "The tree cover will make winching her out tricky."

"Understood, Hackley. I will get things ready. I will call Bristow and update them. They will advise and contact the nearest hospital."

He sat, turning it over in his mind. "What if he is just bullshitting? I'm going to be Bristow's laughingstock. No… I'm going to wait before I call this in."

Hackley touched the child's forehead. "You hang in there, little lass. We'll have you out of here." Hackley was unaware of what was watching him a little distance away in the rough.

Motionless, lips curled back to bare blade-like canines in a silent snarl, the dragon waited. Every time the man reached out to touch his girl, the dragon's hind legs quivered, its tail twitched, and its pupils narrowed on its prey.

Now, the fear of losing the girl was real. The helicopter hovered, searching. Hunting was one thing, but this had intensified the creature's darkness. It fixated on its prey, poised for the kill.

"It is alright, lass; help is on its way."

The dragon couldn't control its emotions any longer; a low guttural growl, loud enough for the man to hear, rose from deep within its chest. Hackley glanced over his shoulder but shrugged it off as a creak from a nearby tree or lapping wave on the shore. But as he turned back, the monster erupted from its hiding place with such ferocity it hurled the winchman through the air. He landed a few metres away with an ear-splitting thud, cracking his head on the gravel, splattering the gravel with blood. His helmet skittered across the ground and bounced into the water. His vision blurred, the world a spinning haze of blood and water. A scream ripped from Hackley's throat, high and raw, before breaking into a choking gasp as the weight crushed his chest. His face soaked with the dripping saliva of the beast standing above him. He gagged on the stench of its hot breath, the heat rolling over him in suffocating waves. Arms flailed, legs kicked, but the weight pressing him down crushed every effort before it could begin. The claws drove deeper, punching into muscle and bone. His orange jumpsuit turned dark red as the blood spread in jagged patterns across the fabric. The dragon reared back, its mouth opening wide for the killing blow, when Aeona groaned.

The sound cut through its frenzy like a blade, ripping it out of its bloodlust. For a heartbeat it lingered there, caught between instinct to kill and instinct to protect, before its eyes snapped back to Hackley writhing beneath its claws. It blew out hard through its nostrils in disgust and growled once more before slowly withdrawing its talons. The sound of tearing cloth echoed in the man's ears. "Come on, my girl, I've got to get you out of here before the other human comes," whispered the dragon. "You've got to help." Lowering its head, it pushed its snout under the girl's left leg and up under her arm. Then wrapped its frills around the child's left thigh and around her body, holding her like a blanket. "Here we go," it muttered, trying to keep its voice as quiet as possible.

Hackley's loud moaning drowned out the creature's low whisperings of "One… two… three," before it rolled to its left, lifting the girl onto its back. As soon as it rose, it secured her other side with the rest of its crest and then skulked into the forest.

"Where are you taking me?" Aeona mumbled, oblivious to what had just happened.

"To somewhere safe, Aeo … somewhere safe!"

At the edge of the trees, Thomson struggled towards Hackley, carrying the SAR kit he had slung across his back. The pack felt heavier than usual, not because of its weight, but because of the urgency pressing down on him with every step. After covering some distance, he reached an opening where the ground sloped gently towards the tarn. "Wow!" he exclaimed. Like Hackley before him, the beauty of the spot stole his breath away. It was different from the view in the air, where everything seemed flat and two-dimensional except for the mountain ridges and high hilltops. The cool breeze drifting over the rippling water refreshed him as he paused for a moment. "Well, enough of that," he sighed. "Better get a move on." Rocks crunched underfoot as he followed Hackley's prints along the eastern shore. In the distance, he spotted a slash of orange standing out against the surrounding foliage. At first, he mistook it for an abandoned buoy adrift from its anchor, but as he drew closer his heart stopped. "Hackley!" he called, dropping his helmet as he sprinted to his partner.

He fell to his knees, ripping the pack from his back. "What the hell happened to you?" he asked, staring at the gaping hole in his partner's suit. He glanced around, half-expecting whatever had inflicted the wound to still be lurking nearby. He had completely forgotten about the girl who had fallen from the sky. His main priority was to care for his partner. The captain swung the bag from his shoulder and yanked at the med-pack, noticing the fan of blood around Hackley's head on the stones. With a swift tug on the zip, half its contents spilled onto the ground. Assessing Hackley faster than he would have done for anyone in the field, he propped him against a boulder and checked where the blood was coming from. "Shit, that's a nasty head injury you have, mate. I will have to bandage that up," he said, trying to pull some of the hair out of the way. It was difficult to see which to treat first, the head wound or the blood streaming from his chest.

"Fuck!" winced Hackley as he felt Thomson prodding, trying to stop the bleeding in the deep gash at the back of his head. "It all… happened so fast, Thomson… I didn't even have a chance to see what… it was," he groaned.

"Hold still, mate. We'll cross that bridge once I've patched you up. Lie still!"

The pilot worked fast, trying to wrap the bandage around the poor man's skull. "Right… that will hold for now!" But looking down at his chest was a different story altogether.

He pulled open the torn front of Hackley's suit and saw five large puncture wounds, pulsing as the ripples of life flowed from his chest. Now, it was Thomson's turn to swear. "What the hell…. and you didn't manage to get a look at this thing?"

He tried to produce a positive tone but had never seen anything like this before. Sure, car accidents and falls had specific injuries that went with them, but this was an apparent animal attack, not the usual Search and Rescue scenario. Claw marks and deep lacerations could prove fatal. "We've got to get you to a hospital ASAP, but first I need to bandage you up," he said, placing a thick wad of cotton over the wounds.

A little to the north, the dragon carrying the girl came to a narrow track that cut through the trees. The birds sang in the air, and everything seemed to settle now that they had put some distance between themselves and the helicopter. It paused, listening for any sign of people, before crossing the track and moving on. The trees stopped abruptly. "Left, or right?" it thought, choosing right to follow the tree line for as long as possible. Then, it reached a stone wall, blocking their way. It thought it best not to take flight at the moment. It would wait until it reached the summit of the hill, where it could glide unseen over the far side.

Following the wall seemed its best hope of evading the hunters behind. At least it provided some cover for now. It skirted a hundred metres along the wall to a corner, crouched low, crept ninety degrees left for twenty metres, crouched again, then ninety degrees right to a clump of trees, before the ground opened ahead.

"Alright, my girl, we're nearly home free."

"Thanks, dragon," she whispered to its surprise.

"No thanks needed, my girl; I'm just glad you're back with me," it said softly, unfurling its wings. "I'm going to take it low and slow and head for that wall on the horizon." The dragon did as it said and fly-hopped across the field. It flew ten metres, then ran five, repeating the pattern. It made it to the wall in no time. A small section of the old drywall had fallen, weathered beyond repair. On a barren, wind-swept hill, no one cared for the wall or the land anymore, leaving it to the elements and the hardy Swaledale sheep to roam. Climbing through, the dragon sat down, allowing the girl to dismount on her own this time. She was shaky on her feet, but able.

"I'm sorry, my girl," it said apologetically. "I should've warned you. Please forgive me."

"It's okay, dragon. I shouldn't have panicked like that."

They both fell silent for a moment.

It was the dragon who broke the silence. "I've to go and get something," it said. "I'll be quick. There is something I need to fetch."

"No," pleaded the girl. "Why?"

"It's important. I'll not let anyone see me."

"Please don't leave me here, I need you," she begged again.

"I'm not going to leave you again; I promise." It said solemnly.

Aeona gently reached up and stroked its snout. "I believe you, I do; please hurry back. I'm tired. I'm just going to curl up here for a bit... I think what happened must've drained me."

The dragon bowed its head in silent apology, then leapt through the gap in the wall and vanished from sight.

Thomson knelt by the backpack and retrieved the sat-phone from a side pouch. When the red light indicated it was on, he got up and made his way to the shore, away from the trees. The handset quickly locked onto a signal, and with a firm press of his index finger, he held down number one. With a beep, it registered the programmed number of the Aeronautical Rescue Coordination Centre in Fareham, about ten miles from Southampton. He waited for the call to connect.

A voice crackled through the line. "This is ARCC Fareham, come in. Over."

"SAR-nine-one-two, Captain S. Thomson reporting. We're currently at Malham Moor, coordinates fifty-four point one-zero-zero-four-seven-five degrees north, two-point one-seven-zero, five-seven-two degrees west. Requesting immediate support. Winchman casualty. Over."

"SAR-nine-one-two, this is ARCC Fareham. Copy location and status. Emergency support requested Bristow Cumbria." There was a short pause, and then the voice continued, "SAR AW-one-eight-nine en-route. ETA 24 minutes. Over."

"ARCC-Fareham, the casualty has been attacked by a large animal of some sort. Requesting ground support. Over," explained Thomson.

"SAR-nine-one-two, requesting response from local police."

"ARCC, copy that, awaiting SAR AW support. Out!"

Putting the phone on the boulder, he knelt beside his injured partner. 'Okay, Hack, we've got a bird inbound in twenty… how's that bandage holding?" he said, reaching forward. When he pulled the torn jumpsuit aside, he was met with a blood-soaked bandage. "Better get that IV on you. Hang in there, buddy. We've got this."

It didn't take long for him to set up the whole thing and prepare for the hard part. Giving a needle is one thing, but ever since he was a child, Hackley never liked being on the receiving end. "Hold still, you big baby. You know the size of this thing!" he scolded with a grin as the needle slid home in his vein. "Sorry mate… all done… Let's get this little beauty in you and do something for the pain."

"Cheers, Cap!" he said, forcing a smile. "Have you seen what happened to the girl?"

"Shit… I was too busy patching you up to even think for a second," he quickly turned to his right. "I can't see any sign of her. There's no way she has walked away from that fall!"

"She was there, lying against that tr…," finishing with a wince of pain, the cannula disagreed with being waved around; through gritted teeth, he continued, "…We both saw her! I checked her vitals!"

"I believe you, Hack. I believe you."

He didn't want to say he thought he was pulling his leg earlier, but when he radioed the girl was alive and they both saw her from the chopper window. That much was certain.

"Yes, we both saw her, but…" Thomson trailed off. He stood puzzled, surveying the area. "The girl was lying beside that tree, so what has happened to her?" he asked. "…you don't suppose that thing what attacked you has, you know, dragged her away or something? Like eaten her?"

It was the imprint in the grass that caught his eye. "The grass there is pressed down, you can see the impression, so she was there." He was not really speaking to his partner at this point. He was running through the puzzle in his mind, confused and like a dog with a bone. "Something is off!"

There was evidence that something had pushed through the undergrowth and went north. A few snapped branches indicated that. Then, he noticed the prints, erratically scattered around where he stood. They didn't form a uniform pattern; it looked as though whatever made them had been pacing left and right in front of where the girl lay.

"Hey Hack, you would expect this thing to have paws like, Milly, my cat, wouldn't you? But these are strange, man… really strange."

He was referring to his tabby, which he had owned for about two years. It always ran into the garden whenever his partner visited. Then, trying to get her to return in the evening was a real pain. Thomson would have to spend an hour or so doing the usual: "Puss-puss, puss-puss…puss. Come on, Milly, where are you?" to get it back in. Eventually, she would come padding through the flowerbed and edge her way into the house, only to the disgust of his wife, Adlin, who would pick it up and wipe its paws with a wet cloth, before it jumped onto the couch.

"I'm no expert Hack, but looking at those prints, that's no

cat!"

Thomson stood on a boulder to better view the surrounding area. He was able to pinpoint ten to fifteen noticeable tracks scattered from the water's edge to the tree line. The discernible scrapes in the mud showed two different sizes of footprints that zig-zagged the area. The larger ones lay farther back, nearly twice the size of the others, shaped more like four-fingered handprints; the animal had small elongated fingers with sharp, deeper intrusions in the ground. Long lines at the front of each digit, pushed forward slightly splayed like sharp talons, as it walked. Thomson saw that they were more like a bird's than a cat's retractable claws. "Where the mud was clear of stones, perfect prints revealed finer details: delicate, intricate ridges of scale running in symmetrical patterns along each appendage."

Like a human, the back feet were more profound than the front, with perfectly rounded heels. Another distinct feature that stood out on the shore was a deep, continuous line, perhaps a tail, snaking between the feet. Every piece of evidence littered around contrasted with that of a cat or dog, whatever it was. The spacing between the toes, a half-moon curve between each, like the webbing of a duck.

Scratching his head, he turned to his partner, "Whatever attacked you, Hack, was big. Damn big!"

After leaving the girl in safety, the dragon retraced the same route. However, when it reached the wall, instead of continuing south, it diverged into the trees to the left, making sure to stay out of view.

Skirting from tree to tree, it kept the road to its right, just in case anyone was walking. It was wary of heading back to where it had attacked the man. It felt it had gone a little too far, but the animal within couldn't be subdued and reared its ugly head to protect the girl. Especially since Aeona was unconscious, it felt helpless in getting her out of there.

After a hundred metres or so, it came to a couple of outbuildings, possibly an old stable or something similar, with deep red shutters that blocked the windows. A large gate to the left barred any entry. A close inspection of the loose panels revealed nothing of any interest inside. The smaller building to the left was also fruitless. It quickly scurried into the shade on the right of a parked hatchback; its windows would be no match for its claws if needed, but only a spare wheel looked back at it from the boot.

"Nothing here!" it exclaimed, then moved on, edging its way to the next corner, with a house on its left.

It then crouched to crawl under two large windows and paused at the corner. A small plaque indicating the 'Pennine Way' two miles down the lane meant nothing to the dragon without Aeona's help.

Suddenly, an old man dressed in a dirty green boiler suit came across the grass, pushing a lawnmower. He sat on a broken bench and removed his Wellington boots. Luckily, the dragon had frozen just in time. The mottled wall and large bush hid it to some degree. That, along with the old man's poor eyesight, kept it from being detected.

"Better head the other way around," it whispered, slowly stepping backwards. Passing the outbuildings again, it came to the other side of the house. "This looks more promising," it said, raising its head a little too high for a creature trying to stay hidden. Several cars, of different sizes and colours, makes and models were irrelevant to its search. It could neither tell the difference nor care. It was only after one thing: food.

Something. Anything. For the girl.

When it was run-hopping across the field taking Aeona to safety, it saw several sheep, and its stomach started rumbling. It realised it had not eaten anything since the hare it had caught. It seemed so long ago, and with this realisation came the guilt that the girl had not eaten anything other than the chocolate and the biscuits in the forest the night before. It needed to find something fast. It didn't want to enter the house, but if need be, it would have to.

Jumping from one car to the next, it peeked through the windows, searching for anything useful. "Nope... Next... Nope... Next... Nope..." Five cars down and still nothing.

It glanced at the window of the house; a group of people gathered around a table, holding what appeared to be plates of food. "Damn. Too many in there to make a snatch and grab. Carry on..."

The next car was a large seven-seater, with a brown jacket loosely thrown over a blue and white striped hold-all. "Jackpot!" it shouted with joy.

The dragon had seen people open doors before, so using one of its claws, it tried to lift the handle of the driver's door. It was met with the obvious: locked. The same with the other doors.

The concept of locking all doors with a push of a button cost it a minute in reaching its goal. It wondered how much force it would take to break a window without making any noise. It lowered itself as best it could, its massive body contorting to fit into the small space. It reached up a claw, and with careful precision, it pressed at the corner of the back window. The dragon's muscles tensed as it applied more and more pressure until suddenly, the tempered glass shattered inside the vehicle. The sound, from the dragon's perspective, was like the explosion of a bomb, instantly followed by the blaring of the horn: beep... beep... beep... beep... beep... beep...

In fright, it dove through the window to snatch the things, expecting the people to come running out, but none did. They were wrapped up in conversation, distracted by the little ones making a mess in their high chairs.

Taking the jacket in its right claw, it yanked at the hold-all with its teeth and pulled itself out of the window. A pair of walking boots fell from under the bag onto the floor as it did.

"Good, good, good," it repeated, throwing the jacket and bag to the ground before diving back in to get the boots.

It fled over a wall and into the forest, not stopping until it was clear and near the wall again, at the northern end.

There, it stopped to inspect its haul. "Jacket, boots... bonus!" it smiled. "Please tell me there is some food!" The zip strained to hold the contents. Trying to grab the slider was tricky, with its large claws, but it managed to open it bit by bit. When the bag was half open, the dragon grinned again.

"Well, that went better than expected," it said, smiling with delight. "My girl is going to love this!"

Off it bounded, with a spring in its step.

***

Just outside Malham, Constable Williams and Officer Collins

had gathered the volunteers, thanked them and announced that the girl had been found, so they were calling off the search.

"Great job! Thank you so much." Williams called out. "Now, you all deserve a hot drink; let us go home." This was met with claps and cheers from everyone.

However, Williams and Collins stood there, confused. The helicopter crew had said they had the girl, but it was unclear what they meant by 'in the clouds.'

It took about twenty minutes to drive to the Malham Tarn estate. Along the way, they discussed how they were going to write their report and how strange life was. One moment all was quiet in the Yorkshire Dales, and the next... whoosh, they were in the thick of the strange mystery of a missing child. They drove up the Pennine Way, the glacial lake stretching out to their left. It was always a beautiful drive for Williams. Unlike Collins, he knew the area like the back of his hand. He was a wealth of information, an oracle of knowledge, and Collins was about to be on the receiving end.

"Do you know, Collins, the Tarn is one of the highest glacial lakes in England, formed in the last Ice Age," he said with a smile.

"I didn't know that, Will... that's an interesting fact," Collins responded, gritting his teeth every time Williams tried to navigate through the minefield of water-filled potholes that littered the single-lane dirt track.

Williams didn't need an excuse, but Collins noted that 'interesting facts' were all he ever needed.

"And did you know... another surprising feature is that it is only four metres deep? You wouldn't believe it just by looking at it!"

He hoped to distract the constable enough to stop him spouting useless information. "What's the background on this girl, anyway, Will?" He was not a country person; it was a little too quiet for his liking.

Twenty minutes of the Tarn, the trees, and "oh, look… do you see that sheep?" was, in his mind, a curse rather than a blessing.

It didn't take long for the joyous creature to arrive back at the girl, who was curled up in a ball, right where it had left her. Her arms wrapped around her bent legs, shielding herself from the brisk wind that blew over the Yorkshire Dales.

Sensing the movement, she lifted her buried head out from her folded arms, shivering. "What took you so long?" she asked. Then she saw the bundle of things it had.

"Surprise!" her friend said. "Look what I've got."

With a little shiver, Aeona got to her knees and lifted the enormous golden-bronze coat the dragon gave her.

"Do not just look at it!" the dragon coaxed impatiently. "Put it on."

The girl brought it around her shoulders and slid one arm in, then the other. The sleeves dangled on the ground, her arms lost inside the fabric. She wormed her hands out and fumbled to reach the zip. It took a while to put the two ends together, and then, reaching home, she pulled it up to her chin. "How does it look?" she joked, lifting her arms. The dragon couldn't see where the voice came from, as the hood completely buried her little friend within.

It laughed. "It looks warm! Look, I also got you these," it said, pushing the boots towards the girl.

She threw her head back, her eyes popping wide in surprise. "Seriously?"

A second went by, and then, they both fell to the ground, rolling around with laughter. "There wasn't a choice," the girl laughed, almost screaming. It had been so long since she had

had anything to laugh about, and this was what she needed.

Pulling herself together, she rolled up the jacket's sleeves so she could use her hands. She then picked up the boots and placed them sole to sole with her slippers for comparison. To her delight, there was not much difference in size, "These should fit nicely, dragon." The colour matched the jacket, a gold-bronze pair, well-worn, with dried mud caked into the tread. Not the best thing wearing boots without socks, but definitely better than slippers," she said with a smile. "Thanks, dragon, what's in the bag?"

"That's the best part.... open it."

Aeona reached over, pulled it closer, and yanked at the zip. "You hit the jackpot here, dragon!" Her mouth watered at the sight: sandwiches, an orange, a couple of apples, some fitness bars, and a few juice cartons. Jumping up, she threw her arms around the dragon's neck, "This is great! Thank you so much!" She first picked up one of the sandwiches, Egg mayonnaise, according to the label. She was not a fan of eggs, but beggars can't be choosers. She peeled back the label and passed half to her friend. It sniffed it curiously, snorted and shook its head, "What on earth's that white thing?"

"Egg!" responded the girl.

"Egg, that isn't an egg. Eggs are like water and runny!"

"Not when you cook them, they don't," smiled the girl, taking a bite.

"I'm hungry, but not that hungry," it scoffed, turning towards the broken wall. "I'll be back in a tick," it said, before darting off again.

The sandwich disappeared quickly, and she crunched her way through an apple. By the time she got a juice carton from the bag, the dragon was back, but this time, it didn't come with a bag but the limp carcass of a sheep. "Sorry, my girl, but it goes with who I'm, not my table manners." It apologised, "I'll take it over here, out of your way."

The sound was enough to put her off, but it was part of being friends with a carnivore. She knew the poor creature had not eaten in a while either. Now that they had both eaten, they rested beside the wall and thought about the day.

"It's going to get dark soon, dragon." The girl sighed. "Any idea where we're going to spend the night?" she said. "It'll get cold, so we need to find some sort of shelter."

"I think I know a good place for you, not far from here,"

it answered, "but we'd better wait until the sun goes down. It'll be easier to fly out of here then."

Aeona gave a nod of agreement, and slipped back behind the wall for shelter from the wind. Even with the gift of the clothes, the cold still bit through to her bones.

***

The police car pulled into Malham Tarn Estate, thankful the tyres had survived the never-ending crunch of gravel and loose stones, which finally ceased as they entered the driveway.

"Do you know, Collins…"

Collins had been listening to Williams talk about the Tarn, Highfolds Scar, Fountains Fell, and Water Sinks for the last twenty minutes, and now, the estate!"

Seeing light at the end of the tunnel, Collins forced a smile. "No, no, of course, go ahead. What about it?"

"I'm glad you asked… well, the building's a three-hundred-and-fifty-year-old hunting lodge. It has had many owners, but now it belongs to the National Trust."

"So, happy you told me, ma… hey what's this then?" Collins was cut short mid-sarcasm by a group of people waving their arms in the air. Williams pulled to a stop, wound down the window and stated the obvious, "Good afternoon, what seems to be the problem?"

They all started speaking at once, "Someone has broken into our car!"

Not waiting for the details, Collins answered from the passenger seat, "Oh dearie me, strange thing to happen in this neck of the woods. Totally unheard of. Sorry to hear it," he said. "But…"

"but… but, what?" asked the woman, "Are you not going to do something about it? After all, you are the police!"

Much to the woman's disgust, Williams said, "Unfortunately, we've got much more pressing matters at the moment, so if you do not mind, please call the local police station or 999. Preferably, the station in Skipton'll send someone out to take a report. Oh, and another thing: sorry, but it closes at five today, so it's better to call tomorrow after nine. Sorry, but we've got to go." Williams closed the window and accelerated away without giving the woman time to respond. "Do you think I was a bit harsh?" asked Collins.

"There's only so much we can do," Williams said with a smile as the car slipped beneath a canopy of trees. "It was probably a fox or something. Anyway, you are not wrong. We've got more pressing matters, and we can't be too far from the helicopter now." The branches above arched into a living tunnel before giving way to the sheer stone walls of a canyon. Once through the canyon, the expanse of the Tarn appeared on the left, beautiful even with the clouds rolling in. The road snaked nearer the water's edge, bordered by a wooden fence that guided ramblers through the trees before stopping just short of the shoreline. "Here we are," Williams announced, pulling into the layby beside the road. Collins got out and looked around, then poked his head back into the car through the open door and asked, "Any idea exactly where they are?"

"He said he was around this location." Williams pressed hard on the horn for a few seconds and listened.

"Hey! Over here!"

"That was easy!" Collins said, trying to understand where the voice came from.

Not too far away, towards the water, Collins spotted the flash of an orange sleeve being waved. "There, spotted him, Williams, just through those trees there!" The constable was already at the car's boot, pulling on his Wellingtons.

"All done, come on, let's go!"

Thomson was standing beside Hackley when the police officers met them. The winchman was still lying on the ground. The captain had firmly wrapped his head in a fresh bandage, and the one on his chest seemed to hold.

"Shit!" Williams grimaced. "What happened?" he asked Thomson.

"It appears to have been an animal attack, judging by the injury to his chest. And look at those prints. Careful not to walk over them, more than I have!"

The three men turned at the same time. Over the far end of the water came the …ToccaToccaTocca… of the rotors. "SAR AW-one-eight-nine inbound, with four crew," came a call. It didn't take long for the captain and co-pilot to spot Thomson's waving arms in his orange jumpsuit. As they got closer, the winchman had already opened the door and was hooking the stretcher into the hoist…. Potta, potta, potta, potta… roared the engines as it hovered above the rescue site. It was kept away from the tree line at the water's edge.

When a few metres from the ground, the chopper glided gently forward until Adams had landed his feet on the shore.

"It's good to see you, Adams. It's been a while," Thomson

said, stretching out a hand.

"You said barbecue, not to come and rescue your ass!" He laughed. "How's Hack holding?"

"Hopefully, he'll be fine once we get him to the hospital."

"I've brought the Street Doc with me," he said, pointing. "He'll soon have him sorted out."

Collins and Williams waved a welcome to Adams and helped carry the stretcher a little closer to the injured man.

"Here we are, Hack. We'll have you out of here! Now, lie back while we lift you up. Are you ready? On three… one… two…up we go!" With a slight grunt of pain, they had him strapped in and, a minute later, securely fastened to the cable.

"Cheers, guys," he said, thanking the policemen. "Thomson, I'll send Rescue-tech down in a tick." With that, he signalled for the crew to hoist them both.

The constable and Collins turned their attention to the animal tracks.

Williams walked over, crouched, and placed his hand next to a clear print. "Umm, I've not seen tracks like these before," he said, bewildered. "I'm wracking my brains, Collins, but these have me stumped. Far too large for anything native to these parts. Claws like a bird. I don't know, an otter?" He laughed at the absurdity of it. "These are a good ten inches from heel to point. I'm totally lost." He stood back up and turned to Collins. "We've got to call in the experts on this, Collins. It's above our heads, I'm afraid."

The captain said, "Whatever that thing is, look at the damage to my partner. That girl's as good as dead. It dragged her off and had her for lunch." He pointed to the tree where the body had been and the disturbed undergrowth. "I'm just saying, you're looking for what's left of her, not a missing-person."

"When it rains, it pours," Williams shook his head at Collins. "We need more men. If that thing has eaten the girl, we must catch it fast before it takes anyone else."

"It just does not make sense, non-of it," Collins told the constable. "How did the girl get from Winwick to here?" he said, answering himself before Williams could interrupt, "That's nearly sixty miles! Only to be dragged off by a wild animal. What's it with this girl? Let's get back to the car and radio it in. It is getting dark. It is going to be a long, long night, Williams."

They both walked back in silence, the thought of the beast and the girl running around their heads with many scenarios. The last sighting was a few years back in 2022; nothing had happened since then, so where had the animal been hiding? The poor kid… eaten. What exactly would they be searching for? Would they change the focus to the animal or the missing child?

Both men got into the patrol car, Williams, in the driver's seat, let out a short sigh, reached forward, and picked up the handset. "Williams-2268 to Control, come in. Over."

There was a pause, then: "Control here, come in 2268."

"Williams-2268 and Collins-356 reporting on the missing girl from just north of Malham Tarn. There was a sighting of her from SAR, but suspected large wild animal in the area."

There was a short pause of confusion, then, "So, what are you reporting… Do you have the girl? What's this got to do with a wild animal?"

"Not exactly, Control; a large animal may have taken the girl. The SAR helicopter encountered an animal; it had its claws tore into one of the crew's chest, nearly ripping it open. He has been airlifted to hospital. Requesting immediate emergency services and requesting wild animal experts as well as trackers, over," he reported. This was the hardest thing that Williams had ever had to say over the radio. Sure, he had had a few car accidents and petty crime, but adding a missing child, a mauling, and a girl feared eaten… this was the kind of nightmare he never wanted to end his career with.

"Control to Williams-2268, we've alerted Mountain Rescue (MRT) and NPAS Carr Gate. Will report back shortly with Police helicopter ETA from Wakefield. Over."

"Thanks Control, awaiting orders, Williams, out."

Collins waited until the constable had finished before jumping in, "I do not suppose you…"

But Williams stopped him before he could finish, "Yes, glove box. Help yourself and pass me one."

Collins moved his knees aside and popped the button. "Star man. Knew you would." He said retrieving Williams's hidden supply of chocolate from the glove box and putting them on the dashboard. "This will keep us going until everyone arrives."

"Control, to Williams-2268. Over."

"Williams-2268."

"MRT first responders, UWFRA and CRO en route, ETA fifty minutes."

Williams looked at Collins and shrugged. "Do not you just love it when they throw acronyms at you?"

"2268 to Control, who are Uniform-Whiskey-Foxtrot-Romeo-Alpha and Charlie-Romeo-Oscar. Over."

"Mountain Rescue from Upper Wharfedale Fell and Cave Rescue."

"Thanks for the clarification." She mumbled with a mouthful of chocolate, then let go of the button and smiled to Collins "If you don't ask, you don't know!"

"Okey-dokey! Nothing to do now but wait, I guess."

Less than ten minutes later, exhaustion overtook them, and the two men were out cold as twilight crept in.

***

Unbeknownst to the girl and the dragon, a massive rescue operation was already underway, and they were now the hunted.

The girl had eaten and drunk enough to last her for the day. Now, snug in her new coat and feet properly covered, she was set for whatever the weather threw at her. She discarded her slippers beside the wall, leaving them behind, and stood to stretch her legs. "Okay, dragon, do you think it is safe enough for us to head out now?" asked the girl.

The dragon looked up towards the horizon and paused for a moment before responding. "A little longer, maybe. A little longer."

Aeona followed its gaze in acceptance and then asked a question that had been on her mind. "You still haven't told me what it is you wanted my help with."

"Sorry, child. I've been meaning to talk to you about this, but with everything that's happened today, there hasn't been time. Let's get you somewhere safe to sleep, and I'll tell you everything, tomorrow."

The sky glowed with a deep purple-blue as the clouds darkened the way ahead. The wind had not let up, and now he was standing, the brunt of it whistled round his ears. "We've got a bit to go before we can rest for the night. We need to put some distance between us and that flying machine." it explained. "You had better get on so we can get moving. It'll be dark soon so that we'll have some good cover."

Aeona inspected what food remained in the bag. There were

still a few sandwiches and cartons of juice, enough to last her a day or so. Pulling the zip closed, she slid the bag onto the dragon's back and climbed on.

"Pull that hood down over your face to stay warm, my girl. Don't worry, I'm holding you tightly. You're not going anywhere." It crouched low, then ran forward until it gained enough speed to tuck in its legs and skim gracefully above the ground. It stayed low enough to follow the troughs and gullies of the land to avoid the attention of any wandering ramblers and so ramblers wouldn't have time to raise their torches and glimpse what it was.

In no time, they had covered the four miles to the top of the high outcrop crowned with a large cairn of limestone. The dragon sat briefly to check on the girl, "We've got to be a little careful around here; lots of caves to watch out for." With a muffled reply from within the coat, it carried on. Like a dark snake, a narrow road wound through the heather and bracken on the windswept hills, but no car headlights or people hindered their progress. When the ground dropped, a thunderous stream emerged, cutting a ravine through the land, sharp as a blade, and every so often, the roar of cascading water rose from below.

A few miles ahead, it diverged east, but the dragon's instincts followed Polaris in the broken sky. The higher it flew, the smoother the going, until its goal appeared below: a mountain bothy, perched high on the summit of the fell. It came to land near a lone tree, surrounded by a rock wall. It sat quietly, listening and watching for any sign of life. Nothing stirred from within, and no light shone through the windows.

"I think it's empty, my girl," it whispered. "Safe for the night." The bothy was in excellent condition for its desolate location, battered by constant Helm wind and rain. With a tired yawn, Aeona slid off the dragon's back and stamped her feet on the cold ground. "Go inside to get out of this wind," the dragon urged.

"Are you not coming?" she asked.

"It's better to check inside first," the dragon told her.

Aeona turned, walked to the door, and pushed at the handle. It was firmly shut. She glanced over her shoulder, silently questioning what to do next, then realising there was a latch just below it. With a press, the door clicked ajar.

It opened into a little mudroom entry with a couple of plastic chairs, and then to the right, another door opened to a large living area. "Quiet, cosy," she said to herself, looking around.

Brown plastic chairs ran along the wall, and to her surprise, an old guitar was propped against the corner. Signs on a notice board on the far wall, with various instructions on the toilet and rubbish. High on the wall was a painting of a smiling man sitting on some rocks with a plaque to its right, which read: "In memory of John Gregory." Aeona opened another door to its right to find a room with a raised sleeping platform and a fire. "This is great. I will have to bring dragon!" she said, turning for the exit. She quickly made for the door, pulled it open and collided with a man at the doorway.

"Whoa, little lass!" said the startled stranger as Aeona bounced off him and landed in a heap. The man moved quickly forward and helped her to her feet. "Sorry… sorry, up you get, up you get!"

The man swung his rucksack off his right shoulder and let it drop to the floor. "Pretty cold out there; looks like the weather is closing in for the night. Good job we landed at Greg's place, eh?"

"Erm… yeah, sure. Good job!"

"What's your name, girl? My name is Danny. You can call me

Dan," he smiled.

She was too busy thinking about the dragon outside, she gave herself a little shake and thought quickly. "Erm… yeah… Hi Dan, my name is Sara. You can… erm… call me Sara, with or without an 'h'… I suppose." She said, trying to stay calm.

The man grabbed hold of the strap of his rucksack and pulled it over to one of the chairs, the door swinging shut behind him. "You all settled for the night, Sara? It was a beautiful day today, but that soon turned, did it not? Well, let us get some food on. I'm pretty starving, are not you?"

He seemed to know where everything was in the hut, quickly jumping from one place to another. Within no time, he had his lantern on, the gas stove burning, and the water slowly coming to the boil.

"I can't seem to see your rucksack, little lass. Do not tell me you came up here without any supplies?" he asked, scanning the room.

"Erm, yeah…" She thought quickly. "Yeah, my dad was supposed to be following up behind, but he must've got delayed or something. He will be coming soon." She hoped the man would buy it.

"No worries. I'm going to put some noodles on. Do you fancy some?"

She couldn't just walk out; the man would report her to the police. It would look too suspicious, so it was best to play along for now. "Sure, that would be great, thanks," she replied and sat down on the chair beside the guitar, knocking it over with a clatter that echoed around in the silence. "Sorry," she said automatically, leaning it back against the wall to the smile of Dan, who was busy stirring the food. The smell made her mouth water; it had been so long since she had smelt or had anything hot to eat.

"Here you go, girl," the man said, handing her a small metal mess tin and a spoon containing the piping noodles. "Watch yourself, they're hot."

She reached over and took it, raising it to her chin to inhale the spicy aroma, which made her eyes water.

"This is so good, thanks."

"Most welcome, little lady. Sorry, I only have a spoon," he apologised.

Aeona blew on the steaming noodles; she loved the warmth of the tin in her hands.

They sat quietly eating, and suddenly, the silence was broken by a sharp bang outside. The girl's heart pounded as she sat bolt upright, nearly dropping the tin off her lap. Looking at the man, she begged under her breath, "Do not come in, do not come in, do not come in."

"Well, good timing, that's probably your dad!" The man smiled.

The look of horror in Aeona's eyes caught the man off guard. "Are you alright?" he questioned.

She was too busy praying to respond, "Please do not come in!"

They both stared at the door for what felt like a lifetime. No one or anything came in. Dan got up and walked across and pushed the door open to the darkness outside. The hinges groaned as the wood swung wide, and a sudden blast of cold, damp air rushed in, tugging at the lantern flame and carrying with it the sour tang of wet earth. He stood for a minute on the threshold, shoulders squared, listening. The fog pressed thickly around the hut, a grey blanket that swallowed even the sound of his own breathing. No torches, no footsteps, nothing but the wind scraping along the stone wall.

"The noise must've been the wind knocking something

over," he said as he sat back in his place again. "I do not think your dad will make it here tonight, not in that fog. Did he have the tent and sleeping bags with him?"

"Erm… yeah, sure did!" replied the girl. "I'm sure he is alright. He has been camping since he was a kid, so he will be fine." She tried to cover as many bases as possible to stop the man from asking too many questions. She broke eye contact and continued with her noodles.

"He must be worried sick, though." Dan's voice softened, but the smile he had worn earlier had slipped away. He tapped the rim of her tin absently, though his eyes lingered on her face, probing for the truth. "Are you sure he knows you made it to this hut?" The question hung heavy in the air, more measured this time, as if he was weighing her every word.

The girl had to end this conversation; it was not going her way. "Do not worry, he isn't going to be concerned at all," She yawned, scrunching up her face. "It has been a long day. I better get to sleep. It is getting late. Got to get up for that sunrise, hey."

"Maybe you are right," he said, bending down to his bag. "Here, Sara. I can't have you just sleeping in your coat. You have to make do with this, for tonight, it's all I've got I'm afraid."

He pulled a small, rolled-up blanket secured with a Velcro strap from his bag and passed it to her. "Take this as well. You can use the jumper as a pillow if you like."

"Alright, Sara, I'm shattered," yawned the man, "See you in the morning, sleep tight." The man made his way to the back room, slid his sleeping pad onto the wooden platform and unfurled his sleeping bag. "Come on let me turn the light off. I've got a long day tomorrow," he called.

"Sure, right behind you," she said, going to the window. She pressed her nose against the cold glass and peered into the darkness. The wind had picked up and whistled around the hut, but there was no sign of the dragon. She couldn't step outside to check, not with the man still awake. To keep her cover, she decided it was best to go inside and lie down. The man was already curled up in his sleeping bag, zipped up to his chin, and didn't turn around when Aeona walked in; he just called, "Are you in for the night?" Not waiting for a response, he paused for a second, then turned the light off. Aeona barely had enough time to throw the blanket on the shelf, slip off her boots, and climb onto the raised platform. She spread half the blanket across the rough wooden boards, turning it into a thin mattress that offered just enough padding to dull the hard surface beneath her. The other half she dragged up over her shoulders and chest. It took her a while to drift off to sleep, thinking about the dragon and the relentless howling of the gale outside.

Just before dawn, the first glimmer of a change in the sky woke the dragon from its slumber. It stood, gave itself a rippling shake from head to tail, and then peered over the wall, listening. It was still dark enough for it to remain hidden. Upon hearing nothing from inside the hut, it climbed over the rocky wall and edged to look inside.

The man sleeping near the small window was covered with condensation, which distorted the view inside. It couldn't tap on the window, certain it would wake the man. "How am I going to wake her?" it thought. The only solution was for it to go into the hut and somehow, wake her. Making its way to the door on the right, it nudged the latch open, then slowly eased the door forward with its snout. Now and again, the door creaked softly, but not enough to draw attention. When the gap was wide enough to allow its bulk to enter, it crept inside. Once in the entryway, it stood listening again, then edged cautiously into the main room. "Easy, dragon. Easy now," it whispered to itself.

The room was empty in the middle, which made navigating easy, but as soon as it placed a clawed hand on the decking floor, the pressure of its weight caused a tiny creak. It froze. It didn't matter what it did, releasing the pressure made it creak, pressing down harder made it creak again. Not daring to move, it looked forward, left, right, and down at its feet, trying to guess where the damn floor wouldn't creak. A small grunt from the room at the far end indicated that someone stirred; whether it was Aeona or the man was difficult to tell. It had to do something quickly, either forward or retreat, but it was unsure which.

The dragon paused for a second and looked at its legs, then went to the window and back to its legs. "It looks doable?" it questioned itself, "it can't be more than a couple of metres. Here goes!" Lowering its hindlegs, it crouched to the floor and extended its clawed toes, but with every little movement came a creak, audible but still too low for a human to hear, supposed the creature. It released a burst of energy and leapt for the windowsill. A loud creak echoed in the room, followed by a thud as the dragon slammed into the window and nearly bounced back off the pane. A second later, a loud snort came from inside, followed by silence.

"This is going better than expected," it praised itself. "Well, that's the floor covered. Now, get that door open. Here goes."

Four plastic chairs, lined against the wall, made an easy bridge to the door without a sound to give it away. Balancing on the last chair, it reached toward the handle, but as it did, the painted man's eyes seemed to glare, daring it to enter. The fright sent the dragon stumbling back onto the chair behind, which crashed into the next, then toppled into another, until silence swallowed the room. "Phew, that was close," the dragon muttered under its breath.

Before the last word had left its mouth, behind it, a scraping sound, like a mouse scratching at the wall. Then, in quick succession, another, then another, until the head of the guitar slid down the wall, resonating its strings as it fell. The loud thud and the ka-plang exploded on the wooden floor, sending shivers through the hut's startled occupants.

"What the hell!" The man and the girl shrieked together, sitting bolt upright, half-asleep and listening. Nothing answered them from the dark. When the guitar cried in annoyance, the dragon skidded across the room, claws raking against the wooden floorboards with a splintering scrape, then barrelled out of the door. A rush of cold air burst in as it bounded over the wall and vanished beneath the tree.

Cocooned in his sleeping bag, the man sat motionless for a minute, unsure if his eyes were even open. The fog of exhaustion pressed heavier than curiosity, and with a weary grunt he dismissed the noise as a trick of his half-dreaming mind. Rolling onto his side, he tugged the bag up over his chin and let sleep swallow him again. Aeona, however, sat, heart pounding in her chest, and listened. She opened and closed her eyes a few times to try and get them to adjust to the darkness.

Outside, the night wind had brushed away the gloom, and the first glow of dawn began to appear. The ink blue-black faded to a subtle hue of deep purple, signalling the day's approach.

The girl quietly slid herself to the edge of the wooden platform, lifting her weight as best she could, using the palms of her hands. She searched for her boots with her sockless toes. When her foot found home, she leaned forward and gingerly picked them up, along with her bag, and held them tightly against her stomach. As if holding her breath made any difference, she traversed the minefield of creaks and slipped stealthily out of the hut. Oblivious to the disturbance, Dan breathed in the peaceful rhythm of sleep, unmoved as dawn crept on.

The girl stood by the door and looked around in the dim light but couldn't see her friend. Too afraid to call out, she crept to the corner of the building and then walked around the back.

"Where are you?" she whispered to herself, her voice swallowed by the mist. The sting of the cold bit into her bare feet, snapping her attention downward. She perched on a rock, the chill seeping through the seat of her jeans, and tugged her boots on before pulling the legs of her trousers tight around her ankles to guard against the biting air.

Restless, she paced a slow circle around the bothy, peering into every corner until she found herself back at the door again. Nowhere for it to hide. Was it still asleep somewhere, or had it gone off to find something? The questions crowded her mind until her gaze lifted and caught on the tree, standing proud at the heart of its stone fortress. The wall in front of the door offered no place for it to hide. She gingerly made her way over to the tree, ensuring not to dislodge any loose chippings or rocks on the way. Placing two hands on the wall, she stood on the tips of her toes and looked into the black hole.

"You are awake," the dragon said, popping its head up.

"Aah!" cried the girl as she toppled backward, landing with a thud on the cold earth.

"I'm here creeping around, and you go and frighten the life out of me!" she hissed in a sharp whisper. "Why did you not just shout Boo or something?"

"Sorry! I thought the man would come running out from the noise of the..."

"That was you? What were you thinking?" she scolded. "Anyway, this has to wait. Let us get out of here before he wakes up. And when we're clear, you ARE going to tell me where we're going, right!"

The dragon nodded its head and climbed over the wall.

"On you get," it urged, lowering itself. "Let us move."

The Upper Wharfedale Fell and Cave Rescue team were the first to arrive at Malham. Within two hours, Malham National Park Visitor Centre had been transformed into the central emergency headquarters, bristling with urgency and command. Radio masts and communication centres were erected, and thirty minutes later, coordinators were briefed and designated teams to search grid by grid. Three teams were dispatched south to scour Janet's Foss, Malham Cove, and Gordale Scar, while others pushed north towards Malham Moor and Darnbrook Cottage. When the media caught wind of the news, reporters both local and national, from the Yorkshire Post, BBC, and Leeds Radio to name but a few, rushed to cover the event. Cameras flashed, microphones were shoved forward, and shouted questions cut through the chill air as live radio reports crackled into the night. Whether they were interested in the missing girl or the animal sighting was anyone's guess. It didn't take them long to sensationalize 'The Beast of Malham,' which spread rapidly across the region in headlines and whispers.

The public also turned out in force, clutching torches and hope, but as the temperature dropped and the light diminished, only the true searchers remained, while the others slipped back to the warmth of their homes and the glow of their televisions.

The police helicopters kept sweeping the moors long into the night. Yet the thermal readings showed nothing but scattered smudges of heat and the wandering silhouettes of ghostlike figures on the ground. Weariness and frustration began to creep through the Command Centre, where every fifteen minutes the officer demanded fresh updates. Coffee cups piled up in corners, and tired faces glowed in the harsh light of the screens.

"HQ to Alpha-Team, come in. Over."

"Alpha to HQ, nothing to report at Janet's Foss. I've got a party at the waterfall and the cave entrance. Awaiting dogs and Cave Team to enter."

"HQ to Alpha, report when done… then continue south, following the Beck, towards Stone and Little."

"HQ to Charlie-Team, come in."

"Bravo to HQ, nothing at Malham Cove. Nothing to report. The party has searched Eastwood, and we're just heading over the beck and sweeping towards Westwood."

"HQ to Charlie-Team, come in. Over"

"Charlie to HQ, nothing at Gordale Scar… Nothing to report. We thought we'd found something, but it turned out to be some discarded litter and an old campfire. An extensive search area is going to take some time. I've got dogs and Cavies checking."

Meanwhile, on the ground near the Tarn, others worked with equal urgency. The RSPCA and North Yorkshire Police Wildlife Crime Officers cordoned off the area and lit the whole of the north-west corner of the Tarn with search and spotlights. Generators broke the usual silence as they were busy taking photographs and carefully preparing casts from the clearest prints. "This is no cat. Look at the way the toes splay, and the gait, see that sideways shift, it is unnatural." One expert said to the other.

More and more people arrived throughout the night from farther afield. Mountain Rescue Teams from Calder Valley and Scarborough & Ryedale MRT moved to cover the north and east. The Department for Environment, Food & Rural Affairs turned its attention to the place where the girl had been. Under the watchful eye of Williams and Collins, the DEFRA team got to work, mixing some yellow powder with liquid into large gardening spray bottles. Curiosity got the better of Collins and he had to ask. "Hey, chief, what's that?"

The Lead gave a smile and answered. "Simple. We spray the area with this, and if there is any blood around, it should light up when we shine this at it," he answered, holding up a strange purple torch.

Collins, in his excitement, had not been involved in anything like this in his years of police work. "Great, I can't wait," he said, momentarily forgetting the weight of being a police officer.

The two men set up several tripods, fixing cameras on top, all aimed at the spot where the SAR crew had been attacked and at the tree stump. Other cameras were positioned to capture the wider area and the tracks in the mud. They began at the fallen tree and walked backward, spraying the liquid in a steady line as they went. When they had finished, they smiled and stood next to Collins.

"Time for the magic, guys. Kill the lights." And with a flick of a switch, the commotion of people stopped as the generators purred into silence. "Here we go, everyone," he said, raising the UV lamp. "Let's see what we've got," he called, pressing the button.

The ground glowed greenish-blue from the winchman to the trunk. Outlines of claws zig-zagged everywhere, the ultraviolet light making it even more terrifying. Sharp and deadly footprints ringed the site, stark as a murder scene. "What… the… fuck!" Collins finally managed, his voice catching in his throat. He stumbled back a step, eyes fixed on the glowing prints clawed into the earth, each mark flaring under the UV light like the scar of some nightmare dragged into the world. "I'm no expert," he muttered, almost to himself, "but I will tell you this much. Whatever left those marks, it sure as hell isn't a cat."

"Everyone, stay put," announced his colleague, holding the UV lamp. "We need to leave the cameras for a minute to capture the evidence."

He had worked in forensics for over ten years, photographing murder scenes, corpses, and routine incidents, but the novelty soon wore off, and the constant exposure to death drained him. For the past year, he had considered a move into the Department for Environment, Food & Rural Affairs: DEFRA, as everyone called it. As the name suggested, it was nothing like his old job. It was calmer, and for the first time in years, he could sleep without nightmares or panic attacks. He had used Luminol many times in his previous job, especially when murder was suspected or when a scene looked suspiciously too clean. This call-out was different. He had never been summoned for an animal attack before, and in his mind, it was the best of both worlds.

"Okay, guys. Flip the lights back on. The cameras are done. I'm sure we've got some good stuff," he called, then turned to Williams. "Have any of the farmers reported any missing sheep or cattle?"

Williams thought for a minute, glancing at Collins for confirmation. "Not that I know of. What about you, Coll?"

"Nope, but I'm sure we're going to get some soon enough."

At Headquarters, coordinators barked updates into radios, but out on the moor, the search dragged on fruitlessly. Nothing fruitful was found other than the animal tracks leading to the north end of the forest, but then nothing.

The temperature dropped through the night, and the winds from the northeast battered the search party fanning out from the Moor towards Darnbrook Cottage. Faces were pinched against the cold, breaths came ragged, but still they pressed on, sticks beating the heather in stubborn rhythm. Twenty volunteers walked along the wall to the left of the bleak road, their chatter and slashing of sticks drowned by the whistling wind. They were trying to flush out the creature and find any remains of the girl, or clothing at least, which would bring some finality to their search in the cold night.

It was not until two o'clock in the dark hours that the Ryedale search team, who were fanned out along the top of the Moor heading east when one of the dogs stopped about twenty metres north of the wall, nose twitching as it caught a scent. It looked around and then circled back to its owner. It let out a confused grunt and snuffled back to the clearing once it picked up the scent again. The man gave a short yank of the lead and coaxed it back to the search, "Come on, Tank, where is it?" he asked his dog.

Tank froze, nostrils flaring, then circled sharply as though chasing something invisible. His whine cut through the wind, confused, almost frustrated, before he dropped his nose to the ground again. "It can't have disappeared into thin air, boy. What is it?" he muttered to his dog.

He turned to his son, who joined him. "It does not make sense; Tank has never lost a scent before, has he?"

"No… it is like the trail just vanished, Dad."

"Joe," the farmer called through the biting wind, "Joe. Tank's lost the scent again; he definitely had it. Better radio it in. Something is fishy here, the scent and those slippers. Aye, something is afoot."

"Nah… he is just muddled with the smell of sheep, lad. Do not go spinning one of your yarns!"

"Just do it, Joe, will you? It is too cold for messing about."

Joe and Tom's banter was legendary around Malham, and no rain, hail, or snow was ever going to stop it. They were used to being out in all types of weather and had lived in the Dales all their lives. For generations, their families had reared sheep and seemed to be able to make ends meet, but they always managed to complain about it. Deep inside, they wouldn't change it for the world.

As the wind picked up, the search party joined the sheep, hugging the walls for protection. The flocks of Swaledales huddled in groups to stay warm from the gusts. Farmers like Joe and Tom usually let them stay out until much later in the season, but the weather looked like it was making a turn for the worse. "Bloody forecasters," thought Joe, looking from under his hood.

"Hey Tom, I think that stupid forecaster got it wrong again. I think we need to get the Swales down from here tomorrow. It looks like winter is on its way in. It does not look good, not good at all."

"You are not wrong. I will let you have this one, Joe. Now, radio Malham and let them know what we've got."

Joe pulled his radio from his breast pocket and pressed the button.

"Ryedale MRT to HQ, come in, over."

"HQ to Ryedale, go ahead, over."

"North-west of Malham Tarn, high on the Moor. One of the dogs picked up a scent but somehow lost it, and we found a pair of red and green slippers over."

"Ryedale, did you say slippers? Over."

"Affirmative, over."

"HQ to Ryedale, confirmed, over." Officer Janna looked over her shoulder and called her supervisor.

"Sir, Ryedale reports they lost the scent and found a pair of slippers. What should I respond?"

"Did you say slippers?"

"Yes, Sir. They said slippers."

"Who would take slippers up on the moor?" He frowned. "ask Ryedale to take some photos and send them in."

At 6:15, Officer Janna radioed for all teams to report in.

The teams searched through the night, and as the first rays of dawn began to appear, all they had was some litter, a cold campfire, and a pair of slippers.

"No one has anything else to report, Sir."

With a heavy sigh, the Incident Commander told her to send a team-wide message for everyone to reconvene at Malham Estate, ending with, "Officer Janna, also update Gold-Command." For the next ten minutes, the radio buzzed with communication between the police-SAR helicopter, Mountain Rescue, and Team leaders as everyone slowly made their way back.

***

Ten miles northeast of Greg's hut, the dragon skimmed over a river and landed beside a large warehouse. The place was still, broken only by the distant drone of a passing car and the muted roar of a waterfall. It looked around for somewhere secluded to rest and give the girl enough time to eat and drink. It made its way along the structure, entered a row of trees, and descended into a grassy outcrop.

The dragon stood beside a wooden bench, listening. The stream flowed gently over the rocks and under a rickety old bridge, just wide enough for one person to cross at a time. "Here is a good place for breakfast, my girl. Come on, tuck in," it said. Then, it walked to the stream and started to drink.

Aeona opened the bag and pulled out a sandwich wrapped in clear plastic, its edges smeared with pale cream. She set the bread aside to see what was inside. "Ugh! Who puts eggs in sandwiches?" she scoffed, holding it at arm's length. "Dragon, do you like eggs?"

"Yes, but not cooked, thank you," it said, curling its lip in disgust.

She pulled out an apple, a packet of crisps, some biscuits, a carton of juice, and at last another sandwich. "Yay! This one does not have egg," she said, stuffing a slice of cheese into her mouth. "This is so good, dragon. You are missing out. Are you sure you do not want any?"

"No, I'm good!"

In front of them, through the trees, the sound of a waterfall echoed up from the ravine where they sat. The peaceful atmosphere and the singing birds relaxed them for the first time since leaving her home, which felt so long ago. Every now and then, a refreshing spray from the crashing water drifted toward them.

Aeona finished her sandwich and closed her eyes for a moment, listening to the sounds around her. "This is so nice, dragon, just to sit here listening to the water and the birds," she sighed.

After a minute, she opened her eyes and looked around for her friend. The dragon was sitting by the water, mimicking her with its eyes still closed, listening just like the girl. "Alright, my friend, now that we've got the place to ourselves, come on, out with it. Where are you taking me?" she asked, placing her palms on the bench and swinging her legs.

It padded over to the girl and sat like an eager puppy.

"Okay... So, while I was away, I was trapped in this strange void. Many things, strange things, weird images, like dreams but not dreams. You know what I mean?" it asked, leaning forward, its eyes bright with anticipation.

The girl paused, considering its words. She felt no need to share what had happened to her while it was gone. Deep down, she wanted to reply, "Yes, actually, I do. Being drugged up does give you weird, dark, strange…" She hesitated, the word 'nightmares' rising to her lips but feeling too small for what she had endured. But she did have some idea of what it was talking about.

"Right, in these dream-like things, I saw dragons, lots of them, like me. Some were dead, some alive, and everywhere skeletons lay scattered on the ground."

The dragon sat up and moved closer as if to whisper a secret.

"Some were… like… asleep… "They were trapped inside dark, swirling bubbles, words drifting like smoke around them. I know those words are important. They must be."

It paused, waiting for Aeona to offer her thoughts, but when none came, it asked directly, "So, can you make any sense of it?"

"Did you say bubble?" the girl asked.

"Yes, dark navy swirling spheres, evil things, that locked the living inside." It explained, "I could see them shouting, screaming, punching at the sides."

Aeona leaned forward, brow furrowed, fingers tightening on the bench as she tried to piece together the dream.

"So, the creatures are trying to get out?" she prompted.

"Yes. And not only creatures. I saw a human in there, too," it added. The girl waved her hand impatiently. 'Human? Do you mean a werewolf, a vampire, or some kind of demon?"

"…and I could hear them all… faint, shallow, all of us shouting to get out." It paused, trying to remember the finer details.

"Stop, just tell me everything; the suspense is too much!" she pleaded.

"Shhh… I'm," it closed its eyes and lowered its head, then gasped, "I heard, I heard… Aeoniks, Aeoniks… shouting and other creatures… there were so many, 'Lint-Lint… Ddraig-Ddraig… Uff-Uff…" So, so many sorrowful cries." The dragon began to shake at the remembrance of the ghostly echoes.

"So, what do you make of it?" the curious dragon asked.

The girl didn't answer; she just looked down at her boots in thought, noticing one of the laces was undone and bent forward to tie it. When she had pulled at the loops tight, she looked back at the dragon, inhaling deeply through her nose.

"So?" it puzzled.

"I really do not know. Are you expecting me to figure this out? Maybe, if you give me some time, let me think," she replied, raising an eyebrow.

"I do not know. I thought you might know something about these things from books and school," the dragon said, a little disheartened.

Aeona put a hand under the dragon's chin and gently lifted it, "We'll figure it out, okay? So, what do we have?" She systematically repeated what she understood from the dragon. "Dead dragons, sleeping dragons, bubbles surrounding them, a girl and letters... Wait, what did the letters say?" She sat up, suddenly interested by the clue.

"I'm a dragon. Do you expect me to know?" the dragon asked, confused.

"You said you saw letters, so what did they say?" Aeona pressed, her curiosity growing.

"I do not know. I can't read!" the dragon said, shaking its head.

The girl wrinkled her nose, frowning. "I'm sure I taught you the letters a long time ago. Do not you remember any of them?"

Aeona asked. "Sure, I do," the dragon replied. "They were 'ell-l... ah-ah... em-m-m... be-ee..." It closed its eyes as if the memory were burnt into its mind. "Tee-ee...oww-w...enn-n, I think."

The girl rummaged around for something to write with.

"Okay, again, sorry... the first one was... what did you say... ah-ah, so that's A," she said, scrawling it in the mud with a twig. "What next?"

The dragon seemed a little put out; it had struggled enough the first time, but after searching for the memory, it was able to say the letters in order. Once it had finished, the girl stood up to read the word, if any.

"Okay, dragon. It says AMBTON. Have you heard of it?"

Dragons aren't known for their sarcasm, but the dragon just shrugged its shoulders and asked, "Have you?" It read through the letters again.

"ah-ah... em-m-m... be-ee... tee-ee...oww-w...enn-n." Then it shook its head. "No, no, no, this isn't right. You missed one. The first one was, ell-l."

"Oh! So, it reads Lambton. I've heard of it somewhere..." she murmured, frowning.

"Lambton... I do not know where, but the name feels... old... like something I should remember." She scratched her chin in thought. She didn't know why, but the name gave her a strange feeling, like the edge of a memory brushing past her. It felt both familiar and far away. "We need access to the internet. If only I had brought my phone. But we could check it in a library or somewhere. Yes, that's it, we need to find a library. There must be a town around here somewhere. But we've got to stay off the radar, so I can't ask anyone."

Aeona frowned at the thought, hugging her bag. "So, first step, a library. Somewhere quiet, where no one will ask questions."

The dragon dipped its head. "Then we go searching, my girl. Tell me which way, and we'll find it."

With that, it lifted off and flew north, keeping the road to its left until it reached a junction.

"What way, my girl? Left or right?" it asked, hovering in place.

"Urm… Take a right… No left," she stuttered undecidedly.

On it went, and after a couple of miles, the road broke, and they followed a cycle track; it felt a little less conspicuous. The dragon called for instructions every mile: "Left or right?"

"I do not know," the rider hesitated. "Just forget the road. It looks like it is heading back to where we came from. Stay straight."

"Righty oh! Captain, will do."

They continued to skirt beside the river and followed the track with thick foliage following its banks. It offered protection if anyone happened to be cycling or walking in the brisk morning.

It also allowed it to fly at speed, with the occasional curve in the river, which proved not too tricky on the wing. A bridge suddenly appeared, causing it to barrel roll through an arch, almost losing the girl in the process. The crests along its back instantly wrapped around the girl's legs in time, her head missing the stone wall by inches, blasting through in a flash. "Shiiit! You trying to kill me?!" she screamed, half furious, half terrified.

The dragon landed a second later on the east bank to give the girl time to calm down from screaming at it.

"Sorry, it just appeared, like BAM!"

"Are you trying to kill me?" she panted, catching her breath.

"Sorry, but… did you see me? Did you see me? I was like,

Woah, and then I was like, SPIN, and then back out of it. And I grabbed you and… and…and…”

“Okay, okay. You were awesome! Big head. But I could’ve died!”

“But, you didn’t. I got you!” it smiled.

The bank, lined with trees, gave them good cover from the road above. When the dragon stopped, they could hear people talking but couldn’t pinpoint from where. Aeona pressed a finger to its lips, shushing her friend, then pointed through the trees to her right. “There are people, there.” She mouthed, pointing her finger. “Stay here, and I will go and look. Okay?” showing her palm so it would keep quiet.

The girl slowly climbed the bank to the top. Staying low to the ground, she could see a petrol station forecourt and a shop in front of her. “Great, someone should know if there is a library around here.”

Aeona crouched low, waiting as a nearby car took forever to leave, strapping a child in, doors slamming, the sluggish whine of the engine starting. Finally, the vehicle rolled away. She exhaled, brushed dirt from her oversized coat, straightened her hair, and whispered, “Okay, here goes.” With a casual cough, she stepped out from behind a parked car, whistling as though she belonged, and strolled toward the petrol pumps. Her eyes flicked across the forecourt, weighing who might know the area best.

She scanned the people nearby, most looking more like tourists than locals in their hiking clothes and boots. There was a man in his twenties dressed in jeans and a black shirt, “I will try him,” she said under her breath, then plucked up the courage to ask. “Excuse me, but do you know if there is a library around here?”

The man looked strangely at her, eyeing her repeatedly,

"library? A library?"

"Yeah, sorry, my dad is parked in the car over there," she said, pointing. "He needs to print something off, like for work. Do you know if there is one?"

"Sorry, kid. I haven't got a clue. I thought they had closed them all," he said, removing the nozzle from his car and replacing it in the petrol pump. "It may be better if you ask inside; they should know." He called back as he headed inside to pay.

The girl waited for a second and then followed him to the shop. The cashier inside was just as unhelpful, her bored expression suggesting books were not exactly her thing. "Okay, thanks for your help," she said, turning to leave.

Then, an elderly woman standing by the cash machine called over to her, "Excuse me, pet. I couldn't help hearing, did you say you were looking for a library?"

"Erm… yes. My dad needs to print something, and he sent me in to ask if anyone knew where a library was." She quickly responded, keeping to her original alibi.

"Well, as luck should have it, there is one a minute up the road. Just carry on up Station Road," she pointed out the window, "and take the left into Front Street. It is in the town hall, tell him."

She had to keep herself from running out of the shop. "Thank you so much. He will be so happy." She smiled brightly at the woman.

"You are most welcome, my love."

Walking out from behind the tree was far easier than sneaking back again. The car she had crept behind was no longer there, and no one was about, but glancing back, the fiery eyes of the girl at the counter met hers. She froze with raised eyebrows. Thoughts raged through her mind: She knows. Oh God… she knows! Don't run, don't run, don't run, played on a frantic loop in her head.

She only broke eye contact when a white van pulled in behind her. It gave her just enough time to hurtle around the corner and dive into the toilet on her left. The cashier was left in a daze, scanning the forecourt for the disappearing girl.

It felt like a lucky break slipping away from the cashier, finding the library, and now, as a bonus, a toilet. Finally, a place to sit, breathe, and gather her thoughts. When she was done, she skulked out of the toilet, slipped left behind the shop, climbed a low wall, and disappeared back into the trees.

Back by the river, the dragon paced anxiously, frantic about what might have happened to the girl. "Hey, did you miss me, dragon?" she whispered, looking for her friend, who, upon hearing Aeona, came from under the bushes.

"You had me worried. Where did you go?"

"Well, we're in luck. There is a library not far from here."

"What's a library?" it questioned.

"That does not really matter. I think it is best if you wait for me here. I was told it is only down the road, and this seems a good place for you to stay," she said, patting the creature's neck.

"Do not worry, I will be fine."

In a worried tone, it relented, "If you are sure. Hurry back."

She couldn't go back up the same way she had earlier; the girl in the shop would certainly be even more suspicious of her.

Walking a little farther up the bank, she turned just past the spot she had returned earlier and stood at the roadside before heading left.

The old lady's directions were correct.

Not far down the road, she reached a junction where the road sloped gently uphill, and to the left stood a wonderful old building. Its Victorian-Gothic Architecture rose proudly, the spire towering high above the neighbouring houses. The clock had fallen into disrepair years ago, its hands frozen at ten forty-five, as though crying out to be set free.

The library was small, cosy, and well-stocked. A circle of reading chairs sat at the centre, and along the wall, two computers seemed to smile back at her. An old gentleman sat behind a small counter at the far end of the room. He seemed happy to see the girl. "Good afternoon, me young'un. Welcome, come in. I've not seen you in here before."

"Hi, nice to meet you. May I use one of those computers over there for a bit?" she motioned.

"Sure, lass. Just press the button. The login information is written on the wall. If you need any help, give me a shout," he said with a smile, waving her toward the computers.

She made her way over, sat down, and muttered, "Well, that went smoothly enough."

Opening the browser, she typed: 'What's special about Lambton?' Instantly, a long list of sites appeared on the page.

The first three, along with different small logos: 'About Lambton College, offers smaller classes." "Top Reasons: Why You Should Study at Lambton College. Their college offers…' 'Lambton College.' She stopped. "Well, that isn't working," she thought, glancing around the library as she held her finger on the delete key until her question disappeared.

Trying to focus herself, she took a deep breath. "Stay cool; stop acting so suspicious!" She thought about what the dragon had told her, but she couldn't think of how to search for strange symbols in the bar. "I can't seem to find anything, but let us give this a shot. Here goes nothing," she muttered, pressing ENTER. Instantly, the screen went white and right in front of her eyes… six images appeared, three so shocking they nearly made her fall off the back of her chair.

Her pulse kicked as the images loaded. "Bingo!" she blurted before clapping a hand over her mouth. Heart racing, she lowered her voice. "The dragon was right."

"Okay, let us go through what the dragon dreamt. I better get this down; I will not remember any of it."

She slid the chair back a little and went to the librarian. "Excuse me," she said, trying to be well-mannered. "May I borrow a piece of paper and a pen, please?"

"Wouldn't it be better just to print what you want? It only costs twenty pence a page, my dear," he replied.

"Sorry, I didn't bring any money with me today," she admitted, embarrassed.

"No worries. Here you go. Take these. Please return the pen when finished, will you not, lass?" he said with a smile.

Returning the smile, she thanked him and went back to the computer.

"Before I forget," she said, jotting on the paper: skeletons, sleeping dragons, creatures striking, bubbles surrounding them, a girl, Aeoniks, and the floating word 'LAMBTON.'

The image on the far right showed a knight locked in battle with a snake. Aeona couldn't call it a dragon. It was clearly a snake to her. There was no mistaking what it portrayed: spiky armour, a comical head, and a swinging sword. She rose from the chair and leaned closer to the screen. She was right. Each picture showed the creature with nine black spots from its nose to its neck.

Her eyes quickly scanned the other two pictures. Apart from the added colour and a strange arrow-shaped tongue, the dragons bore the same nine spots as the others.

She began to scan through the page, 'The Lambton Worm is a legend from North-East England in the United Kingdom. The story takes place around the River Wear and is famous local folklore, having been adapted from written sources and transformed into pantomime and song. The story revolves around John Lambton, an heir of the Lambton Estate, and his battle with a giant worm-dragon that had been terrorising the local area.'

"Okay, nothing to note down here," she continued.

'The Battle with the Worm'

Alden Squire was under the banner of the noble Lambton family…' "Squire… Squire?" Aeona stopped, puzzled. "Squire?" 'tasked with assisting John with his return from the Crusades. He harboured an ambition to become a knight…'

Aeona stopped and ran her finger over the mouse and opened another tab: 'What is Squire?' she searched.

'During the Middle Ages, a squire was a knight's shield or armour-bearer, tasked with looking after the knight's horse and weaponry. Other responsibilities included serving the knight's meals, particularly carving the meat. It was a prestigious role that also provided valuable training for those aspiring to become knights.'

"My family… Knights! No way!" she gasped.

'TAP!' Back to the main tab. 'But Alden Squire was troubled by a deep yearning to understand the forces of magic and the mysteries of the land. He had heard whispers of ancient secrets, of a great power hidden beneath Lambton hill, and of the family's dangerous pact with a fearsome creature, the very creature that had once protected the land and granted the Lambton their wealth. John Lambton now made the mistake of vowing to rid the land of the creature.

One night, Alden ventured deep into the forest to seek out the old crone who knew the secret of the land, the only one who could unlock the path to the power. The crone was rumoured to be a witch, a sorceress who had lived for centuries, bound by ancient magic and forgotten pacts. Her name was Elda, but Alden never learned her true name, as she was known only by the Keeper of Secrets.

She instructed him on how to defeat the worm, telling him that in order to kill it, he would need to build special armour and sword that would protect him. Most importantly, once the creature was dispatched, he must kill the first thing he sees.'

Armed with this knowledge, Alden instructed John Lambton on how to face the worm. With the tools in hand, John then instructed Alden and his father on what to do when they heard the sounding of three horns.

Unfortunately, they were so excited when they heard the horns that they forgot to release the hound and rushed out to congratulate him. John couldn't bear to kill his father or his dear Squire, so he killed the hound instead. But it was too late, and nine generations were cursed, doomed never to die peacefully in their beds. Thus, the story ends.'

"I'm related to a knight!" she gasped, quickly glancing over at the librarian who was stamping books behind the counter.

"I'm Aeona Knight… and now I've got a dragon. This is unbelievable!" She chuckled, then paused. "I can't wait to tell dragon about this!" Her expression changed as a thought hit her. "Oh … if I'm related to this Alden … then my family is responsible for …" Her mind raced to the fire, to Mary, to Nyxa… She took a deep breath, processing the shock, and then came to a final realization: 'The curse!'

With a newfound zeal, she pressed for more information. "Right,
Squire Aeona," she muttered, "going off the pictures, this must've something to do with … nine. Okay, let us see."

'Why is 9 important for the worm?' she typed and pressed enter.

A picture of a knight wearing spiked armour was swinging his sword at the Worm. A distant memory popped into her head of magazines she used to read with Nyxa. She pictured herself on the bed, a book in her lap, finger slowly passing over a line of words as clear as day... *Whispers call, unseen be, Gone in One, trapped you will be. Do not read - ME!'*

Then a flash of white, dark, piercing eyes stared back at her through a curtain of long black hair.

"AEONIKS! Aeon ... do not read ... me?" Like a lightning bolt, she screamed, "AEONA, NYXA!"

The man came running as fast as his old legs would carry him, his heart pounding. "What's wrong, lass? Is everything alright?"

"Nyxa!" she gasped.

"You nearly frightened the life out of me," he puffed.

She quickly reached across and turned off the monitor. "So, sorry, I... I... I... I was daydreaming, and I saw..."

"It is okay, my dear," he comforted. "You are safe here." He saw the girl's shocked look and tried to distract her by changing the subject.

"You've been a busy little bee today, haven't you? May I ask what you are researching? Maybe I will be able to point you to a book that will help. You know, those things with lots of pages," he finished as a mischievous grin beamed on his face.

"No... No... thank you, the internet is much faster. I... I... I'm writing stuff down about erm... Egypt... yes... Egypt," she panicked.

"Oh, wonderful stuff, just there on shelf C," he pointed, "but unfortunately, we're only open half-day today."

"It is okay. I'm done. Thanks," she said, quickly getting up from her chair, still clearly shaken, and making her way to the door.

The old man fixed his glasses, returned to stamping books and stacking them onto his trolley. "Dearie me, kids nowadays, eh?

They haven't a clue what they're missing. What a shame, I tell you! What a shame!" he muttered under his breath.

CHAPTER TWENTY-FOUR 'REACTIONS'

The sun shone through the broken clouds and streamed in through the window on Cross Fell. The rays glared into the man's eyes, making him roll over in annoyance. He was not a morning person, but his love for nature and the freedom of the outdoors always managed to soothe his soul. He knew that once he had his morning coffee, the world would transform into a place of wonder. It was the loud noise that had disturbed him in the early hours, and although he dropped straight back to sleep, the damage had already been done.

When he finally screwed up his face and forced the morning tiredness from his eyes, he arched his back to stretch, moving his head from side to side to get the crick out of his neck. Not having a proper pillow when hiking was the only drawback he ever had. Once he had brought some life into his stiff body, he opened his eyes, expecting to see Aeona lying on the wooden platform, but the girl was not there. With a sigh, he sat up and looked around. His jumper was rolled up where the girl had laid, but the blanket was on the floor.

After putting his boots on, he opened the door and entered the main room. That was when he saw the culprit: the guitar lay sprawled on the floor, its big eye staring back at him, strings curled into what looked like a mischievous grin, and its saddle teeth slightly askew. "So, it was you!" smirked the man, waving his fist.

"Hey, kid, where did you go?" he called from the main door, but no reply came from outside. He shrugged his shoulders, her dad must've come in the night and made their way down, but when he thought about the weather, it just didn't feel right.

At the library, Aeona wrote down as much as she could about Lambton and the mystery of the worm. There was too much information, but she judged that she had enough to please the dragon, folded the paper, put it into her jacket pocket, and returned the pen to the man, thanking him as she did.

"Anytime, my lass. Have a wonderful day." He waved as the girl made her way out of the door.

The weather had changed since she entered. Now, it was only mid-afternoon, and it was slowly getting dark. She followed the route she came. Before the garage, she looked around, then slipped back over the wall and edged her way down the bank towards her friend. "Drag… drag… I'm back," she called. She thought it better to shorten it from dragon, just in case anyone above in the car park heard her.

She thought it would be too conspicuous to have a dog named, Dragon. Better to be safe than risk drawing attention to herself. The creature, a majestic being with shimmering scales and piercing eyes, came out from its hiding place and smiled. "So, were you followed?"

"What am I, a spy?" she laughed. "Why would anyone follow me?"

"I do not know. Maybe because you look like a homeless kid, wearing a coat and boots you found at the side of the road, five times too big for you!" the dragon responded. They both burst out laughing uncontrollably, and it took them a while to pull themselves together. Then, they sat at the side of the clearing. It was best to be ready for anyone wandering along the river path.

When all was quiet, Aeona took the paper out of her pocket and showed it to the dragon. She explained what she had discovered in the library but stopped short of revealing that she might share the same bloodline as Alden Squire.

***

Back at the Town Hall, the librarian had finished stamping and slowly pushed the trolley to put the books back onto the shelves. As he picked up a book on ancient Egypt, his mind went back to the young girl who had used the computers earlier. "Well now, this would have come in handy for the little lass," he said to himself. "I will keep this to one side; she might be back tomorrow." With that, he straightened the fallen hardbacks and placed the one in his hand, flat on its back at the end, with a smile. All the books had been put to bed, and glancing at the clock, he decided it was time to call it a day.

The only things left were to shut down the computers, turn off the lights, and lock up. He only lived across the road, which was fortunate for the ageing man, who was a year from retirement. He had kept putting it off but loved being surrounded by literature and the quietness of being in such a place. With a happy sigh, he sat down in front of the screen. "Egypt, eh," he chuckled to the monitor, reaching for the mouse. But, instead of being met with images of pyramids and the River Nile, The Lambton Worm stared back at him. He went over it in his mind again, "…Yes, she definitely said Egypt… I'm sure of it," he muttered, glancing across at the "Historical 900-999" shelf; he had just placed the book. "She must've changed her mind, I suppose!" he said, as he moved the cursor to the START menu, clicked SHUTDOWN and turned off the screen.

The dragon and the girl looked up at the sky. "It is going to be dark soon," it said, "which is good for us; we can make some distance through the night. Do you have any food left in the bag?"

"I still have … erm … an apple and a packet of … yuk … prawn cocktail crisps," she said, unzipping the bag by her feet with a grimace. "We also need to find somewhere warm for you to sleep for the night," it thought aloud, then addressed the girl with a hint of worry in its voice, "Come on, eat first and then we can make a move. Your safety is my priority."

***

In Winwick, Aeona's aunt and daughters, Olivia and Cassidy, sat in the living room with two policewomen. Small talk was uncomfortable, but they tried as best they could, waiting for any news of the girl. It had been a couple of days since her strange disappearance at night. The area was cordoned off, and a police car parked just outside. A lone news van, staked out not too far away, waited alongside them. At around six in the evening, Officer Wendy and liaison Officer Gemma Plinter turned into Hollins Lane from the A49 in their police car. This time, no blue lights nor siren blared their arrival. When Wendy pulled beside the other patrol car, she leaned across to her colleague. "Here we go, Gemma. You ready?"

"Not really," she replied, "but it is what it is."

They made their way up the path and gently knocked on the door. It was not the time to ring the bell, especially with the news they carried.

Officer Gilan opened the door with a hello and welcome. She knew too well why Gemma was there, but she gave a dry smile all the same. "You had better come in," she said, leading them into the living room.

Standing, hands clasped tightly, Melanie anticipated the news. As soon as she saw the headlights pull up, she knew. She was sure good news would have been by telephone or over the police radios. None of these came!

Officer Gilan spoke first, "I think it would be better if you sit down, Ms. Squire." Eyes shot from one to the other before all the blood drained from Melanie's face. Her legs gave way as she fell backwards onto the chair, with her head in her hands, wanting, but not wanting, to hear what they had to say.

"I'm very sorry…"

Melanie didn't let her finish. Bursting into tears, she wailed into her lap, "No… No… No…" she wailed into her lap.

"I'm very sorry," Wendy repeated, "but I've got some bad news, I'm afraid." As soon as she finished, Gemma picked up: "I can't imagine how you must be feeling right now. Please know we're here to support you in any way we can." It was a very difficult double act, but this was not the first time they had been requested to deliver unfortunate news to a parent. Melanie said nothing. The officer took a deep breath before the next delivery: "I know this is overwhelming, but we're investigating the circumstances behind her passing."

Olivia panic-stricken, threw an arm around her sister. "Where is she? When can we see her? Where are you keeping her?" she cried.

Wendy glanced at the other women officers, who stood behind the settee, listening wide eyed. 'I'm sorry to say this, but we've not found the bo… sorry… Aeona. We believe she was taken by a wild animal." She paused before continuing. "Despite our efforts, we're still searching for her bod…"

"So, how the hell do you know she is dead?" screamed Melanie, standing with tears streaming down her face.

The ferocity of her anger took Wendy by surprise, and she jumped backwards. "Sorry, we want to share what we know, but we want to spare you some unnecessary details!"

"'Unnecessary! Unnecessary details!' she screamed."

"Whatever it was, attacked one of the Search and Rescue and pu…" she stopped short of saying, he was alive and in hospital. "…We've got all of our resources searching for her bod… her."

Silence filled the room for a moment before it was broken by a knock at the door.

The officers looked at one another, and Officer Sia took it upon herself to see who it was. "I will get it," she said sympathetically.

"No… it is okay, I will go," said Cassidy, slowly rising.

As soon as she opened the door, a spotlight blinded her, and a microphone was thrust into her face. "Good evening. Charlotte Luna from the Gazette." A cameraman stood inches behind. "…we're very sorry for your loss, but we're hoping you could share your thoughts about an animal attack that has also put a man in hospital?" she said at speed, not waiting for a reaction until she had finished.

It took Cassidy by surprise. The shock of the news was not even a minute old. "How dare you! Do you even know what we're going through?" she shoved the microphone aside, swiping it away from her face.

"We completely understand this is extremely diffic…" she persisted. The door slammed in her face. "…ult time, but…" she trailed off. Turning to her cameraman, she questioned, "Did you get that on? We can at least use it for a reaction."

Cassidy composed herself before entering the living room so as not to make it worse for her mother. As soon as she entered, she explained, "Just some reporter. I just told them, no comment, and closed the door." The slam indicated otherwise, but they took it at face value.

Silence filled the room again.

The officers stayed for the next hour in silent support, making a cup of tea and irrelevant small talk cut through the solid atmosphere. Officer Wendy glanced at her colleagues and raised her eyebrows, indicating that they had done all they could tonight. With a slight cough, she said: 'We know this is a lot to process, and we want to ensure you have all the support you need." Gemma slowly slid her card onto the coffee table as Wendy continued.

"Gemma has several bereavement counsellors who will pop in tomorrow morning. They will be able to offer help and advice. We know you might need some time to process this, and we'll leave you in the safe hands of Olivia and Cassidy for the night." She paused, but no response came, as expected.

With that, the three police officers edged their way to the living room door. Gemma stepped forward, crouched beside Melanie and stroked the back of her hand with care. "Please call me anytime," she said to Melanie before she followed the other officers out of the house.

Aeona and the dragon made their way along the riverbank until the voices from the garage faded. The pair climbed through the treeline into an open field, devoid of people. At the far end, some two hundred metres away, a lone person watched their dog run around, too distant to notice them. The two creatures locked eyes briefly, but both soon became bored. The dog barked and then ran off towards its owner; the dragon looked at the darkening sky, then cocked its head towards the girl. "Are you ready?" it asked. "Come on, get on."

Aeona stuffed the remaining food into her pockets, dropped the bag by her feet onto the grass, pulled up the zip, and put her hood up. "All ready now," she said, climbing aboard.

She shuffled from side to side to get comfortable. The frills on the dragon's back slowly began to curl around her thighs, while further down, others arched to form a seat ridge that held her securely in place. With an unspoken "Off we go" pat on its neck, the dragon crouched and leapt into the night sky. The thrust sent the bag rolling like a tumbleweed into the trees and down the bank. It was wonderful to be up in the air again, to feel the freedom and the peace, away from the cares of the world below.

She breathed in deeply and closed her eyes. The gentle beat of the dragon's wings, whoosh…
whoosh… whoosh, rhythmically buffeted her chest. Then, the dragon elevated the aerodynamic frill behind its head to protect her from the headwind.

The dark patchwork of land below, dotted with the occasional light of a car or a secluded farm, was the only thing that showed Aeona their immense height. The firmness with which her trusted friend held her in place was a comfort, and she raised her arms, feeling a tranquillity and joy in the silence.

They flew over a few tiny hamlets and a village, then landed by a large, triangular reservoir to search for a place to stay. "It's so cold down here!" the girl said, trembling as a biting gale blew from the east. A man-made straight edge cut down its side from top to bottom, as if channelling the rushing water into a fang-like icicle. She shivered violently. "We can't stay here. Let's carry on a bit further; we might find something better." The dragon took flight and banked left, away from the water and into the fields farther north.

Not more than five minutes later, Aeona looked down from the heights. Below was a strange line of trees, different from a wood or forest. They seemed purposely planted to form an enormous fortress. Rows upon rows of tiny rectangular segments created the intricacy of a beehive. Four paths cut through the darkness towards seven or eight grey structures, with an occasional light illuminating their corners. At the northeast point, a long line of white headlights led the way, whilst red brake lights flickered, edging the drivers forward.

The dragon came in low over the field and, seeing no movement, glided silently before settling gently at the southern corner of the trees. They would at least offer some protection from the wind for the night.

Following the road to the end of the trees, they came to a courtyard with a huge, open-sided building on the opposite side. As they crossed the open ground, a number of black-and-white mottled faces looked curiously back at them.

The sheep, quickly realising the dragon was not human, began to panic. They ran as a herd to the far corner, bleating loudly. The intruders felt it best to retreat as quickly as they could, back into the darkness from where they had come. The dragon's mouth dripped with saliva as it imagined the feast. "Not a chance, dragon," the girl whispered, patting her friend's rump. "It looks like people live here, so we've got to be quiet. Let's check out the other end; it looks quieter."

To their left, four other large sheds stood in a row. Animals stirred inside, but they were different from the sheep. These curious creatures had long necks, and in the dim light, it was difficult at first to identify them. Aeona had never seen them up close before. A number of alpacas and llamas stood watching curiously.

The llamas stood back from the fence, their long necks stretched out and their ears erect. More curious than their cousins, the alpacas came to the fence to inspect their visitors.

They stood nose to nose with the dragon, each smelling the other, unsure whether it was a friend or foe. Two Highland cattle glanced over from the neighbouring pen and snorted, shaking their long horns in annoyance. "Come on, dragon, leave them alone and let's check farther along," the girl called from the corner. When the dragon finally bid farewell to the animals, it caught up with Aeona, who was standing in front of a bungalow. Its doors were almost black, and an unlit sign on the stone wall was unreadable in the night. The girl made her way up the steps and, for the sake of it, tried the door. Not expecting it to budge, she was shocked when it creaked ajar. Her heart stopped. "What the...?" She instantly crouched behind the panelled window, hiding. There were no lights inside, apart from the small LEDs of a display counter. "Why is it open? More importantly... why is it not locked?" The questions raced through her mind.

After a minute, she peeked through the window but could see no one and no movement within. She eventually plucked up the courage. Her hand trembled as she reached out, her fingertips brushing the cold handle. With a shallow breath, she gently pushed the door with her index finger, her heart in her mouth. Thankfully, the hinges remained silent and it swung with ease. The dragon stood waiting at the corner beside a stone pillar and some artificial plants. "Come… dragon," the girl beckoned, rising from her crouch.

Inside was a café area with many wooden tables and chairs.

A red standby light from a television glared on the wall at the far end, positioned between indiscernible prints of farm animals. Along the left side was a long grey counter with a glass cabinet containing sandwiches, a couple of cakes, and croissants, all ripe for the taking.

"I don't like doing this, dragon," she said softly. "It's not right."

"I know you don't, my girl, but sometimes you have to, out of necessity rather than for the sake of it," the dragon replied. It knew Aeona was no thief; she didn't have it in her. So it made its way around to the back, gathering what it could. It stuffed food into the girl's pockets and slid sweets and biscuits from beside the cash register to fill her hood.

"Right, now we need to find somewhere to sleep for the night, and I know just the place," it said, patting the girl on her head. "It's okay; you didn't steal anything. I did," it said, smiling.

The creature led the girl back to the alpacas. "Come on, I'm sure they will let us stay the night," it said as it began to climb over the fence. The animals stood without concern, welcoming the creature into the pen.

The dragon stood quietly amongst them, giving them a chance to become comfortable with its presence. A llama tentatively approached, reaching forward with its long neck to take a curious sniff. The pair sat quietly in the corner, surrounded by the alpacas and a couple of the bolder llamas from the herd. The girl ate some of the food, and they chatted until they yawned. Finally, both drifted off to sleep, wrapped in the warmth of the animals' bodies and the musky smell.

Over a hundred people gathered around Malham Estate, awaiting orders from Incident Commander Karsef. Search and Rescue teams camped in nearby fields south of the main buildings, while volunteers headed home for the night. Police helicopters had returned to their bases in Wakefield, Ryedale, and Upper Wharfedale. As SAR teams pitched tents, Constables Williams and Collins called it a night, driving the twenty minutes back to Settle police station to write their reports.

The wildlife specialists from DEFRA and the RSPCA had departed hours earlier, after photographing the site where the girl and the winchman were attacked. They were utterly baffled, stating they would need to study the prints in detail back at Westminster.

Everything they had was laid out on the table: the litter, the slippers, and photographs of the paw prints. The Silver and Bronze Commanders sat puzzled. "Right, what do we make of all this?" Karsef asked.

"Well, Sir," began the Operations Chief, "the campfire turned out to be nothing more than a couple of ramblers making their way from Kilnsey towards Fountains Fell, east of Malham." He paused, placing his finger on a location marked with red pen. "Here. The litter was fresh: a triangular box, an egg sandwich identified by its 'best before' date, which is tomorrow; an apple core and a juice carton. However, the juice carton was clearly for a child, with a smiling lion on the front. If we were to prosecute the ramblers for littering, how could we use this against them?" He looked around for support before continuing. "There were no children in their group, so we can disregard that, as it wouldn't hold water."

"So," Karsef interjected, "we only have the slippers, a man in hospital, and the suspected killing of a girl by an unknown creature?"

Officer Campbell from Tactical raised his hand. "Go ahead, Campbell," Karsef said, waving a hand.

"Sir, we also have the slippers," he said. "Something just doesn't fit. We've got a child's juice carton and size three slippers." He picked up a folder and flicked through the pages. "Ah, here it is. It was reported that an old man… where is it… oh, here. Mr. Geoffrey Thomlinson reported that the girl in question was wearing pyjamas and slippers when she entered the shop, Sir. He couldn't remember the colour, but he was certain she had slippers on," he read closely. "His story is supported by an elderly lady who, it says here, gave the child a pound coin. We've obtained the CCTV footage."

He lifted the screen of his laptop to find the file. "Sorry, but it's black and white; the old man hasn't upgraded his system in twenty years. He said there was no need." It took him a minute to locate and play the file. Once it finished, he waited for a response.

Commander Karsef thought briefly before speaking. "So, if the slippers belonged to the girl, as the photos from Ryedale show…" He spoke slowly, working through it systematically, thinking aloud. He traced his finger on the map from the edge of Malham Tarn, along the wall to the north, and in a straight line to where the slippers and litter were found. "Looking at the images… the slippers were… placed… together, next to a wall." He paused, pulling at his lower lip with his thumb and forefinger. "Hang on… Who said this creature, or whatever it is, attacked the man and then dragged the girl off to be eaten? Do we have any drag marks? Blood leading into the forest? Any traces of torn clothing?" He scanned the room, looking sternly into everyone's eyes. "Anyone?"

A heavy silence filled the room, the weight of the situation pressing down on them as they each mentally reviewed the details.

"Well, I can't see a creature dragging someone off to eat and carefully placing a. pair. of. slip. pers. next to each other." He banged the table with each syllable. "Someone better explain this, because THAT girl is alive. I don't know where she is, but someone must know something." He spun around. "Officer Janna, get me Westminster on the line. I need to know what we're dealing with."

Danny was heading down from the hut on Cross Fell, where Aeona had spent the previous night. It had taken him the best part of the day to make his way along the Pennine Way to Alston. The walk usually took around four hours, but he liked to stop now and then to photograph the beautiful scenery and, if he was lucky, a red fox or deer. He had once been blessed to see both in a single day, but it was the view that always amazed him. He loved the late autumn, just before the first snowfall. It was cold, but not cold enough to diminish the awe.

This was his sixth or seventh time walking from Alston to Cross Fell and back. He knew Alston well, a little town in the beautiful county of Cumbria. He always managed to park in the exact spot on Front Street, a great place to have a bite to eat and buy supplies from the local shop before and after his walk.

When he arrived, Jess, his faithful old car, was waiting. He'd owned her for about three years, and the nickname was perfect. "Hey girl, did you miss me?" he said, retrieving his keys from his rucksack. He opened the boot and threw his bag inside. "First things first," he said to himself, rubbing his cold hands together. "Heating on." But there was no hope for warmth for at least the next five minutes. "Come on, girl, it shouldn't take you long to warm up." He chuckled. It was only a forty-minute drive home, and looking at the clock, he guessed he would arrive a little after seven. But first, the yellow light on the dashboard begged for fuel.

"Not to worry, Jess, there's a garage just down the road," he told her.

He sat for a few minutes, letting the engine warm and the windscreen clear, before setting off. The route to the garage took him past the Town Hall and then left at the T-junction, with the garage on his right. It was empty, which he liked; he hated waiting in garages, as the process always seemed to take forever. The rigmarole was a thorn in his side, but a necessary one. Once he had filled up, he went inside to pay.

The cashier behind the plate glass watched him suspiciously, eyeing him up and down as he entered. He made his way to the biscuit aisle and stood browsing the selection. The girl lost interest soon enough and continued flicking through channels on the television mounted on the wall above the cash machine.

Dan glanced at the TV, distracted for a second by the noise, before returning to the tough decision of choosing which biscuits to buy.

She wasn't looking for any channel in particular, having already scrolled through every new post on her social media accounts. In truth, television bored her to death.

She was nine hours into her twelve-hour shift. Alston was quiet at the best of times, but in the late evening, she was lucky if four or five cars came in. With a long sigh, she stopped at the news. Another plane crash flashed up: 103 dead with 55 survivors, search teams still combing the wreckage. A Guy Fawkes warning on fireworks misuse; teenagers hurt in a pre-November 5th prank. A girl missing from Warrington. The Beast of Malham. A man in hospital. The first snow across the area was expected on Tuesday. The girl had zoned out after the fireworks report and was jolted from her stupor by an abrupt, "Just these, thanks. I nearly forgot. Petrol on pump…" Dan strained to see the pump number through all the posters on the windows. "The white banger out there, is that number two or three? Anyway, it's the only car you have sitting out there."

"Biscuits and number two, that will be…"

"It can't be…" the man said, staring at the television as he interrupted her. "It is… I know that kid!" he said, turning to the cashier. "Hey, that girl, her name's Sara!"

She gave him a rough stare, unimpressed. Then her eyes flicked to the screen. "Oh my God… I know that kid too!" They locked eyes.

"I've to call the police!" they both shouted in unison.

Not far from the garage, Albert from the library sat in his bedsit, receiver in hand, already tapping 999, waiting for an answer. "Emergency. Which service do you require?"

"Hello, good evening. May I have the police, please?"

"I'll connect you now. Please hold the line."

After a few seconds, a woman answered, "Good evening, police. How may I help you?"

"Good evening," the old man began. "I was watching the television and saw the terrible news about the plane crash, poor souls. I think it said more than one hundred dead."

"Yes, sir, terrible news, but what are you reporting?" the confused policewoman asked, waiting for relevance.

"Oh yes, very sorry. After the fireworks and the unfortunate goings-on with those teenagers…"

The sigh from the woman was audible. Two incoming calls lit up her switchboard. Albert, however, was committed to recounting the event in his mind. That was how he was going to tell it: all the details, from start to finish, whether she liked it or not. "Anyway, after that, I saw the girl!" She placed her hand over the microphone and mouthed to Officer Rachel to take the other calls.

"The girl, you said?" She waited for him to elaborate, but he stayed silent, expecting her to speak first. "Hello, Sir. Are you still there?"

"Yes!"

"You said a girl; which girl are you referring to?" she pressed.

Albert waited a minute. "Why is she asking me which girl? There is only one girl," he said to himself aloud. "Maybe she is confused with the fireworks," he added. "Sorry, I'm not discussing the fireworks now, my dear. I'm talking about the one that was eaten, but she wasn't, you see."

"I'm sorry, Sir. I don't think I'm following you."

"I'm talking about the girl that you say was eaten by the beast, the one that put that man in hospital."

"Oh, okay. I'm with you now. Can you tell me your location, please?"

"I'm in Alston, just down the road from the Town Hall," said Albert.

He was caught off guard by her next question. "Can you describe the person you've seen?"

"Now, why would I want to do that? You put her picture on the television," he chuckled. "Is there anyone else I can speak to, dearie?" Albert was approaching seventy-one, but he could still put someone in their place and recall many facts. The benefits of working at the library for so many years kept his mind active.

"Sorry, Mr… May I take your name, please."

He shook his head. "I don't think it's an emergency. After all, a person who was not eaten by a wild animal may not be in a hurry. Here we go. My name is Mister Albert Bainbridge. That's

A for Alpaca, L for Lion, B for Bingo… should I continue, love?" He thought this game was better than watching the news and enjoyed teasing the officer. He had tried to rush things along, but he didn't like how she was now handling it as urgent.

Officer Laura felt the same. She was tired of being a dispatcher, especially when old people phoned in. True, it was for real emergencies, sometimes, but she could tell by their tone that it was usually a missing cat, a lost remote control, or a suspicious washing machine. The weekends were enjoyable when things were busy, and she managed the logistics of guiding officers to incidents. Albert's call fell into the former category, or so she thought.

"Thank you, Mr Bainbridge, I'm familiar with the spelling," she stopped him. "How certain are you that this is the girl on the news?"

"I never forget a face, you see," he said sternly. "One hundred per cent, it was the girl in the picture. Her scars were better than a fingerprint, poor lass."

"Thank you, Mr Bainbridge. We'll dispatch officers to your location as soon as possible."

He looked at the clock before answering. "Very well, you can reach me on this number. Good night!"

She leaned back in her chair, relieved the call was finally over. "Good night," she said, rolling her eyes at her colleague Rachel, who had just finished with the second caller.

Rachel smiled back. "Another old fogey, I'm guessing. What was it this time? Cat or crossword?"

"No, he was going on about a girl on television who resembled the one that was eaten down in Malham," she laughed. "These old people, eh? What about your calls?"

Rachel's face straightened, her eyes wide. "You are not going to believe this!"

It was not until the following morning that police were dispatched to take statements from the three individuals who had reported seeing the girl supposedly killed by the Beast of Malham. One officer was sent to interview the cashier and the elderly gentleman in Alston, while another was sent forty minutes away to Hexham.

At the garage, Officer Megan entered and waited at the side of the counter for the girl to finish serving a customer. "Hello, Chloe. How are you?" she smiled. "It's been a while; keeping out of trouble now, eh?" Chloe, a familiar face in the town, was known to Officer Megan from previous encounters.

The officer had dealt with her on many occasions for various minor offences. Nothing too serious; it was just teenagers hanging around causing a nuisance, random petty theft, or being cheeky to the older residents near the Town Hall.

"I've got myself a full-time job, you see."

"Nice one, Chloe. I heard you're also doing an online course or something," Officer Megan added. "And before you ask, it was your mum. I bumped into her a couple of days ago," she winked. Not giving Chloe time to interrupt, she asked, "So, what's this about the girl on the TV?"

"She was in here last night, around six-ish, I think. Before I recognised her, I thought there was something strange. She was acting a little odd."

Taking her notepad from her pocket, the officer asked, "What do you mean?"

"Well, she had this coat on, about ten times too big for her, and enormous boots that made her walk like an ape. She said something about her father being outside in the car, but she didn't glance out the window like a person usually does." Chloe tapped her temple with a finger. "I've got an eye for these things, you see… Anyway, she wanted to know where the library was. It's definitely the girl you're looking for. No one I know has a scar like that running down her face. It looked great… I wish I had something like that, you know… So," she went on, "Mrs. Fisher was getting some cash…"

"Who?" asked the officer, writing it down.

"Mrs. Fisher. She was getting some cash from the machine, and she told the girl where the library was."

"That's what Mr. Bainbridge called in about," she said, flicking through her notepad.

Chloe wasn't listening. "And then she left. But she didn't walk to any car. She just stood by the door, thinking. I clocked her, and she panicked when she saw me looking."

"I'm going to need to look through the CCTV, if that's alright?" asked the policewoman.

The girl shook her head. "Sorry, but I don't have the key to the back office. You'll have to wait for my supervisor. You know, Johnny. He should be here in about ten minutes."

"No problem. I'll pop back in an hour or so."

She closed her notepad and slipped it into her top pocket. Turning, she walked out to her car, her mind buzzing with the new information.

It took her less than five minutes to drive to the Town Hall to speak to Albert, the librarian. "Good morning, Mr. Bainbridge. How are you?" she began.

"Not too bad. Not too bad at all," he responded. "And how is my little Megan doing?"

"Well, I'm not little anymore, but all is good, Mr. Albert." He had taught her in primary school many years ago but could never break the habit of calling her 'little Megan.' He still remembered the names of all the children he had taught. A few had remained in the town, married, and had children of their own.

These children showed him the most respect. He only needed to mention their parents' names: "If you don't quit messing around, I'll tell your mother." That was enough to make them behave or scurry out of the library.

Officer Megan pressed on. "So, Mr. Albert, the station said you rang last night about the missing girl from Warrington?"

"Well, yes… that was last night… so what took you so long?" he said, somewhat annoyed. She didn't respond. "Anyway, the girl came in and asked if she could use one of the computers. She said she needed to research something about… Egypt."

The officer was scribbling in her notepad when Albert stopped.

"Sorry, carry on, Mr. Albert, I'm listening. I'm just getting it all down," she said, looking up.

He gave a little frown. "Well, the girl said she didn't have any money, so I gave her some paper and a pen to take notes. But when I went to shut the computers down for the night… she wasn't looking at Egypt at all. She had been reading about the Lambton Worm, which I thought a bit odd, because there are no worms in Egypt, you see."

"The Lambton Worm, you said?" she asked.

"Yes. Do you want me to show you?" he said, already walking to the computers. "Come along, Miss Megan, follow me."

The officer stood behind the old man as he sat down and opened the search history. She leaned over his shoulder to look at the long list of website links the girl had visited.

There were no searches about Egypt, the Pyramids, or the River Nile. She pursed her lips in thought. If it was a lie the girl had told the librarian, that wasn't for her to judge. She was here to collect evidence to support his claim.

"Could I have a printout of these pages, Mr. Albert? And I would also like to see the CCTV footage, if I could?" she asked.

The librarian printed the pages and took the officer to the back room where the security computer was kept.

It was exactly as he had reported. The footage showed the girl entering, wearing an enormous coat. It showed the time she was there, how she approached Mr. Albert for paper, and then hunched over, making notes for a good thirty minutes.

The officer was satisfied and asked for a copy of the footage. He had never worked with the security recorder much but was fairly tech-savvy for a man in his seventies. "No problem, my dear, but it might take me a while," he apologised.

"Many thanks, Mr. Albert. I need to nip back to the garage. Would thirty minutes be enough?"

"I'll give it a shot. No promises, but I'll try," he smiled.

"Thanks, Mr. Albert. I'll be back shortly," she said, leaving the library.

***

Twenty miles away in Hexham, another police officer was on his way to speak to the third person who had reported seeing the missing child.

Still in his pyjamas, Danny Hallins opened the door with a steaming cup of coffee in hand. "Good morning, please come in," he welcomed. "Sorry about the mess. I was just about to get ready for work." He beckoned Officer Gary inside. The policeman wiped his feet and followed him down the hall into the living room. "Would you like one?" Danny asked, waving his cup. "The kettle's just boiled."

"I don't mind if I do, thanks," Gary smiled. "So, Mr. Hallins…"

"Dan's fine. No need for formality," he said, handing him a fresh coffee.

"Thanks, Dan," he grinned. "So, I've just come from the garage.

The cashier said you both recognised the missing child on the television last night. Is that right?"

"Yes, we realised at the same time, but I had met her the night before, up in Greg's Hut."

"Could you give me the details for my report?" asked the officer.

Dan drank some coffee and sat in his favourite armchair. "Sure, have a seat, and drink your coffee before it gets cold." He paused, noticing the policeman was struggling to keep up with his notes. When the officer nodded, Dan continued. "I got to the hut late in the afternoon, just before sunset, and she was already there. I asked her who she was with, and she said her name was Sara, and that she was waiting for her father. I didn't think much of it; you meet so many people out walking. Some are great, but some can be a bit odd." He paused again. "She said she was waiting for her father, right... Now, when I looked around the hut, I saw she didn't have any equipment: no sleeping bag or rucksack, nothing at all! I've never met anyone on the moors with nothing but an oversi... Oh, that's another thing. She had on this enormous coat, far too big for her, like she'd pulled it from a lost property bin. I thought it must've been her father's. I should have asked, but I didn't."

"Strange. Anything else?" prompted the officer, pen poised.

Dan thought for a minute, looking at the ceiling. "Let me think... yes, she didn't have any food or even a water bottle."

"No food or water," the policeman mouthed, writing it down.

"We'd some small talk, nothing interesting, as we waited for her dad. Needless to say, he didn't come. I was knackered and wanted to sleep, so I lent her a blanket from my pack and my spare jumper as a pillow. When I woke up, she was gone. I didn't think anything of it until I saw her on the TV in Alston, and that's when I called you."

"Great! Thank you for your help, and thanks for the coffee," he said, placing his empty cup on the table and getting to his feet. "I'd better get this written up for my supervisor."

"You're welcome. If I remember anything else, I'll call," Dan said, leading the officer out and closing the door before running upstairs to get ready for work.

The three reports and the CCTV footage from the garage and the library were sent to Incident Command by early afternoon. Commander Karsef and his team watched the footage carefully. The garage's forecourt was their primary focus, but the girl was seen stepping out from behind a tree at the far end of the car park. There was no father, as she had claimed. The library video showed her wearing the enormous coat, rolling the sleeves into bulky cuffs, and her strange gait as she walked about.

"So, as I see it," began Commander Karsef, "the girl was somehow taken from her house in Winwick, a mystery in itself, with a great hole in the bedroom wall. I can't rule out kidnapping, but this seems more like a jailbreak. She has left a trail of breadcrumbs across the country, whether deliberately or not." He paused, and everyone nodded in silent agreement. "Now, here in Malham, what do we have? A man in hospital and a girl supposedly eaten by an unknown creature with claws like a crocodile. I've never seen anything like it! I've got over a hundred people outside who searched all night. The best we've got is some litter and a pair of slippers." He paused again, pulling at his bearded chin. He turned to Officer Janna. "How far's it from here to Cross Fell, as the crow flies?"

It took her only seconds to reply. "Just under fifty miles, Sir."

"And from Cross Fell to Alston?"

"Not far, Sir, about ten miles."

"Either way, ten miles is ten miles," he glanced at the map. "Right, so anyone can jump in. This girl has somehow covered about sixty miles. She hasn't walked it, so how on earth did she get to Alston?"

The group debated for the next hour, but no one could devise a believable explanation for her travelling north from her home. Now, they knew her direction.

Commander Karsef was on the phone for over thirty minutes, updating Gold Command in Carlisle.

"Yes, Sir… Yes, Sir… Of course, Sir… Will do, Sir… Right away, Sir." He ended the call, stood up, and looked back at the map. "Well, everyone, we've got to move fast." He looked around the room. "We know the direction she's heading, so let's beat her to it." He tapped his finger vigorously on the map. "Janna, get me the Northumbria Police Chief Constable; we need all their available officers on this."

"Yes, Sir," Officer Janna answered.

"Oh, and Janna," he said with a frown, "we need the liaison officer to update the guardian. Give her the news." He raised his eyebrows. "I wouldn't like to be in their shoes… 'We're searching,' 'we found her,' 'she's dead,' 'we found her.' What a rollercoaster. At least we finally have some good news."

CHAPTER TWENTY-EIGHT 'RACE'

A cold October wind swept across the fields, pushing clouds at speed. Grey mountains loomed, blurred by the wintery gusts from the east. The windscreen wipers swept away a drizzle that sliced like needles as Officers Wendy and Gemma drove to deliver the news to the girl's aunt.

It was an uncomfortable task her supervisor had assigned. She didn't know if she would face the aunt's anger, but she hoped the good news would overshadow the sorrowful message she had delivered previously.

Pulling up, she turned off the car and looked across at Gemma, a tall, slender woman with piercing blue eyes. Her hands still on the wheel, she leaned forward to peer under the sun visor. The upstairs curtains were open, suggesting the occupants were awake. "Here we go again, Gem. You ready for this?" she asked, taking a deep breath. "Why is it always us?"

"All in a day's work, Wen. Come on, you've got this," Gemma replied, undoing her seatbelt. The sheer force of the wind took her by surprise as she opened the door, nearly wrenching it from her grip. The hinge groaned as it swung wide.

"I've got this if you've got that door!" Wendy laughed, opening her own door and holding it firmly with both hands. She battled the gale and finally stepped out. They made their way to the door, and a minute later, Olivia, Aeona's cousin, answered.

"Good morning," she said, confused by their appearance. "How can I help you?"

"May we come in? We've got important news about Aeona," said Officer Wendy.

"Please, come in," Olivia replied, her reluctance clear. Her mother was still distraught, unable to process any more details about the loss of her niece.

"Mum, the police are here again." She led them in, put an arm around her sister, Cassidy, and sat on the arm of the chair.

"How can we help you?" asked Melanie. "Don't you think we've been through enough?"

"I know this is difficult, but we… have some… good news."

"Good news?" Melanie's voice was sharp with disbelief. "How could you possibly have good news? Have you found her body? Is that your good news?"

"It's okay, shh… let them talk," her daughter said calmly.

Officer Wendy glanced at her colleague, who remained silent.

Clearing her throat, Wendy continued. "We believe we may have misread the situation. We think she might be alive, but we need you to look at some footage to confirm her identity." She braced for another outburst, but the news was so overwhelming that Melanie simply froze.

Wendy didn't wait. "We've had several sightings of a girl in the north of England who fits Aeona's description." She paused, gauging their reaction.

Melanie sat upright, edged closer to the table, and pulled the laptop towards her. Without a word, she gave a slight nod. The video was already open, paused on the screen. She tapped the space bar.

The file had been edited by the crime scene department, who had sharpened the image and cropped out irrelevant areas like the backroom and the rows of confectionery.

The clip began with an outside view of the car park. After a few seconds, a girl stepped out from behind a white car parked at the far end. Melanie gripped the edge of the table, leaning so far forward her daughters instinctively mirrored her. She held her breath, afraid to blink. Then the child moved closer. The woman studied her gait, the set of her shoulders. Something deep inside her spoke louder than reason. It was her.

Her hood was down, her face blurred in shadow, but Melanie didn't need more. She pressed a hand to her lips, eyes stinging. The camera shifted to inside the shop. When the girl addressed the cashier, she lowered her hood. That was enough. Tears of joy spilled down Melanie's cheeks.

Olivia and Cassidy were already pressed to her side. Cassidy clutched her sister tightly, whispering, "It's her, Liv… I knew it." Olivia wiped her own eyes, unable to stop smiling.

"She's alive. She's alive! Oh my God, she's alive." Their voices broke in unison, trembling with relief.

The room filled with their sobbing joy. Wendy and Gemma exchanged a look, saying nothing, allowing the family their moment. When the clip ended, Wendy moved the cursor to the next file. The emotional outburst had already confirmed everything.

This screen showed footage from the library, the girl hunched over a desk, scribbling notes and occasionally speaking to the elderly man.

After a few minutes, Wendy slowly closed the laptop. "I've got to ask this formally. Can you confirm that the girl is Aeona Squire, your niece?" she asked softly.

"Yes. It's her." Melanie smiled through her tears.

"And can you confirm these are her slippers?" she asked, sliding two photographs across the table.

Cassidy picked them up and looked closely. "Yes, they are. I bought her those. Now please, where is she? When will you bring her home?" she asked excitedly, wiping her eyes with a tissue Gemma had handed her.

"Well, we're s…" A knock at the door interrupted her.

"I'll get it," Olivia said, standing.

"So when will she be here?" Melanie leaned forward, her

voice cracking. "They're bringing her home?"

"As I was j…" She was stopped again by a commotion at the front door.

As Olivia opened the door, a wall of microphones and cameras surged forward. Flashes burst in her eyes as reporters jostled against each other, voices colliding in a deafening roar: "When will she be back? Is she hurt? Where has she been?" The questions crashed over her in a relentless wave.

Amid the shouting, a familiar voice cut through. Charlotte Luna from the Gazette had her foot braced in the doorway, preventing it from being shut. "How did it feel when you heard the news?" she pressed, leaning in with her microphone. Olivia scowled, pushing against the door, but it bounced back on its hinges. "Come on, give me something to work with," Charlotte begged.

"Get out of my house!" Olivia screamed, kicking at the intruder's foot. "I'll call the police!"

Wendy quickly pushed past her. "Come on, get back! No questions at this time," she barked, waving the microphones away. "When they're ready to release a statement, you'll have it." She planted herself firmly in the frame and pulled the door half-shut. "I've got nothing more to say. Please give the family privacy. You'll get your press conference."

Most reporters backed onto the pavement. Some turned to their cameras, updating their studios for the evening news. But one lingered.

"Charlotte Luna, Gazette," she announced sharply, microphone still raised. "How can the police tell a family their loved one is dead and then say, 'Sorry, we made a mistake'?"

It took every ounce of Wendy's restraint not to snap. Her voice was loud and clipped: "As I said, no questions. When we have a statement, we'll release it. This is private property. I need you to leave. Right now. Miss… what was your name?”

“Charlotte Luna, Gazette,” she repeated, unflinching. “The public has a right to know.”

“I understand you’re doing your job, Miss Luna, but…”

“Are we breaking any laws by being here?” Charlotte interrupted, lifting the microphone. “Yes. I would call it trespassing,” Wendy said, her stare hardening. “Shall I continue?”

The reporter finally relented and lowered her mic. Her voice dropped to a whisper meant only for Wendy. “Can’t you give me something? Where is she?”

“I would if I could. But I can’t.” Wendy’s tone softened a fraction, and she added a quick wink. “Now, let me get back inside. Thanks.”

Charlotte’s shoulders sagged as Wendy shut the door, leaving her stranded among her colleagues. When she returned to the living room, Melanie, Cassidy, and Olivia were by the fireplace, discussing what had happened. “Sorry,” she said, “that should keep them away for a while.”

“So, where is Aeona now?” her aunt asked.

“Truthfully, we’re still searching, but from what the librarian said, we suspect she might be heading to Lambton.” She explained. “We’re sending a team there, so we should find her soon.”

Melanie looked completely confused. “I’ve never heard of it. Why would she want to go there?” She looked back and forth between the officers.

“It’s near Sunderland. We’re hoping you could tell us if you have any family in the Northeast?” Wendy asked.

“No… I don’t think so…” She looked at her daughters for confirmation. “Do we?” They both shook their heads.

“Any cousins, friends, or anyone Aeona knows from

school?" she pressed. "We're at a loss. The videos show she's acting on her own accord... so, no one?"

They stood quietly for a minute, thinking, but couldn't provide an answer. Many relatives had been in touch, aware of the situation from the news, but none had come forward with information. The aunt and her daughters caught each other's eyes in a sudden, silent understanding. Then, in one fluid motion, the three walked out and went upstairs. The officers were left in the room, wondering, but decided to give them space and sat on the sofa to wait.

After five minutes, heavy footsteps sounded as the three quickly returned, each carrying a small bag. "Right, let's go," said Melanie. "It shouldn't take long. Let me grab the keys." She snatched the keys and her purse from the mantelpiece.

"Come on, Cassidy, I'll drive. You find us somewhere to stay on the way."

The officers were taken aback, though they had anticipated this reaction. "But..." Wendy pleaded, "It's only a lead. We don't know for sure she's going there. We need you to wait here, in case she calls."

"That's why they call it a mobile. She doesn't even know the home number," Melanie explained.

"You two stay and wait by the telephone. We're going to Lambton," Cassidy said to the policewoman. Without waiting for a reply, she turned to Olivia. "Find the place on your Satnav. We'll figure out the rest on the way. Let's go." She swung her bag and headed for the door.

There was nothing Wendy or Gemma could do but run after them. "Wait, the reporters!" Wendy called.

By the time the officers caught up, the family was already in their car, reversing out of the drive. The waiting reporters scattered to the sound of screeching tyres. Others jumped into their vehicles to give chase but were blocked by the two officers standing firmly in front of the lead car.

Wendy knew they couldn't catch the family, not with an ensemble of reporters in pursuit. "Okay! We're ready to make a statement. Gather round!" Wendy shouted as Gemma slammed her shins against the lead car's bumper.

The driver glared through the window, engine revving, ready to thrust forward after its prey. He edged forward, but when he saw the ferocity in Gemma's eyes, he lifted his foot from the accelerator and accepted defeat. A slow gathering approached Wendy, reluctant to listen.

All except one. Just as she was about to start, one car screamed over the grassy bank to her right, its back end sliding from side to side. "That stubborn bitch!" spat Wendy, as it sped away after the escaping vehicle.

Aeona had managed only broken sleep over the past few days, but being wrapped in the warmth of the alpacas was a welcome respite from the elements. The animals' occasional, rhythmic snores amplified the tranquillity of the night. It was the dragon who stirred everyone just before sunrise, to the confused looks of the other animals. "Girl," it whispered, gently shaking the child. "Girl… we've got to go."

The alpacas raised their long necks, looked at the dragon, then curled back into themselves to sleep. The creature briefly questioned its own judgement for waking them, but it knew they couldn't stay. What if the farmer did his morning rounds? The thought of outstaying a welcome they never truly had was a risk they couldn't take. "Sorry, girl, but up you get," it said, lifting Aeona by her foot.

"I heard you!" she moaned. "Five more minutes?"

"But…" it conceded, "not a minute longer… okay?" It received no reply from the squirming girl as it lowered her back into the warm pool of alpaca fleece. It shuffled to the side and out into the cold.

The forecourt was quiet; the dawn shift in the sky had begun. Bats darted around the buildings, feeding on the wing before their daily retreat, while a fox looked on, unable to catch one. It turned instead to the torn black bags of discarded rubbish near a wall. Other nocturnal animals had already beaten it to the previous day's scraps. The fox sniffed for any morsel but found only empty food packaging. With nothing left, it scurried into the hedge.

The dragon listened quietly, taking in the brisk air of the fading night. Then a flicker of light caught its eye, a reflection in a window some fifty metres away. The dragon skulked back, listening and watching for a door to open. Nothing stirred. "I don't like this," it said to itself. "That's enough… five minutes are done!" It moved swiftly to extract Aeona from her huddle. "Time's up, my girl. Up you get!"

Disturbed by the dragon, the alpacas trumpeted in unison, disgruntled, as the creature tugged the girl's foot. "I'm coming!" answered Aeona, coughing on a mouthful of straw as she was dragged out on her stomach. Once her friend let go, she pushed herself up and pushed back her hood. Her eyes were half-closed; with a yawn, she rubbed her face to wake up. "Can't we sleep a bit longer?" she asked. "What's the matter?"

The dragon listened, moving its head as if trying to pick up the faintest sound. "I think the coast is clear," it said. When confident, it continued. "I'm sorry, but I saw a light come on in the house at the end of the yard. We don't know when the farmer will wake; I don't want to press our luck." Its tone was increasingly concerned. "It's a big place with lots of people. It might be difficult to leave without being seen."

"Okay, you're right," she said, looking back at her bedfellows.

Before they climbed out into the brisk morning, Aeona stroked one of the gentle creatures and whispered goodbye to the alpacas' mournful hums.

The morning was as cold and damp as the last. The distant light urged them to take flight. They moved across the yard to a clearing. "We're good to go. Climb on," it whispered, crouching to let her jump onto its back. Aeona was getting the hang of mounting now.

"Just like riding a bike. Once you know, you know," she smiled. Except she had never learned to ride one. She was only four and a half. Her father had wanted to buy the twins bicycles, but their mother always said they were dangerous. He had once bought them as a surprise, only for her mother to return them.

She soon lost faith in asking for anything, and a quiet resentment towards Father Christmas began to burn within her.

It didn't help much; it just buried the dark thoughts. It had taken a while to replace Nyxa, and then the dragon disappeared, too. The frills held her in place and rose against the seat of her pants. "You'll be a pro soon enough," the dragon smiled.

Suddenly, the creature turned at the faint sound of footsteps behind it, too low for Aeona to hear. The shudder running from its head to its tail made the girl spin around, searching the increasing light.

"What is it? What do you hear?" Aeona whispered.

The dragon didn't need to answer; the girl knew something was wrong.

"Go… take flight!" she croaked.

With a push of its powerful hind legs, it beat its wings and thrust into the sky. The force sent gravel and stones clattering against the shed walls, shattering the silence. The footsteps below skidded to a halt, then thudded as a man in Wellington boots ran to investigate. He found nothing but the bobbing heads of the humming alpacas. They came to greet him as he switched on the lights.

He walked the site, checking the livestock. The alpacas and llamas pressed at the gate, eager for pasture, while a few goats and ewes called in chorus. Beyond them, Highland cattle grazed the frost-crusted field, their thick coats protecting them as they stood like dark silhouettes against the dawn. Finding all present, he stretched, yawned, and started his day.

Picking up the mess from the rubbish bins was not the best start. "I'm going to bloody kill Steve for this!" he scolded, punching the air. "I told you to use the skip! Wait till you come in, you stupid sod!" He stuffed the contents of the black bags into the overflowing wheelie bin, cursing with every handful.

"Going to have to do somethin' 'bout those effin' foxes, too!"

Even the hungry fox became the scapegoat. It didn't take him long to clean up; it was too cold a morning to break his back bending down at fifty-three. He had had better days, but the joys of working on a farm in the small, cold hours eventually took their toll. Through his aches, he adjusted his wellingtons and decided to start properly with a cup of tea before the regular chores: feeding, milking, collecting eggs, and mucking out the stalls. The latter awaited Steve as punishment, a thought the farmer relished as he walked to the small on-site café.

He didn't want to go back into his house; he would wake his wife and endure a shouting match. It was an earful he could live without. The café was the beginning of his day, which he always enjoyed. He never tended to lock the door; the farm was on high ground, generally off the beaten track, though close enough to Newcastle. It got busy at weekends, with a steady stream of families, providing a good income that kept several workers on the payroll.

He pushed open the door and walked to the counter, barely noticing the empty boxes stacked there. He bent and picked up a chocolate bar near a chair. "What the heck, Steve? First the bins, now this?" he frowned. "That's strike two; there better not be a third." He made his way behind the counter to the small back room and clicked the kettle on. It already had enough water for one cup.

While waiting for it to boil, he fumbled in his coat pockets for his phone but realised he had left it at the house. "Damn," he said, going back into the main café. It was here he noticed something was amiss. A sandwich and a packet of biscuits were squashed on the floor beside the counter, as if stepped on. Cartons of milk and juice were scattered inside the fridge. An empty box that once held chocolate bars lay on its side by the cash register. "I'm sure…" he muttered, trying to shake his memory to life, "I checked everything before Steve left." He paused, looking around the large room. "Steve wouldn't… couldn't have done this. I dropped him at the bus station… so… no!" he shrugged. "It can't have been the bloody foxes… never had them push the door open… so who? What?" His thought was broken by the click of the kettle, but his mind trailed into mystery.

Aeona was again buried within her coat, hood pulled down, protected by the frills behind the dragon's neck as they put distance between themselves and the farm. Lambton was only ten miles away; at a moderate speed, the dragon made the trip in fifteen minutes. It was good the dragon had woken the girl before sunrise, as the dull morning hid them from early drivers going to work or returning from night shifts.

They landed near the War Memorial beside the river. A stone monument surrounded by an iron fence, its inscription stood proud: "For the servicemen who fell in the Great War, 1914–1918, and also of those who fell in the Second World War, 1939–1945. Their names live forever in the hearts of those who knew them." It was a fitting tribute.

They stayed within the dark shapes of the trees, skirting a grassy bank. The road was empty; a parked car sat alone near several buildings. Its engine rattled in the cold; ghost-like breath snaked from the exhaust. The occupant's face was dimly lit by a phone screen. Aeona and the dragon stopped and looked around.

"Do you know where this place is?" the girl whispered.

"I know it's here," replied the creature. "I sensed it from above, but down here is different for us fliers. I'm a little disoriented. Give me a minute!" It looked around, stretching its long neck, trying to lock on. Aeona had asked before, but it couldn't explain its navigation; it just could, like a magnet in its head.

Sometimes the pull was stronger, depending on how hard it thought of the place. The dragon told her it felt weird, like a self-induced headache. It was its superpower, the way a child might tiptoe through a dark house without knocking anything over, a story Aeona knew too well and was best left unsaid.

It was not that easy. By day, it needed to see distinct shapes from above; by night, it had the stars.

"Come on, where are you?" it asked itself, the frills on its back twitching. "It's okay, I've got a plan," the girl said, patting its neck. "Stay here!" She made her way across the grass toward the parked car. When she was about seven metres away, her dark silhouette caught the driver's attention, his face harsh in the flickering phone glow. The taxi sign on top of the vehicle sprang to life as he pre-emptively pressed the meter.

Aeona didn't dare knock and gave a short wave. A second later, the window whirred down slightly. The driver sat silently, waiting.

"Excuse me, do you know where Worm Hill is?" she asked.

His response was so stern the girl didn't know how to take it. "What do I look like, lass, a tour guide? I'm a taxi driver," he replied. "It's behind Biddick."

"Biddick? What's a Biddick?" she asked shyly.

"You're not from 'round here, are you?" he asked sarcastically.

The tone made Aeona lean forward to peer into the unlit car. No smile greeted her. The driver just nodded toward a large grey house sandwiched between two bungalows. A sign hung above the windows in bold capitals: 'THE BIDDICK INN.' Realising he was not going to drive her, he turned his meter off, sighed heavily, and gave directions. "Walk to the corner, there," he nodded again. "Turn left, and just past the bus stop; you'll see it on the left." The girl looked in the direction he indicated.

"Thanks," the girl said, forcing a smile as the window slid shut. She sensed the dragon watching and thought it best to follow the instructions. Nearing the pub, she could read the unlit sign: black letters contrasted against the white background stretched above the Georgian windows. The wooden frames held the many panes, creating a historic, foreboding ambience. She walked to the corner, across the car park, and came to a road curving left. As the driver had said, there was a bus stop at the corner of a large grassed area. A blanket of clouds tried to suppress the morning light, but it silhouetted the rising hill against the skyline.

Aeona scanned the area. With no one around, she stepped over the low decorative barrier. Just as she was about to walk toward the hill's base, she noticed a poster on the bus shelter. She stepped back to investigate as the dragon appeared from the side, causing her to slam her leg into the post. With a yelp, she lost her balance and fell, clutching her shin. "Stupid post," she muttered.

"Sorry," her friend apologised. "I came from behind the houses when I saw you. But this isn't the place."

"What do you mean?"

"I can feel something, but I know this isn't what we're looking for."

"But look," the girl said, taking her notes from her pocket to compare with the poster. "It's the same as mine... Okay, this poster is better written, but I got the gist. My drawing is pretty bad, but..."

The dragon looked at the poster and growled at the image of a man swinging a sword at the Worm's neck. "What does it say?" it asked, uncurling its lip.

"Okay," she began, clearing her throat dramatically. "The Legend of the Lambton Worm." She raised her voice for effect. "The subheading: The Fisherman. John Lambton, the young heir, missed church one Sunday to go fishing. After a long time, he caught a strange, slimy black creature with sharp teeth. Horrified, he called it a devil." Aeona stopped. "A devil is an evil thing, okay?"

The dragon nodded.

"So, he tosses it down a well. An old man warns him his actions will bring misfortune upon his family." She stopped. "Did you get that?"

The dragon couldn't understand most of it. "Sort of… but give me the short version. We can't stay here long."

"You're right. Speed read." She ran her finger over the text. "Years later, while John is away fighting in the Crusades, the creature grows into a fearsome serpent. It emerges from the well and coils around Worm Hill, terrorizing the countryside. It devours sheep and cows, destroys crops, and demands a daily offering of milk. Its strength is unmatched. It could also heal itself from any injury." The girl widened her smile. "Wow! Can you heal yourself?"

"I don't know. I've never had to," it answered.

"I hope so," she replied, patting its snout. "Right, continue. John returns home to find his father's lands in ruin. He seeks a wise woman. She tells him the only way to slay the Worm is to forge a suit of armour covered in spikes and confront it in the River Wear. However, there's a catch."

"String? Do you mean a rope?" asked the dragon, confused.

"No, not that string… It means a condition. Like, if I give you an apple, you have to do something for me. The apple isn't really free." She felt she had explained that well. "So, the condition is he must kill the first living thing he sees after defeating the Worm, or his family will be cursed for nine generations."

"The Battle: John prepares, lures the Worm into the river, and as it wraps around him, it is cut by the spikes. He slices it into pieces, carried away by the current.

The Curse: Triumphant, John blows his horn. His father runs to him, forgetting to release a dog. John kills the dog instead, but this does not satisfy the terms, and the Lambton family is doomed to tragedy for generations."

Aeona stopped. "Does any of this mean something?" she asked.

"I don't know, except I don't like this person. But I feel something is wrong," it stressed. "This isn't the place."

"Okay, let me finish. The bottom says it's commemorated in songs and sculptures. The tale carries themes of redemption and consequences." She glanced at the dragon. "Someone even wrote a song." She read the first part to herself and decided it wouldn't help. "I'm not singing it. It has weird words."

A worm illustration curled around the poster's border, its head in the bottom corner. On the left, John Lambton stood over the slain creature.

"That's all here. Let's look around the hill. Maybe you'll sense something," she said, scanning the poster and her notes. Then her eyes froze on the bottom corner: a sketch of a Greek temple with the word 'Penshaw' beneath it.

"Penshaw Hill! Why did they write 'Penshaw' and not Worm Hill?" she thought aloud. "Why?"

They left the bus stop, climbed over a low fence, and went around a small electricity station. Ahead, Worm Hill rose, its rounded shape bulging against the skyline like a dark mound. Nine metres high and forty long, it loomed squat and bare. "Come on, this way." The dragon followed her around its base to a larger field. From there, the hill's full bulk was barren and exposed. Aeona set off up the slope with the dragon close behind. "Are you sensing anything?" she whispered.

It looked around. "No, nothing."

At the summit, a square concrete foundation jutted from the earth, remnants of a long-gone structure. Aeona frowned; neither the poster nor her research had mentioned it.

A biting wind blew across the top, offering no protection from the trees. Aeona retreated down the opposite side. The dragon wandered ahead, brushing aside foliage. They came to a small clearing on the western side, with a dune of soil and rocks left by a glacier, part of it collapsed to reveal the sand beneath.

Aeona scooped up a handful of wet soil and idly plucked at the grass. She was surprised she didn't miss her phone; playing with the soil felt like pure fun. Life felt different now. She had not spent much time in her garden or played outside in years, but with the dragon, everything had changed. Flying and evading pursuers felt like life itself. She smiled at the squish of dirt.

The dragon disrupted her play. "I can't sense anything here," it said, confused. "I felt it in the air."

"It would help if I knew what we were looking for," she said. "Shall we dig? We might find something." Aeona fell to her knees, tearing up clumps of earth. "Come on, let's dig!"

The dragon dug a huge claw into the earth, held it, and slowly withdrew it with a disappointed "No!" It raised itself on its hind legs, breathed deeply, and let out another exasperated "No!" before settling heavily.

"Come on, I'm making a nice hole. Why aren't you helping?" she laughed, holding up her dirty hands. Sensing something was wrong, she said, "Oh, sorry. I wasn't listening."

"We're in the wrong place. It's near, but not here," the dragon said, ears twitching.

"I told you!" she burst out.

"Told me what?"

"I told you, I wrote Pen…" she said, clapping her hands to remove the mud. When that didn't work, she wiped them on her coat and fumbled for her notes. "Here, look!" she thrust the paper at the dragon. "Penshaw Hill. It's on my notes and the poster. That's where we need to go."

"We need to fly so I can regain my senses," it told her. "The sun is coming up, and I'm worried we'll be spotted."

Aeona was ahead of it. "Nope, I've got it covered. I'll just ask the taxi driver again. It can't be far."

At the police station in Lambton, Commander Karsef had just finished a call with Northumbria Police Chief Constable Appleson, briefing him on the situation. A comprehensive report was sent, including video footage and a photo of Aeona Squire. It detailed her disappearance from Winwick and the trail of clues leading them to believe she was heading toward Lambton. The final clue was tenuous but all they had: the girl had researched the Lambton Worm on a library computer.

Chief Constable Appleson met with his Deputy and Assistant Chief, and within an hour, they had assembled a team to organise a task force to locate and safeguard the girl. What troubled Appleson most was the lack of a vehicle registration or any description of a potential abductor. He didn't know who was holding her or what to expect.

In the briefing room, thirteen CID officers listened to Appleson's report. "Ladies and gentlemen, you've seen the video and have the printouts. We need to cover all locations identified: Worm Hill, Penshaw Monument, and The Lambton Worm restaurant near the Drum Industrial Estate. Officer Moore is in charge of coordinating the task force," he said, gesturing. "Moore, over to you. Good luck." Moore stood and thanked the Constable, who then left the room with the two Chiefs.

"Right, everyone. Gary and I will be in the radio van by the monument entrance. The rest of you'll cover the approach roads and the restaurant. Keep your eyes sharp; we don't know how many we're dealing with. Let's find the child without incident. Any questions?"

The room stayed silent, officers shaking their heads. "Okay. Smith, Jones, Taylor, and Liaison Officer Williams in Team

One; Lauren, Rebecca, and Liaison Officer Evans in Team Two; Wilson and Thomas in Team Three; and Johnson and Robinson at the restaurant in Team Four. Let's go."

Many CID officers had worked stakeouts before, but a case involving a child was always different and more dangerous. It was vital to keep radios ready to call for backup at the first sign of a sighting.

An hour later, the teams were in place, using plain clothes and unmarked cars to blend in. Near the roundabout by the monument's entrance, Officer Moore and his partner were crouched in a black van tucked behind a bright yellow grit bin. From this vantage point, they had a clear view of the three main roads leading into Penshaw. The October roads were quiet, the car park empty.

Moore scanned the area, his eyes flicking between the street and his colleagues. The radio crackled with static. "Team One, everything's quiet here. Over," came the voice of Officer Wilson.

"Roger that, Team One," Moore replied.

Gary stayed silent, eyes on his binoculars. Then Moore murmured, "You'd think I'd be used to this by now."

Gary lowered the binoculars and smirked. "Maybe. But this one… it feels different."

Moore didn't reply, but the look he gave was enough. Years on the job had made them numb to pretty much everything, but this case felt off.

Gary shifted in his seat. "I guess we'll see how it plays out," he muttered, refocusing on the road. Moore nodded and continued his survey. No matter how many times they'd done this, every case carried the same weight.

"Moore to teams. Come in, over."

One after the other, they all responded: "In position."

The officers in Team One, Smith, Jones, and Liaison Officer Williams were sitting in a café, drinking coffee and eating cake. The waitress had told them they were the first customers of the day. The warm aroma was a blessing against the cold outside.

Carrie Williams didn't know how long they had to sit, but she didn't mind. She happily removed her coat, scarf, and gloves. "I think we got the better end of the stick, lads," she said, smiling as she looked out at the frost forming on the forecourt. The two other officers followed suit, removing their coats, which drew a smile from the waitress at the counter.

"You glad I put the fire on?" she asked, wiping a spill. A vintage metal fireplace, its flue running through the ceiling, set the style of the café. Logs were piled to the side. "Should I turn it down?"

"No, no, it's alright. Thank you!" responded Officer Smith. "What's your name?" he asked with a smile.

"It's Sally," answered the girl, who was no more than nineteen.

"My name is Tony. Thanks for the coffee, Sally," he winked, causing her to blush.

"We can't take you anywhere." Carrie smirked, nudging him with her elbow. "Behave yourself. We're supposed to be undercover, not flirting."

The tearoom had beautiful wooden tables and chairs. Their chosen spot overlooked the forecourt, its double-glazing fending off the autumn wind. Outside, carved garden furniture and rows of autumn shrubs brought colour to the dull buildings and dark sky.

Officer Taylor stood in the butcher's near the entrance, leaning against the wall and chatting with Graham, the butcher. He didn't know what was colder, the chillers keeping the meat fresh or the draught from under the door. He had chosen a spot in the corner, away from the cold. Through a small window behind the man, he could see the service road, and through the door window, he saw his colleagues laughing in the café. Taylor stamped his feet, trying to get blood flowing into his frozen toes. "I always get the shitty end of the stick," he muttered jealously. "Next time, guys!" He scoffed, turned his back in frustration, and carried on chatting. "When I'm done here, I'll take you up on that offer, Graham. A kilo of steak for how mu…" His question was cut short.

At the roundabout, a car approached. "Team One, Team Three, I've got a white Ford Focus, just turning in. Over," Officer Gary alerted from the van.

Even though he had been briefed, the butcher began to panic. Taylor had to explain his presence, or the man would have questioned why he was loitering. "Okay, so what do I do?" he asked, pacing and waving his knife. "What do I do?"

"Nothing… just act normal, just chill!" Taylor responded. "Here, this'll give you something to do. Sort me out a couple of kilos of sausage from the back. That will keep you out of the way until I give the all-clear." He smiled, pressing his earpiece in more securely. Then he responded, "Taylor understood!"

"Team Three, we've got eyes on the Ford!" Wilson and Thomas called from the car park. Their seats were reclined so the car appeared empty. They had parked at the far side, away from the building, binoculars in hand, though they didn't need them from this distance. Only six other cars were parked near the main building.

In the café, the three CID officers were halfway through sharing an egg custard and a Manchester tart when the call came through. Tony, his mouth full of cake, jumped to the mic. "Um-rit-tover," he mumbled, to his colleague's disgust.

"Come again?" questioned Constable Appleson.

"Shut it," scolded Officer Williams. "You'll get us into trouble. Swallow your food!" Instead, she pressed the mic to answer, "Officer Carrie Williams, Team One, understood," to the sound of muffled coughing from across the table. The waitress watched from behind the counter, trying not to laugh.

The white Ford pulled in, took a left, and parked close to the entrance. Wilson and Thomas watched as a man and a teenager got out and entered the building. "Sir, I have a white male and… could be a teen, but unclear from here… a shorter individual entering the building. Team One, do you have eyes?"

The officers in the café were alert, pretending to converse. Carrie clocked the pair first as they entered the central area near the ornamental furniture and plants for sale. The man sat on a bench with intricately carved deer heads and antlers of contrasting black wood. It was now clear the other individual was a female, approximately the same age as their suspect. It was safe for Carrie to report. "Sir, the kid's age fits the description."

"Appleson here. All teams, stand by! Let's wait to see where they go."

"Will do." She replied; the other officers, all linked via earpieces, heard the instruction. Wilson and Thomson slowly edged their car towards the Ford and reversed into a space a few spots away, ready to block its exit if needed.

The man stood from the bench, rubbed his hands together, and spoke to the young person. He then entered the butcher's. Taylor was ready, his back to them. "Graham," he called loudly. "Hey Graham, where are my sausages? You're killing that sheep… oh, sorry, hi…" He turned, greeting the strangers.

"Hullo," the man said with a smile and a strong Durham accent, before turning his attention to the meat behind the glass counter.

"You from these parts, then?" Taylor asked, making small talk while inconspicuously trying to see the face of the silent teenager, whose head was buried deep in a black hoodie with a strange image of animal-headed people.

"Sort of, we're from Seaham by the coast, just headin' back doon," he answered, as Graham gingerly emerged from the back room, avoiding eye contact.

The man returned a question to Taylor: "And you? Ye don't come frae round these parts, div ya?"

"No, my accent gives it away," he said, then attempted to draw the teen into the conversation, reading the slogan on the hoodie. "Snapped Bough Baby fell... um, I don't think I've heard of them; who are they?" he asked.

"Shattered Petals," grunted the voice.

"Nice," said the officer. "I think my nephew is into them. He says they're awesome."

"Ah cannae see it, like," returned the voice from the black void.

The man interrupted. "C'mon, pet, be nice," he scolded. "Lads these days... don't mind him. Have ye finished?" he asked the officer, who responded with a quick nod. Then, the man leaned forward to the counter. "Can ah hev some fresh chicken?" he asked the butcher.

"How many would you like?"

"Fowah, pleez."

Taylor left the shop and locked eyes with the officers in the café.

He shook his head and reported on the radio. "Everyone stand down, not our target. I repeat, not our target! It is a boy."

"Nice." Tony smiled, raising his hand. "Sally love, could we have another round of cappuccinos... sorry, wait a second. Jones, do you want a cappa or something else?"

The dragon waited in the woods near the base of Worm Hill while Aeona returned to the taxi driver. The man was still parked in front of The Biddick Inn, engine running. In the morning light, he seemed less formidable. Before she reached the car's boot, he had already lowered his window. "How was it, kid?" he called sarcastically. "Everything you dreamt it to be? See the Worm?" he chuckled.

"It was… um… nice," she stammered. "I wanted to ask you about something else," she paused. "My mum and dad were telling me about Pens…"

"Why are you out so early? Kids your age are usually in bed till noon," he quizzed.

Aeona struggled to keep her composure. "Well… I just couldn't sleep and needed the toilet. Then I went to the kitchen for a drink," she spluttered.

"Okay, okay, kid. I don't want your life story," he moaned. "Right, so what now?" he leaned out to look at her.

Aeona kept her face hidden beneath her hood. "As I was saying, my mum and dad want to go to Penshaw Monument later. Do you know how far it is?"

"You're being sarcastic. I'm a bloody taxi driver," he said. "Tell them it's less than ten minutes by car." He passed her a card. "This is the local taxi firm. It'll cost about seven quid." He then reached down and pulled out a brochure. "Here, take this too. Some people from Liverpool left it yesterday." Aeona stood by the car and began to read it. "Now what? Anything else?" the man asked.

"No, thanks, Mister," she said. "I'll give my parents your card." With a short wave, she returned to Worm Hill, where her friend was waiting. The brochure contained the same information as the bus stop poster, but on the back was a map showing both hills. "This is great," she thought, walking over the grass to get her bearings. When the coast was clear, she called dragon, which emerged from a clump of bushes. "Hey. Look what I've got," she said, holding up the leaflet. "We're here." She pointed and ran her finger along the river. "The river is over there. It should be straightforward from here. We just need to get you over that bridge without being spotted. Come on, let's go."

She folded the leaflet, tucked it into her pocket, and walked along the pavement towards the bridge. A woman was walking her dog at the end of the road, but the street was otherwise deathly quiet. Aeona had lost track of the days since her disappearance and no longer cared what day it was.

Once they confirmed the taxi driver was on his phone and couldn't see them in his rear-view mirror, they ran across the road. The dragon bounded over a fence into a hedge of nettles and brambles. The girl walked quickly along the pavement and began to cross. The bridge was too low over the water for the dragon to fly under; its launch required a crouch and a powerful wing thrust, which would be too visible. The metal structure was in full view of houses on both banks, making the risk too great. However, it looked up at the substructure, where wide beams crisscrossed to the other side. "You're not the only one with a great idea," it said with a smile. "Watch this." It reached up, twisted its body, and grabbed the girders with all four claws. Suspended upside down, it stealthily made its way across. But halfway, it looked down at the water and froze in terror. It began to shake and whimper, the sound rising to a pitiful cry. "My girl, help! GIRL!" it bellowed. "HELP!"

Aeona had already reached the other side and was leaning against the railing. The dragon's cry made her leap the fence and run back, nettles and brambles ripping at her clothes. "DRAGON, I'M COMING!" she shouted. Her fear shifted to a smile at the comical sight, though her friend, clinging for dear life, didn't see the humour.

"It's not funny, I'm panicking! Help me!" it begged.

Aeona was confused. "Come on, silly, just come across."

"I can't swim!" it whimpered.

"What do you mean…?" Her smile vanished. "Oh, no! What can I do?" she shouted. "Okay, listen! You're almost across. Just…"

"Just what? Don't say just!" the creature shouted back, its claws stripping paint from the girder as it began to slip.

"Okay! Hold tight with three claws, move one! That should do it. Listen, tight with three, move one!" she called. "Come on, say it with me." She chanted louder, "Hold tight with three, move one!" It took a second for the dragon to follow. "Tight with three, move one! Tight with three, move one!"

"I'M DOING IT!" the dragon screamed.

"I know… Tight with three, move one! Come on, you're nearly over!" called the girl. "Three more! Tight with three, move one!"

The dragon landed with a thud and leapt about wildly. "Did you see me? Did you see me? Whooo-ooo!" it roared.

"Quiet down!" shouted the girl, trying to cover its mouth. "QUIET… shh!" she hissed, diving at her friend and wrapping her arms around its snout. The drone of a car's wheels above echoed like thunder under the bridge.

When the dragon had composed itself, Aeona, from the cover of the bridge, looked at the map and plotted a course. "I'll be on the path up there," she said, pointing. "When I whistle, you can come out, okay?"

It was not until she climbed onto the path that flames seemed to erupt across her legs. A sharp stinging, like a thousand pinpricks, shot through her as her jeans offered no protection against the nettles. Her ankles took the brunt. She pulled her jeans up to her knees; small white welts and red hives spread from her shins to her thighs.

She quickly looked for dock leaves, the only remedy she knew. The more she rubbed, the more she needed to. She spotted a bunch near the hedge, right beside the nettles and dagger-like brambles. She threw herself onto the grass and rubbed her shins vigorously. She never knew if it was truly medicinal, but the placebo effect took hold. She lay on her back, looking at the dark clouds, waiting for the stinging to subside to a throb. Getting up, she rolled her jeans down and followed the pathway tracing the river behind the houses.

When she reached a bend in the river, she found the path deserted and whistled for her friend, who promptly appeared beside the bank.

"From here," she said, indicating, "we need to cut across this field. But we've got to be careful; it's quite open."

"Understood," the dragon noted. As they crossed the open ground, Aeona read through the song, or at least what she could understand of the strange dialect.

It was a north-eastern ballad about the Lambton Worm. It was tricky, but parts made sense. "Okay, I've read it a few times. Are you listening?"

'Catched heuk, queer kind, carry'd doon, whist tell ye boot, vary seun forgat. Penshaw Hill, myest gannins on, Penshaw Hill, myest gannins on. Gat bowld Sor John, craaled aboot, lapped ten times. Gat bowld Sor John. Hyem he cam' an' catched the beast, an' cut 'im in three halves. Noo ye kaa hoo aall the foaks, byeth, leaeved. One Sor John, frae myekin halves,

319

famis. Aall Aa knaa aboot clivvor, wi' the aaful Lambton Worm.'

She translated as best she could:
'Caught on hook, a strange kind, carried down. Will tell you about, it'll very soon be forgot. Crawled about, lapped ten times. Penshaw Hill, most goings on. Got bold, Sir John. Home he came and caught the beast. And cut it into three halves.

Now you know how all the folks - both - left. One Sir John for making famous halves. All I know about clever, with the awful Lambton Worm.'

The dragon cocked its head. "You'd expect it to include how he killed the Worm, wouldn't you?"

Aeona pursed her lips. "Do you know what this sounds like?" she asked, pausing. "It sounds a lot like that damn book in my bedroom!" She bit her lip in thought, and they quickened their pace as if the idea gave them urgency. After a couple of minutes of silence, she asked, "Can you tell me about your dream again?"

"Well, as I said, I saw dragons. Some dead things, and a girl."

"What do you mean?" she asked, confused.

"The girl or the patterns? They were spread about in strange patterns."

"Stranger patterns! You never said that before," Aeona questioned.

"Well," it explained, "like a big axe ... surrounded by water."

"Well, if you got out, maybe the others can too!" she said. "But that leaves us with the question ..."

"What's that?" it interrupted.

"How?" quizzed the girl, stopping mid-step.

"I thought you knew," it threw back.

They came to a long tunnel under a train track. Through the

bare autumn branches on the other side, the monument loomed atop the hill. A path was carved through dense trees, with steps supported by logs to prevent erosion. Puddles had gathered on some steps from the previous rain.

Aeona was completely unaware they were heading into a trap. As they reached the tree line, the dragon stopped, wanting to bound forward, but something held it back. Its instincts flared; its ears shot up, and a shockwave pulsed down its spine.

"I sense it. I can feel it, but I don't think I can step closer. Something doesn't feel right," it said, struggling. The girl saw no movement. "It looks all clear to me," she said, looking for anything unusual.

"Maybe you're right. No, wait," it paused. "I can hear it… calling. I can't make out the words. I know this." It scanned the area, cocking its head. "It is here, somewhere!"

"Come on, let's check it out." She said, pulling its shoulder.

"I think I might have to sit this out. It's too exposed. If you want me to come out, I'll have to change… you know, be invisible."

"So, do it then. At least I'm down here. You're not surprising me with that again." A shudder ran through her at the memory of her previous panic.

"I can't do it on command. It only happens when I'm scared or in danger," it explained.

"What do you want me to do, say boo?" She laughed. "What do you suggest?"

The dragon was at a loss. "I don't know… You go ahead, I'll figure it out."

"Okay, I don't know what I'm looking for, but I'll go first, and you can follow when you're ready," the girl said comfortingly before heading up the hill.

The monument was more impressive from the top. A

formidable replica of the Parthenon in Athens, stood bold in the autumn gloom. Eighteen enormous columns, two metres in diameter, reaching for the sky. Vast lintels stretched around the top. Aeona drew closer and tried to climb onto its base, which was elevated above the ground. The wall reached past her chest. She tried to pull herself up but lacked the strength.

"The only thing for it," she said, undefeated.

She backed away a few metres, crouched, and took a running start. She slammed her toes into an eroded stone for leverage and grasped clumps of weeds growing in the cracks. It was a struggle, but she made it. She lay on her back for a minute to catch her breath, looking up at the grey sky framed by the monument's walkway.

She got to her feet and surveyed the area. The wind whistled bitterly through the columns but didn't lessen the grandeur. She felt like a victorious gladiator. "So, where to start… I don't even know what I'm looking for," she said, walking to a corner column. "If I were to hide a dragon, where would I put it?" She counted the columns. "Four there, and four at that end. That makes eight." She smiled. "And five on each side makes eighteen. Okay! Nine over there and nine over here!" She shook her head; the math wasn't helping. Then she paused… frozen.

Beside one column was a notice board with tourist information on the Lambton Worm and the 'Penshaw Monument.' What struck her most was the drawing of the worm. She took her notes from her pocket and placed them beside the poster. "Nine!" she whispered. "It has nine spots on each side of its head… nine and nine make eighteen. Eighteen columns, eighteen spots… so that means, what? Um…"

She traced the writing on the poster. "It says the curse was put on his family for nine generations, but how long is a generation?" she asked herself. "If only I had my phone! Right, if a generation lasts… say twenty-five years…" She wet her finger with moisture from the Perspex cover and wrote on the stone floor. "Twenty-five multiplied by nine… makes two hundred and twenty-five."

She stood up and reviewed the information. The poster stated the folklore began around the time of the Crusades, possibly the twelfth century, when John Lambton returned. Aeona paused, thinking hard, searching for a connection. She glanced down the hill but saw no sign of her friend.

"…so, the curse should have ended long ago. Nine generations only take the story to just before the 15th century." Rubbing her chin, she walked in a large circle around the board three times, then returned. "If the curse was lifted, something should have been written about the Lambtons rejoicing. But nothing, no celebration, no joy." She was getting a headache from the thinking. She took a deep breath and shook herself.

Back in the van, Officers Moore and Gary watched the road for any vehicle turning into the car park. A few cars and a bus had passed, but none turned in. Gary sipped his cold coffee; he liked watch duty, but boredom was setting in. "Hey, Moore, I was thinking of buying a new car; what do you think?"

Go for it, man; what are you thinking?"

"Well." He sat up straight. "You drive a nice motor. What is it again?"

"A Capri. It's a classic, but ready for the scrapyard. You can't get parts."

"What about a Mustang? I was thinking blue or red."

"So, it's true, you're insane!" He laughed. "Do you know how much fuel that thing uses? It has a five-litre monster under the bonnet."

"Yeah… but… no, not really. I was dreaming online last night. Those GTs look amazing."

Moore elbowed him. "You'd have to live where petrol isn't so expensive! Now, there's a thought."

The officer mulled it over, then raised his binoculars. Through the eyepiece, the blurred heather and foliage on the roundabout came into focus before he moved them up to the hill. "Hey, these things are great! You get a good view," he commented, lowering them to see if Moore was listening. They made eye contact in silent agreement before he continued.

The monument stood proudly for miles. Officer Gary began to count the columns. "Have you ever been up there?" he asked, not waiting for an answer. "One, two, three, four, five, six… I've movement!" He stopped, glancing at Moore.

"Probably ramblers. No other car has come through except that white Ford," said Gary, steadying the binoculars. "One individual looks like a kid… wearing an oversized coat. What colour does the file say?" he asked Moore, who retrieved it from the glove box.

Moore thumbed through the papers. "It says here: dirty brown. What's that person wearing?"

"Yep! A dirty-brown oversized coat. Do you think this could be our guy?"

"But where did he come from? No cars have pulled in. Let me check with Team Two." He leaned forward and picked up the receiver.

"Lauren, come in. Over."

In a lane on the other side of the hill, Officers Lauren, Rebecca, and Liaison Officer Evans sat in the driveway of a bungalow overlooking a dirt track. The owners had permitted them to park there. When questioned, the owners said they had seen no one drive down the lane recently.

The women were chatting when the radio interrupted. "Team Two, Lauren here. Over."

"Have any cars or people made it past you?" Moore asked.

"Nope! All's quiet here. Not a soul."

"Do me a favour: walk up the back lane to the monument. We've got an individual fitting the description there. Take Rebecca with you and check it out."

She affirmed and replaced the handset to her colleague's groans. "Come on, Rebecca, you heard the man. Out you get, you lazy sod!"

"Why me? Take Evans! I don't like walking! I came to sit in the car, it's what I do best," complained Rebecca. "Take Evans! She likes hiking…"

"And get into trouble when he finds out? Not a chance! Get the biscuits out of your face, and let's go!" she snapped, as Evans laughed.

Aeona was in front of the board, running through the numbers. "Definitely nine. But what about it?" Behind her was a column different from the rest, with a metal door encased in a solid white frame.

She went over and pulled at the bars. To her surprise, they swung forward with a loud creak. The shock made her spin around as if expecting a shout. She entered to find a spiral staircase leading to the top. The stone steps were dark, and she held the handrail tightly. Missing a step sent her heart pounding. "Seventy-one, seventy-two, seventy-three… last one, seventy-four," she panted. The metal grate at the top gave way with a clang.

The view from the top was incredible, miles in every direction. The accessway allowed her to walk all the way around. "I can't see anything up here," she said, counting her steps. She was clutching at straws. "What about down there?" She lifted herself onto the stone parapet and looked towards the clearing where she had come from, spotting her friend.

"Hey, dragon!" she waved, arm stretched out while supporting herself. "DRAGON!" she shouted.

"What are you doing!" It shouted back. The fear of her falling terrified the creature, and in an instant, its body sparked blue, ripples shot from nose to tail, and then, in an explosion of light, it was gone. The only sign was the erupting leaves, twigs, and mud flying in all directions.

"You can see for miles from here," Aeona said in awe. "Not like flying, but nice."

"HEY!" shouted the dragon.

Aeona flung herself backwards off the wall. "What the shit!" she screamed, "You scared the life out of me!"

"Thanks for making me invisible! I guess you scared me too!" it responded.

She smiled towards its voice. "I think I figured that out; glad you could join me!" she joked, getting up. "Now listen. I think I figured some of it out. Why has the Worm got nine spots on either side of its face?"

"Well, I've little stripes on my cheeks. They make me look like I've got gills, but I never had them before," it explained. "The book threw me into the darkness. I was in a bubble, like in my dream."

Aeona didn't like to think about it. "I don't really remember when," she said. "What you're saying is that you were away for how long?"

"Yes, a very long time. I'm sorry," it said, lowering its head.

"Right, let me stop you. I think we might be onto something," she replied. "So you never had them before and came out with them… let's say each line means ONE." She grew excited, patting her knees. "Look, dragon," she said, waving the paper. "Say something so I know where you are." The dragon placed a paw on her foot, making her flinch. "Okay! Look at this. It has eighteen spots, but you have lines. What's the difference between lines and spots?" she quizzed.

"It is a lot bigger than me. Do you think it has to do with size?" it asked.

Aeona bit the inside of her cheek. "Size doesn't make sense. I feel it has to do with time. The story talks about nine generations, but that's only about two hundred and twenty-five years. So, whatever the dots mean, it has to be more, or the dragon would be free." The invisible creature interjected.

"But eighteen can't be years; that's nothing for a dragon. What if each dot represents ten years?" it asked.

"That makes one hundred and eighty years. That doesn't work, either. That only takes it to… 1330," she added, "still in the past. It would be great to have a pen." She picked up a loose stone from the wall.

She knelt and used the stone as a pencil. She drew a little ball, wrote an equal sign, and formed a table, multiplying everything by nine and then eighteen until the completed table was scrawled on the floor:

O = 20 × 18 = 360
O = 25 × 18 = 450
O = 30 × 18 = 540
O = 40 × 18 = 720
O = 50 × 18 = 900
O = 100 × 18 = 1800

"Okay, let's have a look," the girl said, rocking back and standing to view her artwork. Instantly, they gasped together.
"NINE HUNDRED!"
"Nine hundred years… Nine hundred years!" the dragon shouted. "My poor friend has been in there for NINE

HUNDRED YEARS! That can't be!"

"Hang on," Aeona said… "The tale began around 1150, which makes it… 2050. It won't be long before it comes out, but even so, the poor thing has been there nearly nine hundred years."

"I'm not leaving it in there another day!" exclaimed the dragon. "I can feel it calling."

The girl jumped to her feet and threw herself onto the parapet. "I've got it. I know where it is! LOOK!" she called, pointing.

Her eyes found it immediately. "Oh my God! Do you see it?" she shouted. "Look down… There in the centre… can you see where the bricks join?" The dragon leaned over, but saw only crisscrossing bricks.

"Bricks? What about them?" it asked.

"Don't you know anything about pirates?" she quizzed. "Don't look at the bricks, look at the pattern."

It was only four hundred metres from the bungalow to the monument, but for Officer Lauren, dragging her struggling colleague, it felt like four miles.

Rebecca complained the entire way, her unhealthy lifestyle taking its toll. "I don't want to do this anymore! Can't I just wait on the grass?" she begged. "Why don't we just drive?" she moaned, dragging her feet and swiping at bushes with her hiking pole.

"Take mine, you big baby," Lauren laughed. "Try planting them into the ground. They'll help."

"If I get blisters, I'm complaining!"

"Come on, quicken the pace; Moore sounded urgent."

"You're joking, right?" Rebecca returned in disbelief.

Her colleague was losing patience. "I shit you not," she answered sarcastically, increasing her speed. "Catch up when you can. I'll go ahead," she said, speed walking to a near jog.

All other teams converged at the car park. Team Leader Moore pulled up next to the unmarked police car and wound down his window. "Anyone got eyes on her?"

Wilson, his binoculars trained on the child, confirmed: "It's definitely her, Sir. No doubt."

"Right, we've got to be careful. We don't know who the abductors are, and they haven't shown themselves. Can we get them without harming the girl?"

Officer Gary scanned the area. "Someone must be up there, but I can't see anyone." He turned his attention to the trees skirting the hill. "It doesn't make sense," he said, binoculars still raised. "What's she doing up there alone? Where are the people who took her?"

So many questions ran through their minds, but the priority

was to secure the girl.

Gary threw the question to the others, "Why isn't she running? If I were her, I'd be running hell for leather down toward the buildings for help." Gary wasn't the only one; Moore wasn't taking chances. The truth was the police had very little information. She was a missing child, taken from a house, later seen in a village, possibly attacked by a wild animal, and now sighted again. But the police had used her internet search history as their ace card, and it was only a matter of time.

"Right, everyone, listen up! Team One, take the right, skirt around from that clump of trees. Team Three, go to the end of the car park, get over that wall," he said, pointing, "and advance low. The others will push her your way if she runs." He lifted the microphone. "Team Two, come in. Over."

"Shit," Lauren puffed. "What am I going to say?" she gasped, slowing to a walk. "Team Two… here… over," she panted.

"Lauren, are you running?" he chuckled. "Please, tell me you're videoing it. Is Rebecca running, too?" He laughed. "I said it as a joke! Well done! Right, any sign of vehicles? How far to the monument?"

"Sorry, no video," she laughed nervously. "Should be there in about five minutes."

"Start running again; I'll give you three minutes, then all teams move in, over," he called, looking at his watch.

After a minute, he called everyone to attention.

"Right, everyone! Gary and I will take the direct path. Watch the wings for any movement. It's imperative we get that girl away from her abductors. Let's go!"

The groups split, following orders. In the lane, Lauren paced in circles, cursing. "Come on, Becca, where are you? Our asses are toast if you don't get here."

To her surprise, a car appeared, racing towards her. Rebecca was behind the wheel, the vehicle bouncing with every pothole. Evans was in the back, screaming and holding on. The car crunched and banged as the shocks took a pounding. Rebecca slammed the brakes, grinding to a halt beside her astonished colleague.

"Are you getting in, or what?" she asked, smiling from the open window. "I told you a car could make it! Now who's puffing and panting? I've a good mind to let you walk." She laughed as Lauren grabbed the handle.

They reached the end of the dirt track in less than a minute. "Rebecca, Team Two, ready to move up, over."

"Team Three, keep your volume off. Be casual. Everyone else, hold until I give the order. Over." A series of clicks confirmed. "Team Three, go!"

Aeona burst from the spiral staircase, her breath coming in short, excited gasps. Her heart pounded as she flung her arms into the air, the surge of realisation flooding through her. The pieces had been right in front of her all along. As she ran to the centre, it finally struck her with the force of a lightning bolt. Her eyes widened, and an icy shiver ran down her spine.

"No, no, no!" she gasped, gripping her head as dizziness washed over her. "How didn't I see it before?"

It was there, hidden in plain sight, woven through every clue. Every fragmented piece of the puzzle, the disappearing dragon, the demon, Mary, even Fluff, led back to the same thing. The answer that had eluded her was in Shadows Chant. The name lingered in her mind, a whisper of truth. Everything stemmed from it. Everything… "Nyxa…" The words crashed into her consciousness. Aeoniks… Aeona-Nyx…She screamed, the truth washing over her like a wave. "The girl!" she shouted, breathless, her heart racing.

"She's not gone." The words rang clear, echoing louder than

anything she had ever heard. For the first time, Aeona felt the weight of everything at stake. Nyxa wasn't lost. She wasn't dead. Just like the dragons, she had been thrown into the void and banished, but she wasn't gone. She was still there, waiting.

A surge of energy exploded within her. Her feet pounded against the stone as she leapt, unable to contain her excitement.

"Nyxa! Nyxa!" she screamed with joy. "SHE'S ALIVE! SHE'S ALIVE!" For the first time in what felt like forever, hope surged through her veins. "Here! Look at the lines!" she shouted, pointing frantically at the ground. "This… this is the key!" Her hands traced the lines, fingers skimming over the ancient paths. It was all connected; every symbol, every marking led back to Nyxa and the path to freeing her. "Dra…" She froze mid-sentence, something catching her eye.

Two men at the far end of the monument stood still, watching. Her breath caught in her throat. She didn't know whether to run or act naturally. She tried to calm herself, turning slowly to study the columns as if nothing was wrong.

The men mirrored her move. It was too uncanny. After a moment, they casually walked toward the information board, giving a polite wave and a smile before turning to the display.

Aeona's heart raced. She scanned the area, then made a beeline for the door, her pace quickening. Just as she reached for it, she froze. Two women, one with hiking poles, appeared at the top of the stone steps, blocking her path. Her pulse thudded in her ears. There was no way around. She glanced at the door, the one safe exit, but it was too late. The women were already moving toward her. Her instincts screamed to stay calm, but she had to figure out her next move, fast.

"Good afternoon," one called. "That was a tough climb," the woman said, puffing. "Not as young as I used to be, eh!" She expected a laugh.

Moore and Gary watched through binoculars from a short distance. "Officers in position. We need Wilson and Thomas to block the western end, then we move!" Gary said, scanning the tree line, but no one appeared to be communicating with the girl. Two clicks sounded on the team leader's radio as the last two officers crested the hill.

"Gary, that's our cue!" Moore said. "We'll have her surrounded. Let's get up there before she realises!"

At the sight of the growing number of people, Aeona panicked. Though none moved on her, she sensed something was wrong. Their side glances and mannerisms didn't seem genuine. The two on the right seemed more interested in reading graffiti. She saw her chance and hurried to the opposite end, but two men were already running up the hill toward her. She skidded to a halt at the edge, jumped backward, and ricocheted off a column straight into an officer's arms, who snatched at her coat. She spun and ran for the side, but another officer stood between her and freedom.

In an instant, the seven officers converged. "Come here, we're not going to hurt you! We're the police!" they shouted.

Watching from above, the dragon wanted to roar, "Run, my girl! Run!" Its heart pounded, ready to attack, but there were too many. It looked on in dismay, waiting for a chance to pounce.

An officer seized her by the hood and yanked her backwards. The zip slashed her neck as her legs flew into the air, causing her to land on her back with a thud. The sharp jolt ripped the wind from her lungs. But she wasn't giving up without a fight. Quickly, she rolled and squirmed free from the loose coat, flung her arms up in the air, and bolted forward. The sudden shock of seeing another officer, arms outstretched, made her try to skid to a halt, but there was no stopping. Using the momentum, she launched herself at the man and exploded with all the force she could summon with her fist. In a splintering crack, his head snapped back, and a spray of blood burst across his cheek from his broken nose. He gave a blistering cry, hands flying to his face, blinded by the shock and the pain.

It gave her a second wind to run, but she only got less than a metre before she was struck from behind by a woman who rugby-tackled her to the ground, followed by another, then another. She struggled with all her might to get out from under the bodies on top of her, but as soon as the multitude of legs surrounded her, she knew there was no escape.

"Cuff 'er Gary," ordered Moore, as she was dragged to her feet. Her arms were roughly yanked behind her, and the cold steel found home with a sharp click. It was only then that the police stepped back in triumph.

"Good job, guys, we got her!"

Aeona looked around frantically, writhing and cursing, trying to break free. But, with so many people around her, there was no way out, except for her friend to rain down its fury from above. She quickly shot a glance up to the parapet to see if she could see the dragon. It remained invisible, watching, its hind legs rocking side to side, waiting for the right moment. It quickly flashed a kaleidoscope of blue and green, giving Aeona its warning.

Suddenly, she stood motionless.

The clarity of the thought hit her. The answer lay in the book.

As evil as Shadows Chant was, they needed it. It was undeniable. It ran through her mind in a flood of truth.

She stopped struggling, lost in the moment. The officers felt the calm in the way her whole body settled, like water around a plan. Officer Moore turned and stared, confused at the sudden change in the handcuffed girl. He didn't see it, but the corner of her mouth curled into a grin. She had to use this to her advantage. They would take her back to where the book was, for sure.

There was no other way but to tell the dragon not to save her.

"No dra! No!" she screamed to the darkening sky.

The unexpected cry jolted the officers, who stared at each other in alarm. "Quickly, check the perimeter," shouted Officer Moore. "She is calling someone. It can only be the person who brought her here!"

Three officers instantly ran to the edge of the monument and scanned the tree line for any movement, while the others bolted to the opposite side.

"It's okay, lass. It's okay. We're the police. We're here to take you home!"

Dragon looked down from the platform above, trying to understand what she was saying. "No! Need book!" shouted again, "Book!" it whispered to itself.

Officer Moore quickly looked from right to left, too distracted to listen to the commotion the girl was making, waiting for confirmation from the others. "Anything?" He called.

Aeona continued to scream, "Book, plan!"

"Nothing this side!"

"Nor this!" returned another.

Officer Gary gave a little tug on the girl's arm, "Will you quiet down? We're the police. What's your name?" he asked, in more of a distraction than a question.

She didn't answer. She just glared at him and yanked her arm back in defiance.

"Say or don't. We know who you are anyway." He paused, then spoke calmly, "You're Aeona Squire."

As the words left his mouth, a shudder ran through the stone beneath her feet. It was a deep, low vibration that hummed up through her boots and into her. It was gone as quick as it came, but the whisper that followed it wasn't. It didn't come from the air. It was just there, right inside her head. A voice like crumbling rock, worn thin by centuries, full of aching weight.

It growled one word.

"SQUIRE!"

From the parapet above, the dragon let out a startled cry. Aeona froze. The shouts of the police, the tight grip on her arms, the cold of the cuffs, faded into a dull buzz.

That vengeful, ancient voice hadn't been her friend's. It was the other: The Worm. It was alive in its prison, and it knew her name.

www.ingramcontent.com/pod-product-compliance
Lightning Source LLC
Chambersburg PA
CBHW072022110726
47910CB00005B/1833